W9-AUJ-022

Hinsdale Public Library
Hinsdale, Illinois 60521

BAKER & TAYLOR

WARNING SHOT

WARNING SHOT

Clive Egleton

St. Martin's Press ⚏ New York

Library of Congress Cataloging-in-Publication Data

Egleton, Clive.
    Warning shot / Clive Egleton.
        p.   cm.
    ISBN 0-312-15685-5 (hardcover)
    I. Title.
PR6055.G55W37   1997
823'.914—dc21   97-7196
                                                   CIP

First published in Great Britain by Hodder & Stoughton,
a division of Hodder Headline PLC

First U.S. Edition: June 1997

10   9   8   7   6   5   4   3   2   1

This book is for two of the finest

Joan Evelyn Egleton
Robert Low Donaldson

Chapter 1

Neil Franklin had lost count of the number of times the mynah bird belonging to his next-door neighbour had fooled him. In addition to mimicking the human voice, this particular bird was able to imitate the distinctive burr of a telephone, a trick that sent Franklin scurrying back into the house every time he heard it when out in the garden. But this was the middle of an unusually chilly night in early autumn, not a warm summer afternoon, and a furious Ella was digging him in the back. In his befuddled state, it was some moments before he realised that the insistent burr had nothing to do with his old enemy the mynah bird. Reluctantly, he reached out for the telephone, lifted the receiver off the cradle and drawing it nearer, greeted the caller with an irritable, 'Yes?'

'Neil?' a tense voice said in his ear.

'Who else?' he growled.

'It's me, Steven Quorn.'

'Well now, there's a surprise.'

'You want another one? I've lost Moresby.'

'You've done what?' Franklin said, suddenly wide awake.

'Moresby's disappeared. John and I were supposed to meet at this bar in the Kreuzberg District but he never showed up.'

'What bar?'

'The *Schwarz und Weiss* on Oranienstrasse. It's open until three a.m. – very popular with the local drag queens.'

'Oh, for God's sake.' Ella grabbed hold of the duvet and

rearranged it to cover her exposed shoulder. 'How much longer are you going to be?'

'Not much longer,' Franklin told her quietly.

'What did you say, Neil?' Quorn asked.

'I was talking to Ella. Where are you calling from?'

'A pay phone near my hotel.'

'Give me the number.'

'It's 262-3419.'

'Stay there, I'll ring back.' Franklin hung up, got out of bed and slipped on a dressing gown before going downstairs.

His study was at the front of the house overlooking a lawn that would not have disgraced Wimbledon. It was, however, questionable how much longer that comparison would remain valid. The Treasury had already reduced the indoor staff to a cook/housekeeper and there was every chance Franklin would lose the services of the gardener-cum-general handyman in the next round of cuts. Stifling a yawn, he sat down at the desk by the window, picked up the phone and tapped out the number he had been given. Quorn answered the moment it rang out.

'Let's start again,' Franklin told him, 'this time from the beginning. Whose idea was it to meet at the *Schwarz und Weiss*?'

'Moresby's. Although he didn't actually say so, I got the impression that our prospective business partner was staying nearby. Anyway, I arrived on the dot of eight thirty and only left a few minutes before closing time.'

'How well do you know Moresby?'

'He's practically a stranger. I hadn't even heard of him before I was called into the office last Friday and informed that he would be accompanying me to Berlin. I was told that he was highly regarded by 'The Firm'. I then had lunch with him the better to make his acquaintance.'

The two men had travelled separately, Moresby on the first flight to Berlin out of Heathrow, Quorn departing two hours later on Lufthansa 4073. Immediately after checking into the Hotel Berliner Hof, Quorn had telephoned Franklin to let him know he had arrived.

'Moresby is staying at Hecker's Hotel in Grolmanstrasse, just off the Kurfürstendamm. He rang me shortly after five o'clock yesterday evening to say he'd heard from our business associate and was on the way to see him.'

'Had they met previously?' Franklin asked.

'No, but Moresby told me they had discussed how they were going to recognise each other and he didn't see any problem.'

'He didn't sound worried to you?'

'Not in the least. In fact, Moresby was positively ebullient when he rang me again to say that the deal was on and would be completed when I arrived at the *Schwarz und Weiss* with the down payment.'

Franklin caught his breath. The down payment amounted to 250,000 US dollars in cash, and while he had not been actively involved in the negotiations, Head Office in London would almost certainly lay some of the blame at his door if Quorn had just been relieved of the whole quarter of a million.

'Where is the money now?' he asked in a voice which betrayed his anxiety.

'Where it has always been – in a safe-deposit box at the Europa-Center. I only took the key with me and I still have it.'

'Good. I take it you haven't contacted the police yet or made any enquiries yourself concerning Moresby's whereabouts?'

'No. I thought it best to apprise you of the situation first.'

'Quite right too, we don't want to draw attention to ourselves.'

More particularly, Franklin had no desire to find himself in the spotlight. He was the twelfth Head of Station, Berlin the Secret Intelligence Service had had since the end of World War Two and had been continually in post since June 1986. He was also destined to be the last Head of Station, which was why he had not been relieved at the normal five-year point. When the city became the official capital and seat of government in three years' time, the

British Embassy would move house from Bonn and he would be made redundant. He could live with that prospect because in two years from now he would be fifty-five and eligible for early retirement on a full pension, never mind the golden handshake he could expect to receive as a senior government official whose career had supposedly been truncated. To be accused of some act which Bonn considered prejudicial to German interests was the last thing Franklin needed at this juncture. If that should happen, London wouldn't hesitate to recall him and he would be compulsorily retired on a much reduced pension.

'What do you want me to do, Neil?' Quorn asked.

'Go back to your hotel and await developments,' Franklin told him brusquely. 'If you haven't heard from Moresby by ten o'clock, check out of the Berliner Hof, collect the down payment from the Europa-Center and go home.'

'I don't think London will like that.'

'London can get stuffed,' Franklin said, and put the phone down.

The builder's yard belonged to the Public Works Department of the Tiergarten Municipal Authority and was something of an eyesore. The one thing to be said in favour of the site was that it was located on wasteland approximately half a kilometre south-west of Lehrter Stadt Bahnhof on the elevated suburban line, an area not exactly renowned for its scenic beauty. When Police President Heinrich Voigt arrived at the builder's yard, Polizei Kommissar Eicke and the detective squad from the Central Division, together with a forensic team, were already on the scene. Voigt also noted that the uniformed branch and the ambulance service were well represented and fast getting in one another's way. The same thought occurred belatedly to Eicke who hurriedly dispatched one of his sergeants to sort out the muddle.

From his demeanour, it was obvious to Voigt that the

4

Inspector resented his presence. He could understand that. No investigating officer, least of all one as touchy as Eicke, liked to have the *Polizei Präsident* of Berlin breathing down his neck. But old habits were hard to break. Only a few months ago, Voigt had been in charge of the *Kriminalpolizei* and his new role of administrator was dull and tedious in comparison.

'So what have we got here, Gerhardt?' he said, endeavouring to put the Inspector at ease.

'A double murder.' Eicke cleared his throat. 'Two men, both disfigured.'

'Before or after death?'

'One before, the other after, according to the medical examiner, but he's unwilling to swear to that. We have to wait for the results of the autopsies and we can't move the bodies until Forensic has finished with them.'

'No reason why we shouldn't take a look.'

Eicke nodded, turned about and led him towards a huge pile of condemned tyres which the public works department used as hard core in their road-building programmes. Stacked six deep, one on top of the other, the wall of tyres extended over approximately fifty metres and was high enough to obscure the perimeter fence in the immediate vicinity. The floodlights erected by the forensic team showed that a gap had been cut into the wire mesh fence large enough for a man to enter the compound without stooping. His legs stretched out in front of him, his back resting against the tyres, the dead man seemed to be contemplating the breach through the empty sockets of his eyes.

'They also cut out his tongue,' Eicke said in a voice that was completely matter-of-fact.

'They?'

'The number of footprints and scuff marks indicate there was more than one intruder.'

Voigt mentally kicked himself; four months ago he wouldn't have asked such a stupid question. He started thinking like a detective again and rapidly came to the conclusion that the victim must have been killed else-where. His throat had been hacked open from ear to ear and although the jacket and shirt-front were soaked, there were very few bloodstains on the ground. The body was cold and rigor mortis already pretty far advanced.

'The medical examiner thinks death occurred some twelve to fourteen hours ago.' Eicke glanced at his wristwatch. 'In other words between 14.00 and 16.00 hours yesterday afternoon. The Herr Doktor also thinks the victim was aged thirty-five to forty-five and was a guest worker, possibly of Turkish origin, judging by his clothes and swarthy appearance.'

'The good doctor could be right. The dead man certainly doesn't look German.'

'We haven't searched the victim yet so haven't been able to identify him. But once Forensic have finished their business, one of my officers will accompany the bodies to the mortuary and collect their personal effects before the pathologists get to work.'

'Where are Forensic now, Gerhardt?'

'With the other victim.' Eicke pointed vaguely in the direction of the S-Bahn. 'Over there by the pyramids.'

'Let's take a look at him.'

The pyramids were mounds of sand dumped at irregular intervals on the opposite side of the compound facing the elevated suburban line. Forensic were still photographing the corpse from every angle, taking measurements and recording every last detail in longhand.

'We weren't aware there was a second victim until a short while ago,' Eicke said, anxious to explain the hold-up.

Vehicles entering the compound to pick up a load did so from Heidestrasse via a purpose-built cinder lane. Since there was no other way in, the municipal authority did not consider the builder's yard to be at risk. A perimeter fence and a night watchman on duty at the gate were considered a sufficient deterrent to any would-be thief intent on stealing a truckload of bricks, builder's sand or hard core.

'The night watchman is supposed to patrol the perimeter fence once every hour,' Eicke continued. 'He's never going to admit it but my guess is he spent most of the night in the warmth of the office watching TV. Anyway, when he did get around to earning his pay, he broke the all-comers record for the 400-metres dash when his flashlight picked out the mutilated body of the guest worker.'

The night watchman had run back to the office and dialled 110. A prowl car in the vicinity of the Brandenburg Gate had been the first to respond to the emergency call; shortly thereafter, mobiles from the Wedding, Tiergarten and Charlottenburg Districts had converged on the builder's yard.

'The night watchman led the uniformed officers to believe he'd patrolled virtually the whole compound before he'd stumbled over the body,' Eicke went on. 'That's why we thought there was only the one victim.'

The killers had gagged and bound their second victim, lashing the wrists and ankles together behind his back so that his body had been arched like a drawn bow.

'Male Caucasian, fair hair, blue eyes,' Eicke said, reading from his notebook. 'Height 1.98 metres, weight 85 kilos.' He paused, then added, 'You understand these are guesstimates, Herr Präsident.'

Voigt made no comment. The first signs of daybreak were beginning to creep above the horizon and beyond the glare from the arc lamps Forensic had rigged to illuminate the immediate area around the dead man, he could now just see what appeared to be a strip of timber lying in the sand. Moving several paces nearer, Voigt saw that it was a batten some two metres in length.

'Don't forget to bag this up,' he said, addressing the officer in charge of the forensic team. 'Doesn't look as if it has been lying there all that long.'

'I don't understand, Herr Präsident.'

'Look at the way the dead man was hogtied. They could have slipped this batten under his wrists and ankles and then carried him between them.'

7

'Suspended like a suckling pig,' Eicke added in a low voice.

'That remark was in bad taste,' Voigt told him curtly, then turned away from the *Polizei Kommissar* and looked back towards the bank of condemned tyres where the first murder victim had been found.

All the evidence suggested to Voigt that the intruders had approached the builder's yard from the direction of the Tiergarten. They would probably have used a van to convey their victims from wherever they had been holding them and he wondered where they had parked the vehicle after crossing the River Spree. It would have to be somewhere well away from passing traffic while being as close as possible to the perimeter fence. The abandoned sidings in rear of the Hamburger Bahnhof which had been converted into a conference hall was one possibility.

'Why do you suppose these two men were murdered, Gerhardt?' he asked, offering the detective an olive branch.

Eicke shrugged. 'It's too early to say but in the end we will probably find it was drugs related. Some cartel reckoned they were being short-changed by these two and it was decided to make an example of them. Offhand, I can't think of a more graphic way to send a warning to any other dealer who might have been tempted to take a leaf out of their book.'

'They wanted maximum publicity so instead of hiding their bodies, they dumped them where they were sure to be found.'

'That's the way I read it, Herr Präsident.'

Voigt turned about and looked towards the embankment again. The arrogance shown by the killers was breathtaking. They had mutilated one man and then slit his throat in full view of the S-Bahn. It had been a clear, moonlit night and they would have had to have allowed for the fact that the surface rail network continued to run one train an hour in each direction between 01.00 and 04.00. So what if the Bellevue and Tiergarten stations were closed for renovation and the trains had a clear run between Lehrter

Stadt Bahnhof and the Zoologischer Garten? They didn't exactly hammer around that long curve. Fifteen to twenty kilometres an hour was about the mark and the builder's yard was in sight from the elevated train for quite an appreciable distance. The timetable would have told them when the trains would be passing the yard but that still would have left a number of imponderables. What if it had taken them longer to cut a gap in the fence than they had allowed for? What if the night watchman had stumbled across them?

'They would probably have cut his throat too,' Voigt said, answering his own unspoken question.

'What did you say, Herr Präsident?'

'I was just thinking what might have happened to the night watchman had he been a little more conscientious.'

'Oh, right.' Eicke cleared his throat. 'May I carry on? Forensic have finished with the bodies now.'

'But of course.'

Voigt retraced his steps to take a closer look at the corpse lying in the blood-soaked mound of sand. He crouched beside the body and, closing his mind to what the killers had done to the dead man's face, went through his pockets. The passport the man had been carrying was due for renewal in January 1995, having been issued ten years previously. Predominantly blue in colour, the motif on the front cover picked out in gold was instantly recognisable even to Eicke.

'An Englander,' he said.

'Correct.' Voigt turned the page. 'John David Moresby – describes himself as a businessman.' He slipped the passport into the inside pocket of his topcoat. 'I'll let you have it in due course, Gerhardt,' he added.

Eicke did not approve and made it known with some pretty heavy breathing, but as Police Präsident of Berlin, Voigt was very much a law unto himself.

To the world at large, Neil Franklin was the owner of the English Bookshop which had first opened its doors to

Berliners on Saturday, 7 June 1986, one week after he had arrived in post. Located on Budapesterstrasse opposite the *Zoologischer Garten*, it was funded by the Secret Intelligence Service whose other business ventures over the years had included a car body repair shop, a small travel agency and an extremely modest hotel in the Wittenau District. At the height of the Cold War, these front offices had been necessary in the interests of secrecy; forty years on, the English Bookshop was an anachronism.

With the Treasury and Foreign Office looking for ways and means of reducing expenditure, the SIS had found it difficult enough to justify the post of Head of Station, Berlin after the frontier had moved eastwards to the Oder-Neisse line following reunification. The closure of RAF Gatow, together with the withdrawal of the Berlin Infantry Brigade and the disbandment of Headquarters British Troops a few weeks ago meant that it was now only a question of time before the Director General was forced to yield to their demands.

It was Franklin's intention to do everything in his power to postpone that moment of reckoning. In furtherance of this aim, he had managed to convince the British Ambassador in Bonn that his continued presence in Berlin was vital until the German government moved house. At the same time, Franklin also had to persuade Chancellor Kohl's people in Berlin that he would always seek approval from the *Bundesnachrichtendienst* before embarking on any covert operation. With Victor Hazelwood temporarily in the chair and calling the shots from London, this wasn't the easiest promise to keep. Franklin had not been told exactly what Quorn and Moresby were up to but clearly the operation had not gone according to plan, which was extremely worrying.

If the day had started badly with the phone call from Quorn, it had rapidly worsened soon after Franklin had arrived at the bookshop. The last thing he had expected to find on his desk was a letter from Fräulein Helga von

10

Schinkel giving notice that she wished to retire on 31 December.

Few people are indispensable but Helga von Schinkel almost certainly was. Fluent in French, English and Italian, she had served every SIS Head of Station since the end of World War Two, when she had been poached from AMGOT, the Allied Military Government Occupied Territories. Initially employed as a shorthand typist, she had never been to a secretarial college and had been incapable of typing more than eight words a minute. Her political credentials had however been beyond reproach; in 1944, when a nineteen-year-old university student, Helga had been a courier for the Bendlerstrasse conspirators. Arrested after the failure of the July bomb plot, she had appeared before the People's Court in January 1945 charged with High Treason and had been found guilty. Sentenced to death by Judge Roland Freisler, she had been taken to the Lehrterstrasse Prison to await execution and had still been there when the Russians had overrun the city.

Helga von Schinkel had forgotten more about Intelligence-gathering than most SIS officers learned in a lifetime and Franklin didn't know how he was going to manage without her. But as she had pointed out when he had tried to persuade her to withdraw her notice, she would be seventy on 25 November and it was time to go.

When Helga tapped on the door and walked into his office shortly after ten o'clock, he was sure that she was going to tell him that she had changed her mind about leaving. He came back down to earth the moment Helga announced that Heinrich Voigt wished to see him.

'You had better show him in then,' he said in a dispirited tone of voice.

Franklin had met the Police President in 1986, shortly after he had been appointed Head of Station, Berlin. In those days, Voigt had been a rising star in the *Kriminalpolizei* and Franklin had followed the German's career with a mixture of admiration and apprehension. Anxiety became the uppermost emotion when Voigt dropped the passport with the Lion and Unicorn motif on his desk.

'I thought you would be interested to see this, Neil,' he said.

Even before Franklin opened it he knew the passport had belonged to Moresby. 'What makes you think I'd want to see it, Heinrich?' he said calmly.

'Because Moresby has been murdered.'

'I think you should inform the British Consul General. His office is in Uhlandstrasse, which is no distance from here.'

'Look at the amendment on page three where the occupation has been altered from government official to businessman by the Consul in Beirut.'

'It doesn't mean anything, Heinrich. Every civil servant is a government official in my country, same as in yours.'

'They cut his throat.'

'I'm sorry to hear that.'

'You've never seen such a mess. It looked as though nature had given Moresby a second mouth under his chin.'

'A sight like that would be enough to turn anyone's stomach.'

'You don't seem very upset.'

'I didn't know the man.'

'His name was John David Moresby.'

'I still didn't know him,' Franklin said.

'I'll take your word for it.'

'Would I lie to you?'

'I hope not, but if I find you have done so, I guarantee you will be leaving Berlin a lot sooner than 1997.' Voigt picked up the passport and started towards the door, then turned about as if some last-minute thought had occurred to him. 'Did I tell you that they had cut off his nose before they killed him?'

'No.' Franklin swallowed. 'Why do you suppose they did a thing like that?'

'I think they were sending you a message. What's that English expression about poking your nose into other people's business?'

Chapter 2

In a little over four years, Victor Hazelwood had gone from Head of the Russian Desk to Acting Director General of the Secret Intelligence Service. Neil Franklin, who was roughly the same age, maintained that he would never have advanced beyond the Russian Desk if the then Assistant Director, Eastern Bloc, hadn't suffered a fatal coronary in 1990, which cynics claimed had been caused by the sudden realisation that his once all-powerful empire was about to be dismembered. There wasn't a grain of truth in Franklin's snide observation; although fate might have contributed to his meteoric rise, Hazelwood had never been overpromoted.

No one had known that better than Stuart Dunglass, who had sent for Hazelwood and invited him to be his deputy the moment he had been informed that he was to be the next Director General. Dunglass had done this because he had spent the greater part of his service in the Far East and had been aware of his limitations. What he'd needed at his right hand was someone who could predict which way Yeltsin would jump even before the Russian President knew himself, and he couldn't have picked a better man than Hazelwood.

Until Dunglass had found his feet, Victor Hazelwood had been the DG in all but name. After twelve months in the appointment, that observation had ceased to apply and Hazelwood had gradually taken a back seat. He had come to the fore again when Dunglass had been admitted to hospital back in April for an operation on the prostate. That had been all of five months ago and there was still no telling when, if ever, he might return. The time, in fact, was fast approaching when the Prime Minister and Foreign Secretary would be invited to either confirm the Acting DG in post or select some outsider for the appointment. More than anything else, Hazelwood wanted the job but he was all too aware of the reputation he enjoyed in Whitehall. Although there was nothing wrong with a little bit of aggression, he was regarded as the apostle of the high-risk strategy which was anathema to the Foreign Office and politicians on both sides of the House. Realising what they wanted was a safe pair of hands, he had made a determined effort to change his image. Now, just when he had reason to believe he was succeeding, there was a good chance that the European Department under the direction of Rowan Garfield had undone all his good work with their shenanigans in Berlin.

Hazelwood turned back to the beginning and for the second time read the proceedings of the Board of Inquiry which he had convened, then placed the folder in his pending tray.

'Doesn't tell us much, does it, Rowan?' he said dismissively. 'The Board takes a statement from Steven Quorn, asks him a couple of questions for the sake of appearances and then comes to the conclusion that no blame can be attached to him.'

'I didn't know we were looking for a scapegoat,' Garfield retorted angrily.

'What makes you think I am?'

'Steven did nothing wrong; he followed his instructions to the letter. When Moresby failed to show, he left the rendezvous and contacted Neil Franklin—'

'Let's talk about Moresby,' Hazelwood said, cutting him short. 'Who put his name forward?'

'Our own people on the Armed Forces Desk. I described the sort of man we were looking for and they consulted the Ministry of Defence who produced a short list.'

'How many names did they give us?'

'Four,' Garfield told him promptly, 'all of them ex-army.'

'Remind me why we agreed to employ a reservist.'

'We were advised to do so. The army said the latest round of defence cuts had left them with a shortage of Arabic speakers whose other qualifications included colloquial German and six months' duty with a diplomatic protection group. They were, of course, being a touch sarcastic. Even before the Treasury went at them with a hatchet, the army would have had some difficulty filling that particular bill.'

Of the four possible candidates, only Moresby had possessed all the necessary qualifications. A former sergeant in the Royal Military Police, he had been made redundant in September 1993 at the age of thirty-two and had subsequently been taken on by Securicor for six months before setting up in business on his own account.

'Moresby looked good on paper,' Garfield continued. 'He had done two tours of duty in the Lebanon, the first back in 1982. This was shortly after Prime Minister Thatcher discovered the Foreign Office was employing a very expensive private security company to guard the British Embassy in Beirut. On her instructions, that lucrative contract was terminated forthwith and the task was given to the RMP.'

'And what was Moresby in 1982?'

'A twenty-one-year-old lance corporal.' Garfield cleared his throat. 'I know what you are thinking, Victor, but he wasn't a tender greenhorn when he went back to Beirut in 1985. Furthermore, he'd been an instructor at the RMP Depot and had taught God knows how many servicemen and women the kind of driving skills that could save their lives if ever they ran into a terrorist ambush.'

'Didn't do him much good in Berlin, did it?'

'Apparently not.'

'I wonder if he tried to make a deal with the people who eventually cut his throat?'

'A deal?' Garfield echoed in a voice a good octave higher than his normal tone.

'Quorn had a quarter of a million dollars in cash; perhaps Moresby hoped the people who had lifted him off the street would spare his life if he helped them to get their hands on the money?'

'Well, that's one thing we'll never know.'

'Unless we do a little digging,' Hazelwood said.

'I thought we were going to take a leaf out of Neil Franklin's book and keep our heads down?'

Hazelwood smiled. 'Don't look so worried, Rowan. I'm not going to do anything rash.'

Unfortunately, he already had. A prudent man would have backed off after the Foreign and Commonwealth Office had declined to alert their opposite numbers in Bonn, but he had never been the retiring type and in his judgement too much had been at stake to observe the diplomatic niceties. So he had given the European Department a green light to go ahead with an operation the Germans knew nothing about even though it would happen in their back yard.

'There's no way the *Kriminalpolizei* can link Moresby to us, Victor,' Garfield said, as if he were blessed with extra sensory perception and could tell what was passing through the DG's mind.

'He wasn't married, was he?' Hazelwood asked.

'Divorced four years ago, hasn't seen his ex-wife since the decree absolute even though she was given custody of the children. He had visitation rights but never exercised them.'

'Any girlfriends?'

'There was a live-in lover but they split up in April. Moresby intimated he was footloose and fancy-free.'

'What about the next of kin?'

'He nominated his father after the divorce. We got that from the Record of Service card, Army Form B2673. We thought it best not to ask Moresby if his father was still alive in case it made him suspicious. I mean, as far as Moresby was concerned, he had been hired to look after a diamond merchant who was going to see a potential client in Berlin.'

It hadn't been a bad cover story and Moresby hadn't been told that he and Quorn were on separate flights until the last moment. There was, however, one small detail which bothered Hazelwood.

'Moresby was briefed on Friday and departed for Berlin on the Monday. Right?'

'That's correct.'

'So where did he spend the weekend, Rowan?'

'At the Cadogan Hotel in Sloane Street.'

'And he was on his own the whole time?'

'Yes.'

'How do we know he didn't go home or visit some friend on the Saturday or Sunday?'

'Because we picked up his itemised hotel bill, and it was all there, every breakfast, lunch and dinner.'

'Did he make any phone calls?'

'Not from the hotel.'

'Let's hope he didn't use a pay phone,' Hazelwood said.

'You're not convinced Moresby was sans girlfriend, are you, Victor? You are afraid he smelled a rat, told her what it was, and the lady is going to sell her story to the highest bidder once she learns he's dead.'

'Something like that,' Hazelwood admitted.

'Well, one thing is certain: we can't afford to go looking for her. That really would be asking for trouble.'

'I'm sure you're right.'

Garfield took the hint and stood up. 'Is there anything else we need to discuss?' he asked politely.

'I don't think so, Rowan.'

Hazelwood waited for Garfield to leave, then took out his pocket diary. If the SIS could go outside The Firm to hire a guard dog to look after Steven Quorn, there was no reason why he shouldn't farm out a little job to an old hand like Peter Ashton. He would have to search high and low for someone to rival his experience – four years on the Russian Desk, two as Head of the Security Vetting and Technical Services Division and a spell as the Grade I SIS representative in the army's Military Operations (Special

Projects) branch at the Ministry of Defence. Furthermore, he was eager to return to the fold. Turning to the memo page at the back of the diary, Hazelwood looked up Ashton's new address and phone number in Lincoln.

Even though Ashton only put himself through it two mornings a week, the régime was still a punishing one. One hour in the gym, working out on the wall bars, horizontal beams, ropes and vaulting horse, followed by a good twenty minutes pumping iron would have been more than enough for most men of his age whose job was not physically demanding. But Ashton was unlike the vast majority of his peer group; five months ago in California he had taken a 6.35mm from a Walther PPK semiautomatic pistol in the left shoulder immediately below the collarbone, and now he was after a lot more than the feel-good factor. Determined to get himself in the peak of physical condition, he started running the moment he left the gym at Lincoln City football club.

The route he took was always the same – along Waterside, across the River Witham, on past St Swithin's Church and then up the long steep hill to the cathedral via Lindum Road and Pottergate. From there on it was level going all the way to the house in Church Lane. By putting in a final spurt over the last hundred yards, he managed to complete the one and a quarter miles from door to door in a fraction over five minutes. The fastest time yet, he told himself with great satisfaction, and he wasn't blowing like a grampus either. Digging into the pocket of his track suit, he took out the Yale key and opened the front door. Four-month-old Edward was a light sleeper and started crying as soon as he heard footsteps in the hall.

'Is that you, Peter?' Harriet called out from the kitchen.

'It had better not be the milkman,' he told her.

'Oh, very funny,' she said, turning away from the gas stove to face him with a saucepan in her left hand.

'What are you doing?'

'Preparing Edward's lunch. What does it look like?'

Harriet was half an inch under six feet. She had large hands with long tapering fingers, and was very self-conscious about the size of her feet which was ridiculous because, as Ashton had told her more than once, she would look overbalanced with anything less than a seven and a half. Following her pregnancy, she had regained her figure by rigorous exercise, slimming down to 143 pounds in the process. With her bone structure, any further loss of weight would make Harriet an ideal model for a War on Want poster. But eye-catching though her figure was, it was the perfect symmetry of her face that claimed everyone's attention and remained firmly imprinted in their minds afterwards. Harriet was, in fact, quite beautiful. Right now, however, she was regarding Ashton through narrowed eyes which were distinctly unfriendly.

'What's wrong?' he asked.

'Your friend Victor Hazelwood phoned while you were out. He wants you to call him back as soon as possible.'

Her tone of voice said it all. Harriet had never been a member of the Hazelwood fan club; as she saw it, loyalty was an admirable quality provided it extended in both directions, but in her opinion, Victor took Peter's for granted and made use of him. No argument of his could persuade Harriet she was wrong; she had observed Hazelwood at first-hand when she had been seconded from MI5 to the Security Vetting and Technical Services Division at Benbow House.

'Well, aren't you going to jump to it?' Harriet demanded.

'I'll help you with Edward first.'

'I can see to our son, you go and phone Hazelwood. I have to be in the office by twelve noon and I'd like to be sure there will be no distractions when you're supposed to be keeping an eye on Edward.'

'You're the boss.'

Ashton went upstairs to the smallest of the four bedrooms, a ten-by-nine box he used as a study, which overlooked the back garden. A month ago he had written

19

to Hazelwood asking whether it might be possible to rejoin The Firm if he repaid the eighteen months' salary he'd received as a golden handshake on resigning from the SIS. Mentally crossing his fingers in the hope that Victor had secured his reinstatement, he picked up the phone and tapped out the direct link number which bypassed the switchboard at Vauxhall Cross and went straight through to the Acting DG.

'Hi,' he said when Hazelwood answered, 'it's me, Peter.'

'Thank you for ringing back. I've got a job for you.'

'A permanent one?'

Hazelwood chuckled. 'No, I'm afraid that's still in the pipeline. This is a short-term commission, same daily rate of pay you would receive as a Grade I officer, plus expenses but no Inner London Weighting Allowance.'

'I don't know,' Ashton said doubtfully.

'I'm guaranteeing one month's salary for what is a few days' work.'

'I've heard that one before.'

'Let me ask you a question. Can you afford to walk away from £2,746?'

'You're in a generous mood, aren't you, Victor? I was on 32K a year when I left.'

'There's been a pay award in line with inflation since then. Now, are you interested or not?'

It took Ashton less than five seconds to make up his mind. Why else had he undertaken such a gruelling fitness programme if it wasn't to get himself ready for just such a contingency?

'When do I start?' he asked.

'What's wrong with today?'

'That's pretty short notice.'

'This inquiry won't wait.'

'You want to tell me what it's all about?'

Hazelwood wasn't prepared to do that over an open land line. Instead, everything Ashton needed to know would be delivered by special messenger. To this end, he was required to make his way to the East of England Showground outside Peterborough where he was to wait in the car park behind the Hare and Hounds opposite the exhibition site.

'The special messenger will arrive between two forty-five and three o'clock,' Hazelwood continued.

'Fine. How are we going to recognise one another?'

'He'll know the registration number of your Vauxhall Cavalier,' Hazelwood said, and hung up.

Ashton did the same, then went downstairs wondering how he was going to break the news to Harriet. He was still groping for inspiration when he walked into the kitchen and found her burping Edward.

'Well?' she said in a voice that warned him that trying to pull the wool over her eyes would not be a good idea. By the time he finished telling her what Hazelwood had said to him, they were out in the garden, Edward was back in his pram on the patio and Harriet was burning on a slow fuse. 'You've done it again, Peter.'

'Done what?'

'Allowed Victor to twist you around his little finger.'

'I want to be reinstated,' he said tightly. 'If I'd turned him down, he might just wonder why the hell he should go to bat for me.'

'I don't understand why you want to go back.'

'We need the money.'

'There are other ways of earning a living,' Harriet said, and walked back into the house.

Ashton agreed there were other ways of earning a living and reminded her of just how many CVs he'd filled out since returning from California. Unfortunately, German linguists were two a penny and it seemed there wasn't too much demand for fluent Russian speakers in the business world. He had done some freelance work, translating glossy catalogues of beauty products for Moscow housewives, but even that source of income was rapidly evaporating. So was the golden handshake he had received from the SIS. Eighteen months' salary came to £48,000 and his share of the deposit on the house had accounted for half of that. Although Harriet's parents had given her a similar amount as a wedding present, they had still needed a mortgage of £60,000 to buy the property.

'How much longer do you think we can keep up the repayments?' he asked, following her into the hall.

'I'm working.'

'Yeah, five half-days a week with an estate agent who happens to be a friend of your father's.'

'That's uncalled for.'

'Well, I'm sorry . . .'

'So you should be. Anyway, if the SIS did take you back, how do you propose to repay the £48,000?'

'I'd persuade the bank to give us a second mortgage.'

'Brilliant,' Harriet snorted.

'Listen, the only thing I'm good at is Intelligence-gathering.'

'And it's what you want to do?'

'Yes, it is.'

'I knew we'd get to the bottom line eventually.' Harriet went upstairs, then stopped on the landing and leaned over the banisters. 'Anyway, you can't go to Peterborough this afternoon. Who's going to look after Edward?'

'Your mother?'

'She's gone to London for the day. Remember?'

'Oh shit, I forgot.'

'And while Alec Peters is one of Daddy's oldest friends, he has made it very clear that he doesn't want me bringing our son into the office.'

'Then stay at home.'

'Don't be silly, we need the regular income I bring into the house.'

Ashton gritted his teeth. 'OK then,' he grated, 'I'll take Edward with me. We've got a special car seat for him.'

It was not, Harriet told him, a good idea. Disturb Edward now when he was about to drop off and he would be in a crotchety mood all afternoon. Their son would probably yell all the way to Peterborough and back, which Ashton would find very distracting at a time when he needed to have his wits about him.

Ashton retreated to the kitchen, bubbling under the surface like a volcano about to erupt. He was tired of being dependent on the Egans whose daughter also happened to be the breadwinner in all but name, and he was mad at Harriet for using Edward in order to thwart him. If she would only be honest with him and admit that she was frightened of being widowed at the age of thirty, he wouldn't get quite so riled. He also recognised he wouldn't be anything like as angry if much of what Harriet had said hadn't been true.

He heard a faint ping and instinctively looked over his shoulder to see if Harriet had left something cooking in the microwave and was unable to account for the noise when it became apparent that she hadn't. Then his head of steam dissipated as rapidly as it had built up and more than anything else he wanted to declare a truce, so much so that it didn't matter who was the first to raise the white flag.

'I'm sorry.' Ashton returned to the hall and repeated the message. 'I'm sorry,' he called out.

'I'm sorry too,' Harriet told him from the landing.

'I'll ring Hazelwood and tell him I won't be there to meet his special messenger.'

'That would be unfortunate.'

Ashton started up the staircase. 'What was that?'

'I've just rung the office to say I won't be in this afternoon,' She leaned over the banisters and smiled at him. 'Blame it on the time of month.'

Harriet had changed out of the sweater and slacks she had been wearing into a blouse and skirt and then, acting on an impulse, she had used the extension in the study to call the estate agents, Alec Peters and Sons.

'You're terrific,' he said.

'I know.'

'And I'm an idiot.'

'Tell me something new,' Harriet said with a laugh.

'How the hell are we going to manage if I'm away all the time? I mean, what are we going to do about Edward? We

23

can't expect your mother to become a permanent babysitter.'

'We'll think of something.'

They were only a foot apart now and she smothered his mouth with hers before he could voice yet another imagined difficulty.

Neil Franklin was still trying to explain to an irritated, middle-aged lady why it would be difficult to obtain a copy of a title written by an obscure English novelist which had been out of print for the past sixteen years when 'Attila the Hun' walked into the bookshop. Whether the nickname was appropriate or not, it sprang instantly to mind the moment Franklin laid eyes on him. Although lacking the beard, long hair and droopy moustache, the man certainly had the gloomy, fierce and heavy countenance common to many artists' impressions of the barbarian. Listening with only half an ear to the complaining matron, he watched the man approach Helga von Schinkel and idly wondered if *Mein Kampf* featured amongst his personal list of the best top ten of all time. Then the man turned his head to look at him as Helga also glanced in his direction, and Franklin knew Attila hadn't dropped by the store to purchase a book. With a muttered apology, Franklin left the middle-aged lady to see what he wanted.

'This gentleman is Herr Polizei Kommissar Eicke,' Helga informed him.

'From the detective squad, Central District,' the Kommissar added and produced his ID.

'He wishes to have a word with you, Herr Franklin,' Helga said, not to be outdone.

'What about?'

'Is there somewhere we can talk privately?' Eicke asked.

'My office at the back,' Franklin said, and led the way.

He didn't need to ask Eicke again what he could do for him. With maximum dramatic effect, the German detective took out a batch of colour photographs and one by one laid them face uppermost on the desk. Franklin was not a squeamish man but the sight of what had been done to Moresby sickened him.

'The Police President instructed me to show you these,' Eicke said in a harsh voice. 'The Englishman you have seen before. The other victim is not a Turkish guest worker as we had originally thought but a Palestinian who was expelled from Kuwait for allegedly co-operating with the Iraqis during the Gulf War. His name was Gamal al Hassan . . .'

There was no stopping the German. Every time Franklin tried to say something, Eicke simply raised his voice and talked him down. By the time the Detective Inspector had finished, the Englishman knew where Gamal al Hassan had been staying in Berlin and how the Palestinian had got there.

'Why should I be interested in all this?' he asked when the well finally ran dry.

'Because Herr Voigt said you would want to pass the information on to London.' Eicke frowned. 'I was told your friends at Vauxhall Cross would be interested.'

Somehow Franklin managed to keep a tight rein on his temper. Only the Chief of the *Kriminalpolizei* and the Police President knew the identity of the SIS Head of Station. That was the accepted rule, but Voigt was determined to get rid of him once and for all. The bastard was going to send every Tom, Dick and Harry on the Force to the English Bookshop on Budapesterstrasse until the lowliest traffic cop in the city knew who he was and what he did, which would make it impossible for him to continue in post.

'My compliments to Herr Voigt,' he said with a grimace that passed for a smile. 'Be sure to mention that I hope one day to be in a position where I can do the same for him.'

Ashton could not have timed it better had he tried. Five minutes after arriving at the Hare and Hounds, the special messenger roared into the car park on a Harley Davidson. Ashton was asked to produce his driving licence for identification purposes and was then required to sign for a large Jiffy bag, after which they went their separate ways. Heading back to Lincoln on the A15, Ashton pulled into the first lay-by he came to and examined the contents of the Jiffy bag. Pinned to the personal documents of Sergeant J. D. Moresby was a long typewritten note from Hazelwood which he had neglected to either sign or initial.

Chapter 3

What had drawn Moresby to York when he had set up in business was a mystery to Ashton. According to the Record of Service card, there was no family connection and he'd never been posted within a hundred miles of the city. Moresby had been born in Cambridge on 16 July 1961 and his father, whom he had nominated as his next of kin following his divorce, had been living in Dartmouth when he'd left the army. For the last nine months of his service, Moresby had been stationed at Woking where he'd taken every opportunity to prepare himself for civilian life. Apart from attending a vocational training course, he had applied for several jobs and had been taken on by Securicor before his actual release date. On 7 March 1994, barely six months after joining the security firm, he'd handed in his notice and moved to York where he had formed a company trading as Sentinel Alarms Limited.

Sentinel Alarms Limited was sandwiched between a betting shop and a gents' hairdresser on Parliament Street. Amongst the documents Hazelwood had sent to Ashton was a sketch map of York which pinpointed the location of the firm and indicated some of the prominent landmarks in the area. The only thing Victor had neglected to tell him was where he could park the Vauxhall Cavalier. York was a walled city full of narrow one-way streets and double yellow lines policed by an eager band of traffic wardens.

It took Ashton the best part of half an hour to discover

there was nowhere he could leave the car in the city centre. In due course, he also discovered that every car park outside the walls was full. Working outwards in ever-increasing circles, he eventually found a vacant space at the kerbside in Fulford on the southern outskirts and caught a bus back into town.

Before leaving for York, Ashton had taken the precaution of phoning the offices of Sentinel Alarms to make sure somebody was going to be in and had found himself talking to the company secretary, a Mrs Anthea Vise. Moresby's body had been found during the early hours of Tuesday morning; forty-eight hours later, news of the murder had yet to be reported in the British press. In his covering note, Hazelwood hadn't indicated whether the next of kin had been informed but from what she had said on the phone, it was evident that Mrs Vise had learned of Moresby's death. From the tone of her voice, Ashton had concluded that she was upset; on meeting her, the dark smudges under both eyes told him she hadn't slept much since hearing the news. He also saw that she had cried a lot.

'My name's Ashton, Mrs Vise,' he said, introducing himself, then flashing his old identity card at her which Hazelwood had enclosed with Moresby's documents. 'I'm in the Consular Department at the Foreign and Common-wealth Office. We spoke earlier this morning.'

'Yes, I remember.'

'I'm sorry to bother you at a time like this but . . .'

'The German police would like to know what Jack was doing in Berlin,' she said, finishing the sentence for him.

'Yes. Is there somewhere we can talk without fear of being interrupted?'

'We could go upstairs to the flat.'

'Well, if it's not too much trouble,' he said.

'It's no trouble at all, Mr Ashton.'

The offices of Sentinel Alarms Limited consisted of two rooms at the front of the shop and a large store at the back where Moresby kept the smoke detectors, burglar alarms, infra-red intruder systems, surveillance cameras, ground sensors and various other security gadgets. There wasn't enough shelf space to hold all the stock and the overspill in cardboard boxes had simply been left on the floor. To reach the staircase which led to the flat above was like picking a way through an obstacle course.

The flat was neat and tidy. The flowers in a cut-glass vase on the hall table provided further evidence of a woman's touch. It was, Ashton thought, yet another sign that Anthea Vise and Moresby had been lovers. He wondered how and where they had met, wondered too if she had money and that had been part of the attraction for Moresby. The first to admit that he was no good at judging a person's age, Ashton still reckoned that Anthea Vise was unlikely to see forty again. A natural redhead who even in high heels was no more than five feet six, she was not unattractive, but the fact remained that she didn't have the figure to get away with a micro mini-skirt.

Aside from that observation, Moresby must have been eight, maybe as much as ten years younger than Anthea Vise, and if his army ID photograph was anything to go by, a lot of young women would have found him attractive. But the one really relevant point was the fact that he had told the SIS he was footloose and fancy-free when he clearly hadn't been. Perhaps Moresby had been afraid he wouldn't get the job if he had admitted to an involvement, but whatever his motive, it showed he'd been prepared to embellish the truth. It also showed that whoever had vetted him hadn't done a very good job.

'What would you like to drink, Mr Ashton?' Anthea Vise walked over to the sideboard in the adjoining dining alcove and, crouching down, opened the side cupboard farthest away from the serving hatch in the kitchen. 'We've got gin, whisky, brandy, sherry, Grand Marnier . . .' She looked over her shoulder, frowning. 'I think there may be a couple of beers in the fridge.'

'Thanks all the same,' Ashton told her, 'but it's a little early for me.'

'Well, it's not for me, I need a drink.'

Anthea Vise poured herself a very stiff whisky from a bottle of Vat 69 and filled the rest of the tumbler with lemonade. Waterford Crystal, Ashton decided, eyeing the glass in her hand as she returned to the sitting room. It went with the G-Plan three-piece suite and the hand-carved nest of occasional tables. Either the lady had brought a considerable sum of money into the partnership or else the two of them had been living above their means and were in hock up to their eyebrows.

'Did Mr Moresby tell you why he was going to Berlin?' Ashton asked, diplomatically keeping up the pretence that Anthea Vise and the former RMP sergeant had simply been business partners.

'I didn't know Jack was going to Berlin until he rang me on Sunday night. I thought he'd sugared off for the weekend with some woman he was seeing on the side.'

There were any number of questions Ashton wanted to ask her but he was supposed to be an official from the Consular Department and if he went outside his brief, she might become suspicious. His best course was to play the sympathetic listener and hope she would unburden herself. He had already learned that contrary to the instructions Steven Quorn had given Moresby, the man had contacted Anthea Vise after he had been briefed.

'It wouldn't be the first time Jack has done that to me, Mr Ashton. That's why I didn't believe him until he rang me again from the hotel where he was staying in Berlin. He gave me the phone number so that I could ring back and satisfy myself that he wasn't lying. Had to go through the switchboard at Hucker's Hotel to get his room number.' She took a stiff drink of whisky, then said, 'No, I'm a liar, it was Hecker's Hotel.'

'Did Mr Moresby sound nervous to you?'

'Jack – nervous?' Anthea Vise threw back her head and laughed. 'You've got to be joking, he was too stupid to know when to be frightened.'

'The German police think he was in Berlin to buy

heroin from one of the East European cartels and the deal went sour.'

There was a grain of truth in the allegation. Ever since the collapse of the Warsaw Pact, the SIS had been looking for a new role. According to the brief Hazelwood had sent Ashton, they had found one in waging war against the drug cartels. Steven Quorn had gone to Berlin to buy information from an insider and had used the hapless Moresby as a go-between.

'The Germans are barking up the wrong tree, Jack wasn't into drugs.' Anthea Vise swallowed the rest of the whisky, then got up and, teetering on high heels, went into the dining alcove to fix herself an even stiffer drink. 'He despised anyone who smoked pot, snorted cocaine or shot themselves up with heroin.'

'Well, you should know,' Ashton murmured.

'You're right, I do. Jack was a damned good military policeman. You should have heard him on the subject of drug pushers and what he would like to do to them.' Anthea Vise returned from the alcove and sat down again, spilling some of the whisky and lemonade over her mini-skirt in the process. 'Mind you tell that to the German police,' she added.

'You can't blame the *Kriminalpolizei*. They're just looking for a motive, and robbery is out. Whoever killed Jack wasn't after his money, credit cards or traveller's cheques.'

'What about Mr Quorn, was he also murdered?'

Ashton managed to conceal his surprise. 'Who's Mr Quorn?' he asked, feigning innocence.

'The diamond merchant Jack was supposed to be protecting.'

'The police didn't mention his name when they contacted our Consul General in Berlin.'

'Can't say I'm surprised. Chances are he doesn't exist. I mean, how would a diamond merchant in Hatton Garden know that Jack would make a good bodyguard?'

Her speech was getting a little slurred and she was

finding it difficult to get her tongue around words of more than two syllables. Although a long way from being drunk, Anthea Vise was beginning to be affected by the whisky.

'Doesn't make sense, Mr Ashton.'

'I don't know what to make of it either.'

'Jack told me he only took the job because the business was going down the pan. As if I needed telling.' Anthea Vise finished the rest of her drink and placed the empty glass on the arm of her chair while she opened her handbag and took out a packet of John Player. 'Do you smoke?' she asked.

'No, I gave it up twelve years ago.'

'Well, good for you,' she said, and lit up. 'Sentinel Alarms, now there's a joke. Those smoke detectors you saw downstairs? We can't even give them away, that's how successful we are.'

'I'd say it was a sign of the times,' Ashton told her. 'The country's still in recession.'

'None of the local firms wanted to know us,' Anthea Vise continued in a monotone. 'Jack even tried selling door to door – same story.'

'Is that why he decided to branch out?'

'It couldn't have been a conscious decision because he was offered the job. At least, that's what Jack told me. This diamond merchant was supposed to have called him while I was out of the office.'

She spoke slowly as if suddenly aware that her annunciation wasn't all it might be. Even so, conscious was pronounced with a slurring 'shush'. There was, however, nothing wrong with her mental faculties.

'I don't understand how this Mr Quorn knew he had been trained as a bodyguard. I mean, the army wouldn't have broadcast the fact, would they?'

'Maybe somebody who'd served with Jack put in a good word for him?' Ashton suggested.

'I wish I could believe that.'

Ashton didn't like the way the interview was going. It was to have been a damage limitation exercise; there had been an almighty cock-up in Berlin and Victor had hired him to make sure the incident was kept under wraps. Unfortunately, he had merely succeeded in arousing Anthea Vise's suspicion. The only remedy he could think of was to rubbish Moresby.

'Have you ever spoken to this Mr Quorn?' he asked snidely.

'I just told you, he phoned Jack while I was out of the office. I'd gone to Marks and Spencer across the road.'

'So Quorn could have been a woman for all you know?'

Anthea Vise took the bait, just as he had hoped she would. 'The bastard,' she said breathlessly.

'Sorry?'

'Two days after Mr Quorn got in touch with him, a woman phoned asking for Jack. She had a real lah-di-dah voice; when I asked who was calling, she hung up.'

Ashton immediately said he was sorry, he hadn't meant to imply that Mr Moresby had gone to Berlin on an illicit weekend. But of course that had been his intention and the more he tried to persuade Anthea Vise that she was jumping to conclusions, the more certain she became that Moresby had been having an affair with a woman called Quorn. He gave her sympathy and in return she told him all there was to know about her relationship with the dead man. By the time Ashton left, he fancied he had dispelled any notion she might have had that Moresby had been recruited by a government agency.

There were however a number of disturbing facts he needed to discuss with Hazelwood. Before returning to where he had left the car in Fulford, he rang the Acting DG from a pay phone, told him what was on his mind and asked for a meeting.

Fräulein Helga von Schinkel left her apartment in Charlottenburg and started walking back to the bookstore. It was not her usual practice to go so far afield during her lunch hour but she had done so today for business reasons. After nearly seventy years of living under the same roof, she had decided to put her flat up for sale. When she retired on 31 December, Helga planned to up sticks and spend the rest of her days in Venice with Sophia, her Italian-born cousin.

She had, in fact, started the ball rolling two months before informing Neil Franklin of her intention to retire. Until today, her agent had been unable to find a prospective buyer for the apartment. The trouble was, the young couple who had expressed an interest had insisted on making an appointment to view the property at twelve noon. Their take-it-or-leave-it attitude had angered Helga; she had become even more enraged when they had arrived forty-five minutes late and offered no word of apology. Things had gone from bad to worse as they found fault with everything: the rooms were too big, the ceilings too high, the windows too small and there weren't enough power points. The apartment on Kantstrasse had belonged to Helga's parents; it was where she had grown up, it had survived the war when lesser buildings around it had been reduced to rubble and brick dust. To listen to their snide observations had been almost unbearable. But the lowest point, the nadir of her discontent, had been the young woman's reaction to the sight of Hans Dieter's photograph on her dressing table.

'A Nazi friend of yours, Fräulein von Schinkel?' she had enquired pointedly.

Hans Dieter Best, officer cadet 16 Oldenburg Airborne Regiment, patriot and resistance fighter, condemned to death for high treason in 1943 and beheaded at the second attempt by a clumsy axeman. The Gestapo had taken great pleasure in showing Helga photographs of the execution when she was being questioned at the Prinz-Albrecht-Strasse Headquarters. Hans Dieter Best, the man she had planned to marry, the man she still mourned fifty-one years later.

The young woman did not know how close Helga had come to striking her. The husband had in mind to make an offer for the apartment but she had refused to listen to him and had ordered them both to leave. Long after they had left, she had still been in a blind rage. Although the S-Bahn station was no distance from the apartment, Helga chose to walk the length of Kantstrasse through Savignyplatz to the junction with Joachimtaler Strasse near the empty shell of the bombed-out Kaiser Wilhelm Memorial Church. By the time she reached the English Bookshop, she was in a more equitable frame of mind, and tired.

On most afternoons at this time of the year, not too many people walked through the door, but there were always exceptions to every rule and this particular Thursday happened to be one of them. There were several young men and women whom Helga assumed were university students and an elderly couple who had buttonholed Herr Franklin. The couple had their backs to her; catching Franklin's eye, she tapped her chest and pointed towards them, a gesture that asked if he wished her to rescue him. The way he held his right hand close to his side and gently moved the index finger like a pendulum told Helga there was no need. Well, that was all right; she had work to do, invoices to check, the books to balance.

As Helga walked towards the cubbyhole, which served as her office at the back of the bookstore, she heard a man with a guttural voice call out to Herr Franklin. A split second later, she received a violent blow in the back which hurled her through the door to her office.

Ashton turned off Hampstead High Street into Gayton Road, went on down the hill towards the Heath and then wheeled into Willow Walk. After the unnaturally dry and hot summer, the leafy chestnut and lime trees which lined the pavements like well-disciplined soldiers on parade were already beginning to turn. In another fortnight or so, the leaves would be ankle-deep on the ground and small boys would be knocking the husks down to get at the conkers inside.

The house which Hazelwood owned was called Willow Dene. It formed part of what had once been a magnificent residence built in 1900, when things were done on a grand scale. Under one slate roof there had been six large bedrooms, two bathrooms, a study, library, games room, parlour, dining room, drawing room, conservatory, kitchen and scullery, as well as the servants' quarters in the attic. Over the years, various builders and interior decorators had converted the house into three maisoncttes, carefully subdividing the property so that each residence had a minimum of three bedrooms.

Ashton parked the Vauxhall Cavalier close in to the kerb, collected a much-battered suitcase from the trunk and, aiming the miniature transmitter at the vehicle, activated the central locking and newly installed alarm. Opening the wrought-iron gate set in the hedge, he followed the footpath to the front door at the left side of the house and rang the bell. A frequent visitor to Willow Dene, he had never stayed overnight before and he wondered if Victor had consulted his wife before issuing the invitation. Victor's suggestion that he should leave his suitcase in the hall while they adjourned to the study left Ashton with the uncomfortable feeling that Alice had had little or no forewarning.

'Dinner's at eight,' Hazelwood told him grandly. 'Gives us plenty of time for a chat before you need to bath and change.'

The study was Victor's domain; it was the one place in the house where he was allowed to smoke. The curtains in the sash windows, the books and the wooden shelves themselves, which were now a dull yellow instead of a high-gloss white, all testified to his love of a good Burma cheroot. Given Hazelwood's addiction, Ashton was flattered that he should take time out to pour him an ultra-large whisky with just a dash of soda before raiding the ornately carved wooden box on the desk, one of a pair he had bought in India while on a field trip to Delhi years ago. The other had graced his office in Century House and had presumably accompanied him to the new SIS Headquarters at Vauxhall Cross.

' "And a woman is only a woman," ' Hazelwood paused to blow a smoke ring towards the high ceiling, then added, ' "but a good cigar is a Smoke." Know where that quotation comes from?'

' "The Betrothed",' Ashton told him, 'by Rudyard Kipling. And the quotation isn't apt because you are smoking a cheroot which is open at both ends.'

'You're being pedantic.'

'Maybe that's why you keep on hiring me.'

'Could be you're right. Now suppose you justify the generous commission you'll receive from the SIS?'

'Somebody made a boo-boo when they hired J. D. Moresby; the man was about as leakproof as a colander. He was a cock-happy Romeo who didn't know the meaning of discretion.'

Keeping the narrative as brief as possible, Ashton repeated everything Anthea Vise had told him about her relationship with the deceased whom she had met while on holiday in Cyprus roughly eight months after her husband had got himself electrocuted trying to reconnect a power line that had been struck by lightning.

'Moresby was stationed in the Sovereign Base of Akrotiri at the time and he picked her up in a bar called Simeon's in Limassol. I don't know when Mrs Vise told him about the £425,000 she had received in compensation, but I'm willing to bet the money was the major attraction for Moresby. Anyway, they became a number and they eventually set up house together in Woking when he was posted back to the UK.'

That had been her first big mistake; others had followed quickly. Against her better judgement, Anthea Vise had been persuaded to become a Name at Lloyd's and had then compounded the error by lending Moresby the necessary capital to set up in business.

'Why York?' Hazelwood asked.

'She came from there, had a council house which she and her husband bought when the Thatcher government was encouraging home ownership.'

The house and most of her capital had gone when the Lloyd's syndicate was hammered by a series of insurance disasters, but she had made sure that the money she had put into Sentinel Alarms Limited couldn't be touched. That had been the one hold Anthea Vise had had on Moresby whenever he strayed, and the threat of liquidation had always brought him to heel.

'Of course, he wasn't aware they were steadily going broke,' Ashton continued. 'Anthea Vise kept the books and didn't apprise him of the facts. They'd had another blazing row just before Moresby left for Berlin. She was convinced he had another woman in tow and put the fear of God up him. Which is why Moresby phoned her when he was in London and again from Hecker's Hotel in Berlin. He also told her he was looking after a diamond merchant called Quorn.'

'Shit.' Hazelwood aimed the cheroot in the direction of a cut-down 40mm shell case and spilled ash all over the desk and himself. 'Oh shit,' he said wearily.

'I did the only thing I could and convinced her that Quorn was a woman. It wasn't difficult given that she suspected as much.'

'You did a good job, Peter.'

'Let's not be too hasty with the congratulations. We could have a problem if the *Kriminalpolizei* ask Interpol for information on Moresby. We don't want the police knocking on her door.'

'Yes, that would be rather embarrassing.'

'Could we prime the Interpol cell at Scotland Yard, Victor? You know, tell them to sit on the request for a week or so and then send the *Kriminalpolizei* some plausible feedback which will satisfy their curiosity?'

'Consider it done,' Hazelwood said airily.

'Good. That only leaves Moresby's father down in Devon. He knows Anthea Vise; in fact, he broke the news to her after he was informed of his son's death. Now, I don't think he is going to take it too kindly if he learns that his son's reputation has been rubbished. My gut tells me he is not going to be anything like as pliable as Mrs Vise. So the question is, do you want me to go down there or should we give him a wide berth?'

'I'm a great believer in nipping things in the bud.'

'Right.'

'Just be careful, that's all. Walk on eggshells . . .'

The phone rang before Hazelwood had time to explain precisely what he had in mind. Answering it with something like a grunt, he suddenly sat bolt upright, then touched the button on the cradle and told the caller to go ahead. His face gave nothing away and apart from the odd 'yes', the conversation was entirely one-sided. But at the end, he asked to be kept fully informed of developments and, as if in a hypnotic trance, slowly replaced the receiver. Ashton had never seen him look so shocked.

'What's wrong, Victor?' he asked quietly.

Hazelwood turned to face him. 'Neil Franklin's been killed,' he said bleakly. 'Some murderous bastard planted God knows how many pounds of Semtex in the bookshop and blew the place to smithereens.'

Chapter 4

Heinrich Voigt stopped the BMW just short of the barrier which sealed off Budapesterstrasse and got out. Acknowledging the salute from the patrolman on duty, he ducked under the plastic tape stretched across the road and walked on past the Inter-Continental Hotel towards the heap of rubble that had been the English Bookshop. Sixteen hours after the bombing at 15.20 yesterday afternoon, the emergency services had been scaled down to one ambulance and a fire engine. The arc lamps that had been rigged to illuminate the building so that the rescue team could work through the night were no longer required and were being dismantled by an electrician. Only a dog handler with his *Schäferhund* were still searching the rubble, looking for signs of life; the remaining personnel were clustered round a mobile kitchen breakfasting on coffee, rolls, cheese, ham and frankfurters.

'How are you doing, Chief?' Voigt asked the senior fire officer on the spot.

'I think we are about finished here.' The fire chief pointed the mug of coffee in the direction of the dog handler. 'Soon as he's completed a final check of the building, we'll be moving on and the *Kriminalpolizei* can have the place to themselves.'

Voigt nodded. His men would have their work cut out delicately sifting through the rubble like archaeologists on a dig. Only they wouldn't be looking for artefacts from a bygone age; they would be searching for fragments of the bomb which would enable Forensic to determine what type of explosive had been used. If they were lucky, they might also recover sufficient evidence to identify the terrorist organisation responsible for the outrage. Although the initial report had spoken of a possible gas leak, Voigt had known from the outset that it wasn't an accident, an opinion that had been rapidly confirmed after the emergency services had arrived on the scene.

'It's a bad business,' Voigt said to himself.

'It certainly is,' the fire chief agreed wearily. 'We've brought out another four bodies since you were here last.'

That had been around midnight when the total number of known fatalities had already risen to eight. Now it was in double figures, with a further twenty-one injured, some of them seriously. None of the injured had been inside the bookshop; all had been cut by shards of glass when the windows had blown out and they had also suffered varying degrees of shock. But the pedestrians who had been in the immediate vicinity of the premises when the explosion had occurred had suffered multiple compound fractures and were now in intensive care.

'These latest casualties,' Voigt said tentatively; 'was one of them a woman in her late sixties?'

'Well, yes, there was a woman and I suppose she could have been about that age, but it's hard to be really sure because she was pretty banged up. I mean, I've never seen injuries like it.'

The dead woman was Helga von Schinkel; Voigt had no doubt about that because he had repeatedly telephoned her apartment throughout the night and there had been no answer. He already knew Franklin was dead because he had been there when the firemen had recovered his body less than half an hour after the explosion. Despite the Englishman's terrible injuries, Voigt had recognised him immediately. Although Franklin had lost both legs, one below the kneecap, the other above, and his right arm had been blown off at the shoulder, his face had been virtually untouched. His cheeks had sunk and were drained of blood, leaving them the colour of chalk so that he had suddenly looked an old withered man in his nineties, but there had been no need to resort to dental charts for identification purposes as would undoubtedly be the case with most of the other victims.

Voigt thought it strange that Franklin should have been the first victim to be dug out of the rubble. His office was at the back of the store and logically his body should have been amongst the last to be recovered. Of course, he might have spotted the bomb and tried to get out before it detonated, but whatever else he might have been, Franklin had never been a coward and Voigt had dismissed the notion almost as soon as it had occurred to him.

The effects of blast, especially in a confined space, were frequently unpredictable. He recalled what his father had told him of his experiences when in command of a *Technische Nothilfe* battalion during the war. There was the block warden who had discovered that, after the adjoining tenement had been levelled by a 1,000-pound medium capacity bomb, four of the sixty-two occupants of his basement shelter had died without a mark on them. And how, during one daylight raid by the Amis, a naked man denuded by a high-explosive bomb as he was running to the nearest shelter, had walked into his command post. The man had come virtually from one side of Berlin to the other which was not a healthy thing to do in February '45 when there were a thousand B17s over the city. He had died later, so Voigt's father had maintained, from delayed shock.

'I see we've still got a couple of vultures with us, Herr Polizei Präsident.'

Voigt glanced to his right in the direction of the Zoo. Although the news-gathering teams from the two public service broadcasting channels had departed, Berlin's local TV station was still represented. He also recognised a reporter from *Der Tagesspiegel*.

'A bit different from yesterday evening, eh?'

'A distinct improvement.' Voigt scowled. Yesterday evening it had required a strong cordon of police officers to hold back the press, and their baying as they called to him asking for a statement had sounded like a pack of jackals.

'They're hoping you will give them an updated briefing.'

'There's nothing wrong with hoping,' Voigt growled.

He had had enough of that yesterday. He had faced the pack twice, the first time shortly after Franklin had been brought out of the building. He had answered their questions in a monotone, all too aware of the shameful voice inside his head which told him over and over again that something good had come out of the incident, that at least it would be a long time before the British SIS became a thorn in his side again, if ever. Racked with guilt, he had been unable to face Ella Franklin and had taken the easy way out, leaving it to the British Consul General to break the news that her husband had been killed.

'Looks as if we're back in business.'

The quiet voice of the fire chief jerked Voigt out of his dark reverie.

'What did you say?' he asked.

'The dog's found another body.'

'Do you have to be so damned cheerful?' Voigt turned away from him and started walking back to the BMW. 'Isn't the death toll large enough already?'

'Hey, don't get me wrong, I didn't mean it literally.'

'And I didn't mean to jump down your throat.' Voigt waved a hand above his head. 'Let me know what you find.'

He walked on, ducked under the tape and got into the BMW. Ten minutes to seven, the sun well above the horizon now and everything pointing to a fine September day. He would go home, spruce himself up a bit and have breakfast; then he really would have to pay his respects to Frau Ella Franklin. He had put off that awkward duty long enough and he had run out of excuses.

* * *

Hazelwood chose to hold the inquiry immediately after the usual morning prayers with Heads of Departments had been concluded. He could have asked Rowan Garfield to stay on in the conference room while his PA sent for Steven Quorn, but that would have been a little too informal for his liking. After what had happened in Berlin, he preferred to summon both men to his office, a subtle way of letting them know they were on the mat. There was another reason for the venue: his office was the only place in Vauxhall Cross where smoking was permitted, a privilege which Stuart Dunglass had reluctantly agreed to shortly before he had been admitted to hospital.

'I assume we all agree that whoever planted that bomb knew the English Bookshop was run by the SIS?' Hazelwood gazed quizzically in Garfield's direction. 'Rowan?'

'I don't think there can be any doubt about that.'

'And we can be equally certain that Neil Franklin had been targeted for assassination?'

'One is forced to that conclusion,' Garfield admitted.

Hazelwood opened the ornate wooden box on the desk, the duplicate of the one he kept in his study at home, and took out a cheroot. He savoured the aroma first, then lit it, all the time looking thoughtfully at Steven Quorn. A Grade III desk officer in the European Department, Quorn was twenty-nine, a fact which, on first acquaintance, most people found hard to believe. He had a pleasant, somewhat immature face, curly light brown hair, and eyes which occasionally looked doleful enough to remind Hazelwood of a St Bernard dog.

'Do you believe that Franklin was hit as a direct consequence of the operation you were running in Berlin?' he asked Quorn.

'No,' Garfield said, before his subordinate could answer for himself. 'There's no evidence to support the accusation.'

'I wasn't aware I had accused anyone.'

'It sounded that way to me, Victor.'

'I think you are being oversensitive.'

Garfield leaned forward, arms resting on his thighs. It was a posture he always adopted when he was fighting his corner. 'Look, Neil wasn't involved in the operation; no one went near him, his only function was to provide additional resources should Steven ask for help. There was no contact.'

'At least, not physically,' Quorn added. 'I did however phone him twice. I had been instructed to let him know that I'd arrived in Berlin and this I did as soon as I'd checked into my hotel. And naturally I rang him again when Moresby failed to show up at the RV.'

'Yes, so you told the Board of Inquiry.' Hazelwood contemplated the cheroot, then drew on it and slowly exhaled the smoke. 'The thing is, what did you tell Moresby to do in an emergency? I mean, suppose it had been the other way round and you had failed to turn up at the *Schwarz und Weiss*?'

'He was to go back to his hotel and wait.'

'For how long?'

'Twenty-four hours.'

'And then what?'

'He was to catch the next flight to Heathrow.'

'What about the money?' Hazelwood asked, chipping away. 'The 250,000 dollars that were in the safe-deposit box in the Europa-Center? Did Moresby know how that was to be recovered?'

'No.' Quorn glanced to his right as if seeking support from Garfield for what he was about to say. 'No, he didn't need to know. Franklin had been told where the down payment was to be lodged. He had also been told that I would leave the duplicate key to the safe-deposit box with the concierge at the Hotel Berliner Hof. It was his job to recover the money.'

'Those were the arrangements, Victor,' Garfield said, backing his subordinate.

Hazelwood nodded. He had vetted and approved the plan submitted by the European Department and he had been prepared to take on trust their assessment that Moresby was the ideal choice for a go-between. But Ashton had thrown a new light on the former RMP sergeant and it was evident he had seen through Quorn's story and had been clever enough to worm a lot of information out of him.

'I believe Moresby knew he was working for the SIS,' Hazelwood announced bluntly.

Quorn went a little red in the face. Anger was not the cause; he was the kind of man who blushed when he felt guilty or was embarrassed.

'I know what you are thinking, Director, but I never mentioned Neil and I didn't tell him about the English Bookshop.'

'No one is saying you did,' Hazelwood told him.

According to the source who'd demanded a quarter of a million dollars up front, there was a *Mafiozniki* involvement. If there was any truth in that claim, it was likely the opposition already knew the identity of the SIS Head of Station and the real purpose of the English Bookshop on the Budapesterstrasse long before Quorn had arrived in Berlin.

'The truth is, Franklin should never have been allowed to remain in post for eight years; his face became too well known. The KGB had him tagged, just as we knew who was running their show in East Berlin.'

'What are you implying, Victor?' Garfield asked.

'There are a lot of ex-KGB men in the Russian Mafia. I'm saying they either carried out the bombing or else they pointed their friends and business associates in the right direction.'

'And when did they do this?'

'I imagine soon after the friends got their hands on Moresby. Up to that point, the poor man had thought he was dealing with the source, but Gamal al Hassan was already dead. They had killed him after he had told them how to get in touch with his SIS paymaster.'

'That's pure guesswork,' Garfield said dismissively.

'You're right, it is. But there would be no need to use one's imagination to anything like the same extent if Neil Franklin hadn't been quite so determined to keep his head down.'

The withdrawal of the Berlin Infantry Brigade had left Neil feeling exposed. He no longer had access to the crypto-protected communications provided by the detached squadron of 13 Signal Regiment and now had to rely on either a secure speech telephone or the diplomatic wireless link at the British Consulate. It had been his belief that both facilities could be monitored by the German Intelligence Service. He had therefore deliberately kept all his Intelligence reports short and sweet to minimise the risk of interception. In the forty-eight hours prior to his death, Franklin had sent just two messages to Vauxhall Cross: one to notify the SIS that Moresby had been murdered, the other a day later reporting that the second murder victim had been identified as Gamal al Hassan. He had ventured no opinion as to who had been the first to die, nor had he attempted to find out.

'Still, there's no profit in bemoaning the lack of information we've had from Berlin.' Hazelwood bent down, picked up the metal wastebin by his desk and used it to stub out the cheroot. 'What we have to do now is put things right. Who's looking after Ella Franklin?'

'The Consul General visited her yesterday evening and again first thing this morning. He will be taking care of the funeral arrangements.'

'Better get one of our people up from Bonn. Ella ought to be told what her pension rights are and so on.'

'I'll see to it, Victor.'

'Good. Have we tried to contact Helga von Schinkel?'

'I've rung her flat several times but no one answered,' Garfield said.

'What about the other Germans on Franklin's payroll? Have you managed to raise any of them?'

'Oh, come on, Victor. You know what Neil was like, he ran his own show and didn't tell us any more than he had to. Sure, I've heard of a guy called Willie but I don't know his surname or what he does for a living.'

'I bet Ashton does.'

'Ashton.' Garfield reared back in his chair as if somebody had struck him. 'You're not planning to use him again, are you, Victor?'

'Do you have a problem with that?'

'Where are you going to put him? The Administrative Wing has left Benbow House, we're all under the same roof now and he doesn't have the requisite security clearance to enter Vauxhall Cross.'

'Don't you worry about that,' Hazelwood said airily. 'I've got just the place for him where I guarantee he won't get in your hair.'

Garfield looked as if he were about to raise some other objection but then apparently had second thoughts and decided to let the matter rest. He also correctly assumed they had nothing else to discuss. Soon after the two men had left his office, Hazelwood picked up the phone and rang his home number.

Ashton was no stranger to the semi-detached house at 84 Rylett Close in Chiswick. It had been acquired by the SIS in 1992 at a knockdown price from the building society which had repossessed the property a year earlier when the young couple who'd purchased it on a hundred per cent mortgage had fallen seriously in arrears with their repayments. He had stayed there a few weeks after it had been purchased and again on his return from Moscow's Lefortovo Prison in October 1993. Apart from the unkempt front garden, the other distinctive feature was a 'For Sale' notice erected by a firm of estate agents across which there was now a sticker bearing the magic words, 'Sold Subject to Contract'.

The London suburb of Chiswick instead of the seaside resort in Devon represented a drastic change of plan for Ashton. However, Franklin's death plus the fact that some stringer in Berlin had at last picked up on the Moresby story had put paid to the idea of going to Dartmouth in order to interview Moresby's father. So he had stayed on at Willow Dene awaiting further instructions until, much to Alice's relief, Hazelwood had telephoned the house and told him to get his body over to Rylett Close.

Approximately ten minutes after a District Line train had left Ravenscourt Park on the way to Stamford Brook, the familiar figure of the Assistant Director in charge of the Administrative Wing entered the close. Roy Kelso was responsible for courses, clerical support, internal audits, claims, expenses, departmental budgets, control of expenditure and Boards of Inquiry. His empire included the financial branch, the motor transport and general stores section and the Security Vetting and Technical Services Division which at one time had been Ashton's bailiwick. To run such a diverse and compartmentalised organisation required a sense of humour which he conspicuously lacked. Roy Kelso was fifty-three, tired, disappointed, embittered that he hadn't gone any farther in the service and small-minded. He was, in short, a real pain in the arse.

'Hello, Roy, nice to see you again,' Ashton said brightly, trying to sound as if he meant it.

'The feeling's mutual.' Kelso pushed the gate open and walked up the front path. 'But much as I'd like to reminisce about old times with you, I'm a busy man. So let's get this over and done with.'

'I'm not with you.'

'This house is going to be your office, it could even become your permanent abode.'

'What about the signboard?'

'Pure camouflage.'

Kelso took a bunch of keys out of his pocket, unlocked the door and steered Ashton through the hall into the dining room next to the kitchen at the back of the house. He placed the executive briefcase he had been carrying on the sideboard and opened it up.

'Recognise this bit of kit?' he asked.

'Yes, it's a Brahms.'

'Wrong,' Kelso said triumphantly. 'This is the Mozart – it's an updated version.'

He unravelled the flex attached to the built-in transceiver and plugged it into a power point. He then ran a tape through the crypto machine which resembled a small vice. 'Normally, this would be good for a week but we're already into the fifth day so you'll get a new tape on Monday.'

'Right.'

'There is an ordinary BT phone in the kitchen which is still on line, but the alarm and surveillance systems have been shut down. Here are the keys to the front and back doors.' He slapped them down on the table and turned to go.

'You're leaving?'

'Like I said, I'm a busy man.' He walked out into the hall, then snapped his fingers and turned about. 'Nearly forgot, there's no food in the house.'

'That's OK. If I remember correctly, there's a mini market not far from here.'

'Good.' Kelso progressed a little farther down the hall. 'I think Victor is making a big mistake bringing you back into the fold.'

'Everyone's entitled to their opinion,' Ashton said mildly. Then he reached past the older man, opened the door and stood to one side. 'Trouble is, Roy, nobody seems to take any notice of yours.'

Kelso looked as if he were going to have an apoplectic fit. Unable to think of a cutting riposte, he stalked off down the front path, slammed the gate behind him and continued his splay-footed way to the Underground station.

Closing the door on him, Ashton returned to the dining room and called Victor on the Mozart.

'Hi,' he said, 'it's me.'

'Hello, you,' Hazelwood said. 'Settling in all right?'

'Yes. One thing puzzles me though. Roy Kelso said this

place could become my permanent abode. What did he mean by that?'

'We're looking for a new housekeeper. I thought the job might interest Harriet. We could probably offer her ten thousand a year.'

There were to be other fringe benefits – rent-free accommodation, the chance eventually of buying the property for the same price the SIS had paid for it.

'What do I have to do in return?' Ashton asked when Hazelwood finished listing all the attractions.

'What was the name of that German who did odd jobs for Neil Franklin? Willie something or other?'

'Baumgart.'

'That's the fella. What's he do for a living?'

'Willie is a dispatcher for Blitz Taxis in Theodor-Heussplatz. But that was a year ago and he may have moved on since then.'

'Have you got the number of Blitz Taxis?'

'Yes, I've still got one of their cards in my wallet.'

'Good. Get on to them, run Willie to ground and put him to work. I want to know if Helga von Schinkel is still with us.'

'Anything else?'

'Yes, I'd like to know what the German police have on the bombing.'

'You've got it,' Ashton said and put the phone down.

The Franklins lived in a large secluded villa at the corner of Grunerweg and Alsenstrasse in the Wannsee District of Berlin. Apart from being located in a highly desirable neighbourhood, the house lay within easy walking distance of the golf club where Ella had won the Ladies' Championship in 1993. In all the years he had known Franklin, Voigt reckoned he could count the number of times he had set foot inside the place. On further reflection, he could only recall two occasions when he and Jutta had been invited to socialise with the Franklins. There had been a drinks party one Sunday lunchtime in the dim, distant past and a barbecue fifteen months ago when both sides had been anxious to mend fences.

Voigt turned into the sweeping driveway of 41 Alsenstrasse and pulled up behind a wine-coloured Audi A6. Beyond it was the inevitable Volkswagen Passat; knowing that the Franklins owned a dark blue Mercedes, he wondered just how many friends had rallied to Ella. Given his reluctance to call on her, it wasn't very difficult to convince himself that it would be wrong to intrude. With a sense of relief, he switched on the ignition and was about to start up when a short dark-haired woman in a black skirt and jacket opened the front door and beckoned him to come inside. There was, he decided, no ignoring her imperious gesture; putting a brave face on it, he got out of the car and walked up to the house.

'My name is Heinrich Voigt,' he told the woman.

'Yes, I know,' she gushed, 'you're the Police President. I saw you on television last night.'

Her name, he learned, was Frau Inga Klintsch; her husband, she informed him, was the Finance Director of the City Trust Bank. In Voigt's experience, rich middle-class women usually treated all police officers from a lowly patrolman to a Kommissar with regal disdain. Frau Inga Klintsch was an exception; she positively fawned on him.

'I really came to offer my condolences to Frau Franklin,' he told her, 'but I can see this is not a convenient moment.'

'Not at all,' Frau Klintsch said emphatically. 'Ella would never forgive me if I turned you away.'

There was no escape. Before he knew what was happening, Voigt found himself in Ella's drawing room and shaking hands with four other equally well-dressed matrons. At Inga's suggestion, all four of them decamped to the kitchen to assist her in making a fresh pot of coffee.

Ella was a slim, athletic woman in her late forties. As always, she looked very composed and in control of herself. Except for the rather drained expression, there were few visible signs of grief, and people who weren't aware of the facts would never have guessed that she had just been widowed.

'I wanted to say how very sorry I am,' Voigt began awkwardly.

'Thank you, Heinrich.'

'I also wanted to tell you that you won't be asked to identify Neil. That has already been taken care of.' Voigt mentally kicked himself. How could he be so crass? He sounded like an officious bureaucrat dealing with a particularly obtuse member of the public. 'I'm sorry,' he murmured. 'I don't think I expressed myself very well.'

'It's all right, Heinrich, I understand.'

'Neil was a good friend,' he said, going over the top in an effort to make amends. 'And I for one am going to miss him. We all liked him.'

'There are many who would say my husband was abrasive and a law unto himself.' A faint smile touched her lips. 'And they would be right,' she added.

'I'm sure that's not true.'

'Is there any news of Fräulein von Schinkel?' she asked, abruptly changing the subject.

'No. Technically speaking she is missing. However, it is by no means certain that she was in the building.' He thought a small blatant lie was permissible in the circumstances.

'Have you tried phoning her apartment?'

'A couple of times. There was no answer, but I wouldn't read too much into that. She may have gone away for a few days or she could have simply been out when I rang.'

'Yes, I imagine Helga would have a lot to do.' Ella nibbled her bottom lip, then looked up. 'Did you know she had given in her notice and was leaving at the end of the year?'

'No, I didn't.'

'Well, she is almost seventy and way past the normal retiring age.'

'Quite so.'

'Neil loved this city.'

'Yes?' Caught off balance, Voigt didn't know what else to say.

'And the people of Berlin. He wanted to spend the rest of his life here, and now his wish has come true.'

Ella Franklin was in a state of shock and was unable to concentrate on any subject for more than a few minutes. He should have recognised the symptoms.

'You will find who killed him, won't you?'

'I shan't rest until I do,' Voigt assured her and meant it.

'I blame London for his death. They ran an operation on Neil's territory and deliberately kept him in the dark. All he ever knew was that a lot of money was going to change hands and there was some sort of Russian involvement.'

He waited to see if there was anything more Ella could tell him but it soon became apparent that her mind was up and running on yet another different track. Anxious to get away, he glanced pointedly at his wristwatch.

'You have to go,' Ella said, taking the hint.

'Yes . . . the investigation.'

'Of course. You must be very busy. It was good of you to come, Heinrich.'

He pressed her hands between his. 'If ever there is anything Jutta and I can do . . .' He left the rest unsaid, raised her right hand to his lips and bowed slightly. So polite, so correct, so false. He walked out of the house uncomfortable with himself, got into the BMW and backed out of the driveway.

The car phone started bleeping as he was driving through Zehlendorf on the Chaussee Potsdamer. The dulcet tones of his PA informed him that the *Kriminalpolizei* had passed on a message they'd received from the fire chief.

'And?' he asked impatiently.

'They've recovered another victim from the rubble of the bookshop. An old woman, identity unknown.'

'Alive or dead?' Voigt barked.

'Alive. She's been taken to the St Francis Hospital on Budapesterstrasse.'

'Was the woman in a coma?'

'No. She was, however, in great pain.'

'But coherent?'

'Oh yes. The firemen said she knew what was happening to her.'

'Check with the hospital, find out when we can talk to her,' Voigt said and switched off the phone.

A survivor, a witness who wasn't gaga. Unable to contain his sense of triumph, Voigt pounded the steering wheel with a clenched fist.

Chapter 5

It took Willie Baumgart less than an hour to discover that Helga von Schinkel had been taken to the St Francis Hospital on Budapesterstrasse. From Admissions, he learned that she was in intensive care, and on the Friday evening that had been all anybody had been prepared to tell him. He had phoned the hospital on Saturday morning and again in the afternoon when the Sister in charge of Intensive Care had informed him that Fräulein von Schinkel had been transferred to Women's Surgical.

The nurse he had spoken to in Women's Surgical could have been a budding Counter-Intelligence officer; before answering his enquiry, she had demanded to know his name and address. She had also wanted to be assured that if he wasn't a relative, he was at the very least a close personal friend. Once he had managed to satisfy her on that score, she had given him the nearest thing to a medical bulletin.

Helga von Schinkel was practically family. She had, in fact, recruited him to work for British Intelligence a few weeks after he had been forced to resign from the *Kriminalpolizei* back in 1979. She had also persuaded Blitz Taxis to give him a job. So there had been no need for Peter Ashton to alert Willie; he had started looking for Helga as soon as he'd heard about the bombing.

On Sundays, visiting hours were 14.00 to 16.00 and 18.30 to 19.30. Clutching a large bunch of red roses, Willie arrived at the St Francis Hospital on the dot of two o'clock.

Ashton had urged him to be discreet and keep a low profile, meaning he shouldn't draw attention to himself. Although Willie couldn't see it, he knew the Englishman found his sartorial tastes decidedly flamboyant. Franklin too had always shuddered at the sight of the electric-blue or emerald-green silk shirts he liked to wear. As a mark of respect for the late SIS Head of Station and in deference to Ashton's wishes, he had chosen a double-breasted brown pinstripe that had been out of fashion when he had bought it in 1974 and a pure white shirt. The tie was plum-coloured, the only one in his wardrobe that wasn't gaudy.

There were, however, certain physical features which were impossible to disguise. He was the sort of individual who once seen remained firmly imprinted in the mind and not because he was 1.75 metres tall, weighed 61 kilos and had light brown hair. When a young up-and-coming detective sergeant, he had lost his left eye. A drug pusher had gouged it out with a thumb and the surgeons had been unable to put it back. He had thrown his assailant down a flight of steps with the result that the pusher had ended up in a mortuary with a broken neck. Although Willie had acted without malice aforethought, a number of people had tried to prove otherwise. The pusher had been a well-connected college kid; there had been plenty of money in the family and they'd had a lot of influence, sufficient at any rate to finish Willie's career in the police force.

In addition to the empty eye socket, his left leg was almost totally rigid following injuries sustained in a traffic accident three years ago which had resulted in the loss of a kneecap and had left the foot at ninety degrees to the shin. The other visible reminder of the accident was a broad white scar across the forehead where he had nearly been scalped. These later injuries had been incurred in the line of duty while watching Ashton's back. He had not, of course, received a single pfennig in compensation.

He found Helga in a sorry state. Her face was battered and bruised; the right eye was closed to a narrow slit and there was a diagonal line of stitches extending from the bridge of her nose into the hairline above the left ear.

'It looks worse than it is,' she croaked.

Willie didn't see how it could be. The staff nurse he had spoken to yesterday had told him that both legs had been crushed, the pelvis badly fractured and the right arm broken in three places between the wrist and elbow. If that wasn't enough, the spinal cord had been damaged in the lumbar region and it was questionable whether she would ever walk again. Although not qualified to say how long Helga was likely to spend in hospital, the staff nurse had spoken in terms of months rather than weeks. He hoped British Intelligence was paying for the private room off Women's Surgical because they certainly owed it to Helga.

'Are those roses for me, Willie?'

'Yes, they are.' Mesmerised by the extent of her injuries, he had forgotten all about the flowers. 'You don't seem to have a vase,' he said, looking round the room. 'Shall I ask the staff nurse to find one?'

'There's a jug of water on the locker; put the roses in that for the time being.'

Flower arranging had never been his forte and in his opinion, the roses had looked far better wrapped in their original Cellophane than they did after he had finished stuffing them into the makeshift vase. But Helga said they looked lovely.

'Have you had any visitors?' he asked, feeling his way.

'Heinrich Voigt was here this morning asking a lot of questions. It was entirely due to him that the hospital authorities moved me into this private room.'

'That was decent of him.'

'I am very lucky.'

'It's no more than you deserve,' he said, thinking she was referring to Voigt's act of kindness.

'Herr Franklin was killed in the explosion. Did you know that?'

'Yes, Herr Ashton told me; he rang me at Blitz Taxis. He was very anxious to find out if you were all right.'

'I still can't believe he is dead,' Helga said in a listless voice. 'He was talking to an elderly couple by the round display table when I returned to the bookshop. I made signs asking him if he wanted me to take over, but Herr Franklin indicated he was happy to deal with them. So I went on through to my office.' Helga swallowed. 'And then it happened,' she said, on the brink of tears.

Willie Baumgart told her that she mustn't distress herself, but to no avail. It was as if a dam had suddenly been breached and the words spilled over in a torrent. Helga remembered thinking that some unseen assailant had punched her savagely in the back and subsequently the whole building had trembled in the shockwave from an earthquake, which, of course, was ridiculous because Berlin was not sitting on top of a fault. The plasterboards had snapped, crackled and popped and she had been pinned to the floor under an enormous weight of rubble. Dust had filled her mouth, nose, ears and eyes.

'I couldn't see anything. I couldn't hear and I couldn't breathe. I have never been so frightened, Willie.'

Unable to move either arm, she had spat the dirt out of her mouth and taken a few shallow breaths. Helga had suffered from claustrophobia ever since the Gestapo had held her for questioning at their Prinz Albrecht Strasse headquarters. Willie reckoned that a lesser person would have panicked and died had they been entombed in a confined space in pitch darkness. Helga had survived because she had courage and willpower in abundance and had forced herself to keep calm in order not to burn up her precious supply of oxygen. She hadn't, of course, told him any of this; there had been no need for her to do so when he knew her well enough to be quite certain that that was the way she had behaved.

'It seemed a lifetime before the firemen digging in the rubble found me and got me out.'

'I can imagine,' Willie murmured.

'There was so little I could tell Herr Voigt. There was a brilliant flash, a loud bang, then darkness and pain.

I wanted to help him but I couldn't. I feel really inadequate.'

'You mustn't,' Willie told her firmly. 'I know policemen. Take it from me, Voigt was merely hoping you could tell him something, but he wasn't banking on it. There are other lines of inquiry he can pursue, especially if the police officers who sifted through the rubble did their job properly. From tiny pieces of metal, Forensic can tell how big the casing was, how much explosive it contained, and the sort of timing mechanism that had been used to initiate the detonator. There's a fifty-fifty chance they will even be able to put a name to the bomb maker.'

'What if they didn't find any recognisable fragments?'

'They will have done.'

'How can you be so sure, Willie?'

He was about to say that when they performed their autopsies, the pathologists would find enough pieces of junk to satisfy Voigt – but thought better of it.

'I just know,' he said, and left it at that.

'I told him I heard a man call out to Herr Franklin just before the explosion.'

'Yes? That's interesting.'

'Herr Voigt thought so too. He asked me if I could describe the man but unfortunately I didn't turn around. I should have been more inquisitive.'

'Is that what Voigt said?'

'No, he was too much of a gentleman, but I could tell what he was thinking.'

'Now listen to me,' Willie said forcefully. 'You're reading too much into this. It doesn't follow that this man carried out the attack. I mean, the bomb could have been planted days ago.'

'No.' Helga shook her head. 'No, the more I think about it, the more I'm convinced he wanted to make sure he killed the right man.'

'I find that very hard to believe.'

'He wasn't a German,' Helga continued, ignoring what he'd just said. 'This man had a curious, harsh-sounding voice and he had difficulty pronouncing Herr Franklin's name properly. He was young.'

'Yes? Forgive me, but if you didn't see him, how do you know?'

'Because my instinct tells me he was under thirty.'

'Well, I suppose that's young enough to be a student and let's face it, all the universities in Berlin are crawling with foreigners. But whatever this guy was, he didn't walk into the bookshop and kill Herr Franklin. You said yourself that the bomb had exploded seconds after he had called out to him. That means he would have blown himself up as well, and who in his right mind would do such a crazy thing?'

'An Islamic fundamentalist,' Helga said.

Willie stared at her. 'Are you saying this man was a Muslim?'

'I think he was born in the Middle East.'

'And what did Voigt make of this?'

'I haven't told him. The thought has only just occurred to me. What do you advise me to do, Willie? Should I contact the office of the Police President?'

'Why don't I ask Herr Ashton what he makes of it first? Maybe British Intelligence has been keeping an eye on Muslim extremists.'

'You don't like our Police President, do you, Willie?'

'He's not my favourite law enforcement officer.'

Willie Baumgart could not forget what had happened the night he had been watching Ashton's back and a truck driver had deliberately side-swiped his Audi off the road. He had ended up in hospital but the girl with him had been decapitated. Voigt had been convinced that Baumgart was lying when he said it was an accident and had refused to believe that torrential rain had made it impossible for the unknown lorry driver to see his Audi in the wing mirror when he'd pulled out to overtake the truck. Unable to prove his contention, Voigt had charged him with reckless driving. The court had imposed a stiff fine and banned him from driving for twelve months. But for the wily German lawyer whom Franklin had covertly hired to

defend him, he might well have gone to prison.
'Matter of fact, I wouldn't lift a finger to help that man.'
'I presume you are referring to Herr Voigt?'
'Who else?' Willie said.

When built in 1908, the semi-detached house in Rylett Close had cost the first owner £350; eighty years later at the height of the property boom, it had changed hands for £200,000. In 1991, the building society which had repossessed the house had been glad to sell it to Roy Kelso for a mere £65,000. If things worked out, Hazelwood had promised Ashton he could have it for the same amount. Although the housing market was still in the doldrums, the asking price for number 84 Rylett Close was nevertheless an absolute bargain. It was a point Ashton had repeatedly made to Harriet when selling her the idea of moving back to London.

He had expected a lot of resistance from Harriet but she had proved surprisingly objective. It was no secret that she did not care for Hazelwood and believed the Acting DG exploited Ashton's loyalty and made use of him. But Victor's name hadn't been mentioned, not even when Ashton had told Harriet about the job offer the SIS had made her. What had concerned her were the financial implications. They had a mortgage of £60,000 on the house in Church Lane and it was likely they would lose a substantial amount of their original deposit if they wanted a quick sale. There was also the little matter of the golden handshake Ashton had received on leaving the SIS. If the Intelligence Service did agree to reinstate him, the Treasury would demand repayment in full, which would be highly embarrassing since half of it had already gone into the house in Lincoln. Harriet had also been anxious to know how they were going to meet the existing mortgage repayments until the house was off their hands, and that could mean anything up to eighteen months.

'I work for an estate agent,' Harriet had reminded him

when he had wondered if she wasn't being a little pessimistic.

And while on the subject of estate agents, Harriet had let it be known that she was pretty unhappy about doing the dirt on Alec Peters, especially since he was an old friend of the family. He had found a niche for her when things had been difficult and it just didn't seem right to ring him at home on a Sunday morning and baldly announce that she wouldn't be in on Monday or any other day. But in the end, Harriet had grasped the nettle and, full of apologies, had explained to Alec Peters why she wanted to leave his employ without giving the usual notice.

Ashton turned into Rylett Close and pulled up outside number 84. Harriet hadn't had much to say for herself on the journey down from Lincoln and the nearer to London they got, the quieter she had become. He wished he knew what she was thinking but she had elected to sit in the back of the Vauxhall with Edward and he couldn't see her face in the rear-view mirror.

'Here we are,' he said unnecessarily. 'What do you think of the house?'

'It looks solid enough.'

'Well, they built them to last back in Edwardian days.' Ashton got out of the car, walked round the front and opened the nearside rear door. Leaning inside, he unclipped the safety harness on the child seat and picked up his son. Resentful at being woken up, Edward opened his eyes and started yelling.

'Better give him to me,' Harriet said when she joined him on the pavement. 'I expect he's hungry.'

'He can't be.'

Harriet had breastfed him at noon and again at four o'clock, shortly before leaving Lincoln. Now, less than two and a half hours later, it seemed Edward needed topping up once more.

'He's a big lad,' Harriet told him. 'Takes after his mother.'

Ashton handed his son over, opened the gate for Harriet,

then darted ahead to unlock the front door. He showed her into the dining room at the back of the house, switched on the light and drew the curtains to give her some privacy, then unloaded the Vauxhall and carried their bags into the house. Besides getting in enough food on the Friday to feed an army for a week, he had also bought a cot from a local furniture store.

'Where did you put it, Peter?'

'In our bedroom until you decide which one we should use as a nursery. I thought I might do the basement up, turn it into a playroom for Edward when he's older.'

He had lots of other plans for the house. Once the place was theirs, he would dig up part of the front lawn and concrete it over to provide a hard standing for the car. And he would get a landscape gardener to redesign the wilderness at the back.

'Enough of the Ideal Homes talk,' Harriet called to him from the dining room. 'Put the kettle on and let's have a cup of tea before I get the supper.'

'I was about to suggest the same thing.'

Ashton filled the electric kettle, plugged it in and switched on the power point, then moved to the fitted cupboards. As he reached for the tea caddy, his eye went to the Dialatron phone on the worktop below and saw there was a message on the answer machine. He depressed the answer button and listened intently to what Willie Baumgart had to say for himself. By the time the German had finished talking, the water had come to the boil and the kettle had automatically switched off.

Lost in thought, Ashton measured six heaped teaspoonfuls of Yorkshire Tea into a pot he had omitted to warm first, then compounded the error by filling it with water that had gone off the boil. Willie had made his phone call over an open link satellite but it was unlikely that an unfriendly Intelligence service was still targeting 84 Rylett Close when the house had stood empty for several months. On the other hand, Hazelwood's abode in Willow Walk would certainly attract a great deal of attention, especially now that he was the Acting DG. There were also matters arising from what Willie Baumgart had told him which merited a security classification of Secret.

He found a cosy in one of the kitchen drawers, jammed it over the teapot and went into the dining room to collect the Mozart. Harriet was now upstairs putting Edward to bed and there was no need to move the crypto-protected phone.

The Hazelwoods were always at home on a Sunday evening. It was also the one night of the week they religiously kept to themselves. The number rang out for almost two minutes before a somewhat testy Victor came to the phone.

'I was watching a play on television,' he complained.

'You want me to ring back later?'

'No. Now that I'm here we might as well get on with it.'

'Can we switch to secure?'

'I don't see why not,' Hazelwood said, still irritable.

Ashton waited for the tonal change, then told him what he had learned from Willie Baumgart, deftly paraphrasing what had been a long-winded message.

'Did he say anything about the police investigation?' Hazelwood asked.

'Willie indicated they were hoping Forensic would come up with something they could get their teeth into. And, of course, they are still waiting on the pathologists. But if you want my opinion, Willie hasn't been near the police, nor will he.'

'You want to tell me why?'

'I'll give you three good reasons. He doesn't like Voigt, and most of the men he knew when he was a detective have now left the *Kriminalpolizei*. In short, Willie has run out of contacts.'

'And the third reason?'

'Voigt didn't like the way Franklin operated and he knows Baumgart was one of Neil's foot soldiers.'

'Pity, I was hoping Willie would be able to keep us apprised of developments.' There was a loud clatter as Hazelwood put the phone down. A few moments later,

Ashton heard him open the carved wooden box on his desk, then strike a match. 'I think we may have to send you to Berlin, Peter,' he said between puffs. 'Someone's got to size up the situation and none of our people in Bonn has met Willie Baumgart.'

'When is this likely to happen?'

'Monday, maybe the day after. Depends on what comes out of the woodwork.'

'Terrific.'

'You were saying just now that Helga thinks the bomber may have followed her into the bookshop.'

The sudden change of direction left Ashton floundering. 'Well actually, she is pretty sure he did,' he said, recovering quickly.

'Interesting.'

'It gets better,' Ashton said grimly. 'If Helga's right, it means the guy deliberately blew himself up to make sure he killed Franklin. She told Willie that the man spoke German as if he had a lot of phlegm at the back of his throat. Apparently, this is a fairly common trait with language students from the Middle East.'

'Piffle.'

'I'm only repeating what I got second-hand from Willie. Anyway, in her book this makes the man who murdered Neil Franklin an Islamic fundamentalist.'

'It's still a fairy tale,' Hazelwood said dismissively.

'Maybe it isn't the only one. You told me Quorn and Moresby went to Berlin to buy information about the activities of a drug cartel.'

'So?'

'So I can see the drug barons deciding to hit Franklin, especially if some ex-KGB man pointed them in the right direction. But I don't see one of their underlings deliberately sacrificing his own life in the process.'

'Hasn't it occurred to you that the bomb he was carrying may have exploded prematurely?'

'No, I have to admit it hasn't,' Ashton said.

'Then you're slipping,' Hazelwood told him, and hung up.

Chapter 6

Morning prayers on a Monday always lasted far longer than on any other day of the week. The various SIS stations around the globe had not been silent during the sixty hours from close of play on Friday, and while no crises had arisen in that time span, Heads of Departments felt it encumbent upon themselves to deliver an Intelligence summary of events within their particular domain. Had anything of consequence occurred during that period, the duty officers would have been notified immediately and passed it on to the appropriate Assistant Director who in turn would have alerted the DG. Stuart Dunglass had thoroughly approved of these expositions which he said brought everyone up to speed and started the week off on the right foot. The one change which Hazelwood had made while he had been keeping the chair warm for the DG was to limit each Head of Department to a maximum of ten minutes. Assistant Directors like Roger Benton, Head of the Pacific Basin and Rest of the World Department, who felt their fiefdoms were under threat, had come to believe that the longer they held forth, the more the continued existence of their particular establishment was assured.

There was no greater exponent of this philosophy than Rowan Garfield, the one person who had the least to fear. Listening to him as he tried to compress everything that had happened in Bosnia, Chechnya, Russia and the Baltic States into his allotted ten minutes, Hazelwood needed no convincing that his organisation was overloaded and undermanned. The European Department was too big an empire for one Assistant Director to handle. The Russian Desk, which had looked after the whole monolith of the old Soviet Union, needed to be reinforced in order to take account of the newly emergent states. What was required was the financial wherewithal to send bagmen into Russia, Belorussia, the Ukraine and Kazakhstan to find out what was happening to the surplus stocks of nuclear warheads and plutonium within those countries.

'Berlin,' Garfield announced. 'There have been no fresh developments in the past sixty-plus hours.' He paused, then added, 'I would like to discuss the future of the station with you, Director.'

'Yes, of course, Rowan, but later – say around noon. Check with my PA, I should be free then.'

Hazelwood had deliberately left Garfield until last on the assumption that he would have more information to impart than all the other Assistant Directors put together and would therefore need more than his allotted time. Now that he had finished his dissertation, Hazelwood had no intention of allowing morning prayers to drag on a minute longer. All Heads of Departments had had their say with the exception of Roy Kelso. Before the Administrative Wing had moved from Benbow House to Vauxhall Cross he had rarely attended the daily conference and had only been invited to become a regular member as a matter of courtesy.

'Well, that's it,' Hazelwood said, before Kelso had a chance to prolong the proceedings. 'Except for you, Jill,' he added. 'Perhaps you wouldn't mind staying behind for a few minutes?'

Jill Sheridan ran the Middle East Department. At the age of thirty-six, she was the newest, youngest and easily the most attractive Assistant Director. She was also ambitious, selfish, inconsiderate of others and motivated by self-interest. Her peers felt threatened because she was obviously in the fast lane and was well placed to become the first woman to be selected for the appointment of Director General.

Her 'Yes, Victor?' when they were alone in the conference room made his hackles rise. It wasn't so much what Jill said but the way she said it, in a tone which suggested that somehow their roles had been reversed, that got under his skin.

'Gamal al Hassan,' he snapped. 'I want you to give me a complete rundown on this A1 completely reliable source you so kindly bequeathed to Rowan Garfield.'

They had been seated at opposite ends of the long refectory table. Vacating her chair, Jill Sheridan came and sat next to him, reminding Hazelwood of a tigress stalking her prey.

'You make it sound as though I did the dirt on the European Department.' A smile touched her lips and almost made it to her eyes. 'I could hardly continue to run Gamal after he had moved into Rowan's area of responsibility, could I? Anyway, I thought all this had been agreed at a meeting between the three of us at least a fortnight before Quorn was sent to Berlin?'

She was right of course; that was the thing which really annoyed Hazelwood. 'Shall we get on?' he said curtly.

'Gamal was a Palestinian. He was employed as a bus driver in Kuwait City, a lowly paid job beneath the dignity of a Kuwaiti, all of whom are pampered by an oil-rich state. He had been recruited by our resident in the sheikdom a few weeks before I was posted to Bahrain.'

Jill had been appointed to run the Intelligence network in the United Arab Emirates from Bahrain in October '89. On paper, she had been an ideal choice for the post. Her father had been an executive with the Qatar General Petroleum Corporation and she had spent most of her childhood and adolescence in the Persian Gulf, so that Arabic had naturally become her second tongue. Persian or Farsi was an additional language she had acquired at the School of Oriental and African Studies.

'Palestinians, Jordanians and Baluchis from Pakistan

account for more than half the population of Kuwait,' Jill continued. 'All of these nationalities are treated like second-class citizens even though the economy would collapse without them. When it comes to applying for a better paid job, there is positive discrimination in favour of Kuwaitis regardless of qualifications. Anyway, Gamal al Hassan was hired to keep his eyes and ears open for signs of disaffection among those second-class citizens. Specifically, we wanted to gauge their attitude towards the ruling family. Of course, Gamal could do no more than take a random sample but what he produced was at least as good as any opinion poll.'

But Gamal had really come into his own when the Iraqis had overrun the sheikdom. Before being sacked to make way for a Kuwaiti, he had worked for Cable and Wireless where he had been regarded as a competent telegraphist. Provided with a shortwave transmitter by his case officer a month before the invasion, he had sent back invaluable Intelligence reports on the standard of training, morale and discipline of the Iraqi army throughout the occupation.

'So why did the Kuwaitis expel him after their country was liberated?' Hazelwood asked.

'He was accused of collaborating with the enemy. There was even talk of trying him for war crimes. Fortunately, Gamal's old case officer was able to persuade the Kuwaiti authorities that the information he had provided had saved thousands of Allied lives.'

'Could he have been a double agent, Jill?'

'He might have been friendly with the Iraqis, he may even have betrayed the odd Kuwaiti to them, but he was loyal to us. I analysed the information he sent in and it was good, very good.'

'Did you have an opportunity to interrogate Gamal after the Gulf War?'

'Not directly.' Jill Sheridan crossed her legs and brushed an invisible speck of fluff from the hemline of a short, charcoal-grey skirt. 'You know the restrictions I had to cope with out there.'

Hazelwood certainly did. Although in British eyes Jill had been tailor-made for the appointment, the Arabs were not accustomed to dealing with a woman on an equal footing. In order to function at all, it had been necessary to disguise her true status and she had been shown as the Personal Assistant to the Second Secretary Consul on the embassy staff list. If that wasn't a big enough handicap, her writ did not officially extend outside the United Arab Emirates. With a British Embassy in Kuwait, Intelligence-gathering operations within the sheikdom had been the responsibility of the SIS Head of Station. She had only inherited that area after Saddam Hussein's troops had occupied the country.

'I can tell you, it was a frustrating experience, Victor.'

Nevertheless, she had stuck it out for twenty-one months before requesting a transfer. Posted back to London, she had been given the Persian Desk, a sideways move rather than a demotion, which was an indication of how highly she had still been regarded.

'I ran Gamal from the beginning of August 1990 to the end of Desert Storm on 28 February 1991. And the moment the British Embassy reopens for business in Kuwait, I lose control of him. I had to address all my questions to Gamal through the SIS Head of Station. Do you wonder I was sick with anger?'

Hazelwood ignored the question just as he had managed to ignore the expanse of thigh Jill Sheridan was showing. Although not as naturally beautiful as Harriet Ashton, she was undeniably attractive and unlike the former MI5 officer, she made the most of her charms.

'Where did Gamal al Hassan go after he was kicked out of Kuwait?'

'Jordan first, then the Lebanon where he approached our Military Attaché in Beirut claiming he had information concerning the whereabouts of some of the hostages. Most desk officers in the Mid East Department believed he was simply looking for a hand-out and had made it up. They couldn't believe he could have got that close to Hizbollah.'

73

'You, on the other hand, believed he had.'

'Yes. I said that what he had told us was probably true, but nobody wanted to act on it. Later, when the hostages were debriefed after they'd been released, my colleagues had to accept that his information had been one hundred per cent accurate.'

And you had been proved right, Hazelwood thought. No doubt she had rubbed that in, but he wondered how loudly she had protested when her peers had decided to cold-shoulder Gamal. Not so loudly that she was in danger of putting her career on the line. Jill was a natural-born survivor with an eye to the main chance. Five years ago, she had been engaged to Peter Ashton and they had taken out a joint mortgage on a flat in Surbiton. But when the posting to the Persian Gulf had come up, a career had taken precedence over marriage and she had put Ashton on hold.

Eight or nine weeks after her arrival in Bahrain, Jill had broken off her engagement to Ashton, possibly because she had already met Henry Clayburn and had decided he was a better bet. Pompous old Henry, sixteen years her senior and moribund with it. There was a plus side: Henry was fairly rolling in money and had raised no objections when, for professional reasons, Jill Sheridan had elected to retain her maiden name after they were married. It might be cynical, but the way Hazelwood saw it, Henry Clayburn had been her personal equity plan in case her career went completely haywire. The joke was that she hadn't needed Henry. Early on in his tenure, she had so impressed Stuart Dunglass that he had seen fit to promote her to Assistant Director in charge of the Middle East Department over the heads of more senior colleagues.

'And after the Lebanon, Gamal resurfaced in Tehran. Correct?'

'Yes, Victor.'

'Where he approached the British Embassy offering his services once more, and was taken on at your insistence.'

Jill sighed. 'We've had all this out before,' she said. 'Why are we going over the same ground again?'

'Humour me,' Hazelwood told her with a bleak smile.

'Well, all right, everyone knew that Head of Station, Tehran, was against the idea but he wasn't aware of Gamal's track record. In the end, however, even he had to admit the man was a jewel.'

'Except that practically all the information arrived too late for anyone in London to make use of it.'

'And whose fault was that, Victor? A little boldness would not have come amiss from our people in Iran.'

Jill Sheridan was overstating her case but she did have a point. Worried that the Iranians might intercept or jam any signal from the British Embassy, Head of Station had held everything back until the next time a Queen's messenger passed through Tehran. However, the fact remained that the best material had invariably been delivered to Head of Station a mere ten days to a fortnight ahead of the event.

'Remind me again of the date Gamal alleged the Islamic fundamentalists made him a member of their operational planning staff.'

'Early in May; we heard about it on 21 June.' Her eyes narrowed spitefully. 'And I don't like the word alleged, Victor. It implies he was conning us.'

'And you don't think he was?'

'No, and neither did you. After all, you agreed we could offer him 250,000 dollars as a down payment. Cheap at the price, you said, if we can stop these people getting their hands on enough plutonium to make a nuclear bomb.'

'I'm not talking about money, Jill. What I would like to know is when these people realised Gamal was one of ours. Can you shed any light on this?'

'Me?'

'Well, you were the last person to have any contact with him. You spoke to Gamal when he was in Cairo on Friday, 9 September, just forty-eight hours before he was due to arrive in Berlin. I wondered if he sounded at all worried.'

'He was relaxed.'

'You didn't have any reason to suppose that a third party

was listening to your conversation?'

'Of course I didn't. Do you think I would have told him who to ask for at Hecker's Hotel if there had been the slightest doubt in my mind?'

'And then you took Gamal through the recognition procedure?'

'Yes.' She raised her jaw pugnaciously. 'What's this all about, Victor?'

'I'm trying to decide how much I should tell Ashton before I send him into Berlin.'

'Oh yes, I heard you were using Peter as a sniffer dog.'

'Does that bother you?' Hazelwood asked mildly.

'Good heavens, no. Why should it? I've got nothing to hide.'

He wondered about that, wondered too if there might be something in Jill Sheridan's background which the Security Vetting and Technical Services Division might have overlooked when they had reviewed her clearance at the five-year point. Hazelwood made a mental note to ask Kelso for her file. When a failed operation resulted in the death of a senior SIS officer you didn't leave anything to chance.

Blitz Taxis was having a quiet day. Occasionally, a cab driver would call in to report a fare and the ultimate destination of same, but for the most part all that came through on the radio transmitter in the dispatcher's office was a lot of background mush. Things were so slack that Willie Baumgart wished he'd thought to bring a paperback with him when he'd clocked on for the noon-to-20.00 hours shift. When one of the girls on the front desk buzzed him on the intercom to say his presence was required by Kriminalpolizei Kommissar Eicke, he wished he hadn't bothered to come in.

Eicke was the sort of intimidating person most people would be afraid to encounter in a lonely place on a dark night. With his heavy countenance and fierce expression, he looked type-cast for a walk-on part as a thug in a

Hollywood crime movie. Baumgart thought the Kommissar was nudging forty, which should have made them
contemporaries, but to the best of his recollection, their
paths had never crossed when he had been a detective
sergeant in the Kripo.

'I'm Willie Baumgart,' he said, introducing himself.
'What can I do for you, Herr Kommissar?'

'I'm here representing the Police President,' Eicke
growled.

'Yes? So how is good old Heinrich?'

'Watch your lip.'

Baumgart grinned. 'Are you threatening me, Herr
Kommissar?' he enquired sweetly.

'Is there somewhere we can talk in private? Your office,
for instance?'

'I don't have one.'

Eicke rested both elbows on the counter and leaned
forward, his eyes glittering. 'Then maybe we had better go
on down to the central police station on Tempelhofer
Damm. Plenty of privacy down there.'

Baumgart sized up his man and rapidly came to the
conclusion that baiting Eicke could be a dangerous
pastime. He asked Karen, the senior girl on the front desk,
to hold the fort for him in the dispatcher's office, then
raised the counter flap and joined the Kommissar on the
other side.

'You ever been to Bertholt's?' he asked.

'Can't say I have,' Eicke grunted.

'Then you're in for a treat.'

Bertholt's was in Pommerallee just round the corner
from Blitz Taxis in Theodor-Heussplatz. A back-street
Frühstückskneipe, the café opened at three o'clock in the
morning and served breakfast right through the day until
late at night. The menu consisted of ham, liver sausage,
salami, cheese and pickled herring with rye bread and
pumpernickel.

Baumgart fancied something lighter and ordered a cup
of hot chocolate and two four-minute boiled eggs, shelled

and served in a glass. Eicke, who claimed he wasn't hungry, settled for a glass of beer, salami and pumpernickel.

'So why has Herr Voigt sent you to see me?' Baumgart asked after the waiter had taken their orders.

'Yesterday afternoon you went to the St Francis Hospital and were with Helga von Schinkel for over an hour.'

'Since when has that been a crime?'

'British Intelligence had a number of questions they wanted to put to Fräulein von Schinkel and you were their messenger boy.'

'Rubbish.'

Baumgart grimaced in pain as Eicke stretched a leg under the table and crushed the toes of his right foot under the heel of his shoe.

'Don't waste my time by lying to me,' he hissed. 'We know you were running errands for the British before the late Herr Franklin even arrived in Berlin.'

'I've known Fräulein von Schinkel for longer than you have been on the force. I went to see her because she is an old and very dear friend . . .'

Eicke increased the pressure on his toes. 'I hear the British wanted to know if she was still alive.'

'You've got it all wrong, Herr Kommissar . . .'

'Shut the fuck up and listen to me, asshole. Whoever planted that bomb in the bookshop virtually destroyed the British Intelligence network in this city. Now, knowing this, Herr Voigt is convinced the British will attempt to rebuild it. And when they do, you will be the first man they approach. So that being the case, Herr Voigt expects you to ring him the moment one of your English friends gets in touch.'

'Otherwise?'

'What?'

'There's always an otherwise,' Baumgart said, gritting his teeth.

'Oh, yes. Well, it goes without saying that if you fail to co-operate with us, we will make life exceedingly difficult for you.' Eicke removed his foot and stood up. 'Tell the waiter I've changed my mind,' he said, and walked out of the café.

It was only the second time Ashton had set foot inside the Atheneum. On the previous occasion, Hazelwood had been late and he'd had to cool his heels reading all the notices in the entrance hall until Victor arrived. This evening, the shoe was on the other foot, except that as a member, Hazelwood could enjoy a large whisky and soda in the bar while he waited.

'You're late,' he growled by way of a welcome.

'Signal failure on the Underground outside Hammersmith,' Ashton told him glibly.

'I've heard better excuses. What'll you have to drink?'

'The same as usual, please.'

Hazelwood beckoned to the barman, asked him to bring another large whisky with just a splash of soda, then made small talk, mostly about 84 Rylett Close. Following a stiff grilling by the House of Commons Ways and Means Committee, the Cabinet Secretary had directed that, along with other government departments, the SIS was to dispose of all property surplus to current requirements. The safe house Ashton was occupying, and several others dotted about the country, fell into that category. Selling the house at cost to a former member of the SIS was not what the finance committee had had in mind and Ashton wondered how Victor would get away with it.

'I haven't been exactly straight with you,' Hazelwood said when the barman was safely out of earshot.

'In what respect?'

'Steven Quorn wasn't sent to Berlin to flush out some drug cartel; we were after a bunch of Islamic extremists who are in the market for plutonium.'

Ashton smiled. 'That's a relief; for one awful moment I thought you meant the house.'

'What do you take me for?' Hazelwood asked indignantly.

A bent corkscrew, Harriet would have said, but she was notoriously prejudiced.

'I'm sorry, Victor, I should have known better.'

'Quite so.' Hazelwood drank some of his whisky, then started afresh. 'Have you ever met Police President Heinrich Voigt?' he asked.

'Not as far as I'm aware.'

'Is there something wrong with your memory?'

'No. Remember when Harriet was injured during a race riot in the Kreuzberg District fourteen months ago? I visited her every day for a week when she was in St Thomas's Hospital. I don't recall seeing a plain-clothes officer in the vicinity of her private room but that doesn't mean to say the *Kriminalpolizei* weren't keeping a discreet eye on her. Maybe Voigt got a photograph of me.' Ashton frowned. 'I gave my name to the Herr Professor who operated on Harriet; he may have passed it on to the police.'

'Anything else you want to tell me?'

'Well, if Voigt doesn't know my name, he will probably have associated me with the anonymous letter I sent him, blowing the whistle on one of his detective sergeants who was an active member of the neo-Nazi Party. I doubt if that made me the flavour of the month.'

'You'll have to do everything through Willie Baumgart.'

'Oh, come on, Victor, you know as well as I do that Voigt's really got a thing about Willie. I've told you before, he doesn't like us operating on his turf and he identified Willie as one of Neil Franklin's foot soldiers long ago.'

'Then you will have to be very careful how, when and where you contact him.'

'You've come to a decision then,' Ashton said. 'You are going to send me to Berlin, aren't you?'

'How else are we going to learn what's in the post mortem reports?'

Hazelwood wanted to know the estimated time of death for both Moresby and Gamal al Hassan. His shopping list also included details of the forensic evidence recovered from the bookshop and how it was that the *Kriminalpolizei* had been able to identify Gamal al Hassan and discover that he had been expelled from Kuwait after the Gulf War. Beyond that, Ashton was required to ascertain what leads the police had got from questioning eyewitnesses to the bombing, and how the investigation was proceeding.

'That's a pretty tall order,' Ashton said, 'even for Willie Baumgart. In the last resort, we might have to go to the police for some of the information.'

'It had better be the last resort,' Hazelwood said grimly.

'You can take that as gospel. The question is, how much can I tell Voigt if push comes to shove?'

'You can say that Gamal al Hassan was a member of Hizbollah and was regarded as an A1 source of information.' Hazelwood finished the rest of his whisky and put the glass down. 'He contacted Head of Station, Cairo and informed him he was on the way to Berlin with the rest of his cell.'

'To do what?' Ashton asked.

'It wasn't to buy plutonium.' In Hazelwood's opinion, the German Government would question why they hadn't been advised earlier, especially as their *Polizei* had intercepted more than one illegal consignment of plutonium. 'Better stick to a close version of the truth and tell him Gamal didn't know but was hopeful he would have something definite for us by the time they reached Berlin. All right?'

'Yes. What's the name of our Consul General?'

'Willmore, Gerald Willmore. Why do you ask?'

'He's the logical man to ask Voigt for the results of the post mortem on Moresby. Perhaps someone could tell Willmore that I might want to have a word with him?'

'Consider it done. Is there anything else?'

'Yes, when do you expect me to leave for Berlin?'

'What's wrong with tomorrow?'

'Harriet will love that.'

'She will take it in her stride,' Hazelwood said with all

81

the confidence of a man who didn't have to break the news to her. Reaching inside his jacket, he took out an oblong-shaped envelope and handed it to Ashton. 'You're on the 07.55 British Airways flight tomorrow morning. As well as the plane tickets, the envelope contains two thousand Deutschmarks in folding money in case you have to grease the odd palm. Make sure you account for it properly, otherwise Roy Kelso will have a fit.'

'Right.'

'We've booked you into Hecker's Hotel.'

Ashton looked up from the envelope. 'That's where Moresby stayed.'

'Well, yes, it is. I thought you could ask a few discreet questions of the staff. You never know, maybe they will put you on to something.'

And maybe, in the process, somebody would use him for target practice. 'Thanks a bunch, Victor.' Ashton said to himself, 'you're a real prince.'

Chapter 7

A personal security file was like a critical biography which was constantly being updated. The one which was still being compiled on Jill Sheridan began with a subject interview some four months before she had joined the SIS at the age of twenty-three. The vetting officer who had conducted the interview had had very little to go on other than the testimony of various referees, all of whom had been nominated by Jill. Her tutor at the School of Oriental and African Studies had been interviewed, so too had the headmistress of The Cheltenham Ladies' College, which she had attended from the age of thirteen. The vetting unit had also managed to trace the former headmistress of the English Primary School in Qatar, but not surprisingly, her recollection of Jill Sheridan had been vague.

Nobody had been able to think of a single reason why Jill shouldn't have constant access to Top Secret material. Reading the initial assessment for the second time, Hazelwood couldn't help thinking that everyone who'd known Jill Sheridan then had looked at her through rose-tinted spectacles. No one had had a bad word to say about her. Described as a popular girl and academically bright by the headmistress of The Cheltenham Ladies' College, she had represented the school at hockey and had been a prefect. Her tutor had considered her to be a sensible and well-balanced young woman. All her friends agreed that she was not the least bit promiscuous, had never experimented with drugs, didn't smoke, and while enjoying the occasional drink, had never overindulged.

Before studying Persian, Jill had spent a year at a secretarial college, during which time she had shared a flat in St John's Wood with three other girls, one of whom had definitely been gay. The flatmate who had supplied this information had been adamant that Jill had never shown any lesbian tendencies. While in London, she had received a generous allowance from her father and he had also found her a job with the Qatar General Petroleum Corporation when she had completed her secretarial training and had nine months to kill before taking up a vacancy at the School of Oriental Languages. Financially prudent had been the verdict of her bank manager in St John's Wood and the office manager she had worked for in Qatar. In fact, the more he read, the more difficult Hazelwood found it to recall meeting such a paragon of virtue in real life.

Since the initial clearance, a quinquennial review of Jill Sheridan's positive vetting status had been carried out in 1986 and again in 1991. In the main, these reviews had consisted of written reports by her superior officers with a further subject interview at the ten-year point. The file also contained three Change of Circumstance reports. The first had been submitted when she had become engaged to Peter Ashton, the second after she had broken it off, and the third when she had announced her intention of marrying Henry Clayburn. The vast majority of security dossiers were graded Confidential; Jill Sheridan's had been upped to Secret after she had been debriefed on her return from Bahrain. But that wasn't the reason why Hazelwood had flagged up the file before sending for Roy Kelso.

'We've got a missing folio,' he told Kelso. 'I'd like to know what has happened to it.'

'Missing?'

'The folios are numbered consecutively from 1 to 87, then suddenly we jump to 89. And that isn't the only irregularity.'

Stapled to the back of the front cover of the security file

was a card headed 'Registration of Secret Material'. A standard pro forma produced by Her Majesty's Stationery Office, it comprised columns for the originator's reference, the date the document had been signed, the subject matter and the folio number where it could be found on the security file. There were two entries on the card, the Bahrain debrief at folio 87 and a demi-official, undated, unreferenced letter from the Foreign and Commonwealth Office which should have appeared at folio 88.

'I see the missing folio was downgraded from Secret,' Kelso said, after examining the file.

'On whose authority, Roy?'

'I don't know. I would have to ask whoever was the Head of the Security Vetting and Technical Services Division at the time.' Kelso dodged backwards and forwards through the file, silently whistling to himself. 'Well, folio 89 is the Change of Circumstance report which was submitted after Jill had informed the then Assistant Director in charge of the Mid East Department that she intended to marry Henry Clayburn. So the missing folio must have been removed during Ashton's tenure.'

'But not by him,' Hazelwood said. 'He had been engaged to Jill Sheridan and therefore wouldn't have been allowed to see her file. That's laid down in standing orders under the paragraph dealing with personal involvements. Right?'

'Yes.'

'So her file would have been kept in your office safe the whole time Peter Ashton was in charge of the division?'

'Yes,' Kelso said unhappily.

'Which means you removed folio 88.'

'I must have done.'

'On whose orders, Roy?'

'You are making things very difficult for me.'

'Do I have to repeat the question?'

Kelso shook his head. 'The instructions came from Stuart Dunglass. This was when he was still the Deputy DG. He told me that the Director General had decided that the memo from the Foreign and Commonwealth should be downgraded to Restricted and removed from the file. If you look at the Registration of Secret Material you will see the words 'Downgraded and Deleted' followed by my initials. I told Stuart that there should be an insert to show what had happened to the original document, but he said it wasn't necessary. I got the impression that it would be filed with the Director General's personal correspondence.'

Hazelwood opened the cigar box on his desk, took out a cheroot and lit it. 'Correct me if I'm wrong,' he said, 'but you don't think I will find it amongst his papers?'

'I'm pretty sure Stuart Dunglass destroyed the letter. I'm equally convinced the then Director General knew nothing about it.'

'But luckily you registered the document and put it on the file.' Hazelwood was almost purring like a sleek cat. 'And naturally you would have read it first, so all is not lost.'

Kelso hesitated, but not for long. 'It was about Henry Clayburn,' he said, and then went on to prove what a good memory he had.

Clayburn was an astute businessman who had made his fortune on the back of the oil revenues enjoyed by the Gulf sheikdoms. He had started at the age of twenty-six in Abu Dhabi when the money was really beginning to flow into the country from the Dás Island strike and the nomadic way of life in the sheikdom was changing from goats, dates and camels into something vastly more sophisticated. The new oil-rich population had wanted Chevrolets, Cadillacs, Ford Mustangs, Lincoln Continentals, Oldsmobiles and Pontiacs, all of which Clayburn had sold quicker than they could be shipped over from Detroit. He had also done a roaring trade in fridge-freezers, TVs, cameras, watches – particularly Rolex – and music centres. After establishing other emporiums in the neighbouring Emirates, he had moved on to Bahrain in 1979. He had been faced with some pretty stiff competition but he had overcome that to a large extent by making himself useful to some of the well-connected young blades about town.

'In what way?' Hazelwood asked.

'Well, he pampered to their not-so-little foibles. You know how it is.'

'No, I don't, Roy.'

'Some Arabs are fascinated by European women and like to fantasise about them. I guess you could say Henry Clayburn made their dreams come true . . .'

'I must be getting dense in my old age. You'll have to spell it out for me.'

'He procured women for them. One member of his stable was said to be the wife of an insurance under-manager who worked for the British Bank of the Middle East.'

'Who made that accusation?' Hazelwood asked.

'A British contract officer serving with the Bahrain police force. He had been recruited by the Crown Agents at the request of the Bahrain Government. Of course, I have to say his contract had just been terminated on the grounds of unsatisfactory conduct.'

'Would you please get to the point, Roy?'

'The point is, he wrote to our ambassador enclosing a colour snapshot. It had been taken indoors and the definition was poor. Anyway, the subject was a young woman who had discarded all her clothing except for a pair of high-heeled shoes, black stockings and suspender belt. She was wearing a yashmak so that all that could be seen of her features were her blue eyes.'

'And that's it?'

'No. Henry Clayburn was standing behind the woman, cupping her breasts in the palms of his hands.'

'Well, thank you, Roy, you've been most helpful.' Hazelwood closed the security file and pushed it across the desk. 'You can return this to your registry,' he added.

As soon as Kelso had left, he told the PA to Stuart Dunglass that he wanted to see the Director's demi-official file and the one belonging to his predecessor. She didn't like it and said so, but Hazelwood was in no mood to brook any argument from her. There was, of course, no trace of the missing folio or the photograph on either file. He wondered how far he should pursue the matter, wondered too what possible bearing it could have on the task he had set Ashton in Berlin. Ash spilled from the cheroot on to his shirt front and a tiny glowing ember burned a neat round hole in his silk tie, but he was completely unaware of it.

Berlin-Tegel reminded Ashton of a small municipal airport which gave an equally small town a certain amount of kudos. The baggage claim area was no size at all and the concourse in the terminal building was scarcely wider than a basketball court. He rang Willie Baumgart's home number from a pay phone near the exit but after a minute or so, it was evident the German was out. Retrieving his loose change, he picked up his suitcase and went on down the concrete spiral staircase to the cab rank on the approach road below. Some twenty minutes later, he checked into Hecker's Hotel on Grolmanstrasse.

He was faced with a choice of three possible lines of inquiry – Willie Baumgart, Gerald Willmore, and the hotel staff whom Hazelwood had suggested might be able to tell him something about Moresby. Ashton didn't share his opinion and preferred to leave them until last. With his connections, there was nobody better than Willie Baumgart at digging for information. Given something he could get his teeth into, he could well be twice as effective. And the only man who might be in a position to supply the necessary kick-start was Gerald Willmore. A glance at the street map which Ashton had bought the last time he was in Berlin showed that the Consulate in Uhlandstrasse was a lot nearer the hotel than the offices of Blitz Taxis.

Her Majesty's Consul General in Berlin reminded Ashton of one of Michelangelo's cherubs in the Sistine Chapel. The monk's patch and receding blond hair was more than counterbalanced by a countenance that was as round and smooth as a baby's bottom. His face was unlined and there were no pouches under his remarkably blue eyes; it was not unreasonable to suppose that twenty years on he would look pretty much the same as he did now.

'I hope you were warned to expect me,' Ashton said as they shook hands.

'Yes, indeed.' Willmore flashed him a smile. 'About three-quarters of an hour ago,' he added.

Ashton spread his hands. 'That's Whitehall for you.'

'I was told you were concerned about Moresby.' His smile became even more conspicuous. 'They did get that right, didn't they?'

Willmore didn't wait for confirmation. He assumed Ashton wanted to know what action he had taken and proceeded to give him a detailed account of the arrangements for returning the body to England.

'The autopsy's been completed?' Ashton said, interrupting him.

Willmore nodded. 'On Thursday of last week to be precise. The police wanted the next of kin to formally identify the body but Moresby's father was reluctant to do it, said he wanted to remember his son the way he had been. Naturally, the Kripo weren't very happy about it but they had got Moresby's passport and even though his nose had been sliced off, he was still recognisable. And as I pointed out to them, what would they have done if there had been no next of kin?'

'Have you seen a copy of the post mortem?'

'No. I wouldn't have understood half the medical terms anyway. I was, however, given a very full briefing by the senior investigating officer, a Kommissar Eicke from the Central Division. The other murder victim, Gamal al Hassan, had been dead for more than twelve hours before his body was dumped in the builder's yard, whereas it appears Moresby had been alive when he was taken to the compound. The medical examiner thought he had been mutilated after death but the pathologist reached a different conclusion. He was of the opinion that the killers had cut off his nose before they slit his throat.' Willmore grimaced. 'The theory being they wanted to inflict the maximum pain before killing him.'

'What else did you learn from Eicke? For instance, do the police have any idea why Moresby was murdered?'

'Kommissar Eicke told me that they had contacted Scotland Yard to ascertain if Moresby had had a criminal record. He appeared to think it was a revenge killing, possibly drug-related.'

Ashton was prepared to bet that Voigt didn't share the Kommissar's opinion. Only a few hours after the bodies had been found, he had walked into the English Bookshop and in so many words had made it clear to Franklin that he believed Moresby had been an SIS agent. Voigt wouldn't have levelled such a charge simply because the victim had had a British passport on him which had been amended on page three to show a change of occupation from government official to businessman. The Police President might have a strong aversion to British Intelligence operating on his patch but he was a rational man. Somehow he must have learned that Gamal al Hassan had been an SIS source.

'Eicke came to see you the day after the autopsy had been completed. Would that be right?'

'Yes, it was on Friday towards one o'clock.'

'Nearly twenty-four hours after the English Bookshop had been bombed,' Ashton said meaningfully. 'Did he say anything about Neil Franklin?'

'No, but then he might not be involved in that investigation. Alternatively, he may have known that Police President Heinrich Voigt had already been to see me to offer his condolences.' Willmore frowned. 'Speaking of Voigt, the funny thing is he seemed to associate the two incidents, that Neil Franklin had been killed as a direct consequence of what Moresby had been up to.'

'What exactly did he say?'

'Oh, words to the effect that Moresby had walked into a trap and exposed Neil as a result. I got the impression that it wasn't unfounded speculation on Voigt's part.'

Had Voigt been bluffing or did he have an informer in the Hizbollah movement? Neither possibility seemed likely to Ashton. Voigt was responsible for maintaining law and order in Berlin and there was no earthly reason why he should even have heard of Gamal's Hizbollah cell which only ten days ago had been in Cairo. No, if he had received prior warning, the information could only have come from either the *Bundesnachrichtendienst* or else G7, the élite anti-terrorist force.

'Are you attending the funeral?' Willmore asked, interrupting Ashton's mental speculations.

Ashton wasn't sure whose funeral he was referring to. 'When is it?' he asked.

'Tomorrow afternoon, three o'clock.'

'I'll still be in Berlin.'

'That's why I asked. Neil Franklin is going to be buried in the Forest House of Peace Cemetery off the Potsdamer Chaussee. The funeral service will be held in the chapel.'

Ashton wondered why he should be surprised. Neil Franklin had never made any secret of how much he loved Berlin and its people. He had connived, wheedled and used every bit of influence he had to ensure he remained in post as Head of Station long after most incumbents would have been relieved. It was perhaps only natural that he should want to remain in his adopted city for ever.

'Yes, I'll be there.' Ashton paused. 'Do you happen to know the name of the funeral directors?'

'Karl Graber Incorporated.'

'Thanks.' Ashton took out his wallet. 'Do you think fifty Deutschmarks would be enough for a wreath or a decent spray?'

'More than enough,' Willmore assured him.

'Would you do me a favour and order it?'

'Why can't you . . . ?'

'Officially, I'm not in Berlin.'

'I see. What would you like me to put on the card? "With deepest sympathy from all at Vauxhall Cross"?'

'In fond memory will do. And sign it Peter.' Ashton felt

guilty about the hypocrisy of the message because he and Neil Franklin had fought like cat and dog on the only two occasions their paths had crossed.

'Anything else I can do for you?' Willmore asked.

'Not at the moment.'

Ashton shook hands, apologised for taking up so much of his time and thanked him for being so helpful. It was a little too fulsome but Willmore seemed to appreciate it and there was no knowing when he might need another favour from the Consul General.

He left the Consulate, walked back to Hecker's Hotel and went up to his room on the fourth floor overlooking Grolmanstrasse. On hotel stationery, he wrote a brief note to Willie Baumgart asking the German to get in touch with him when he came off shift. Back down on the street again, Ashton hailed a cab and told the driver to take him to Theodor-Heussplatz.

The last time Hazelwood had gone to Montrose Place he'd had problems looking for somewhere to park his Rover 800 in the square. Unless, like Stuart Dunglass, you happened to be a resident, your chances of finding a vacant unallotted space were remote. In fact, since Montrose Place was more heavily patrolled by traffic wardens than anywhere else in Belgravia, you were much more likely to get a ticket for leaving your vehicle on a double yellow line in the vicinity of a fire hydrant. For these two very good reasons, Hazelwood chose to use an official car when he called on Dunglass.

Montrose Place was the sort of location beloved of film directors making period movies. The large Edwardian town houses built just after the turn of the century were tailor-made for Sherlock Holmes mysteries and the life-below-stairs soaps which had been very popular in the seventies. Instead of a chauffeur-driven limousine from the car pool, Hazelwood thought it would have been more appropriate had he alighted from a hansom cab outside the imposing entrance to number 22. In 1903, a butler, cook, scullery maid, footman and two lady's maids would have slept in the attic rooms and dined in the basement; now the domestic staff consisted of a former Royal Marines corporal who acted as a butler-cum-chauffeur-cum-general-handyman, and his wife who cooked for the household.

After instructing his driver to return for him in an hour's time, Hazelwood walked up the front steps and rang the bell. Almost before he had time to blink, the former Marine opened the door and showed him into the study at the front of the house where Dunglass was waiting.

Stuart Dunglass looked exceptionally well, as did most people when they were in remission, or so Hazelwood had been given to understand. He was cheerful, optimistic and buoyant, and that too was said to be symptomatic of his terminal illness.

'I'll be back in the office on Monday,' he told Hazelwood.

'That's tremendous news. I've been keeping the chair warm for you.'

'You haven't been tempted to make any changes then?'

'Absolutely not. I have a simple rule – if it works, don't tinker with it.'

'Very wise.' Dunglass clapped his hands. 'Now, what can I get you to drink? Brandy? Whisky? Gin and tonic?'

'Well, actually it's a little early in the day for me.'

Dunglass looked from Hazelwood to the carriage clock on the mantelpiece above the fireplace that had been retained as a feature when central heating had been installed throughout the house. 'Five minutes to four,' he murmured. 'Time for tea then?'

'A cup of tea would be very nice.'

'With shortbread biscuits?' the ex-Marine suggested.

'What a splendid idea,' Dunglass agreed enthusiastically.

The next moment, he sank into one of the two leather armchairs as though suddenly drained by the effort of putting on a brave face.

'Do make yourself comfortable, Victor,' he said.

Hazelwood took the other chair. Glancing around the study, he thought how impersonal it all was. There were no photographs on the desk, no mementos of a lifetime spent in the service of his country, and none of the leather-bound volumes on the floor-to-ceiling bookshelves looked as if it had been opened.

'Now what is it you wanted to see me about?' Dunglass asked.

Hazelwood wondered how to begin. It was one thing to telephone Dunglass and ask for a few minutes of his time to discuss a delicate matter, quite another to know how to broach the subject when you were face to face with him.

'It's about Jill Sheridan,' he said eventually.

'Now, there's someone who is going places,' Dunglass interjected. 'She's got a good brain and has a tight grip on her department. I know a few eyebrows were raised when I promoted her over the heads of more senior colleagues, but I've subsequently been proved right.'

Hazelwood gritted his teeth. This was going to be even more difficult than he had anticipated. He had come to see Dunglass about a missing folio and hadn't intended to brief him about the failed operation in Berlin, but now it seemed he had no option. He started with the recruitment of Gamal al Hassan and took it from there, compressing the whole sorry tale into as few words as possible. The thing which staggered him was the fact that the bombing of the English Bookshop had made little impression on Dunglass even though it had been fully reported in the newspapers and on television. The media might have swallowed the damage-limitation story which the BND in Bonn had cooked up at his request because they had no reason to doubt that Hizbollah had attacked the bookshop as a reprisal against the British and German Governments for their support of Israel. But Dunglass should have seen through it.

'I was terribly sorry to hear about Neil Franklin.'

'We all were,' Hazelwood said. 'But you do see why the incident raised a number of questions about Jill's handling of her source before she passed him on to Rowan Garfield's department?'

'Yes. In your shoes, I would have wanted to satisfy myself that all the procedures had been correctly followed.'

'Good. That's why I would like to know why you removed folio 88 from Jill Sheridan's security file?'

'Folio 88?' Dunglass frowned as though perplexed. 'Folio 88?' he repeated.

'Yes. It was a letter from a discontented British contract officer with the Bahrain police who alleged that Jill's husband was a pimp. Attached to the letter was a snapshot of Henry Clayburn fondling one of his amateur whores. According to Roy Kelso, you told him that you were removing the folio on the instructions of our then Director.'

'That's correct.'

'Kelso also says he understood the folio was going to be placed on the Director's demi-official file, but I couldn't find it.'

'I'm not surprised, Victor. I destroyed the letter.'

'I don't believe I'm hearing this,' Hazelwood said, aghast. 'One of our vetting officers should have confronted Jill with the letter and interviewed her in depth.'

'She was. I did it, and was satisfied with her explanation, as was the DG.'

'Perhaps you can satisfy me as well?'

'What?'

'I want to hear what Jill told you.'

'I think you are forgetting who you're talking to.'

'No, I'm not,' Hazelwood said in a harsh voice. 'You're a sick man and I'm the Acting DG who's faced with a crisis in Berlin. That gives me the right to ask you any damned question I like. Now, please let's hear it.'

Dunglass looked shocked. It was doubtful if anybody had ever spoken like that to him before, and Hazelwood regretted having to do it. He owed a lot to this man who had chosen him to be his deputy, but at the end of the day, he didn't have any choice.

'I'm waiting, Stuart,' he said in a friendlier tone.

'It was an old snapshot,' Dunglass told him in a low voice, 'a self-portrait taken by Henry Clayburn with his first wife who could best be described as a nymphomaniac.'

Clayburn had ultimately divorced her for adultery years before he had met Jill Sheridan. The contract officer had been one of the co-respondents he had named in his petition.

'Naturally I took steps to verify Jill's statement and Henry Clayburn's. After discussing the matter with the DG, we decided to destroy the record. We felt that if the account was left on her security file, it could prove damaging in the future. Somebody who wasn't aware of the facts might conclude there was no smoke without fire.'

Hazelwood wasn't sure whether Dunglass wasn't having a dig at him but he didn't care either way.

'Satisfied, Victor?'

Hazelwood nodded. All the same, he couldn't get rid of the uncomfortable feeling that Jill had successfully managed to pull the wool over their eyes.

Chapter 8

Ashton left Hecker's Hotel, walked up Grolmanstrasse towards Sauvignyplatz and turned left immediately beyond the railway bridge. He had met Willie Baumgart in some strange places over the years; these had included a bar on Seydelstrasse which boasted porno movies and a lewd girlie cabaret every two hours, a dreary tea room in East Berlin, Bertholt's *Frühstückskneipe* and an open-air café in the Zoological Gardens. But the S-Bahn station at Sauvignyplatz was definitely in a class of its own. He continued on past the display windows of a furniture store, electrical goods supplier and an art gallery situated beneath the arches of the elevated railway. On the west side of the square, a narrow alleyway flanked by market stalls on either side led to the S-Bahn station. Climbing the steps which led to the island platform above, Ashton fed three Marks fifty into a ticket vending machine which allowed him to use the entire network for one hour.

He had dropped his hand-written note to Willie at the Blitz Taxi office and had then returned to the hotel. Shortly after four thirty, the girl on the switchboard had put the German through to Ashton's room and in his inimitable way, Baumgart had indicated where and when he was to meet him. Ashton crossed over to the down line and walked to the far end of the platform. Willie Baumgart would be coming in from the direction of the *Zoologischer Garten* and had told him to look out for a train going to West Potsdam after 18.15 hours. At eleven minutes before the appointed time, one going to Wannsee pulled into the platform and departed a shade over forty-five seconds later. It was followed by one going to Werder and then by a third terminating at Nikolassee. Used to the vagaries of the London Underground where the timetable was regarded as a rough guide, Ashton was pleasantly surprised when the West Potsdam train appeared right on schedule.

Willie Baumgart was where he'd said he would be – in the first car standing by the second set of automatic doors. For once, his sartorial tastes erred on the conservative side. Instead of the usual colour clash, he had chosen to wear black loafers, faded Levis and a thin, roll-neck green sweater under his favourite black leather jacket. The patch over the left socket that had practically been his badge of office had been discarded in favour of a glass eye. He looked better in dark sunglasses but that really wasn't on when there was less than an hour of daylight to go before the onset of dusk.

Had Willie not joined the police, Ashton reckoned he could have made a reasonable living as an actor. The bravura performance he put on for the benefit of the other passengers in the car could not have been bettered by a fully paid-up member of Equity. Surprise gave way to pleasure as he went into his 'fancy meeting you here' routine without ever once striking a false note. Ashton followed his lead and made small talk in fluent German. There was a large exodus at Wilmersdorfer; after the train pulled out of Westkreuz, they had the car to themselves. Beckoning Ashton to follow him, Baumgart moved forward towards the motorman's cab and took a seat by the window in a vacant foursome.

'I'm supposed to let Herr Voigt know you are in town,' he said.

Ashton sat down opposite him in the other window seat and leaned forward, arms resting on his knees. 'Would you care to enlarge on that statement, Willie?'

'Kommissar Eicke of the Kripo dropped by the office

yesterday afternoon and had a quiet word with me. It seems our illustrious Police President thinks I'll be the first person British Intelligence will approach when they decide to rebuild their shattered network.'

'I'm not here to do that.'

'Well, that's a relief. I wouldn't like Eicke to step on my toes again, he's got a heavy foot.'

'Are you talking literally?'

'You want I should take my shoes and socks off?'

'No, that won't be necessary.' Ashton studied his man thoughtfully. 'Have you, in fact, contacted the police?' he asked.

'What do you take me for? You think I'm going to snuggle up to the Kripo because some moron tried to break my toes? Hell, if Voigt had deliberately set out to make an enemy of me, he couldn't have done a better job.' Baumgart smiled. 'That being the case, what can I do for you?'

'When are you going to see Fräulein Helga again?'

'I haven't decided yet. Tomorrow perhaps. Why do you ask?'

'I'd like to know if she has recalled anything more about the bombing,' Ashton told him. 'Did anything happen in the days leading up to the incident which with the benefit of hindsight now seems odd? That kind of thing.'

'OK. Anything else?'

'Depends if anyone in the police force is still talking to you.' Ashton told him everything he had learned from Willmore, how Voigt had connected Moresby's death with the bombing of the English Bookshop and the fact that he knew Gamal al Hassan had been expelled from Kuwait for collaborating with the Iraqis during the Gulf War. 'You know anyone who could tell me how the Police President of Berlin obtained that sort of information, Willie? Someone in the Criminal Intelligence Bureau, for example?'

'Most of the guys I served with have left the force, the few who are still in it are leery of talking to me these days.'

'What about crime reporters? I don't know how it works over here, but back home, they all have their well-placed sources who keep them abreast of what is going on. You know anybody like that?'

'I might.' Baumgart rubbed his thumb and index finger together. 'Question is, are you willing to pay him?'

'How about 500 Deutschmarks as a sweetener?'

'Try doubling it,' Baumgart advised him.

Ashton took out his wallet, peeled off a thousand in fifty D-Mark notes and handed the bundle to the German. Kelso expected him to account for the money and he was tempted to ask Willie to sign for the cash just to see the expression on his face. 'I hope your friend is going to earn this,' he said.

'He's the best.'

'Good. I want everything he's heard about Gamal al Hassan and the bombing.'

'What else is on your shopping list?'

'I need a good photographer, one who can keep his mouth shut. Ella Franklin is burying her husband tomorrow afternoon at 15.00 hours. I want to know who's who amongst the mourners at the church service and at the graveside.'

'You don't think you've seen too many Hollywood movies?'

'The front row of the circle is where I learned my trade,' Ashton said drily.

'That's very droll. Where did you say they were burying Herr Franklin?'

'The Forest House of Peace Cemetery off the Potsdamer Chaussee. I want the prints delivered to my hotel as soon as possible after the mourners have dispersed.'

'Maybe I should do it?' Baumgart wrinkled his nose. 'I could pay my last respects at the same time. I didn't really like Herr Franklin but he saw me right when the police were going to press charges of manslaughter, and I owe him.'

'Do you think Voigt will attend the funeral?'

'It's possible,' Baumgart said, and looked even more undecided.

'How well do you know Ella Franklin?'

'I don't, we've never met.'

'Then she isn't going to feel hurt if you don't put in an appearance.' Ashton paused, then said, 'I'll tell you something else, the best way you can pay your last respects to Neil Franklin is to help find the people who killed him.'

'You're right,' Baumgart agreed eagerly.

'One other point. When you go looking for a photographer, try to get one who does freelance work for the newspapers. He would then have a logical reason for being at the cemetery should Voigt take it into his head to question him.'

Ashton said he saw the photographer playing the human interest angle. Why did well-known proprietor of the English Bookshop choose to be buried in his adopted city? Does widow intend to settle permanently in Berlin?

'That's a bit sick, isn't it?'

'Come on, Willie, it's just a cover story, he won't be doing it for real.'

'I should hope not.'

There was no doubting Baumgart's indignation and it was a side of his character Ashton had not seen before. Until now, he had regarded him as a hard nose without too many scruples.

'Better make it snappy,' Baumgart told him. 'We're parting company at the next stop.'

Ashton glanced to his left in time to catch a final glimpse of a platform as the train pulled out of the station. 'Where was that?' he asked.

'Nikolassee, and my advice still holds good.'

'I want you to have a look at the photographs, see if there are any faces you recognise. Can you get time off tomorrow, say around eight o'clock?'

Baumgart didn't see a problem. It seemed he owned a slice of Blitz Taxis and could come and go pretty much as he liked, which was something else Ashton hadn't known about him.

'You're a man of many parts, Willie,' he said.

'Oh, I'm a regular chameleon.'

With a fine sense of anticipation, Baumgart got to his feet and moved up to the automatic doors. A few moments later the train pulled into Wannsee. He did not look round or wave goodbye before he stepped out on to the platform and made his way to the exit.

Ashton stayed on to the end of the line for no good reason other than to humour Baumgart. It seemed a ridiculous precaution, but Willie was almost paranoid about Voigt and had run all kinds of checks to make sure he wasn't being followed between leaving the Blitz Taxis office and boarding the S-Bahn at the Zoo station. Ashton supposed the German believed that the longer they were together, the greater the risk of being spotted.

At seven o'clock in the evening, Potsdam was already beginning to resemble a ghost town. It was a hangover from the days when the place had been a major garrison and the local civilian population had been all but swamped by the Red Army. Ashton left the station, walked as far as the Schillerplatz and dropped into a *Gasthof* for a quick beer before retracing his steps.

The return journey to Savignyplatz seemed to take twice as long. Back at Hecker's Hotel, he rang Harriet to see what sort of day she had had, then went out for a steak at Tanzler's on the Ku'damm. Before turning in, he walked up Budapesterstrasse as far as the heap of rubble that had once been the English Bookshop.

The late-night weather forecast for the next twenty-four hours on SFB, the local TV station, had painted a gloomy picture for the funeral. Instead of another fine, bright day, Berliners could look forward to frequent showers, some of them heavy, with a maximum high of fourteen centigrade or fifty-seven Fahrenheit. The sullen, lowering overcast which greeted Ashton when he drew back the curtains was a grim portent; there was more to come after he retrieved the complimentary copy of *Der Tagesspiegel* which the hotel staff had left on the mat outside his room. At the foot of the end column on the front page were a brief four lines stating that the bombing had claimed another victim, an elderly housewife aged sixty-two who had never regained consciousness. There was also an article on page four which had obviously been written before the unfortunate woman had died. It was the kind of rehash the quality Sundays at home went in for when nothing too disastrous had happened in the world the day before and the editors were hard pressed to fill the centre pages. The article included a photograph of Heinrich Voigt who reminded Ashton of Chancellor Schmidt, who was only marginally less handsome. The Police President had gone on record to assure readers of *Der Tagesspiegel* that the Kripo would leave no stone unturned, no avenue unexplored in their quest to bring the perpetrators of the outrage to justice. The literal translation was so coy and banal, it was almost nauseous, but on reflection, Ashton supposed the eulogy was no worse than some of the in-depth interviews of pop stars that regularly appeared in the trade mags.

With little to do before the funeral at 15.00 hours, Ashton enjoyed a leisurely breakfast in the dining room, then went out and bought himself an umbrella from Bilko's opposite the Kaiser Wilhelm Memorial Church. From there, he took a cab out to Berlin-Tegel and rented a Volkswagen Passat from Avis. He had never met Ella Franklin, nor had he ever been anywhere near 41 Alsenstrasse but to call on her now would, he decided, be intrusive. Better to put that off until tomorrow when she might be marginally less overwrought. He wished Harriet were with him; she would know what to say to Ella, how to deal with her and maybe learn something in the process. From the airport, he drove across town to check out the Forest House of Peace Cemetery and found the only place he could park the car was on the approach road outside the main gates.

Ashton made a three-point turn, got back on to the

Potsdamer Chaussee and headed towards the town centre through the Steglitz and Schöneberg Districts. At the top of Potsdamer Strasse, he turned off left and went through the Tiergarten, crossed the old east-west axis near the Brandenburg Gate and carried on over the Spree.

Franklin had been pretty vague concerning the precise location of the builder's yard in the cables he'd sent to London so that it took Ashton some time to find the place. One quick glance at the compound was enough to make him wonder if his journey had really been necessary or why, having driven there, he should have bothered to get out of the car. Seeing at first-hand the spot where Moresby had been butchered didn't add to his understanding of the incident or the morality of the people who had murdered him. He thought there was no more desolate place to die than this barren wasteland with its backdrop of giant cranes in the direction of the Unter den Linden. And to cap it all, it started to spit with rain as he turned about and walked back to the Volkswagen. On the spur of the moment, he decided to have a look at the rendezvous where Quorn had waited in vain for Moresby to show up.

The *Schwarz und Weiss* looked like any other bar in the Kreuzberg District, at least from the outside. To go through the swing doors, however, was to enter a cocktail bar reminiscent of the late forties, early fifties, replete with chrome embellishments and plush leather upholstery set off by a black and white décor. At one thirty in the afternoon, there were only five other patrons – two men who looked as though they had been sleeping rough and three overdressed women, all of whom were crammed into one booth. Ashton barely had time to settle on a high stool at the bar before a woman with bright red hair detached herself from the others and joined him.

'Hi,' she said in a deep husky voice. 'My name's Claudia. What's yours?'

'Peter,' Ashton told her.

Claudia was tall and slender; she had a nineteen-inch waist firmly held in place by a black patent leather belt with a gold buckle, and a thirty-six-inch bust which formed two sharply defined pyramids under a chiffon blouse. She wore false eyelashes and fingernails which had been painted with a bilious green varnish. To go with the green chiffon blouse, she wore a tight lurex skirt in a matching colour, black tights and high-heeled sandals. Claudia had so much make-up on her face that the pancake was in danger of cracking each time she smiled. The dark hairs on her throat were at variance with the colour of her hair and confirmed a suspicion that she was wearing a wig.

'Are you waiting for someone?' Claudia enquired with a conscious effort to make her throaty voice sound even sexier.

'I'm expecting a friend, a guy called Joachim,' Ashton said and described Moresby as accurately as he could. 'He comes here often.'

'I think I may have met him.'

'Really? What are you – part of the fixtures?'

'I come here every day.' Claudia smiled mechanically. 'A girl has to scratch a living somehow.' A slim hand came to rest on his thigh. 'Will you buy me a drink?'

'Why not?' Ashton signalled to the bartender. 'What'll you have?'

'A brandy sour,' Claudia said and patted his thigh before giving it an affectionate squeeze.

Ashton repeated the order and asked for a Scotch on the rocks for himself. He resolved to give Claudia five minutes of his time to see if she really had met Moresby; he also promised himself that if she moved her hand so much as another fraction of an inch, he was going to break her bloody wrist.

'You're not a Berliner, are you, Peter?'

'I'm no doughnut, that's for sure.'

'That was a good joke against Kennedy thirty years ago, *Liebchen*, but it's got whiskers on it now.'

Ashton gazed quizzically at the transvestite who called himself Claudia. 'Like some people I know,' he said.

Claudia licked her lips thoughtfully. 'Your German is very good,' she said, 'but I think you are an *Ausländer* like your friend.'

Ashton wasn't sure what to make of it. Although he was fluent in German, anyone with a keen ear could tell it wasn't his native language. And on the principle that like socialised with like, it would be a reasonable assumption on Claudia's part that the friend he was allegedly waiting for was also a foreigner. There was, however, a slim chance that this ageing queen had actually met Moresby.

'Let's talk about my friend, Claudia,' he said, and crushed her slim wrist in a grip of iron before she could move her hand any higher up his leg. 'When exactly did you meet him?'

'You're hurting my wrist, Peter. And I didn't meet him.'

'You just said you had.'

'I meant I saw him.'

'When?'

'A week ago.' Claudia shrugged. 'Perhaps ten days, and you're still hurting my wrist.'

She was close; it was in fact eight days since Moresby had told Quorn to meet him at the *Schwarz und Weiss*. On the other hand, Claudia had been watching him like a hawk and maybe he had looked surprised when she had tentatively suggested it had been a week ago and had automatically upped the number of days.

'Did you hear what I said? You're hurting my wrist.'

Ashton relaxed his grip a little. 'Why do you remember my friend so well?' he asked.

'Because he was on his own and I tried to pick him up.'

'And he told you to get lost?'

'No, like you, he said he was waiting for a friend.' Claudia raised her voice until it was shrill enough for her friends in the booth to hear her above the noise of the piped discordant sound of a heavy metal rock group. 'Why do you keep asking me all these questions?'

Ashton glanced over his shoulder. One of Claudia's friends, a beer belly with a brass curtain ring in each ear and a nose stud, was already on his feet and looking menacing. 'You want to earn a cool hundred?' Ashton asked her quietly.

'For doing what?'

'First you tell your friends that everything is all right, then you answer a couple of questions. OK?'

'Let's see the colour of your money.'

Ashton released her wrist, took out his wallet and laid a hundred D-Mark note on the bar. 'Satisfied?'

Claudia nodded, swivelled round on the bar stool and told Karl Heinz to sit down, then huddled close to Ashton again, one hand returning to rest on his thigh. 'What do you want to know?' she asked, giving full rein to her throaty voice.

'Did you see who my friend was waiting for?'

'Yes, she arrived a few minutes after I had spoken to him.'

A woman. When Moresby had phoned Quorn that fateful evening, he had told him that their business associate had been in touch and thereafter everyone had assumed it was a man. The fact that Moresby hadn't bothered to correct the mistaken assumption raised a number of questions, including the possibility that Claudia was lying.

'What was she like, this woman?'

'Small, very sinewy, pointed features. She had jet-black glossy hair and a sallow complexion.' Claudia preened herself like a peacock. 'I can't think what your friend saw in her.'

'You're talking about my wife,' Ashton said.

'What?'

'My best friend ran off with my wife.'

Claudia gaped at him, her jaw sagging. 'I didn't know.'

'Well, now you do.'

Ashton left the hundred-Mark note where it was, slipped off the bar stool and walked towards the exit. Before he reached the swing doors, Claudia found her voice and started yelling about how he owed her another two hundred Marks.

Karl Heinz was three inches taller and forty pounds heavier than Ashton but that was all he had going for him. He was basically unfit, slow to react and lacked the necessary co-ordination to deal with a sudden and unexpected counterattack. Timing it to perfection, Ashton swung round, side-stepped out of his way and then kicked the legs from under Karl Heinz as he thundered past him. The German went down hard, banged his head against a table and rose groggily to his feet only to walk into a forearm smash to the left side of his jaw which put him on the floor again, this time unconscious.

Ashton looked round the bar; five blank faces stared back at him. The piped rock music was no longer coming through the speakers and there was total silence. As nonchalantly as he knew how, Ashton turned about and walked out into Oranienstrasse to find it was now raining steadily. Annoyed with himself for having left the umbrella in the Volks, he ran back to the car, unlocked the nearside door and, diving inside, scrambled across the passenger seat.

There was more traffic about than there had been earlier in the day and it took Ashton longer than he'd anticipated to drive to the Forest House of Peace. The funeral was scheduled for 15.00 hours and the last vehicle of the cortège was just passing through the entrance to the cemetery when he turned into the approach road. Leaving the Volkswagen Passat outside the gates, he grabbed the umbrella and hurried after the procession.

The pallbearers were just entering the church when he caught up with the cortège. Tagging on behind them, Ashton slipped into a pew at the back where he could see what was going on without being seen himself. He counted thirty-one mourners including the widow. Apart from Gerald Willmore, the Consul General, the only other person he recognised was Heinrich Voigt and he would not have picked him out had his photograph not appeared in *Der Tagesspiegel* that morning.

He was no wiser after the service had finished and they

all trooped out to stand huddled under umbrellas by the graveside in the pouring rain. There were more women than men amongst the mourners and Ashton supposed that the middle-aged matrons closest to Ella Franklin were members of the same golf club. He also thought the chunky man in a light blue raincoat who sported a polka-dot bow tie might be an American. On the other hand, if his sartorial taste was anything to go by, he could just as easily be another Willie Baumgart.

It was only after Ashton had pressed hands with the widow and was walking away from the graveside that he noticed the photographer. The man was standing under a fir tree some thirty yards from the open grave and it seemed to Ashton that, in the poor light, he was asking a lot from his telephoto lens camera.

Chapter 9

The question of what he should do about the furore over the missing folio in Jill Sheridan's security file was beginning to haunt Roy Kelso. The trouble was that the DG had kept the news of his prostate trouble to himself until the very last moment. Had he known beforehand just how ill Dunglass was, Kelso would have got him to sign for the bloody document. As was the case with so many of their difficulties, the root cause was the Foreign and Commonwealth Office.

The letter written by the disgruntled police officer alleging that Jill's husband, Henry Clayburn, had made his money operating a call-girl racket had been addressed to Her Majesty's Ambassador in Bahrain. His Excellency, after consulting the embassy security officer, had then sent it on to London in the diplomatic bag. And it was at the Foreign and Commonwealth where things had started to go wrong at the clerical level. The dispatch clerk had correctly addressed the outer envelope to 'The Secretary, Box 850', only to make a howling error with the inner envelope containing the incriminating letter and lewd snapshot. Instead of franking it 'Personal for Director General, SIS', the clerk had marked it 'For Attention Head of Security'. As a result of this error, central registry at Vauxhall Cross had forwarded the sealed inner envelope to the Admin Wing, which in those days had been located at Benbow House. Fortunately, the Chief Archivist of the Security Vetting and Technical Services Division had had the wit to bring the document straight to him instead of showing it to Ashton first.

In view of the previous relationship of Ashton and Jill Sheridan, he, Kelso, had taken charge of the security dossier. He had filed the damaging letter, entered the details on the registration of secret material which was stapled to the back of the front cover, and had then put the dossier away in his safe. He had of course looked at the file from time to time and had studied the lewd photograph with considerable interest, wondering if the naked woman in the yashmak was in fact Jill Sheridan in a wig. But apart from musing over this possibility, he had failed to take any action over the incriminating letter. There had been no follow-up, no subject interview to clear the air. It hadn't been idleness on his part; the truth was, the whole business of positive vetting was a closed book to him and he hadn't known what to do about the damned letter other than file it.

Dunglass had really laid into him when he'd discovered that nothing had been done about the allegation, but in the end, he had accepted his explanation that he hadn't been able to brief any of the three investigation officers on the establishment because Ashton had committed all of them to other tasks. The excuse had contained more than a grain of truth and the Deputy Director, as Dunglass was then, had accepted that he could hardly have asked Ashton to make one of his IOs available without telling him why.

With considerable relief, Kelso had handed over the letter and photograph to Dunglass and had contented himself with replacing the missing folio with a blank sheet of paper. No one on the top floor had ever told him what action had been taken but he'd naturally assumed that everything was OK, especially when Jill Sheridan had been appointed to run the Middle East Department. And there the matter had rested until Victor Hazelwood had called for her security file and had latched on to the blank folio. Yesterday's inquisition by the Acting DG had been bad enough but this morning he'd had Dunglass on to him as well. And unless Kelso's ears had deceived him, Dunglass was now saying that there had been no follow-up and somehow this was due to his negligence.

He had thought of nothing else all morning and by mid afternoon had come to the reluctant conclusion that only Jill Sheridan could tell him what was going on. The Assistant Director Middle East was a very formidable woman and whenever possible he liked to give her a wide berth, but today that was a luxury he couldn't afford. Somewhat apprehensively, he went up to her office on the fourth floor and diffidently asked if she could spare him a few minutes.

'But I can come back later if you're busy,' he added even more diffidently.

'I wouldn't hear of it.' Jill waved a hand at the spare chair. 'Do sit down, Roy, before I get a crick in the neck looking up at you.'

'It's a confidential matter.' Kelso cleared his throat. 'To do with security vetting.'

'I see.' Jill Sheridan stood up and walked round the desk to close the door to her office. 'Has someone in my department been misbehaving himself?' she asked.

Kelso glanced over his shoulder. 'Well, no. This has to do with Henry.'

'Henry?'

'Your husband.'

'Ah. Now I understand why you're embarrassed.'

She walked past him, then turned about and half leaned against, half sat on the edge of the desk, crossing her ankles as she did so. Jill was wearing a beige-coloured outfit comprising a close-fitting mid-calf-length skirt and a single-breasted hip-length jacket with false pockets and a plunging neckline.

'What's Henry been up to?'

She was calm, poised, even sounded amused. It was not the reaction Kelso had expected and he didn't know how to proceed. Lost for words and frequently stammering, he told her about the letter which had been sent to the

Ambassador in Bahrain and the possible security implications for her.

'Are you implying that I was one of these amateur call girls?'

Kelso swallowed, felt the colour rising in his face. 'Good God, no,' he said hoarsely.

'Henry divorced his first wife.'

'I know.'

'Frankly, she was a tart and her antics made life pretty average hell for him.'

'What was the outcome?' Kelso cleared his throat a second time. 'Of the letter, I mean. Was it ever resolved?'

'Would I be holding down this job if my integrity was in doubt?'

'No, of course you wouldn't.' It was not, however, the assurance he'd hoped for and he tried again, this time tackling the issue head-on, which was unlike him. 'Victor Hazelwood's been nosing through your file.'

'Really?'

'He got very worked up about the missing folio and grilled me for what seemed like hours. I had to tell him what I knew about the affair.'

'Of course you did, Roy. After all, Victor is the Acting DG and you would have found yourself in hot water if you had refused to answer his questions.' Jill was all sweetness and light, too damned reasonable, too damned cool, too everything.

'He's hired Ashton to look into all the closets.'

'So I'd heard. I don't know why you are getting so worked up about it; Peter's a fair man and I'm sure he will do a good job.'

'You don't understand,' Kelso blurted out. 'I've had Stuart Dunglass on my back and although he didn't actually say so, he led me to believe that you hadn't been interviewed and that I was to blame. Of course, this was after Victor had been to see him.'

'I see.'

'For Christ's sake, Jill, is that all you can say?'

'Listen to me, Roy. Some of my peers, notably Rowan Garfield, are out to shaft me. I mean to be the next DG but one, and they intend to do everything they can to nobble me. All my life I've done everything by the book. Take Gamal al Hassan for example; he was my A1 source but when he moved from Cairo to Berlin, I agreed control should pass to Rowan Garfield. Unfortunately, his people made a total cock of it and two good men were brutally murdered as a result. Now, since this reflects badly on him, the only way he can save his hide is by denigrating me. And how does he set about that? Simple; he suggests that Gamal al Hassan was something of a con man and a lot of the information he sent us during the Gulf War was supplied by the Iraqis themselves. The inference being that I allowed myself to be duped by him. Everybody knows I was debriefed on my return from Bahrain; one copy of the interrogation is lodged with the Mid East Department, the other was placed on my security file. Victor Hazelwood sent for the latter because he didn't want to alert me, and lo and behold, he finds folio 88 is missing. Stuart should have given you a signature for the document but he didn't and what had been an oversight at the time suddenly looks highly suspicious at a later date when other factors come into play.'

What Jill had said made sense to Kelso and he could think of several examples to support her contention. There was, however, one thing which needed to be explained to his satisfaction before he could accept her hypothesis without any qualms.

'How do you account for Stuart's attitude?' he asked. 'I mean, there's no getting away from the fact that he tried to pass the buck on to me.'

'There are two things you have to remember, Roy. First of all, Stuart is a very sick man, and secondly, you know what Victor Hazelwood is like. Once he's got the bit between his teeth, there is no holding him. My guess is he thoroughly put the wind up poor old Stuart when he went to see him, and our esteemed Director General sought to cover his back. And you have to admit that's not like Stuart.'

Kelso beamed. The one remaining doubt in his mind had been laid to rest and he felt as though a great weight had been lifted from his shoulders.

'I'm glad we've had this little chat, Jill.'

'So am I, Roy.'

Jill straightened up, moved round the desk and sat down. It was regally done, rather like the monarch indicating that the audience was over and her loyal subject was now required to withdraw. Kelso was, in fact, about to open the door when she dropped the bombshell.

'There is one thing I should mention,' Jill informed him quietly. 'Henry and I have decided to separate.'

Kelso turned slowly about. 'Separate?' he repeated in a hollow voice.

'Yes. Things haven't worked out; we have so few interests in common.'

How long had they been married? Two years? More like eighteen months. Jill had returned from Bahrain in '92 and had lived with Henry for several months before he had led her up the aisle. Not the full works, of course, because it had been the second time around for him. They had been married in a registry office and afterwards had been blessed in church, Henry in morning dress complete with top hat, and Jill, the far from virgin bride, in a traditional full-length white satin wedding dress.

'Henry has bought a cottage in Wiltshire, fancies himself as a country gentleman.'

'What are your plans then?' Kelso asked.

'Oh, I'm staying put in Highgate.'

Jill and Henry had sold the flat in Victoria Road, Surbiton, which at one time she and Ashton had been buying with the help of an £80,000 mortgage from a building society. The happy couple had then moved north of the river into a detached four-bedroomed house overlooking Waterlow Park at the top of Highgate Hill – £400,000 minimum but no mortgage because dear old Henry was rolling in money.

'Staying put?' Kelso repeated. 'In the house?'

'Yes. It's part of the settlement. I get to keep the Porsche too.' A smile touched the corners of her mouth. 'You see, I'm not claiming any maintenance.'

Kelso thought that was rich. She had already taken her husband for close on half a million; to then ask him to support her in a style she had only just become accustomed to would be outrageous.

'I'll have to ask you officially to submit a Change of Circumstance Report,' he said pompously.

'I already have, Roy.' Jill opened the top left-hand drawer in the desk and took out a sealed envelope. 'I don't think I've overlooked anything,' she added coolly.

Kelso was damned sure she hadn't. The lady had always shown an uncanny ability to be one move ahead in the game.

Harry's New York Bar was not the sort of rendezvous Ashton usually associated with Willie Baumgart. The name alone sounded expensive; the fact that he had to go round Nollendorfplatz at least half a dozen times before he'd been lucky enough to find a parking space for the Volkswagen Passat led him to think it was likely to be a popular haunt for young, upwardly mobile Berliners. Both suppositions proved correct; the marvel was that Willie did not look wholly out of place amongst the beautiful people, the men in loafers, chinos, granddad shirts; the women in designer outfits that had cost a small fortune.

'I'll have another Bloody Mary,' Willie said when Ashton joined him at the bar. 'I'll grab a quiet table for two while you order.'

Harry's New York Bar was said to be related to the famous American hang-out of people like Hemingway and F. Scott Fitzgerald in Paris in the twenties. The only time Ashton had been to Paris was on a weekend break with Jill Sheridan before she had broken off their engagement in favour of a posting to Bahrain which would reputedly enhance her career prospects. Ashton couldn't recall

117

having visited the original establishment but was prepared to accept the claim that the Berlin version was identical in all respects. Certainly, the black jazz singer at the piano was doing a very fair impression of Fats Waller and 'My Very Good Friend the Milkman', and in case that wasn't atmospheric enough, on the wall behind the musician there was a picture gallery of US Presidents from Woodrow Wilson to George Bush.

'What do you think of it?' Willie asked when Ashton joined him at the table he'd bagged.

'Very up-market,' Ashton said, peeping at the tab the waiter had left with their drinks.

'Yeah, well, you pay for what you get in this world, and this is one place in town where you won't find the Kripo. It's too damn pricey for them.' Willie raised his glass. 'Skol.'

'Mud in your eye.' Ashton tasted the Bloody Mary, then said, 'Your photographer friend still hasn't produced the goods.'

'Rome wasn't built in a day,' Willie said with a shrug.

He had a penchant for English expressions. He had trotted out the same maxim when Ashton had rung him shortly after eight p.m. and even though it was now an hour and a half later, he still wasn't bothered.

'Whatever happened to German efficiency?' Ashton asked him. 'Back home, you can walk into almost any Boots in the high street and get a roll of film developed in sixty minutes.'

'You're not in England now.'

'I had noticed,' Ashton said drily.

'Fräulein Helga asked to be remembered to you,' Willie said, changing the subject.

'I hope you gave her my best wishes?'

'But of course. She also wanted you to know that nothing would please her more than to be of assistance . . .'

Ashton knew what was coming before the words were out of Baumgart's mouth. Helga had been over and over the incident in her mind but couldn't think of anything to add to her original statement. She had heard the suicide bomber call out to Neil Franklin and while she hadn't actually seen him, she would remember the sound of his voice for the rest of her days.

'That's why Fräulein Helga is quite certain he hadn't visited the bookshop before that fateful day.'

'What about your friendly crime reporter, Willie? Have you seen him yet? More to the point, has he earned the fee I gave you?'

'Maybe. Word is the Kripo received two anonymous phone calls the day the bodies were found in the builder's yard. The man said, and these are his precise words, "The traitor Gamal has been executed. Death to the Great Satan." The detective who took the call thought the guy was either drunk or a weirdo, a view shared by his superior officer who told him to log the incident and forget it.'

The anonymous spokesman had called again that evening and this time he had told the Kripo where Gamal had been staying in Berlin since arriving from Cairo.

'And where was that?'

'The Hotel Adlon in the Turkish quarter of Kreuzberg.' Baumgart shook his head. 'The Adlon; the cheek of it, borrowing the name of a once-famous hotel for a fly-blown *pension* in a sleazy area of the city.'

'Never mind the *Michelin Guide*,' Ashton told him. 'What did the police do with the information?'

'They followed it up, went round to the Adlon and questioned the proprietor. He remembered Gamal al Hassan, even had a registration card for him – single room, second floor back. Checked in on Sunday, 11 September.'

'Gamal was on his own?'

'He was when he arrived. The Adlon doesn't have a restaurant so that evening he went out to have a meal. He returned about 21.00 hours with a hooker–'

'Let me guess,' Ashton said, interrupting him. 'The hooker was small, very sinewy, had pointed features, jet-black glossy hair and a sallow complexion?'

'Wrong. She was blonde and a screamer, made all kinds of ecstatic grunts and groans when he was shafting her. The olive-skinned lady turned up the following afternoon around half-past four.' Baumgart stopped short. 'Hey, wait a minute,' he said, 'who told you about the chick from the Middle East?'

'A transvestite who calls himself Claudia; hangs out at the *Schwarz und Weiss.* I had a long talk with him early this afternoon, and when he saw her, she was with Moresby.'

'Yeah? Well, the sleazeball who owns the hotel said Gamal and this woman appeared to be old friends. Anyway, they left the hotel arm-in-arm and that was the last he saw of Gamal.'

'And that's it?'

'How much more do you want for your money?'

Ashton didn't reply. He figured the anonymous caller had rung the Kripo in order to let them know Gamal had been killed for political reasons. The Great Satan was usually the United States, sometimes the United Kingdom or occasionally an individual who was thought to have denigrated the Islamic faith blasphemously. In this instance, the slogan had been a coded message to the effect that the execution had been carried out by Hizbollah. It had also warned the Kripo that the fundamentalists intended to attack the Intelligence agency the dead man had worked for. When it had become apparent that the Kripo had failed to understand the message, the anonymous informant had phoned again, this time giving the police the kind of information that would convince them it wasn't a hoax.

'Has any of this been reported in the newspapers?'

'No.' Baumgart contemplated his empty glass. Taking the hint, Ashton signalled one of the bartenders and indicated they wanted the same again.

'Why not?' he asked.

'Pressure from the source. He knew that if anything

appeared in the newspapers at this stage of the investigation, his neck would be on the chopping block. Wouldn't do my friend much good either. As things stand, he doesn't mind sitting on an exclusive provided he gets a green light to file the story before the rest of his fellow journalists are given an official briefing.'

'The day after the murders, Eicke walked into the English Bookshop, button-holed Herr Franklin and gave him the complete life history of Gamal al Hassan. Is your journalist friend equally well informed about him?'

'If he is, he keeps it to himself. For what it's worth, I believe Gamal's background is a closed book to him.'

Ashton was inclined to think the Kripo hadn't got the information from the anonymous caller. It could have come downwards from the Police President himself. If it had, Voigt could have got the information from one of three sources – the *Bundesnachrichtendienst*, the CIA, or the Foreign Office via the Ministry of the Interior in Bonn.

'You know anybody in the CIA, Willie?' he asked, then described the man in the light blue raincoat he'd seen at the funeral.

'The answer's no,' Baumgart told him, 'and I don't recognise the guy you've just described either.'

'It was a long shot.' Ashton started on the second Bloody Mary. 'You want to ring the photographer?' he asked.

'What's the rush?'

'The funeral was at three o'clock; it is now nine minutes past ten. Do I have to spell it out for you?'

Willie sighed, told him not to go away, then got to his feet and threaded his way towards the cloakroom near the entrance. The jazz pianist reappeared after taking a short break and launched into the definitive version of 'Sweet Georgia Brown'. A buxom woman in a shift dress that was far too tight and far too short for her ample figure was suddenly moved to gyrate around the piano doing bumps and grinds. Willie returned just when she was getting into her stride.

'There was no answer,' he told Ashton.

121

'Did you try ringing him at home?'

'He lives above the studio; the phone rings downstairs, he hears it on the extension in the flat. I would think he's out delivering the photographs to your hotel.'

'Well, there's only one way to find out,' Ashton said.

The four Bloody Marys set him back the equivalent of twenty quid; tips to the bartender and the hat check girl accounted for another five, which he thought was going to please Kelso no end. There was, however, one small consolation for Roy. If Willie had had his way, the Admin king of Vauxhall Cross would have been faced with an even bigger chit for expenses.

There was no package waiting for Ashton at Hecker's Hotel. It also transpired that nobody had left a message for him either, something which even Willie couldn't understand.

'Whereabouts is his studio?'

'It's in Kantstrasse,' Baumgart told him. 'Carry on up Grolmanstrasse, go round Sauvignyplatz and make a left.'

Ashton started the Volkswagen, shifted into gear and pulled out from the kerb. It started raining again for the umpteenth time that day before he reached the elevated S-Bahn.

Kantstrasse was an uninspiring avenue of uniform three-storey blocks, shops on the ground floor, flats above. The studio was on the left side of the road and it was no surprise to Ashton that Baumgart wasn't too sure where exactly it was. When he eventually did spot it, he ordered Ashton to turn right into a side street. It was a last-minute, foot-on-the-brakes, tyres-squealing kind of instruction.

There was a travel agency on one side of the studio, vacant premises on the other. The only sign of life was a light showing in one of the front rooms of the flat on the top floor.

'We need to go round the back,' Baumgart said.

A little way back down the street, a covered passageway near a sex *Kino* for club members only led to a narrow access lane in rear of the block. They didn't need to break into the studio: some unknown person had already effected an entry by smashing a pane of glass in the side window. Taking care not to cut himself, Ashton slipped an arm through the jagged hole, felt for the door lock and opened it.

'I don't like it,' Baumgart muttered. 'The broken glass should be inside the hall, not outside on the concrete path. Looks to me as if the intruder deliberately faked a break-in.'

'What's the name of your friend?'

'Richter, Klaus Richter.'

'And where's the darkroom?'

'To your left.'

Ashton opened the door and walked inside to be greeted by a scene of utter chaos. A dim red light partially illuminated a workbench littered with reels of exposed film, and a mass of old black-and-white prints and colour proofs lying ankle-deep on the floor, saturated with fluid from the developing trays. The man was lying face down in the mess, right arm extended, left leg bent at the knee as though he had been trying to crawl forward on his stomach. There was a deep, ugly-looking gash in the skull that was all of five inches long.

'Is that your friend, Willie?'

'Yeah, that's Klaus Richter,' Baumgart said in a hoarse voice.

'I think we'd better get out of here; there's nothing either of us can do for Richter now.' Ashton backed out of the darkroom and closed the door. 'Did you touch anything on the way in?' he asked.

'I might have put a hand on the doorframe.'

'Then you'd better wipe it down with a handkerchief.'

Baumgart had been a police officer; furthermore, that he had once been charged with reckless driving meant that his fingerprints would be on file. Removing every trace of his presence was, however, a bit of a hit-and-miss affair and they weren't inclined to spend a minute longer in the studio than was absolutely necessary.

Their luck held good; nobody saw them arrive, nobody saw them leave. Even so, it wasn't until they turned the corner into Weimarer Strasse where he had parked the Volks that Ashton began to breathe a little easier. He unlocked the door, got in behind the wheel, then waited for Baumgart to join him before starting the engine.

'Voigt was at the funeral this afternoon,' he said. 'Any chance he can tie you to Klaus Richter?'

'If he saw Klaus there it won't take him long to figure out who hired him.'

'You got a lawyer, Willie?'

'Yeah; looks like I'm going to need him too.'

'I hope not, but if the police do pick you up, you tell him to phone me at Hecker's Hotel and I'll square things with Voigt. OK?'

'Sure.' Baumgart smiled lopsidedly. 'What you've just said fills me with confidence.'

'That's the spirit,' Ashton said drily. 'Now where can I drop you?'

'The U-Bahn station at Wilmersdorfer Strasse will do me.' Baumgart rubbed his jaw. 'About Klaus?' he said. 'Are you thinking what I'm thinking?'

'I'd be surprised if I wasn't.'

'So what are you going to do?'

'I plan to see Ella Franklin in the morning and ask her if she recognised all the mourners at the funeral.' Ashton tripped the indicator to show that he was turning right into Wilmersdorfer Strasse. 'There was somebody there who didn't like having their photograph taken. That's why Richter got his head bashed in.'

Chapter 10

Harriet had told Ashton that when he saw the official residence in Wannsee he would understand why Neil Franklin had fought tooth and nail to extend his tour of duty in Berlin. The moment Ashton turned into the driveway of 41 Alsenstrasse, he realised she hadn't been exaggerating. The house was something out of *Homes and Gardens*, the kind of showplace Franklin could never have afforded in England. As Head of Station, he'd occupied it rent-free; other perks had included a cook, two maids, a manservant, boilerman and two gardeners. But that had been in the good old days at the height of the Cold War; successive reviews, the so-called peace dividend, had whittled the domestic staff down to just two.

Ashton supposed Ella Franklin would be invited to vacate the residence before too long and that raised the question of what he was going to say to her. He had thought about it last night and again this morning over breakfast, and he was still groping for the right approach even now. His subconscious urged him to play it by ear, advice he was only too happy to accept.

Although the drapes weren't drawn, there was an air of solemnity about the villa. It put him in mind of another place, another time, when he was six years old. He had asked his grandmother why she had closed the curtains in the front parlour of her terraced house in Gloucester and she had said, 'It's a mark of respect, there's been a death in the house.'

The woman who answered the door when he rang the bell looked as if she could have thrown the hammer or put the shot with the best of them. Ashton guessed she was the cook/housekeeper, though she could have doubled as a bodyguard for Neil Franklin just as easily. Her sour expression suggested she resented being pressed into service as a maid. Ashton gave her his name, explained that he was a former colleague of her late employer and asked if he could see Mrs Franklin. The woman grunted, closed the door in his face and left him standing there on the doorstep. After what seemed an inordinately long time, she returned and somewhat ungraciously showed him into the living room.

Yesterday afternoon at the funeral, Ella Franklin had worn dark glasses to hide her eyes; this morning she had no need of them. She had, it seemed, done all the crying she was going to do. She had the lean muscular body and weatherbeaten features of someone who, in daylight hours, spent the greater part of her life outdoors. Severe-looking, like an old-fashioned schoolmarm, was the description which immediately sprang to mind on first acquaintance.

'Your name sounds familiar,' she told Ashton, 'but apart from seeing you at the funeral, I don't think we've met before?'

'No, we haven't. However, you may have been introduced to my wife – she was going to spend the night here.'

Ella frowned. 'I don't remember Neil inviting a Mrs Ashton to stay with us.'

'This was a year ago and we weren't married then. Matter of fact, Harriet and I–'

'Harriet Egan,' she said, interrupting him with a warm smile. 'Such a nice girl.'

'I think so too.'

'Is she still with The Firm?'

Ashton shook his head. 'We have a son.'

'I'm glad for you.' Ella swallowed, blinked her eyes

several times. 'Neil and I couldn't have children,' she said in a husky voice.

'That must have been very hard for you.'

'Yes, it was.' Ella forced a smile. 'But we had a good life together.'

'And made a lot of friends.' Ashton paused, racked his brains for some other, more delicate way of broaching the subject, but could think of nothing. 'Judging by the number of mourners,' he added.

'Most of the ladies present were from the local golf club. There were a number of officials Neil had had dealings with over the years – people like Gerald Willmore and Heinrich Voigt.'

'And the chunky man in the light blue raincoat who wore a polka-dot bow tie.' Ashton snapped his fingers and looked vexed. 'What the dickens is his name?'

'Georgi Mugrowski,' Ella said, responding automatically. 'Apparently he did odd jobs for my husband.'

'Funny, I thought he was CIA.'

'No, you must be thinking of Caspar Lemberg at the US Consulate. They are vaguely similar in appearance.'

'So who was the small, very sinewy lady with jet-black glossy hair and pointed features?'

'I don't remember seeing anyone answering to that description.'

Ashton wasn't surprised, he hadn't seen the woman either, but somebody had been there who had been prepared to go to extreme measures to ensure he or she remained anonymous.

'Was there anyone at the funeral you didn't recognise?' he asked.

Ella stared at him, her eyes glacial. 'That's a very strange question, Mr Ashton. What exactly are you doing in Berlin?'

'Trying to find the people who murdered your husband.'

'I remember who you are now.' She wagged an accusing finger in his face. 'You work for that despicable toad Victor Hazelwood, don't you? Well, if you want to know who was responsible for what happened to Neil, you needn't look any farther than your guide and mentor.'

'Do you remember seeing a photographer at the cemetery?' Ashton said, ignoring the outburst.

'Yes. Did you hire him? Silly of me to ask, of course you did. My God, what kind of man are you?'

'The photographer is dead, Mrs Franklin. He was murdered sometime yesterday evening.'

'What are you implying?'

'Nothing.'

'What do you mean, nothing?' Ella snapped. 'I think you owe me an explanation. Your apology can wait until later.'

'It has to do with the bomber. Helga said he called out to Neil, then a split second later there was a brilliant flash followed by a loud explosion. At first, we all thought your husband had been the victim of a suicide bomber, but what if the device had exploded prematurely?'

Hazelwood had been the first to raise that possibility, but at the time he was merely being contentious. Now, however, there were grounds for thinking he had been right all along.

'I wish you would get to the point, Mr Ashton.'

'The point is that Hizbollah wanted to satisfy themselves that you were truly a grief-stricken widow. Oh, your husband's death had been reported in the local newspapers all right, but they weren't satisfied with that. They didn't know for sure that Neil had even been in the bookshop when the bomb went off. The way they saw it, the SIS, with the connivance of the German authorities, could have planted the story of his death in the press. The unfortunate photographer must have captured their observer on film and whoever it was followed the cameraman back to his studio and killed him. That's why I asked you if you recalled noticing any strangers at the church service or later on at the graveside.'

'The short answer is no, I didn't. They were all friends and acquaintances.'

'You're quite sure about that?'

'What do you take me for, Mr Ashton? A complete idiot? Do you seriously believe I can't tell the difference between a Caucasian and an Arab?'

If it was possible to convey an apology without uttering a word, Ashton managed to achieve it with a rueful smile and a couple of empty gestures which could be taken to mean almost anything. There was, he thought, more than a grain of truth in the old adage of like being attracted to like. Neil Franklin had had a reputation for being abrasive, a trait Ashton could personally vouch for. As he'd just discovered, it didn't take much to rattle Ella's cage.

It was becoming obvious to Ashton that he was outstaying his welcome. Any doubts on that score were disabused by Ella Franklin who glanced at her wristwatch and calmly announced it was time she made a start answering the many letters of condolence she had received. They said their goodbyes out in the hall under the watchful eye of Gretl, the cook/housekeeper who had materialised from the kitchen at the sound of their voices. The door closed behind him before he reached the Volkswagen.

Ashton reversed down the drive into Alsenstrasse and headed back into town. Caspar Lemberg and Georgi Mugrowski; two names to conjure with, one a CIA officer, the other a locally recruited foot soldier. He had no idea where to look for Mugrowski but the US Consulate was on Clayallee. Before doing anything else, however, he dropped into Hecker's Hotel. Nobody had left a message for him; it seemed Willie Baumgart was still at liberty.

Clayallee had been named in honour of General Lucius D. Clay, Commander US Army, Europe, who in June 1948 had responded to the Soviet blockade by launching plans for the Berlin airlift. Facing the US Consulate on the other side of the main through road was a small square dedicated to the memory of President Truman, without whose support the plans could never have come to fruition.

The Consulate was housed in a building large enough for

a fully fledged embassy. Whether it would ever be used as such when the German Government transferred to Berlin was problematical. Located in the heart of Dahlem, an elegant residential district, the Consulate was a good seven miles from the Reichstag and therefore somewhat out on a limb.

Ashton parked the Volks outside the Argentine Consulate, which had a much more relaxed attitude to physical security, then walked down the road to the US Consulate. A Marine Corps sentry in full dress uniform directed him to the enquiries desk inside the entrance where a Ms Sharon Pezzi handled his request to see Caspar Lemberg with considerable aplomb. All he had to do was produce his passport, state the nature of his business and fill in a visitor's pro forma. Once he'd completed it, Ms Pezzi invited him to take a chair while she checked to see if Mr Lemberg was available. Ten minutes later, he was issued with a temporary pass and handed over to a Marine Corps sergeant who escorted him up to an interview room on the second floor. Although it was located outside the secure area, he was nevertheless subjected to an electronic body search.

Chunky was not a description Ashton would have applied to Caspar Lemberg. The American was a good deal taller than Ella Franklin had led him to expect and his resemblance to Georgi Mugrowski was only superficial. He wore a double-breasted dark grey pinstripe that hadn't been bought off the peg, a hand-made shirt, a silk tie such as Ashton remembered seeing in Harrods and a pair of Italian shoes.

'It's always a pleasure to meet a fellow operative, Mr Ashton,' he said, shaking hands, 'especially one who's prepared to do a little mutual horse trading.'

In the eighth edition of the *Concise Oxford Dictionary*, liaison was defined as communication or co-operation especially between military forces, an illicit sexual relationship, the building or thickening agent of a sauce, and the sounding of an ordinarily silent final consonant before a word beginning with a vowel. In referring to the purpose of his visit as mutual horse trading, Lemberg had just added a fifth definition. Ashton also had a nasty suspicion that if he didn't watch it, he would end up giving more than he received.

'I've just been to see Ella Franklin,' he said, feeling his way.

'Yeah, we were all pretty cut up when we heard the news about Neil.' Lemberg shook his head. 'It was just terrible.'

'I didn't see you at the funeral.'

'Well, I'd be lying to you if I said Neil and I were real close. The fact is, he didn't like the way we operate. He figured an Intelligence service should be secret, not open and above board like the CIA had been forced to become as a result of the Freedom of Information Bill. Neil said we were making it too easy for the terrorists. So he asked us to keep our disance.'

'And when did this happen?'

'Soon after I arrived, a little over two years ago.'

'A couple of years ago there was still a military presence in this city. At least once a month the American, British and French Intelligence Services sat round a table exchanging information. Are you telling me Franklin boycotted these gatherings?'

'No, of course he didn't.'

'Well, I'm relieved to hear it because you led me to understand all contact had ceased.'

'I was referring to one on one,' Lemberg said, tight-lipped.

'So was there any talk about Hizbollah at the last round table session Franklin attended?'

'There have been no joint Intelligence sessions since the last Allied soldier marched out of Berlin three months ago.'

'Is that another way of saying you are not going to answer my question?'

'Just who the hell are you, Mr Ashton?' Lemberg rested both forearms on the table and leaned forward, his shoulders hunched. Without actually pawing the ground, he looked like a maddened bull which was going to charge at any moment. 'I called your people in Bonn; they say you're no longer with The Firm.'

'You should have rung the number I put on the visitor's pro forma. Why deal with the monkey when you can speak to the organ grinder?'

'We have our own contacts in Bonn,' Lemberg said huffily.

'Well, I really think you should call London on the crypto-protected link and talk to Victor Hazelwood, the Director General.'

'I've never heard of the guy. Why should I believe a word he tells me?'

The brusque, offhand treatment was, Ashton supposed, simply another manifestation of the changed relationship which had come to pass since the man from Arkansas had been inaugurated. On further reflection, he thought much of the chill wind factor could be attributed to Franklin. A native of Newcastle-upon-Tyne, Neil Franklin had been no emissary for that city; he had been an aggressive sod with an uncanny talent for creating hostility where none had existed before. There was a distinct chance that Lemberg had been on the receiving end of his acerbic tongue, which would account for the American's less-than-friendly demeanour.

'Look, would you do me a favour?' Ashton said affably. 'Would you phone Vauxhall Cross and ask for Rowan Garfield?'

'Rowan Garfield,' Lemberg repeated in a deadpan voice.

'Our Assistant Director in charge of the European Department,' Ashton told him through clenched teeth, and then stretched his lips in what was meant to be a smile, albeit a grim one. 'Don't tell me you haven't heard of him?'

Lemberg did his best to maintain a sphinx-like expression while he mulled it over. He was however the sort of card player who should never get into a serious poker school since his face was like an open book. It therefore came as no surprise to Ashton when the American told him to stay where he was. As Lemberg left the room, the Marine Corps sergeant entered it and stood facing Ashton in the at-ease position, feet apart, hands clasped loosely behind him. Ashton said good morning to him again and remarked that the weather was a lot better than it had been yesterday. Both the greeting and the observation fell on stony ground. The sergeant remained impassive, his eyes unfocused, like a mounted sentry at Horse Guards Parade who affected complete indifference to the camera-clicking tourists. Time crawled by, each minute seeming more like five; then just when Ashton was beginning to think Lemberg must be taking an early lunch, the American finally returned and dismissed the Marine Corps sergeant.

'London says you're OK,' he announced. 'Now, where were we?'

'We were talking about Hizbollah,' Ashton told him, certain in his own mind that he didn't need to be reminded.

'They weren't on the agenda at the last tripartite meeting. Discussion centred around the Russians, whether they'd left any unpleasant surprises behind them.' Lemberg smiled. 'I guess I don't have to tell you what would constitute an unpleasant surprise, do I, Peter?'

Ashton didn't say anything. In vouching for his credibility, it seemed to him Rowan Garfield had been a shade too open with the American. Three years ago, Ashton had had to cultivate a lieutenant colonel in the GRU, the Russian Military Intelligence Service. Success had bred rumours that he had become tainted, and on the principle that there was no smoke without fire, he had been transferred to a less sensitive appointment. From what he'd just said, it was obvious that Lemberg knew all about it.

'Hizbollah were here in Berlin,' Ashton said, collecting his thoughts. 'They came to buy plutonium from the Russians.'

The faintly condescending smile on Lemberg's mouth rapidly disappeared. 'Can you prove it?' he asked.

There was an eagerness in his voice which did not escape Ashton. He had a hunch that the CIA had learned that a quantity of plutonium was being offered for sale, but Lemberg would never reveal his source of information unless Ashton gave him something on account.

'Gamal al Hassan,' he said cryptically. 'Ring any bells with you?'

'Yeah, his body was found in a builder's yard nine days ago. Was he one of yours?'

'He was an agent. The case officer who ran him reckoned he was an A1 source of information.'

'Case officers are not infallible,' Lemberg said.

'Agreed, but Gamal had a good track record – did great work for us in the Gulf War.'

He was committed now and there was no point in withholding the rest of the story. In a few brief sentences, Ashton told the American what he knew.

'So you're saying Gamal ran with Hizbollah but worked for you guys?'

'Provided we kept his palm well greased.'

'Agents can get greedy, Peter. If they think you are a soft touch their imaginations can run riot.'

Ashton smiled. Anyone who knew Jill Sheridan would never call her a soft touch. 'Before they slit his throat, they cut out his tongue and blinded him. I don't think Gamal was being inventive when he said his friends were going into the plutonium market.'

'The Kripo said it was a drugs-related crime.'

'The Kripo were being economical with the truth. I hope you're not going to follow their example.'

'What?'

'I don't want to hear you saying, "Jeez, I'd surely like to help you guys because despite Clinton, we really value the special relationship but hell, we don't know shit from shampoo on this one." '

'You've got one hell of a nerve, Ashton.'

'So people keep telling me.'

Lemberg went through all the facial contortions of a man wrestling with his conscience. When he regained his composure, Ashton was supposed to believe that he was about to go out on a limb for him by disclosing information that was strictly For American Eyes Only.

'I know you're not going to believe this,' he said in a suitably earnest voice, 'but all we've got are a few smoke signals. Hell, I don't have to tell you what the Russian economy is like. Getting worse every day. Right? The only people who are making it hand over fist are the *Mafiozniki* and they deal in every commodity under the sun. Since the beginning of this year, the German border police have intercepted two small consignments of plutonium. The smugglers got caught on both occasions because they were stupid enough to transport the stuff in a stolen vehicle–'

Lemberg wasn't telling him anything that hadn't already been reported in the press. In one case, the smugglers had used a Mercedes that had been stolen less than a month beforehand from a lawyer in Frankfurt, and had welded a container to the underside of the chassis beneath the trunk.

'This is history,' Ashton said, interrupting the American. 'I thought you were going to tell me something a journalist couldn't.'

A decidedly hurt expression appeared on Lemberg's face. Ashton didn't think he was acting. 'I was coming to it,' the American complained in an injured tone. Lemberg paused as if expecting an apology. When it was not forthcoming, he launched into a potted biography of a former Red Army colonel turned *Mafiozniki* godfather known to the CIA as The Czar.

'He was Spetsnaz, Special Forces like our Green Berets, your SAS,' Lemberg continued. 'He is said to have had a good war in Afghanistan; he's also reputed to have done a couple of wet jobs in the Lebanon.'

'Do we have a name for him?'

Lemberg shook his head. 'No, all our information comes from a low-grade source in Moscow. Our guy is a gossipmonger, hovers around the fringes of the *Mafiozniki*, frequents the same brothels, casinos, night clubs and bath houses and keeps his ears attuned to what's going on around him. Anyway, the word is The Czar has got himself a tame artilleryman who can supply sub kiloton nuclear warheads. I don't understand the technicalities but these munitions can be fired by a 130mm howitzer. Fact is, roughly three weeks ago, our lowlife in Moscow hears that The Czar has found a buyer for some of these goodies. The actual negotiations were going to be handled by a middleman here in Germany.'

'Where? In Berlin?'

'Or Dresden, Leipzig, even Chemnitz. Take your pick; like I said, all we've got are smoke signals.' Lemberg spread his arms as if he were about to embrace Ashton and smiled ruefully. 'I'm sorry I can't be more helpful.'

'I'm not going away empty-handed,' Ashton told him. 'That's a lot more than I expected.'

The Joint Intelligence Committee usually met on a Tuesday morning, but this week it had been postponed to the Thursday at the request of MI5, the Security Service, which had entertained high hopes that something concrete was about to emerge from the informal talks they'd been having with the Provisional IRA. Nothing had, which meant that instead of being able to take a back seat, Hazelwood had found himself in the limelight. The bombing of the English Bookshop and Franklin's death had already been the subject of a special session with the Cabinet Secretary and the Permanent Under-Secretary of State at the Foreign and Commonwealth Office, and he'd deeply resented having to face a second grilling on the subject simply because MI5 had had nothing to offer. In a foul mood when he returned to Vauxhall Cross, his temper wasn't improved when Rowan Garfield appeared in his office to ask if he could spare him five minutes.

'As long as it is only five minutes,' Hazelwood growled.

'I thought you should know that Head of Station, Bonn has been on to me about Ashton. I had to vouch for Peter before the Americans would talk to him.'

'What Americans?'

'Caspar Lemberg, the resident CIA officer in Berlin. Seems Peter walked into the US Consulate on Clayallee and asked to see him. Bit of a loose cannon, our Peter. I do hope he doesn't exacerbate what is already a difficult situation for us in Berlin.'

Hazelwood gritted his teeth, did his best to control a surge of anger and failed utterly. It was hardly surprising in the circumstances. Smoking wasn't permitted in the cabinet office, the Foreign Office had been wingeing at him all morning because Bonn had lodged a formal complaint about the activities of the SIS and now he had to contend with the unctuous Garfield.

'If it's a question of trying to put out the fire with a can of petrol,' he said caustically, 'I'm sure I can confidently leave that to your department, Rowan.'

There was a message waiting for Ashton when he returned to Hecker's Hotel after leaving the US Consulate. 'This is for you,' the girl on the desk said and gave him a slip of paper folded in two, with his room key. The note, written in beautiful copperplate was brief; it read: 'Herr Rechtsanwalt Josef Weizäcker requests that you phone him on 262-6109 urgently.'

His conversation with the lawyer was equally brief and was conducted in German.

'I'm so glad you called,' Weizäcker said. 'Herr Baumgart has been taken in for interrogation concerning the murder of the photographer Klaus Richter.'

'I have three questions,' Ashton told him. 'Who found the body? When? And who was the arresting officer?'

'The body was found at eight o'clock this morning by Herr Richter's cleaning woman. The arresting officer was Kommissar Eicke.'

'Leave it with me, Herr Weizäcker,' Ashton said. 'I'll have a word with the Police President and straighten things out.'

As of that moment, he hadn't the faintest idea what he was going to say to Heinrich Voigt.

Chapter 11

The office of the Police President was on the top floor of the *Polizeipräsidium* on the Tempelhofer Damm. Gaining access to the lofty eyrie proved to be a time-consuming business. Ashton started with the duty sergeant, was referred to the duty inspector, had a twenty-five-minute interview with a senior plain-clothes officer of the Kripo, then had to get past a very formidable personal assistant who was determined to ensure that only those who had made an appointment to see the Police President could do so. It was only after Ashton had indicated in no uncertain terms that her obstructionism could lead to an official complaint at the highest level that she relented and granted him an audience with Heinrich Voigt.

To progress from the street-level reception to the executive suite on the top floor had taken Ashton the better part of an hour. At every step along the way he had been asked to state the nature of his business so that by the time he was introduced to Voigt, the Police President should have already known why he wanted to see him. His mildly inquisitive expression was, Ashton thought, either a sign of a consummate actor or a failure of communication within the *Polizeipräsidium*.

'It's very good of you to see me at such short notice,' Ashton said in German.

'Please, it is nothing,' Voigt replied in English. 'It would be a poor thing if I could not spare a few minutes of my time to express my sympathies to one of Neil's colleagues.'

'Thank you.'

'You were at the funeral, were you not?'

'Yes, so were you, I recognised your face immediately.'

'Have we met before?' Voigt asked.

'No, your picture was in *Der Tagesspiegel* that morning,' Ashton told him, still addressing the Police President in his native language even though it was beginning to look like bloody-mindedness on both their parts.

'I'm sorry I gave that interview, Mr Ashton. I can imagine what the newspapers will have to say if it becomes apparent that we have run out of avenues to explore. The death toll from the bombing has risen to thirteen, which makes it easily the worst terrorist incident we have ever experienced.'

'Maybe we can help you.'

'We?'

'The SIS, Herr Police President.'

'You people have been carrying out your own investigation,' Voigt said heavily. 'Is that what you are telling me?'

'In a manner of speaking.'

Ashton decided it was time he conceded defeat and reverted to English; the present impasse was ridiculous and had gone on long enough. It reminded him of the time he'd been skiing in Thalkirchdorf in Bavaria while a student at Nottingham University. The ski instructor to whose class he'd been assigned had been just as keen to practise his English as Ashton had been to further his command of German. For practically the whole fortnight, they had conversed in each other's languages, a farcical state of affairs which had only ended when the instructor, looking back at Ashton while busily framing a suitable reply in English, had failed to see a large *Hausfrau* making a diagonal run across the slope in front of him and had ploughed into her. The *Hausfrau* had bruised her rump, the instructor had had his left ankle broken when she sat on him.

'I think you should know that there is reason to believe

the bomb exploded prematurely,' Ashton continued.

Voigt shook his head. 'I disagree. Neil was killed by a suicide bomber. You weren't present and Fräulein von Schinkel was. When I questioned her, she told me that the assassin called out to Neil a split second before the bomb was detonated.'

'Because he wanted to make sure his intended victim was there in the bookshop.'

'I find that hard to believe.'

'Do you? How long did you know our Head of Station? Five years? Six?'

'Eight,' Voigt said promptly.

'As long as that? Then you'll be aware just how infrequently Neil was to be found in the English Bookshop. That was largely Helga's domain. He was out most of the day. When he wasn't liaising with the American and French Intelligence Services or attending one of the innumerable conferences beloved of Headquarters British Troops, Berlin, he was meeting one of the small army of local agents who worked for him.'

Now comes the difficult part, Ashton told himself, the flashpoint where all hell is likely to break loose if it isn't handled right. Building his case layer upon layer, he explained to Voigt why he had decided to hire a photographer to cover the funeral.

'I was certain Hizbollah would want to satisfy themselves that Neil Franklin really was dead.'

'And subsequently you had the satisfaction of knowing that you were right.' Voigt curled his lip in disgust. 'Of course, the fact that Klaus Richter lost his life as a result of your activities is neither here nor there, is it?'

'You think I can shrug off his death just like that?' Ashton said, snapping his fingers.

'I hold you and Herr Baumgart responsible and I intend to bring charges of culpable manslaughter.'

'Willie is not responsible for what happened.'

'You are both guilty of withholding information and obstructing the police.'

'Do you mind telling me how we are supposed to have obstructed the Kripo?'

'You discovered Herr Richter had been murdered but failed to notify us.'

'As you failed to notify the British and American Consulates.'

'What are you talking about?' Voigt demanded angrily.

'A spokesman for Hizbollah telephoned the Kripo the day Moresby and Gamal al Hassan were found dead. He said, "The traitor Gamal has been executed. Death to the Great Satan." '

'Who told you that?'

Ashton brushed the question aside and continued in the same accusing vein. 'When Hizbollah speak of the Great Satan they generally mean the United States, but sometimes the description is applied to us British. The fact is, their spokesman was uttering a threat and your people did nothing about it. They failed to alert both the British and American Consulates. If Mr Willmore had been warned, he would certainly have alerted Neil Franklin who would have taken appropriate security measures.'

'Such as?'

It was a stupid question and he could tell Voigt knew it by the way his voice tailed away.

'Neil would have presumed on his friendship with you,' Ashton told him. 'He would have asked for police protection and if that hadn't been forthcoming, he would have put somebody like Willie Baumgart on the door. But what happened? Nothing. And forty-eight hours later, the bomber walks into the English Bookshop and twelve good Germans are blown to smithereens.'

Voigt was an intelligent man. There was no need to tell him how the media would react if that ever got out. It would be no use his pretending that the threat only became apparent with the benefit of hindsight. He would be crucified on every TV channel and in every newspaper until he was eventually hounded out of office. By that time he would probably be glad to go.

'What do you want from me, Mr Ashton?'

'That's easy. I'd like to see if we can't move this investigation on a bit by pooling our information. But first of all, I want you to call Kommissar Eicke and tell him to release Willie Baumgart.'

'That's not as easy as you think. Eicke is in charge of the investigation; he wouldn't have brought Baumgart in for questioning unless he had reason to suspect–'

'Eicke is your subordinate,' Ashton said quietly, 'he'll do whatever you tell him. He would never have associated Willie with Klaus Richter if you hadn't pointed him in that direction.'

Voigt leaned back in his chair, arms folded across his chest. There were two things he clearly didn't like: being forced to make a hasty decision was one; having his arm twisted in the process was another. For a time it looked to Ashton as though he were going to invite him to go to hell; then suddenly he unfolded, lifted the receiver and punched out a four-digit internal number. As far as Ashton could tell from listening to one side of the conversation, Eicke didn't protest when Voigt ordered him to release Baumgart forthwith.

'Satisfied, Mr Ashton?'

'Very.'

'Then suppose you keep your side of the bargain?'

'OK, let's start with John Moresby. Have you been able to trace his movements before he was murdered?'

'We know he was staying at Hecker's Hotel. Some hours before he was killed, an incoming call was put through to his room. Shortly after that, he again obtained an outside line and rang a local number, subsequently identified as the Hotel Berliner Hof. This was the second time Moresby rang the Berliner Hof, having made the first call minutes after registering at Hecker's. He also made an international call to York. Evidently his friend in York was a woman because she returned the call a little while later and asked for his room number.' Voigt paused, then asked, 'Is there anything you can add about that?'

'Yes. The first incoming call was from a man calling himself Gamal al Hassan. After informing his superior at the Berliner Hof that contact had been established, Moresby took himself off to the *Schwarz und Weiss* to meet Gamal.'

Ashton told the policeman what he had learned from Claudia, the transvestite he had encountered in the same bar, then described the girl who had collected Moresby.

'And the lady in York?' Voigt enquired.

'His partner. She thought he was having an extended weekend with another woman.'

'Obviously Moresby wasn't an SIS officer. If he had been, she would have accepted that, by the very nature of his job, he would frequently be away from home.'

Voigt was smart, very smart, and Ashton knew nothing would be gained if he tried to pull the wool over his eyes.

'He was hired for the job.'

'To do what?'

'Act as a go-between.'

'For all your fine talk, you're not very forthcoming, Mr Ashton.'

'I'm in an awkward position.'

Although Hazelwood had told Ashton not to disclose that Hizbollah were in the market for plutonium unless it was absolutely necessary, his old guide and mentor had stopped short of defining the circumstances in which he could do so. Victor had left that to him. There was an old saying about using a sprat to catch a mackerel and while in this particular instance it could be the other way round, trading information was the only way forward.

'All right,' Ashton said, 'this is for your ears only. Hizbollah sent a team to Berlin to buy a quantity of fissionable material from the Russians. We don't know the identity of the vendor but there is a possibility that he could be a former colonel in the Spetsnaz known to the CIA as The Czar. I say could be because The Czar has access to sub kiloton artillery shells whereas Gamal al Hassan was quite adamant that the people he was playing

footsie with were more interested in acquiring plutonium.'

'Interesting,' Voigt said in a noncommittal voice.

'So how many *Mafiozniki* do business in this city?'

'They're never around long enough to show up on a
census.'

'That's very droll,' Ashton said.

'I thought you would appreciate the humour. The fact is,
the *Mafiozniki* do the greater part of their business just
inside the border with Poland at places like Frankfurt am
Oder and Forst. If they have to come farther west to cut a
deal, they're in one day, out the next. Some entrepreneur
in Moscow wants a top-of-the-range 1994 BMW, they pass
the order on to their German associate, who steals
the requisite model and delivers it to the border. The
Mafiozniki are not the sort of people to take unnecessary
risks.'

'I seem to have struck a poor bargain, if that is your
contribution.'

'This transvestite,' Voigt said, ignoring the complaint,
'the one who calls himself Claudia and tried to pick up
your friend Moresby. Was he close enough to hear what the
small sinewy woman said when she arrived to collect him
sometime later?'

'I didn't ask Claudia. Why?'

'I merely wondered if she was the same woman who
telephoned my office after the bombing of the English
Bookshop.' Voigt smiled. 'We deliberately kept that to
ourselves, which is why you didn't hear it from Willie
Baumgart.'

The woman had rung Voigt's office direct at 15.05 hours
on Friday, 16 September, exactly twenty-five hours after
the incident. The incoming call had been intercepted by
the PA who had then put her through to Voigt.

'She informed me that her brothers in Hizbollah were
responsible for the attack which had been directed against
the Imperialist supporters of Zion. She also said that the
bomb contained five kilos of Semtex, an amount which

was subsequently confirmed by our forensic scientists. She ended by declaiming that the defilers walk in fear. Said it twice, once in German, then in English.' Voigt pursed his lips. 'I thought she was an American,' he added.

'You mean her accent?'

'No, more than that. I think the woman is an American national.'

'It's a pity we can't play her voice back to some expert in phonetics.'

'We have done,' Voigt said triumphantly. 'On her own initiative, my PA listened in to our conversation and recorded it.'

'Would it be possible for me to have a copy of the tape?'

'I don't see why not. You want to take it with you now?'

'If it's not too much trouble,' Ashton said.

Voigt assured him his PA could produce a duplicate in less than five minutes, a claim which proved a shade optimistic. After ten minutes they ran out of things to say to one another and there were awkward periods of silence. After one such lull, Voigt asked when he was returning to London and was clearly relieved when Ashton told him he hoped to be on the first flight departing Berlin-Tegel on the Friday. The PA finally appeared looking hot and flustered, and full of apologies because she'd had to go out to buy a blank cassette, the kind of hiccup that was not unknown in Whitehall.

They parted company on friendlier terms than they had begun. Alighting from the lift on the ground floor, Ashton approached the desk sergeant, asked after Willie Baumgart and was informed that he'd left the building approximately half an hour ago. From a pay phone opposite the car park at Tempelhof Airport, Ashton rang Weizäcker to see if the lawyer had heard from Baumgart, and didn't know whether to be pleased or a little miffed when he learned that Willie had been in touch to say he was out and about.

Ashton put the phone down, collected the Volks from the parking lot and drove back to Hecker's Hotel. Most of the way there, he spent looking at things from Willie's point of view. The Kripo were unlikely to have told him who had secured his release and it was almost certain that Willie hadn't known Ashton was in the same building at the time. To find the German waiting for him in the hotel lobby was therefore both a surprise and a pleasure.

'I wanted to say thanks,' Willie told him.

'Hell, you don't owe me anything. I was the one who got you into trouble in the first place.'

'No, it was largely my fault. I shouldn't have picked a photographer who lived in the same street as Fräulein Helga. It was all too easy for Voigt to make the connection.'

'Perhaps. Anyway, it was a crazy idea and it got us nowhere.'

'So what's the next move?' Baumgart asked.

'Well, I want to see Helga before I leave Berlin.'

'You're too late to see her this afternoon; visiting hours are over.'

'I know. I thought I'd get a bite to eat.'

Baumgart said he knew of a great little café in the Schöneberg District where they served good food at reasonable prices all hours of the day and night. The in-house entertainment was also pretty lively and Ashton thought it was just the sort of place Willie Baumgart would know.

His name was Pavel Trilisser, he was fifty-five years old, a tall, lean, ascetic-looking man. He had startlingly blue eyes that burned with the intensity of an oxyacetylene torch and a manner that had all the warmth of a Siberian winter. A former KGB officer, he had received accelerated promotion to lieutenant general and had been the youngest Deputy Head of the First Directorate, the Foreign Intelligence Service, when appointed to the post in 1987. Described as brilliant and ruthless, Trilisser also enjoyed more than his fair share of luck.

This latter quality had enabled him to survive two attempted coups, the first in August 1991 when the

Hardliners had turned against Gorbachev. Although internal security had not been the responsibility of the Foreign Intelligence Service, a number of Yeltsin's supporters had felt he should have intervened much earlier than he had. His detractors had been convinced that Pavel Trilisser had waited until it had been evident that the coup was going to fail before he had arrested his own chief and assumed command of the First Chief Directorate.

As a result of this suspicion, his career had suffered a setback. Instead of being confirmed in the appointment, a younger, less competent but more politically reliable officer had been promoted over his head and Trilisser had found himself Deputy Chief of the newly formed Russian Intelligence Service. In this capacity, he had been responsible for Operational Planning, Technical Support, Counterintelligence and Computer Services. With this power base as cover, he had raised a secret unit of 325 officers and men recruited from former members of Spetsnaz. The unit had been formed to help Parliament overthrow Yeltsin but weeks before the first 125mm shell from a T80 tank struck 'The White House', Trilisser had changed sides, abandoning Prime Minister Rutskoi. In order to protect himself, he had arranged for his second-in-command to be killed. As Ashton had put it, he had finked on Aleksander Rutskoi and come out of the failed putsch smelling like a rose. From an office in the main building of the RIS complex at Yasenevo on the outer ring motorway, he had moved into the Kremlin to become President Yeltsin's special adviser on External Affairs. It was in this capacity that he had summoned Major General Gurov, the long-suffering Chief of Police, to his office.

'This city has been taken over by the *Mafiozniki*,' Trilisser informed him icily. 'There are now more murders per capita in Moscow than there are in Washington, New York or Los Angeles. Any public official who takes a firm line against them is liquidated; since the beginning of the year, a state prosecutor has been shot to death in his office, one judge was blown up in his official car and a second killed outside his apartment by a hand grenade. As for crusading journalists and TV reporters, they are fast becoming a dying breed – literally.'

'You're not telling me anything I don't already know,' Gurov said wearily. 'If I had more men–'

'More men? Nearly half of your uniformed policemen are on the payroll of some *Mafiozniki* gang.'

'Is it any wonder, considering what the State pays them?'

'And when they are not looking the other way,' Trilisser continued remorselessly, 'they are either killing opponents of the *Mafiozniki* they work for or acting as their enforcers.'

'Since when have you been the President's official adviser on internal security matters, Pavel Trilisser? I thought your remit was external affairs.'

'When the *Mafiozniki* operate outside Russia they become my business.' Trilisser pushed a two-page Intelligence report across the desk to Gurov. 'This is from our resident in Berlin. Seems the *Mafiozniki* were planning to sell a number of sub kiloton warheads to Hizbollah until the British Intelligence Service got wind of it. The man behind the deal is known as "The Czar". What can you tell me about him?'

'Nothing. I've never heard of him.'

'Well, you have now,' Trilisser said grimly, 'and if you want to hold on to your job, you'd better find him pretty damn quick.'

Although Willie Baumgart had described the injuries Fräulein Helga had suffered, Ashton was still shocked by her appearance. If the right eye was no longer closed to a narrow slit, the bruises on her face resembled overripe bananas and the skin either side of the diagonal line of stitches extending from the bridge of her nose to the hairline above the left ear was an ugly shade of pink. A large half-hoop of steel kept the bedclothes off her shattered legs.

'Look who I've brought,' Willie said proudly as they entered the private room adjoining Women's Surgical.

'Why, it's Herr Ashton!' Helga exclaimed and smiled.

She sounded genuinely pleased to see him, which made Ashton glad he'd come armed with a huge basket of fruit. He told her that he was glad to see that she was on the mend and asked if there was anything she needed.

'Everyone has been very kind.'

'You've no worries then?'

Helga pointed to the door and signalled Willie to close it. 'Only about the safe in Herr Franklin's office,' she said in a low voice.

'It's all in hand,' Ashton assured her. 'Herr Franklin's associates in Bonn are taking care of it.'

'There was a lot of money in the safe – about 4,000 Marks.'

Ashton nodded. That would be the petty cash for expenses and payment of informers. There would also have been a number of classified files which Hazelwood had been determined to recover before Voigt could find a cracksman to pick the combination lock. Personally, Ashton was sure the Police President was far too scrupulous to dream of burgling the safe but, quite rightly, Victor was not inclined to leave anything to chance. The crypto material for the secure speech telephone would be regarded as compromised no matter how swiftly the SIS retrieved the safe. As a result, one month's supply of keying material throughout NATO and UK Forces worldwide would have to be replaced within seven days, the current life of a single crypto input. To say it was a communicator's nightmare was an understatement.

'How is Frau Franklin?' Helga asked.

'Ella is bearing up pretty well,' Ashton told her. 'There were a large number of mourners at the funeral and in a way I think she was pleased that so many people had turned up to pay their last respects to her husband.' He paused, then said, 'Although the majority were friends and acquaintances, especially from the golf club, she was very touched that so many of the local agents Neil had recruited were also there – men like Georgi Mugrowski.'

'Who?'

'Georgi Mugrowski.'

'I've never heard of him,' Helga said.

'A chunky man, short hair, pepper-and-salt variety.'

'Not one of ours, Herr Ashton.'

'Ella said he was.'

'Frau Franklin is mistaken.'

Ashton told himself that Helga should know – she had practically run the network. She had kept the imprest account and disbursed many of the payments herself. There was, in short, no way Franklin could have recruited anyone without her knowledge.

'It's ironic,' Helga said quietly. 'All through the Cold War no Head of Station was ever targeted. Oh, the little people were being hit all the time; their bodies would be found on some derelict bombsite, in the sewers, floating in the Spree or in the Havel. But nothing ever happened to the puppet masters until now. No Berlin Wall, no Soviet threat, and a man walks into the bookshop and blows Herr Franklin to pieces. Is that how peace is supposed to be, Herr Ashton?'

There was no answer to that and he steered the conversation on to safer ground. He talked about her plans for the future when she was discharged from hospital, where she would live, the places she wanted to see, the hobbies she meant to pursue now that she would have more time to herself. He even made her laugh with a little help from Willie Baumgart.

They left at ten minutes to eight, shooed out of the room by a ward sister who indignantly pointed out that the evening visiting hour finished at 19.30. It was a crisp autumn night with a clear sky and a nip of frost in the air which should have been invigorating but left Ashton feeling flat.

They dined at the nearest steak house to the St Francis Hospital; neither man said much as they ate their way through spare ribs, French fries and a green salad followed by *Apfelstrudel* and cream. Willie Baumgart wanted to know if the SIS was likely to re-establish the Berlin station, which put Ashton on the spot because he had no idea what Victor Hazelwood had in mind. What he could do was move heaven and earth to get people like Helga von Schinkel and Willie Baumgart decent pensions from the British Government.

When Ashton said goodbye to Willie outside Hecker's Hotel it was in the knowledge that he was unlikely ever to see him again. Sobered by this thought, he collected his key from the girl on the desk and went up to his room. The British Airways flight to Heathrow departed at 08.30 hours, which meant he could pack in the morning. There was, however, one thing he couldn't put off: lifting the receiver, he obtained an outside line, then punched out the subscriber's number. The phone rang out a dozen times before Ella Franklin condescended to answer it. When she learned who was calling, she didn't hesitate to make her displeasure known.

'Do you know what time it is?' she snapped.

'Yes, I know it's late and I'm sorry to disturb you but this won't take a minute.'

'You had better be right.'

'Georgi Mugrowski,' Ashton said doggedly; 'did Neil tell you that he worked for him?'

'No.'

'Well, forgive me for asking but how do you know he did?'

'Because Mr Mugrowski told me so,' Ella said and put the phone down.

Ashton did the same. Mugrowski wasn't Hizbollah but he had certainly been acting on their behalf. Ashton was equally sure the interloper had used a false name when he had introduced himself to Ella Franklin.

Chapter 12

Around Whitehall, T.G.I.F. stood for Thank God It's Friday. For the vast majority of public servants for whom the civil service was a job and not a vocation, this meant they could forget the office over the weekend and work twice as hard at the leisure pursuit of their choice. Hazelwood had been aware of an excited air at the daily conference that morning but it was doubtful if either Jill Sheridan or Rowan Garfield, to name but two Assistant Directors, were looking forward to a weekend in the garden or on the golf course. On the contrary, he rather fancied they were actually looking forward to Monday morning when Stuart Dunglass would be back in the chair.

One of Hazelwood's achievements while keeping the seat warm for the Director General had been to eliminate waffling at morning prayers. However, the session that morning had broken all records for brevity and while nothing too disastrous had occurred in the previous twenty-four hours, Hazelwood suspected that Rowan Garfield, Jill Sheridan and others had deliberately withheld the odd interesting snippet as a welcome back present for Stuart Dunglass.

It had been the same story when he'd returned to his office after the conference had broken up. The files flagged up for his attention had dwindled to only a fraction of the number that usually passed across his desk. When Roy Kelso tapped on his door and asked to have a few words with him, Hazelwood could hardly put the

Admin king off by pleading pressure of work with the in-tray completely empty. The intrusion of the telephone before Kelso had a chance to say anything would, Hazelwood thought, merely postpone the inevitable whinge. It did, in fact, put it off for the rest of the day.

'That was Ashton,' he told Kelso at the end of a long, mostly one-sided conversation, 'calling from 84 Rylett Close.'

'He's returned from Berlin then?'

Hazelwood reached for the last Burma cheroot in the cigar box before he was tempted to bite Roy's head off for asking such a stupid question. Taking his time, he lit the cheroot, then said, 'I hope our Photofit specialist isn't still on holiday?'

'That was last week.'

'Good. Ashton's got something for him to work on, a bogus mourner at Neil Franklin's funeral. There's also a recording of a woman claiming to be a spokesperson for Hizbollah. I want to know if our experts in the Technical Services Division can tell what part of the world she comes from.'

'Right.' Kelso remained seated.

'Well, get on with it, Roy,' Hazelwood said in a mild voice.

'I wanted to have a word with you . . .'

'And so you shall just as soon as we get this little matter under way.'

Hazelwood lifted the receiver, punched out Garfield's number and told the Assistant Director, European Department, that something had come up which required his immediate attention and would he kindly step along for a quick briefing on what was required. With his free hand he waved goodbye to Kelso, forgetting the cheroot he was holding between the index and first fingers. Ash scattered across the desk and a glowing ember landed on his thigh, burning a neat round hole in the dark grey pinstripe trousers before he could brush it away. A whole litany of swear words sprang to mind and fell from his lips just as rapidly. Little imagination was required to guess what Alice would have to say about his habitual carelessness. Head lowered as if in prayer, he inspected the damage, hoping that by some miracle it could be invisibly mended.

'Lost something, Victor?' Garfield asked cheerfully, coming into the room.

Hazelwood looked up scowling. 'Only my patience,' he growled. 'This damned suit cost me £450 from Gieves and Hawkes. Now it's ruined.'

'That is bad luck,' Garfield said with all the false sympathy he could muster.

'I should have bought one off the peg.'

'I always do. Marks and Sparks usually have a very good line.'

'Well, now that we've discussed our respective tailors, perhaps we can get on with the business of discovering the identity of a one-time colonel in the Spetsnaz.'

'You mean he's left the service?'

'That's what we've been given to understand,' Hazelwood said with a cutting edge to his voice. 'The man is in business on his own account now -- head of a *Mafiozniki*. He has a friend in the artillery who can lay his hands on sub kiloton nukes.'

'Which the colonel is going to sell to Hizbollah,' Garfield said.

'We can't prove it yet but that would be my interpretation.'

'I see. What do we know about the colonel?'

Hazelwood repeated everything Ashton had told him. Garfield made a few notes on a scratchpad with a Parker ballpoint, then looked up expectantly.

'Is that it?' he asked incredulously when it became evident that Hazelwood had finished. 'I mean, it's not a lot to go on, is it? How do you expect us to come up with a name on the basis of the information you've just given me? At its peak strength, the Spetsnaz was twice the size of the Americans' Delta Force and our own Special Air Service put together. We're talking about 30,000 officers and men, Victor.'

'A year ago your department identified a bogeyman in the Russian Intelligence Service. He was ex-KGB First Chief Directorate, an organisation of such complexity and size that it makes the Spetsnaz look like a pigmy outfit.'

Garfield shook his head wearily. 'You're referring to Pavel Trilisser and he was not exactly an unknown figure. We had a name, possibly family, maybe patronymic. First time we came across Pavel hc's a sports liaison officer at the Moscow Olympics in 1980, charged with looking after the British Archery Team. Eleven months later we match his face to the Second Secretary, Cultural Affairs, at the Soviet Embassy in Damascus and we are up and running.'

'The colonel had a distinguished war record in Afghanistan,' Hazelwood said unperturbed.

'So you've already told me.'

'You will have to start with the Soviet invasion and seizure of the Darulaman Palace in Kabul on Christmas Day 1979.'

'You want us to go back fifteen years chasing after a will-o'-the-wisp?' Garfield sighed. 'Have you any idea what is involved, Victor?'

It was a silly question to ask someone like Victor Hazelwood who had cut his teeth on the Russian Desk and had forgotten more about the former Soviet Union than Garfield would ever learn. He expected the desk officers to go through every microfilm copy of *Izvestia*, *Pravda*, *Red Star* and the in-house newspapers for the Red Army, Soviet Navy and Air Force.

'Your people are to look for features on war heroes.'

'The Spetsnaz are like the SAS, Victor, they don't like publicity either. You know how it is when our newspapers report some daring-do by the SAS – it's Captain "A", Sergeant "B" and Soldier "C". Names are never mentioned.'

'It's not the same at all,' Hazelwood snapped. 'In this country, any small-scale, apparently undercover operation is always down to the SAS, according to the media. In Soviet Russia, editors didn't speculate, they printed the official party line. In news-speak, the Spetsnaz were simply paratroopers. So start looking for pictures of those gentlemen who wear blue and white striped T-shirts under their combat jackets.'

'It was a long war, Victor; hundreds of officers must have been decorated.'

'Once you've got a list, you can always pare it down. Concentrate on those individuals who were decorated more than once.'

Hazelwood wanted him to liaise with the Defence Intelligence Staff at the Ministry of Defence to see what they had on Special Forces. He also thought it would do no harm to send one of the desk officers up to Hereford for a quiet chat with 22 SAS.

'That's a pretty tall order,' Garfield said with a sickly smile.

'It gets taller,' Hazelwood told him. 'When you have exhausted all our domestic sources, you'd better compare notes with the CIA.'

'Right.'

There was an uncertain note in Garfield's voice and it wasn't difficult to guess what was passing through his mind. But deliverance from an onerous task would not happen simply because Stuart Dunglass was returning to duty on Monday. No Director General could afford to leave any stone unturned when some maniac was only too willing to sell a collection of nuclear warheads to a bunch of terrorists.

'Let's make a start this morning, Rowan,' Hazelwood said with a thin smile. 'Then maybe you will have something to show Stuart Dunglass on Monday.'

Ashton rewound the tape, depressed the play button again and leaned back in the chair, his eyes closed the better to concentrate on the girl's diction. She had a very clear speaking voice and although German was clearly not her native language, her pronunciation could not be faulted. 'The defilers will walk in fear'; it was when she repeated that in English that the American accent came through.

'The defilers will walk in fear'; he reversed the tape just far enough to hear those six words one more time.

'You're trying to place the accent?' Harriet said behind him.

Ashton depressed the stop button. 'Yes. What do you reckon?'

'Sounds transatlantic.' Harriet moved round his chair, plumped herself down on the settee and, balancing the right ankle on the left knee, inspected the sole of her trainer. 'Doesn't mean too much, though. I've heard lots of Russian diplomats with the same accent; comes from improving their English courtesy of the Voice of America broadcasting from Munich.' She frowned. 'Thought so,' she said, 'the sole's split. I wondered why my ankle sock felt damp when I came in from the garden. What are you planning to do with the tape?'

'Someone from the Technical Services Division is coming round to collect it. Kelso will probably send it on to the Home Office for their evaluation.'

'I wouldn't put too much money on the experts. People like Professor Henry Higgins only exist in books. Remember the case of the Yorkshire Ripper and that hoaxer who kept phoning the Chief Investigating Officer to taunt him? Remember how all the dialectologists were quite certain the man came from the north-east, most probably from Sunderland, and it turned out he had never been near the place?'

And then of course there was the Muriel McKay kidnap which Ashton recalled reading about. The Hoseins had claimed they represented M3, the Mafia, and elder brother Arthur had had long telephone conversations with the relatives demanding money with menaces. Listening to his recorded voice, the Home Office experts had come to the conclusion that the caller was an American, possibly of West Indian extraction. When the brothers were finally arrested, it had transpired they were Pakistanis who had lived most of their lives in Trinidad before coming to England in 1955. But the McKay kidnap dated back to

January 1970 and it was not unreasonable to suppose that the experts had become a little more expert in the last twenty-four years.

'You never know, they may come up with something,' he said. 'Anyway, it's worth a shot.'

'I'm sure it is.' Harriet got to her feet, a tall, lithe figure in faded jeans and a pale blue sweatshirt. You could, Ashton thought, dress Harriet in a sack and she would still look highly desirable. 'It's good to have you home,' she said, evading his arms as he reached out to grab her, 'but there's work to do in the kitchen.'

The front doorbell rang as Harriet stepped out into the hall and telling him to stay put she went to answer it. There were some former colleagues she would always be pleased to see and the warmth of her welcome was such that Ashton knew who Kelso had sent to see him even before Harriet announced it was Frank.

Everybody liked Frank Warren, the Deputy Head of the Security Vetting and Technical Services Division. He was getting on for fifty-two and had three years to go before he was eligible for a full pension less five per cent for retiring early. Frank had been an administrator all his life and there wasn't much he didn't know about Vetting and the Technical Services peculiar to the SIS. In Ashton's day, Frank Warren had looked after the crypto material and the authentication tables which were used whenever an operator suspected that a bogus station had joined the net. Basically, the tables consisted of a challenge and countersign which were automatically changed on the hour every hour. Each radio station was issued with three months' supply which had to be accounted for while they were on the shelf and a destruction certificate rendered when they became time-expired.

Frank had also been responsible for the fill guns on charge, a complicated gadget resembling the type of laser weapon issued to the crew of the starship *Enterprise*. Loaded with electronic ciphers from the master grid, the fill gun was used to transfer these key variables to an infinite number of compatible radio sets. By the very nature of the job, there were an infinite number of possible accounting errors, but Frank Warren had never been known to make one. Kelso should have been working for him instead of it being the other way round but Warren lacked self-confidence and always gave the impression he expected to be hauled over the coals for not doing something or other by the book.

'Hello, Frank.' Ashton stood up, turned about, and shook hands with the older man. 'It's good to see you again.'

'And you,' Warren said, pumping his hand. 'Married life evidently agrees with you.'

'You're not such a bad advertisement for it yourself.'

Frank was over three inches shorter than Ashton, and overweight. He had thinning black hair which was retreating from his forehead, a round face and a moustache Clark Gable would have been proud of if some of the old movies Ashton had seen on late-night TV were anything to go by.

'I'm in pretty good shape,' Warren told him.

'How's Mary?'

'Fit as a fiddle.'

'And the children?'

'They wouldn't thank you for calling them children. Barbara is twenty-four and about to make us grand-parents.'

'Congratulations.'

'Thanks.'

'What about Phil?'

'Would you like a cup of coffee, Frank?' Harriet asked before he could answer.

'That would be nice.'

'So what is Phil doing these days?' Ashton persisted.

Phil, he learned, was still up to his old tricks, out of work, living rough and keeping body and soul together on a diet of crack supplemented by amphetamines. Suddenly, all the stares, frowns and rolled eyeballs he had been getting from Harriet made sense. Although she and Frank Warren had only been colleagues for approximately fourteen months, she knew far more about his personal life than Ashton ever had. Men and women of all ages confided in Harriet. Perfect strangers would tell her their life stories at the drop of a hat. If she went to the ladies' room and was gone a long time, it was even money that some distressed woman was using her shoulder to cry on. There was some indefinable quality about Harriet which made people instinctively trust her on sight.

'Regular or decaffeinated?' Harriet asked, rescuing Ashton before he could put his foot in it even deeper.

'Decaff please.'

'Me too.' Ashton ejected the cassette from the music centre and handed it to Warren. 'I think this is what you came for,' he said.

'I'm also here to try out my skills as a Photofit artist.'

'What's this, another string to your bow?'

Warren smiled wryly. 'We all have to double up these days. It's part of the cost-effective programme initiated by the Treasury, who, of course, are neither cost-conscious about their own financial vote nor particularly effective for that matter. Anyway, Roy Kelso sent me on a five-day course run by Scotland Yard so naturally I am now an expert.'

'Terrific.'

'I knew you would be pleased.' Warren placed his executive briefcase on the coffee table in front of the settee and opened it. 'The unknown mourner at the funeral?' he asked. 'What sort of face did he have? Long? Narrow? Round? Tapering?'

'Round, but not like a pudding basin. The chin was blunt as though it had been squared off with a chisel.'

'How wide?'

'The actual chin?' Ashton rubbed his jaw. 'About three inches.'

'And the bottom lip? An inch, inch and a half above the chin?'

'More like two. The lips were thin, top and bottom, and the canal under the nose was very shallow. In fact, his mouth was practically a straight line.'

The briefcase contained a huge choice for every feature that made up the whole face. Assembling the right pieces to portray the suspect mourner was a bit like doing a jigsaw puzzle.

'We're getting there,' Warren said cheerfully. 'Let's talk about the cheekbones.'

'They weren't prominent. I mean, this man was no hungry-looking Slav; he was sleek and well fed like a pampered pussycat.'

The nose had been straight, flared a bit at the nostrils. The bridge too had been broader than most people's. The eyes were either grey or a washed-out blue, Ashton couldn't remember which.

'What shape were they, Peter? Almond, narrow, round, bulging?'

'More oval than round.'

'And the ears?'

'They were very flat, close to the skull as though someone had taped them back when he was a child. Nobody was going to call him jug-ears.'

The man who had called himself Georgi Mugrowski had probably had blond hair in his youth but now it was the colour of pepper with a lot of salt in it.

'It was cut short, no parting and brushed forward.'

'Like that?' Warren asked, capping the head with a suitable hairpiece.

'More or less.' Ashton looked at the Photofit portrait from all angles. 'Something isn't quite right.'

'With the hair?'

'Partly. There was a small cowlick above the right eye.' He snapped his fingers. 'I've got it, the left eye is fractionally higher than the other.'

Warren played around with the hairline, made a fractional adjustment to the eyes, then sat back to admire his handiwork. 'What do you think?'

'Brilliant. What happens now?'

'I photograph the Photofit, we blow up the prints and the rest is down to Hazelwood. What he is going to do with the prints is anybody's guess.'

Ashton didn't say anything. Copies would, he knew, go to Bonn, the CIA at Langley, the US Defense Intelligence Agency in Washington, DC, Head of Station, Moscow – and certain individuals like Heinrich Voigt and Caspar Lemberg.

Hazelwood always feared the worst whenever a colleague asked to have a word with him. In his experience, the request either led to an embarrassing confession of a personal nature or else it heralded a complaint about a third party. When Jill Sheridan appeared in his office that afternoon, he was sure it was the latter, especially when she asked if Roy Kelso had mentioned their little contretemps. The question gave him a shrewd idea why Kelso had wanted to see him earlier in the day. Unfortunately he had sent the poor man on his way before he'd had a chance to say a word. Furthermore, he had forgotten to let Roy know he had finished his business with Rowan Garfield and was therefore free.

'Not in so many words,' he said cautiously.

'Ah. Well, it was really all my fault.' She smiled hesitantly. 'You could say I got out of bed the wrong side this morning . . .'

'Why don't you sit down, Jill?'

'Yes, yes, of course.'

She chose an upright chair, crossed one leg over the other, then leaned forward and clasped her right knee with both hands. Hazelwood could not recall a time when Jill had looked so insecure. Correction – hitherto she had never shown anything other than an icy resolve and a sublime confidence in her own ability. Arrogant, self-centred, intelligent, ambitious; those were the adjectives that usually came most readily to mind.

'What's the matter, Jill?'

'You know Henry and I have separated?'

'Yes. As I recall, you submitted a Change of Circumstance report in writing.'

'I wish it could have ended there.' Jill bit her lip, then said, 'Henry was practically spitting with rage when I arrived home last night . . .'

'Just a minute; in your letter you stated that Henry had bought a cottage for himself in Wiltshire. You're not still living under the same roof, are you?'

'No. Henry drove up from Heytesbury yesterday afternoon after he had been interviewed by one of Roy's vetting officers, a man called Brian Thomas. You know him?'

Hazelwood nodded. Ex-Detective Chief Superintendent Brian Thomas of E District, the London Borough of Camden. They didn't come any harder than him. Or any sharper.

'Don't get me wrong, Victor, I know the vetters have got to ask some pretty searching questions and I wouldn't have it any other way, but Henry is an outsider and doesn't know the form. He was apopletic about Brian Thomas; said he treated him like a common criminal. I gather he dragged up all the distasteful business about Henry's first wife and insisted on knowing her present address. Said he wanted to hear her side of the story. He implied it was Helen who had left Henry and not the other way round.'

Thomas had gone one better and had implied that Jill had given her husband the order of the boot because she had discovered that he was up to his old tricks again. Immediately after the interview had been concluded, Henry Clayburn had jumped into his car and stormed up to London.

'Henry was really hopping mad,' Jill said, repeating herself. 'He demanded to know what I had said to Brian Thomas that could have made him so antagonistic. We had a terrible row but in the end I managed to convince Henry that I hadn't even seen Thomas, let alone talked to him.'

'I imagine you must have been pretty upset,' Hazelwood said soothingly.

'I was.' Jill lowered her eyes. 'And I'm afraid I blamed Roy for what had happened. After the conference this morning, I went along to his office and really tore into him . . .'

Hazelwood could understand how Jill must have felt. If only half of what Henry had told her were true, ex-Detective Chief Superintendent Thomas had certainly been overzealous.

'Anyway, when I eventually calmed down, I knew it wasn't Roy's fault. So I sought him out and apologised for my inexcusable behaviour.'

'And now everything is sweetness and light between the two of you?'

'Well, we've patched things up.' A faint smile touched her lips. 'I just thought you should know the facts, Victor.'

'I'm glad you told me.'

'It was a storm in a teacup as far as I'm concerned.'

'I'm sure it was. Today is Friday, you've got the whole weekend to put it behind you.'

'Thank you for being so understanding, Victor.'

This was a different Jill, one whom he hadn't seen before. She was grateful, and that definitely was a first. Waiting until he could no longer hear the click-clack of her heels in the corridor, he then lifted the receiver and rang Kelso to inform him that he wished to see Brian Thomas.

'He's down in Chideock.'

'Where?'

'It's in Dorset,' Kelso told him, 'about seven miles from Lyme Regis.'

'What's he doing?'

'Interviewing Mrs Helen Clayburn. Look, I know how it must seem but–'

'Did Clayburn give Brian her address?' Hazelwood asked, interrupting him.

'You've got to be joking. He was singularly abusive. We had to go cap in hand to the Department of Social Security to find out where his ex-wife was living.'

Chapter 13

Hazelwood could not recall a Monday when there had been quite so many smiling faces around the table at morning prayers. He did not have to look very far to know the reason for this upsurge in morale. Everybody's favourite headmaster was back in the chair and the assembled coven of Department Heads had been keen to show Stuart Dunglass how much he had been missed. Although a modest man whose head was not easily turned, Dunglass would have had to be a paragon of virtue not to be flattered and secretly pleased by the near adulation he had received. Add the fact that each Assistant Director had withheld some titbit that could and should have been aired on Friday and it was small wonder that morning prayers had lasted double the time it had under Hazelwood's chairmanship.

Rowan Garfield had been the chief offender. He had spent almost thirty minutes on the subject of The Czar, describing in minute detail the steps being taken by the officers of the Russian Desk to identify the former Spetsnaz colonel. Little real progress had been made and the Intelligence analysts were in fact no farther forward than they had been when the task had been given to them on Friday morning, but that had not inhibited the Assistant Director, European Department. Garfield had always been a good speaker who knew how to make the most of his subject matter, and with very little conscious effort had completely enthralled the Director General. After questioning him at length, Dunglass had decided that, in future, Garfield should keep him fully apprised of the progress made by the Russian Desk. He had also directed that Hazelwood would continue to head the Moresby/Franklin investigation as he had termed it.

The hunt for The Czar was the more engrossing project; it was also a lot safer. No political flak would be directed at the Russian Desk whereas there were clear signs that the Moresby and Franklin incidents were about to attract a barrage. Although Dunglass was ultimately responsible for every SIS operation, he was a sick man and had never been consulted about the Berlin job. By steering well clear of the subsequent investigation, it could be said that he was making doubly sure he was fireproof.

If Hazelwood was in a disgruntled frame of mind after morning prayers, ex-Detective Chief Superintendent Brian Thomas was even more so. Kelso had told him that he was to report to the Deputy Director at nine o'clock on the dot; an hour and a half later, he was finally shown into Hazelwood's office.

'Morning prayers overran,' Hazelwood told him. 'One or two people had a bad case of verbal diarrhoea.'

'Doesn't surprise me.'

'Well, it wouldn't, the complaint's endemic to Whitehall.'

'I hear it's contagious too,' Thomas said.

Hazelwood wondered if the former detective was having a dig at him. Had he not been born in Stanmore, Middlesex, on the fringe of London, Thomas could have passed for the bluff, archetypal, no-nonsense Yorkshireman who believed in speaking his mind whatever the personal consequences. A large and weathered-looking man, it could be said he had the physical presence to go with the image.

'I hear you've been treading on a few corns, Brian,' Hazelwood said cheerfully.

'If you mean Mr Henry Clayburn, he started getting hot under the collar before I even had a chance to raise my foot, never mind put it down on anything. I introduced myself, thanked him for agreeing to see me at short notice, then said it was in connection with the Change of Circumstance letter submitted by his wife. That's when he went ape.'

'Had Clayburn been warned what to expect?'

'You'd have to ask Roy Kelso. All I know is he told me that Jill Sheridan had explained the procedures to her husband.'

'When was this?'

'Last Thursday morning when I was briefed. Kelso said I should go down to Heytesbury right away so naturally I assumed he had spoken to Clayburn and warned him to expect me.'

What had clinched it for Thomas was the fact that he had found Clayburn at home. The eruption had started the moment the ex-Detective Chief Superintendent had mentioned Jill Sheridan. There was, Clayburn had announced, no way he was going to answer any questions relating to his private life. It was a gross invasion of privacy and he intended to lodge an official complaint with his Member of Parliament who would undoubtedly raise the matter with the appropriate Minister of State.

'Do you think he's bluffing?' Hazelwood asked.

'Hard to say. Clayburn sounded genuinely angry but that could be because he's got something to hide.'

'Is that a hunch?'

'It was initially.'

After phoning Kelso to explain what had happened, Thomas had visited all the estate agents in the small neighbouring town of Warminster. Eventually he had found the firm which, in conjunction with Knight, Frank and Rutley in London, had sold the cottage in Heytesbury to Henry Clayburn.

'Contracts were exchanged back in November '93. In other words, a full ten months before Jill Sheridan told us that she and her husband were separating. Which means the lady was being economical with the truth when she led us to believe that their decision to separate had only been taken a few days ago.'

'I'm keeping an open mind about that,' Hazelwood told him. 'It could be they originally bought the cottage for a weekend retreat when they wanted to get away from London.'

Thomas grunted, totally unimpressed by this argument. 'Clayburn divorced his first wife because she was a raving nymphomaniac. That's the gospel according to Sheridan, isn't it?'

'More or less.'

'Well, I've talked to Mrs Helen Clayburn and I don't buy it.'

Thomas had gone down to Chideock expecting to find a tarty, lascivious woman whose taste in clothes left very little to the imagination and boldly proclaimed that she was available. Instead, much to his surprise, Helen Clayburn was a polite, unassuming, well-dressed woman in her middle to late forties who would not have looked out of place as the chairwoman of the local branch of the Conservative Party. The woman who'd been photographed in stockings and shoes had been wearing a yashmak which had concealed much of her face. However, Kelso had told Thomas that she'd had very blue eyes and wide cheekbones, a description which in no way applied to Helen Clayburn. He had also rapidly discovered that it was Helen who had divorced her husband and not the other way round.

'A bit different to the story Jill gave us. Right?'

'Maybe.' Hazelwood paused long enough to light a Burma cheroot. 'Have we looked at the divorce petition?'

'We're in the process of doing that,' Thomas told him.

'Did you ask Helen Clayburn about the woman in the photograph?'

'Yes. She said that from the description she thought it was a Lufthansa air hostess called Hanna, last name not known. Apparently Clayburn had a stable of girls drawn from practically every airline passing through Kuwait–'

'Kuwait?' Hazelwood said, interrupting him.

'Yes. This was around '80, '81, when he was setting up one of his import houses. Helen left him in '83, returned to England and started divorce proceedings. By mutual agreement, the petition cited an irretrievable breakdown of the marriage. I imagine Clayburn made it worth her while and it's a fact she would have had a hard time proving her allegations in court.'

It was also evident to Hazelwood that she would have had an equally difficult time establishing her innocence. From what Thomas had said, she had co-hosted the lavish parties which Clayburn had given once a week for wealthy young Kuwaitis who were far from being devout followers of Islam and the teachings of the Koran. To these parties he had invited members of whatever slip crews happened to be staging in the city at the time. Clayburn's particular talent had been his ability to identify those air hostesses who would be willing to turn a trick if the money was good enough.

'He is supposed to have had a client list as long as your arm,' Thomas continued. 'And a list of call girls to match the demand. They literally were call girls; according to Helen Clayburn, he had their private numbers in London, Paris, New York or Rome where he could get in touch with them and arrange a date for the next time they were in Kuwait. He would have his driver pick the girl up from the hotel where she was staying and take her on to meet the punter.'

And this was the man Jill Sheridan had chosen to marry; Hazelwood shook his head in disbelief. So all right, maybe Clayburn had ceased to run a string of call girls by the time Jill had met him but it didn't say much for her judgement.

'The name of the driver was Gamal al Hassan,' Thomas added, choosing the right moment to achieve maximum effect.

Hazelwood leaned over sideways, picked up the metal wastebin and used it as an ashtray in which to stub out his cheroot. He felt physically sick. The A1 source who was

171

reputed to have been a major asset during the Gulf War had, it appeared, been a pimp's assistant before he had been recruited by the SIS.

'You got any more unpleasant surprises for me?' he asked.

'Not at the moment. You want me to have another go at Clayburn?'

'Forget him. If he refused to answer any of your questions the first time around, he's not going to have a sudden change of heart. No point interviewing Jill Sheridan either; she can't tell you what Clayburn was up to before she met him. All you can do is check out the divorce petition and submit a report for inclusion on Jill's personal security file.'

Thomas made no comment, but he didn't have to. The set of his mouth showed he thought the Deputy Director had just made a bad decision. 'I'll get on with it then,' he said and lumbered to his feet.

After he had left the office, Hazelwood picked up the phone and rang the Chief Archivist. Gamal al Hassan had been recruited during the time Miles Dempsey had been Head of Station, Kuwait. However, in late '91 he had resigned from the SIS to become the assistant headmaster of a prep school in Somerset. But nobody ever truly left the Intelligence service; as soon as the Chief Archivist confirmed that the former Head of Station had not moved on to even more greener pastures, Hazelwood rang Ashton on the Mozart secure speech telephone and told him what he wanted done.

The Photofit picture of the unknown mourner which Frank Warren had produced from Ashton's description had been faxed to every NATO Intelligence Service. Copies had also been delivered to the Ministry of Defence, MI5 and Walter Maryck, the CIA Station Chief in London.

Walter Maryck had joined the CIA after completing two tours of duty in Vietnam where he had won a Distinguished Service Cross as well as the Silver Star. A natural for the East Asia Department, he had been transferred to Europe in 1982. Nine years later he had been promoted to Chief of Station, London. That morning he had received a second copy of the Photofit, this time from the CIA at Langley, the Chief of Operations, Europe apparently unaware that the SIS had included him on their distribution list. Langley had also sent him a two-page fax on the suspect, now tentatively identified as Gennadi Yasnev.

Yasnev had been, and probably still was, GRU, the Military Intelligence Department of the Russian Armed Forces. He had first come to notice in 1983 when his photograph had appeared in *Izvestia*. The caption above it read, 'One of our Heroes'; the report below described how he had been awarded the Order of Aleksandr Nevsky for bravery in action against Afghan terrorists. According to *Izvestia*, Major Yasnev was the commanding officer of a motor rifle battalion; four years after being decorated for valour, he had been captured on camera by the CIA cell at the US Embassy in Baghdad who'd secretly photographed every Soviet diplomat. Matching faces to the names on the accredited staff list which the Americans had obtained at a cost of several thousand dollars from a junior official in the Iraqi Ministry of External Affairs had proved a time-consuming process. However, thanks to the publicity he'd previously received in *Izvestia*, identifying Gennadi Yasnev had been almost ludicrously simple. The fact that his military rank had been dropped and he appeared in the list of commercial attachés had convinced the CIA's Baghdad team that Yasnev was a member of the GRU.

In February 1990, Gennadi Yasnev had been recalled to Moscow. For yet another consideration, the junior official at the Ministry of External Affairs had told the CIA that Yasnev was a very sick man. A routine X-ray had revealed that there was a shadow on the upper lobe of the left lung which needed to be investigated had been the official line taken by the Soviet Embassy. However, the Iraqi had heard that the Russian had misappropriated government funds to indulge in currency speculation. Whatever the reason for his recall, Yasnev had not been seen again until he had surfaced at Franklin's funeral using the name of Georgi Mugrowski.

The alias he had adopted was significant. Ten years previously, a Chicago businessman of Polish extraction called George Mugrowski had disappeared without trace in East Berlin. No two men could have been less physically alike than George Mugrowski and Gennadi Yasnev which, in the opinion of the Chief of Operations, Europe, ruled out the possibility that the Russian Intelligence Service was hoping to effect a substitution. Privately, Maryck thought it was also a little late in the day to resurrect the Chicago businessman.

The last two paragraphs of the fax from Langley laid down the ground rules for any meeting Maryck might have with British Intelligence. He could have put it in a sentence. Prune the verbiage and all that remained was a stricture urging him to ensure he didn't give more than he received from the SIS. There were, of course, no guidelines to show him how he was to achieve this desirable state of affairs. To have tendered such advice would have denied the author of the missive the luxury of adopting a critical stance should it appear that Victor Hazelwood had gained more than he'd given in return. But what really angered Maryck was the implication that he was far too pro-British and was likely to be taken for a ride, a charge so far removed from the truth as to be laughable.

'Some joke,' Maryck said aloud, and tossed the fax into the pending tray.

He looked at the battery of telephones on his desk. Although what he had to say to Hazelwood could be conveyed in veiled speech, he decided to use the crypto-protected hot line which automatically bypassed Victor's PA. Knowing which number to try first wasn't a problem. The Deputy DG's office was the one area in Vauxhall Cross where smoking was permitted and he couldn't see Hazelwood denying himself the pleasure of a Burma cheroot after lunch. Lifting the receiver, he punched out the number and was childishly pleased when his deduction proved correct.

'Hello, Victor,' he said casually. 'I think it's time we did a little socialising.'

'So do I. When and where do you suggest we get together?'

'How about the Lansdowne this evening around six. I'll book a court.'

'I'm unfit,' Hazelwood told him, 'and I intend to stay that way. My place, same time, and we'll see off a ten-year single malt. Much better than batting a little rubber ball against a wall.'

The prep school was situated on the outskirts of Luccombe which itself was some six miles west of Minehead and 189 miles from London via the M4 and M5 motorways. One of the prettiest villages in Somerset, Luccombe was part of the Holnicote estate, an area of Exmoor near the Dunkery Beacon which was owned by the National Trust. A narrow lane through fields of red earth bounded by sandstone walls had finally led Ashton to Regina House, home of Bleasedale's Preparatory School for Boys.

Miles Dempsey, senior master and deputy head, was five feet seven inches tall, slender, small-boned and had the reddest hair Ashton had ever seen. He was wearing a dark grey single-breasted pinstripe over a maroon-coloured shirt and a club tie which clashed with everything, a sure sign that Dempsey was a bachelor. His rooms were on the top floor of the west wing of the Elizabethan manor house and overlooked the school playing fields where a rugby match was in progress.

'I hope Victor Hazelwood explained the purpose of my visit?' Ashton said as they shook hands.

'Not in so many words. You know how it is with Victor; he's very security-minded and it was an open line.' Dempsey smiled. 'He said you were on home leave from

Kuwait and were anxious to find a suitable prep school for your son. It took me a minute or two to realise it was all about my time as Head of Station. Incidentally, do you have a son?'

'Yes, he's four months old.'

'Well, there's nothing like putting his name down for a good school at an early age but I doubt if Bleasedale's will still be here by the time he is old enough to be a boarder.'

'Oh, why's that?'

'Falling numbers. It costs nearly £3,000 a term to send a boy to Bleasedale's and taxes being what they are, parents just can't afford the fees. I can't help feeling that I should never have left The Firm.'

'Well, I don't know about that. The Firm's not what it used to be and at least you don't have to rub shoulders with the likes of Gamal al Hassan.'

'Is he the reason you're here?'

'Yes.'

'I see. What's he been up to?'

'You mean you haven't heard?' Ashton said incredulously. 'He got his throat cut in Berlin a fortnight ago.'

'My God.' Dempsey sounded genuinely shocked.

'It was reported in the newspapers.'

'I don't remember reading about it.'

Ashton believed him. Moresby had grabbed most of the column inches in the press while Gamal had barely rated a mention. The bombing of the English Bookshop seventy-two hours later had then captured the headlines and effectively spiked any follow-up on the Moresby story.

'Was Gamal still working for us when he was murdered?'

Ashton ignored the question. 'How did you come to recruit him?' he asked.

'I didn't. I sort of inherited him from the Commercial Attaché. Gamal was a telegraphist with Cable and Wireless in those days and he used to keep the embassy informed whenever he saw anything which suggested a UK firm was being discriminated against by the Kuwaitis.'

'Do you know what prompted him to do that?'

'I guess he felt indebted to the British. Gamal used to work for an Englishman called Henry Clayburn who got him the job when he handed over the day-to-day running of his emporium to a Kuwaiti and returned to his company's head office in Bahrain. This would have been in February 1987, five months before I became Head of Station.'

'How long did Gamal continue to work for Cable and Wireless after you arrived in the country?'

'A little over twelve months. He was replaced by a Kuwaiti in August '88.'

It wasn't difficult to guess how Clayburn had managed to secure a job with Cable and Wireless for his former driver. Some well-connected punter who had enjoyed more than the occasional romp with one of Henry's call girls had had his arm twisted. Ashton thought it must have given the unknown benefactor a great deal of satisfaction to sack Gamal when he'd judged it safe to do so.

'Gamal then got a job as a bus driver?'

Dempsey nodded. 'He was pretty bitter about it.'

'And less effective as a source of information,' Ashton suggested.

'To a degree, but he had his ear to the ground and was very good at discovering what the ex-patriate Egyptian, Jordanian and Palestinian workers thought of the ruling family and how they would react should Iraq invade the country.'

Dempsey had seen the invasion coming and had not been taken by surprise when the Iraqi army crossed the border during the early hours of Thursday, 2 August 1990. He already had an Intelligence network in place for that eventuality.

'And Gamal was the wireless operator?'

'Yes.'

'His hostile attitude towards the Kuwaitis didn't bother you?'

'It was a British-run network and I had no reason to doubt his loyalty to us.'

'So how did you manage to escape from Kuwait City?'

'As easily as falling off a log.'

Dempsey had packed a scram bag and moved out of the embassy to the oil camp at Al Maqwa forty-eight hours before the T72 tanks of the Republican Guard had cruised down the motorway. Even though the Kuwaiti Government had known the Iraqis were massing on the border, they had refrained from mobilising their own army for fear of provoking Saddam Hussein. Convinced the Iraqis would cleave through the few Kuwaiti units which were deployed on the Mutla Ridge like a hot knife through butter, Dempsey had jumped into a Land Rover and driven pell-mell for Saudi Arabia the moment he'd learned the invasion had started.

There was a faint smattering of applause as if the spectators watching the rugby match approved of his action; then a stentorian voice roared, 'That's the way, Bleasedale's, keep running the ball.'

'Tell me something,' said Ashton. 'On a scale of one to ten, how did you rate Gamal?'

'During the occupation?' Dempsey pursed his lips while he considered his own rhetorical question. 'No more than four.'

'Jill Sheridan was running him throughout Desert Storm, wasn't she?'

'Yes. I was shunted off into the sidings. I understand London thought I should have stayed in Kuwait with the embassy staff, and I subsequently became aware that I'd collected quite a few black marks. That's why I left the Service and accepted my brother-in-law's invitation to become the deputy head of Bleasedale's. He owns the school.'

'Jill Sheridan thought Gamal was mustard,' Ashton said, before the conversation went into the realms of personal disillusionments.

'That doesn't surprise me. She is one very ambitious and unscrupulous woman. Half the input she attributed to Gamal al Hassan she had gleaned from the Americans and our own Senior Naval Officer, Persian Gulf. Jill Sheridan was very good at presenting herself in the best possible light.'

And any number of senior officers in all three Services had, it seemed, been only too eager to assist her. Ashton kept reminding himself that Dempsey was convinced Jill had deliberately wrecked his career. But even allowing for the fact that he was deeply prejudiced, what he had said about Gamal al Hassan rang true and was going to alarm Hazelwood.

Maryck paid off the taxi at the junction of Willow Walk with East Heath Road and walked up the gentle hill. There was no earthly reason why he shouldn't have got the cab driver to drop him at the door to Hazelwood's place; although the IRA wasn't exactly dormant, the British were at 'Bikini Black', which was the lowest anti-terrorist alert state. But it was second nature to do everything by the book when you had been targeted by a bunch of psychopaths like the Red Army Brigade as Maryck had on his initial overseas posting to Rome. Never approach an RV without first checking it out; that was one of the basic rules he always religiously observed.

Killing the Deputy Director of the Secret Intelligence Service would be one hell of a coup for the Provisional IRA and it was not unreasonable to assume they had already identified Hazelwood. On this late September evening, however, only the distant throb of a lawnmower disturbed the tranquillity of Willow Walk. In somebody's garden farther up the road, a thin plume of smoke from a bonfire of autumn leaves rose lazily in the still air.

Of all the names to call a house, Willow Dene struck Maryck as the least original. He pushed open the wrought-iron gate set in the tall privet hedge and, keeping to the footpath, walked round to the side of the house. He could only presume that the baggy flannels, thin roll-neck sweater and tweed jacket with leather patches on both elbows which Hazelwood sported were his gardening clothes. With a huge grin, Victor switched off the ignition, abandoned the lawnmower and came forward to greet him.

'Glad you arrived on time, Walter,' he said cheerfully. 'In another few minutes I'd have finished cutting the grass and Alice would have had me trimming the edges.'

Hazelwood ushered him into the house and thence into the study. Maryck thought it was a good thing he hadn't given up smoking because simply inhaling the aroma from innumerable cheroots was enough to give a man cancer. The triple measure of malt whisky which Hazelwood gave him was unlikely to improve his health either.

'Cheers, Walter.'

'Cheers.' Maryck raised his glass in response. The malt looked smoky; it was also as smooth as silk and lit a fire in his belly.

'So what have you got for me?' Hazelwood asked, getting down to business.

'A possible name. The question is, what do we get in return?'

'A really useful present.' From the top right-hand drawer of the desk Hazelwood produced a battery-powered Sony recorder and a cassette. 'How's your German?'

'I can get by,' Maryck told him.

'Well then, listen to this.'

The spokeswoman sounded young, but that was simply guesswork based on the content of her message and she could have been any age. She said, 'British Intelligence is controlled by the Zionists and therefore the English Bookshop on Budapesterstrasse was a legitimate target. The attack was carried out by my brothers in Hizbollah. The bomb comprised five kilos of Semtex packed into a steel container resembling an executive briefcase. After this demonstration of our invincible power, the defilers will walk in fear.'

'I must say the language is kind of flowery. How did you get hold of this tape, Victor?'

'Heinrich Voigt, the Police President of Berlin, gave a copy to Ashton.'

Ashton. They had never met and he couldn't put a face to the name, but Maryck had heard of him. He was Victor's foot soldier and something of a loose cannon, but effective, goddamned effective. Once you let that guy off the leash there was no holding him back.

'Our experts in phonetics are convinced that German certainly isn't her second language,' Hazelwood continued. 'Naturally, they wouldn't put their jobs on the line but they are willing to bet a month's pay that either Arabic or Farsi is her second string.'

'And her first?'

'English.' Hazelwood rewound the tape, then ejected the cassette and gave it to him. 'Like it's spoken by someone who's lived in the Deep South a long time.'

'You want to be more specific?'

'Texas? Arkansas? Mississippi? Alabama? Georgia? The truth is the experts are just guessing.'

Hazelwood wanted a second opinion; that was why he had given him a copy of the tape. Maryck looked at the cassette in his hand, then put it into his pocket. This was really one for the FBI; they were responsible for Counter-Intelligence stateside. The Bureau had files on all the known extremist organisations, including religious sects.

'We may have a description of the spokeswoman,' Hazelwood said idly. 'Small, very sinewy, pointed features, jet-black glossy hair, and is said to have a sallow complexion.'

'How do you know?'

'Ashton went to the lowlife bar where Moresby was last seen alive and met an old queen who was there when this woman picked up our courier.'

Ashton again. The guy seemed to spend his entire time lifting stones to see what crawled out from under. But he knew how to get results. He had put the Kripo on to the queen who called himself Claudia and Hazelwood was hopeful that in due course the SIS would receive an artist's impression of the suspect.

'So how about a little something for us?' Hazelwood said, intruding upon his thoughts.

'What?'

'I understood you could put a name to the unknown mourner.'

'Yasnev, Gennadi Yasnev.'

'What's his history?'

The potted biography took Maryck no more than a few minutes to deliver. The fax from Langley might have run to almost three pages but most of it had been verbiage. That had never been more evident than when Hazelwood began to ask him a load of questions, none of which he could answer.

'I'm not doing a snow job on you, Victor. That's all the information I have.'

'The name alone is enough to please Dunglass.'

'What's it got to do with him?'

'He's back in the chair,' Hazelwood told him laconically.

Though for how long was anybody's guess. In any event, Hazelwood was certain the DG would see things his way and back him to the hilt.

'He has to, Walter.'

'You mean he doesn't have any choice?'

'Of course he doesn't. We've got to find this Gennadi Yasnev before he makes it possible for a bunch of terrorists to make themselves the mother and father of a bomb. That means we have to persuade Mr Yeltsin it's in his interest to make sure we do.'

'Otherwise?'

'Otherwise no more billion-dollar loans and the Russian economy finally goes down the sink.'

Maryck stared at him. 'Are you seriously suggesting that our State Department should lean on him?'

'Why not?' Hazelwood said. 'I mean, how do you know Hizbollah won't use their nuclear bomb on you?'

Chapter 14

Ashton was hard pressed to think of a more unlikely rendezvous than the offices of the Museums and Galleries Commission in Carlton Gardens, and he assumed this was precisely why Hazelwood had chosen the place. It was common knowledge that the mandarins of the Foreign and Commonwealth Office regarded Victor as something of a philistine, the sort of man who would run a mile on hearing anyone mention the word culture. There was some truth in the allegation. Victor had never willingly gone to an orchestral concert, the ballet or the opera and hadn't been inside a museum since he was in knee pants. But conversely, he did know a great many influential people in the arts, one of whom happened to be the Permanent Secretary of the Museums and Galleries Commission.

The next committee meeting was scheduled for Wednesday, 5 October, which meant that, apart from the secretarial staff, they had number 2 Carlton Gardens to themselves. Hazelwood had never made any secret of the fact that he was using Ashton in a freelance capacity. Kelso had delivered a Mozart secure speech telephone to 84 Rylett Close the day Ashton and Harriet had moved into the house and Frank Warren had arrived every Monday to change the crypto. Garfield, Quorn and Jill Sheridan were also aware of the arrangement and, if he hadn't known about it before, somebody would have made it their business to inform Dunglass now that he was back in the chair. Ashton supposed Victor could always claim there had been no breach of security. By withholding the requisite clearance, the Deputy DG had kept him away from Vauxhall Cross. Hitherto, they had either communicated over the Mozart link or met at the Atheneum. The choice of this new venue suggested a need for secrecy. A presentiment that things had suddenly become decidedly sticky was confirmed for Ashton the moment one of the secretaries ushered Hazelwood into the committee room and he saw the grim expression on his face.

'We're in trouble,' Hazelwood announced tersely.

Ashton smiled wryly; Hazelwood wasn't using the word with the royal prerogative.

'It's nothing to smile about. Clayburn has been to see his MP and complained that he is being harassed by the SIS. Now we've got a ministerial inquiry on our hands and the DG is dancing around like a cat on hot bricks.'

'Jill submitted a Change of Circumstance report on herself. What did Dunglass expect you to do? File it and forget it?'

'Of course he doesn't,' Hazelwood said heatedly, 'but he does think I should have limited my enquiries to questioning Ms Sheridan. Going after her husband smacks of a witch hunt in his opinion.'

'Clayburn needs to be reminded he's in no position to make waves.'

'Because of a porno snapshot which no longer exists because Dunglass put it through the shredder?' Hazelwood snorted. 'That will really have him quaking in his boots.'

'What about Kelso? He saw the photograph.'

'Roy won't go in to bat for me, not while the DG shows every sign of remaining in the pavilion. Stuart knows he should never have destroyed that photograph and the letter from the Bahrain police officer, but he's not going to admit it.'

'There's always the first Mrs Clayburn,' Ashton said. 'If you want to keep her out of it, you can get ex-Detective Chief Superintendent Thomas to repeat everything she told him.'

'And a right load of old rubbish it was too.'

It seemed the lady had a convenient memory. From the principal registry of the Family Division at Somerset House, Brian Thomas had learned that, while Helen Clayburn had been granted a divorce on the grounds of an irretrievable breakdown of the marriage, she had neglected to mention that husband Henry had beaten her to it and filed for divorce alleging she had committed adultery with Inspector Leslie North. In the end, their respective lawyers had got together, thrashed out a financial settlement which had been acceptable to both parties and Clayburn had allowed his wife to divorce him.

'The naked lady wearing a yashmak had prominent cheekbones and deep blue eyes; Helen Clayburn's are grey and her face is more round than angular. That's why Thomas believed her when she told him the woman in the snapshot had to be Hanna, a Lufthansa flight attendant. Now he is beginning to think it was probably Helen Clayburn all along. Suddenly it looks as if Henry's version of the divorce is the truth and any questions we ask him about his first marriage are an invasion of privacy.'

'What about the call-girl racket?'

'You talked to Miles Dempsey – did he have anything to say about Henry?'

'Clayburn left Kuwait five months before he arrived in post,' Ashton said, puzzled to know why they were covering the same ground as they had yesterday evening when he'd phoned Hazelwood on his return from Somerset.

'Five months. Are you telling me Dempsey didn't even hear a whisper of what Clayburn had been up to?'

'Apparently not. If he had, I'm sure he would have told me. He's not one of Jill's fans.'

'Who is?' Hazelwood produced a Burma cheroot from the top pocket of his jacket where most people might have kept a folded handkerchief. After lighting it, he looked round for an ashtray but it seemed all the committee members of the Museums and Galleries Commission were nonsmokers. 'Dempsey visited Bahrain in the run-up to Desert Storm. Right?'

'Only on two occasions, Victor. He told me that the less he saw of Jill Sheridan, the better he had liked it.'

Dempsey blamed her for the fact that he had been seconded to the Joint Intelligence Centre which had been established in Riyadh shortly after American and British Forces began to arrive in Saudi Arabia. Although the decision had been taken in London by the Assistant Director in charge of the Middle East Department, Dempsey was convinced that Jill had put him up to it so that she could take over the resistance network in Kuwait which he had organised. The truth was, the Ruling Family, particularly the Minister of Defence, His Excellency Sheikh Salim al-Sabah, had lost confidence in Dempsey and had asked London to remove him.

'If Miles disliked Jill Sheridan so much you'd have thought he would have been only too anxious to trash her husband.'

'If there had been any dirt, Victor, I'm sure he wouldn't have hesitated to pass it on to The Firm.'

'You're right, that's what he would have done.' Hazelwood got up from the table, walked over to the nearest window and opened it. The ash from the cheroot spilled on to the carpet before he could deposit it on the street below. 'I've seen the original memorandum the Ambassador wrote to the Foreign and Commonwealth Office when he forwarded the snapshot and poison-pen letter the embassy had received from Inspector Leslie North.'

'And?' Ashton prompted.

'Helen Clayburn divorced her husband in 1983; eight years later, the odious Inspector North sends his poison-pen letter to the British Embassy in Bahrain. This was after his contract had been terminated following a series of complaints from the public which he believed had been orchestrated by Clayburn.'

'And had he?'

'It's not impossible, but North was a very corrupt officer.' Hazelwood began to pace up and down the room, jabbing the cheroot in Ashton's direction when making a point. In the process, a lot more ash ended up on the carpet. 'Muslims are not supposed to touch alcohol but I understand the desert is littered with empty beer cans. North would shake down any local he caught drinking; same went for any of the ex-pat workers at the Awali oil camp who thought it might be fun to bring along some booze when they went picnicking. And he was mustard on road traffic offences–'

'Tell me something,' Ashton said, interrupting him. 'How did Helen Clayburn manage to have an affair with her police officer when she was living in Kuwait?'

'Easy. The Clayburns were frequently in Bahrain. Henry kept a tight grip on his business empire and made a point of looking in on every branch at least once a month.'

'One other question. How did North get hold of that snapshot?'

'Your guess is as good as mine,' Hazelwood said.

Thinking about it, Ashton came to the conclusion that he could only have got it from Helen Clayburn. She had probably given the snapshot to North as a means of persuading her husband to drop the charge of adultery and allow her to divorce him on less contentious grounds. In securing that concession and with it a much better financial settlement, she must have convinced Clayburn that she would tell everyone the naked lady in the yashmak was one of his call girls. There was no second guessing why North had hung on to the snapshot after the Clayburns had divorced. Had the original petition citing him as the co-respondent gone through, he would have been on the first plane out of Bahrain, his contract terminated without compensation, but it was unlikely he had kept the photograph to remind himself how much he owed the lady who had saved his bacon. Chances were he was the sort of man who always kept a dirty photo in his wallet.

'It must have been an uneasy truce,' Ashton said, voicing his thoughts. 'Between Clayburn and North, I mean.'

For close on eight years they had circled round each other, neither man daring to make a move for fear of the consequences. Then Jill Sheridan had arrived on the scene and because he had fancied her like mad, Clayburn had mounted a campaign to get rid of the Inspector before he went after her, a safety precaution in case North took it into his head to make trouble for him. If Ashton said so himself, it was a pretty neat hypothesis, but unfortunately it didn't lead anywhere.

'It wouldn't surprise me if Jill didn't urge her husband to see his MP.' Hazelwood went over to the window again and this time stubbed out his cheroot on the concrete sill, then turned about. 'She's in trouble and wants to stop our Security Vetting Division before their investigation gets too close to home. Initiating a ministerial inquiry is an effective way of doing just that.'

Ashton raised a sceptical eyebrow. 'You can't be serious, Victor.'

'No? She sold us a duff agent to make herself look good and we mounted a covert operation in Berlin on the strength of her appraisement. But on a scale of one to ten, Gamal al Hassan rated no more than four. Isn't that how Dempsey scored him?'

'Yes. However, it doesn't alter the fact that Gamal must have been on to something. Hell, why else do you suppose the Hizbollah cut off his tongue and put out his eyes before slitting his throat?'

'Jill Sheridan is still making a nuisance of herself and I've got enough problems as it is. Moresby Senior refuses to believe his son had been dealing in heroin and is launching a one-man crusade to clear his name. And the Treasury has begun to ask a number of awkward questions concerning the disposal of 84 Rylett Close, never mind the fact that they can't see why the British Government should award pensions to Helga von Schinkel and Willie Baumgart . . .'

It was a long speech for Hazelwood but there was more to come.

'I want her off my back, Peter.'

'Well, don't look at me,' Ashton told him.

'I thought you might call on Jill and have a quiet word with her.'

'You've got to be joking. Harriet would split me in two with an axe.'

'It would be in your interest.'

It sounded like a veiled threat to Ashton. Hazelwood appeared to be saying that if he would only get Jill off his back, everything else would fall into place and he needn't worry about the Treasury's sudden interest in 84 Rylett Close.

'I don't like being pressured, Victor, even by you.'

'Are you implying that I'm trying to blackmail you?'

Ashton didn't answer. A wall of silence grew between them and in the stillness of the room, he could hear the continuous hum of traffic moving along Pall Mall a block away.

'Gennadi Yasnev,' Hazelwood said, extending an olive branch. 'The name ring any bells with you?'

'No. Who's he?'

'According to the cousins in Virginia, he's the unknown mourner and was, possibly still is, a senior officer in the GRU.'

'Interesting. What are you going to do with the information?'

'Dunglass is passing it to Head of Station, Moscow with instructions to use it as a stick to beat the Russians with.' Hazelwood stopped pacing up and down and returned to the table. 'The theory is Yasnev can lead us to The Czar, which would be a good thing because God knows Rowan Garfield and the Russian Desk are getting nowhere fast.'

'Well, let's hope the Russian Minister for Internal Security is in a co-operative mood.'

'He may need a little prodding,' Hazelwood said.

'Can't the Foreign Office help?'

'Indeed they can. In fact, the Minister of State is sending for the Russian Ambassador this morning to point out the detrimental effect any foot-dragging on their part will have on relations between our two countries. Our Ambassador in Moscow will be conveying the same message to the Minister of Foreign Affairs.'

'That should do the trick,' Ashton said in a noncommittal voice.

'Will it? You know our Foreign and Commonwealth Office; inside the velvet glove there's a limp hand. We need to twist a few arms to get results. The trouble is, Head of Station, Moscow is new to the job and doesn't have the weight to apply real pressure on the Russian hierarchy.'

'Who are we talking about here?'

'Pavel Trilisser, Mr Yeltsin's special adviser on foreign policy.'

'Oh no.' Ashton shook his head vehemently. 'Whatever you've got in mind, forget it.'

A year ago, in one of Moscow's deep shelters, Pavel Trilisser had done his level best to kill Ashton, who wasn't about to give the man a second bite at the cherry.

'I wouldn't ask you—'

'I don't want to hear about it.' Ashton jabbed a finger at him. 'I told you when I went freelance that there was no way I would go back to Moscow. My face is too well known there.'

'Did I say anything about going to Moscow?' Hazelwood enquired blandly.

'You never got the chance.'

'The Poles want to join NATO; the Russkis don't like it, so they are sending a special delegation to Warsaw to see if Mr Lech Walesa can't be persuaded to drop the idea.'

'And Pavel Trilisser is leading the team,' Ashton said flatly.

'Precisely.'

'And what makes you think I'll be safe in Warsaw?'

'Trilisser is wearing a different suit of clothes these days.'

190

'The answer is still no.'

'All I'm asking is for you to think about it.' Hazelwood got up and moved towards the door. 'There's no rush, you've got plenty of time.'

'How long is plenty of time?'

'Trilisser is scheduled to arrive in Warsaw on Thursday, 29 September.'

'That's the day after tomorrow.'

'So I believe.' Hazelwood opened the door, then turned about for one last word. 'Like I said, there's no rush.'

It had been a slack day at the office but then the staff of the British Consulate in Uhlandstrasse didn't exactly go out of their way to attract visitors. In fact, the only entry in Gerald Willmore's desk diary for 27 September was a reminder to the effect that he and Maureen were dining with the French Consul General and his wife at seven o'clock that evening. Having convinced himself that there was no reason why he shouldn't go home early for once, he was on the point of leaving when his secretary announced that Kommissar Eicke of the *Kriminalpolizei* wished to see him.

He had never met Eicke before and considered himself fortunate in that respect the moment he laid eyes on the Kripo officer. Willmore was sure the Kommissar would have felt at home in the Prinz-Albrecht-Strasse Headquarters of the Gestapo had he been around in those days. An utterly humourless man, his brutal features would have inspired terror long before he reached for a lead-filled rubber hose.

'Good afternoon, Herr Kommissar Eicke,' Willmore said in German, then flashed him a wholly synthetic smile. 'To what do I owe this pleasure?'

'Police President Voigt instructed me to deliver this,' Eicke said, and placed a cardboard tube on Willmore's desk.

'What's in this?' he asked genially. 'A bottle of Schnapps?'

'No, it contains a picture.'

Joke over, Willmore thought. Digging his fingernails under the rim of the metal bung at one end of the tube, he prised it free, then extracted a tight roll of glossy paper.

'There are three copies,' Eicke told him.

'So I see.' Willmore unravelled the outside copy and pinned it flat with a paperweight, inkstand, desk diary and the crescent-shaped blotter.

'That is the woman who collected Herr Moresby from the *Schwarz und Weiss* bar on Oranienstrasse.'

The likeness, Willmore learned, was a composite based on a number of descriptions. The Kripo had not only traced and interrogated a fading queen known as Claudia, they had also found the waiter who had served Moresby, pressing one-third-of-a-litre glass of beer after another on him. Nobody was allowed to linger over a drink at the *Schwarz und Weiss* and the waiter had been back to his table several times. He had just served Moresby with yet another small beer and was marking it up on the bar tab when the woman had arrived.

'He was as close to her as I am to you, Herr Willmore. That is why we took more notice of his description than the ones we obtained from the other witnesses.'

The crease mark which the waiter claimed he had seen on the neck would have aroused little interest had the woman been middle-aged but all the witnesses had agreed that she had been in her early twenties. Using the latest computer techniques, the police had played around with the blemish until it had become a thin white scar.

'Forensic reckon her thyroid gland has been surgically removed. They can't say when she had the operation, but if they're right, she will be on thyroxin tablets for the rest of her life. Naturally, we are checking all the pharmacies and doctors' surgeries in Berlin to see if anyone recognises her.' Eicke shrugged his shoulders. 'Of course she may have brought enough thyroxin tablets with her to last several weeks.'

'Do you believe this woman is still in the city?' Willmore asked.

'Personally, I don't think so, but it is necessary to visit every hotel and *pension*. Copies of her picture have gone to all the airlines.'

If I were in her shoes, Willmore thought, I would drive out of Berlin, catch a train from somewhere like Hamburg and give the airlines a miss until I had crossed the border into Denmark, Holland, Belgium or France. No border checks, no passport controls; freedom of movement, that was the great thing about the European Union, especially if you were a terrorist going about your business of killing people. He wondered how much longer the unelected, overpaid bureaucrats in Brussels would allow the UK to remain an exception to the rule.

'We've also advised Interpol Headquarters in Paris,' Eicke added.

'Presumably you would like me to send my copies of her picture on to London?'

'Yes; they are for the information of your Foreign Office in case she asks for political asylum.'

'I would have thought that was extremely unlikely.'

'We want this woman very badly, Herr Willmore. She is responsible for the deaths of at least fourteen people. Consequently Herr Voigt is not prepared to leave anything to chance. He has already been in touch with Herr Caspar Lemberg.'

'Who?' Willmore asked, feigning ignorance.

'The CIA officer at the United States Consulate. The Police President is convinced she is an American national.'

Ashton got off the District Line train at Ravenscourt Park, went on down the staircase and, surrendering his ticket to the collector at the barrier, turned right outside the station. Beyond the railway bridge, he crossed the road, entered the park and followed the footpath which skirted a small pond and sandpit. School was over for the day and when not arguing vociferously amongst themselves, a dozen youngsters were kicking a ball around in a six-a-side match.

He had done a lot of thinking since parting company with Hazelwood and still hadn't come to a decision. Well, that wasn't entirely correct; he had, in fact, resolved to give Harriet a sanitised version of the conversation he'd had with Victor should she ask him what sort of day he'd had. Lousy was the short answer. Hazelwood was in deep trouble and might well go under. If his old mentor was forced to resign, Ashton would be finished too. No house, no job, no prospects. They needed to pull something out of the bag and the solution to that problem appeared to lie in Warsaw.

There had been a time when he wouldn't have hesitated to go in harm's way, but things were different now. He had a wife and son to consider, though if he were honest with himself, they were not the only factor. In Hollywood when the good guy was wounded in the shoulder, he gritted his teeth and blew the opposition away with a cannon. In real life it was a different story. It hurt like hell when you were hit and knocked off your feet by a 6.35mm round and you didn't get up again in too much of a hurry either. In time, you could make a complete physical recovery provided you worked at it as he had, but some of the stuffing had been permanently knocked out of you and the old gung-ho spirit wasn't quite what it had once been. To put not too fine a point on it, you were not going to put your head above the parapet voluntarily, which was the principal reason why Hazelwood could shove Warsaw up his backside.

Completely absorbed in his thoughts, Ashton was surprised to find himself in Rylett Close with no clear recollection of passing the Royal Masonic Hospital on the way. He had left home at eight thirty and it was now twenty minutes after four. Harriet was no fool; she would know that whatever it was Victor had had to say to him couldn't have taken more than a couple of hours at the most and he wondered how he was going to account for the rest of the time he'd been gone. A leisurely lunch? Harriet would never believe it but in truth he would still have been sitting in that dreary pub off Whitehall if the landlord hadn't called time. He pushed the gate open, walked up the front path and let himself into the house.

'Hi,' he said, 'I'm home. Where are you?'

'In the kitchen,' Harriet called out. 'How did it go?'

'Better than I expected,' he said from the safety of the hall. 'What sort of day have you had?'

'Tremendous.' Harriet appeared in the doorway drying her hands on the apron she was wearing, the smile on her lips matching the elation in her voice. 'Mummy rang me today and I think our problem may be solved.'

'What problem?'

'The house in Church Lane which the estate agent said would be difficult to sell because of the recession.'

But now the situation had apparently changed. Her younger brother, Richard, the fighter pilot, had come to the conclusion that a once promising career in the RAF was now looking less than attractive thanks to the on-going Defence cuts. Thoroughly disillusioned, he had applied to leave the service.

'And guess what?' Harriet said excitedly.

'The RAF agreed to make him redundant.'

'Yes, but there's more to it than that. With the golden handshake he will receive, Richard wants to buy our old house. That means we can afford this place without taking out an horrendous bridging loan.'

She hugged and kissed him repeatedly, overjoyed because at last there was hope shining on the horizon. He did not have the heart to tell her they would lose everything if Hazelwood was forced to resign.

'Of course we won't get all our money back,' Harriet continued. 'But you will be able to repay the £32,000 you received from the SIS and we'll still have a place we can call our own.'

A place to call their own. Ashton supposed that was as good a reason as any for going to Warsaw.

Chapter 15

The 'No Smoking' and 'Fasten Seat Belt' signs came on, instructions that were repeated over the address system by a member of the cabin staff in both Polish and English. A few minutes earlier, the captain of Lot Airlines Flight 282 from London had announced they would be arriving on schedule at 14.15 hours. Visibility was said to be good between intermittent showers and the temperature in Warsaw was fourteen centigrade or fifty-seven Fahrenheit. In bright sunlight one moment, the Boeing 737 was enveloped in a grey shroud the next as the plane descended through a murky overcast to emerge below the cloud base in what Ashton could only describe as a downpour.

The view from his window seat was nothing to write home about although Ashton had to admit he was looking at the scenery with a jaundiced eye. Harriet believed he was on a British Airways flight to Washington; in furtherance of this deception he would telephone her tonight at nine and pretend it was the middle of the afternoon and his plane had just arrived at Dulles International. She had accepted that he was going to Washington in order to compare notes with the CIA on Gennadi Yasnev and would therefore not be surprised to hear that the officer in charge of the Russian Desk at Langley had insisted on putting him up. By settling all his bills in cash and posting the receipts on to Kelso after he landed at Heathrow, there would be no telltale evidence to show that he had been in

Warsaw. Clever but contemptible; Ashton hoped that one day he would find the courage to tell Harriet what he'd done and why.

The Boeing touched down, decelerated rapidly, then taxied sedately to its allotted gate at the terminal building. There was a time when it would have taken any visitor from the West an eternity to clear Immigration but this was the new-look, would-be capitalist Poland and unnecessary hold-ups were frowned upon.

That nobody from the British Embassy was there to meet him when he emerged into the Arrivals Hall came as no surprise to Ashton. Hazelwood had told him that there had been a great deal of political in-fighting at Vauxhall Cross before Dunglass had been prepared to authorise the operation. Garfield had been dead against it and had only agreed to disclose the identity of the Polish source who'd tipped them off about Trilisser on the understanding that Head of Station, Warsaw would not be involved. No back-up, no administrative support; as far as the embassy was concerned, Ashton didn't exist. In the circumstances, it was fortunate that both the source and his spouse spoke passable English.

Roy Kelso had provided him with 800 US dollars, a list of suitable hotels and a good deal of advice on all the practical wrinkles a tourist would be grateful to know. Although not yet a freely negotiable currency, the zloty was no longer the Monopoly money it had once been. However, the thirst for hard currency had not diminished and the taxi driver touting for a fare outside the terminal building wanted US dollars up front before taking Ashton to the Marriott Hotel.

The Marriott was full, so were the next two hotels Ashton tried on Jerozolimskie Boulevard. He finally got lucky at the Forum where the desk clerk was able to offer him a double room on the eleventh floor overlooking the avenue. On a less happy note, the room also afforded a view of the appalling Palace of Culture and Science, a prime example of the wedding-cake school of architecture which Stalin had inflicted on Moscow. The Palace had been his gift to the Polish people; as with most gifts from the Soviet dictator, the Poles themselves had had to meet the cost of its construction.

Ashton unpacked, stowed the slimline Revelation suitcase on top of the wardrobe, then went into the bathroom and arranged his washing kit on the glass shelf above the washbasin. Apart from the usual shaving tackle, face flannel, toothbrush and toothpaste, the drawstring bag also contained what appeared to be a small battery-powered razor approximately the same size as a pocket calculator. Known as the Close Quarter Defence System, it had been developed by the army's Small Arms Research Establishment at the request of the Security Vetting and Technical Services Division. The system incorporated a high pitch, ear-splitting alarm and a phial of CS gas. Effective as it undoubtedly was at close quarters, Ashton would have been happier if the DG had seen fit to detail someone to watch his back. There was a first-rate warrant officer from the Special Air Services on the establishment of the Training School at Amberley Lodge whom Ashton had used before but it seemed he was on detached duty elsewhere. Although not expecting trouble before Trilisser arrived in Warsaw, he slipped the combined alarm and gas dispenser into his jacket pocket on the premise it was better to be safe than sorry.

Ashton returned to the bedroom, looked out of the window to see what the weather was like and found it had stopped raining. There were even signs that the sun was trying to break through the overcast. Deciding there was no need to take a raincoat, he went down to the front desk, changed a twenty-dollar bill into zlotys and asked the cashier to include a handful of loose change with the notes. From a pay phone in the lobby, he then dialled the number he had committed to memory. As soon as the subscriber answered, he hung up and left the booth, satisfied he wasn't about to embark on a wasted journey. From the rank round the corner from the hotel entrance, he hired a cab and told the driver he wanted to visit the Botanical Gardens on Ujazdowskie Boulevard. He had to print the address in block capitals on a sheet torn from the back of his pocket diary before the Pole understood him.

Before World War Two, Ujazdowskie Boulevard had been likened to New York's Fifth Avenue. It had also been nicknamed Embassy Row. Following the surrender of the Polish Home Army in October 1944 after sixty-three days of bitter street fighting, the Wehrmacht had levelled every building in Warsaw which had still been standing. During the immediate post-war years, the boulevard, like so many other streets in the capital, had been rebuilt on its former lines. However, although the American, Bulgarian, Yugoslav and Swiss Embassies had reappeared on Ujazdowskie, the equivalent of Saks, Tiffany's and Bergdorf Goodman had had no place in a Communist society and the boulevard was all the poorer for it.

Roman Zborski, the senior civil servant who was Garfield's source of information, lived at the bottom end of Ujazdowskie in an apartment house directly opposite the Chopin monument in Lazienki Park. The Botanical Gardens was about four hundred yards north of the block of flats; after the cab driver had dropped him off there, Ashton spent approximately ten minutes wandering around the grounds before making his way to the Zborski residence.

The apartment house was a solid, grey stone four-storey building constructed on the lines favoured by architects of the Habsburg Empire at the end of the nineteenth century. There were two flats on each floor; as perhaps fitted his status in the Civil Service, Zborski's apartment was right at the top. The one and only lift was out of order.

Rowan Garfield had told Ashton that Maria Zborski was thirty-seven, nine years younger than her husband, but had been unable to describe her appearance. The woman who answered the door when Ashton rang the bell was about five feet six, had dark, tightly curled hair, a heart-shaped face, narrow shoulders and broad hips. She looked about the right age and she was in Zborski's flat.

'My name is Ashton,' he said slowly and distinctly. 'And you are Mrs Zborski. Yes?'

The woman stared at him blankly. Garfield had said that like her husband, she spoke passable English but that was now beginning to look a hundred per cent inaccurate if her lack of response was anything to go by. There were two other possibilities: either this woman was not Maria or else she was being very cagey.

'I am Ashton.' He took out his passport and showed it to her. 'The Englishman Roman–'

'Not here,' the woman said before Ashton could finish and would have closed the door if he hadn't stuck his foot in the way.

'The telephone rang – you answered – no one there.' Ashton put his passport away, showed her his wristwatch instead. 'Half an hour ago,' he said and adjusted the minute hand, putting it back to 16.05 hours to make it easier for her to understand what he was saying. 'That was me.'

A faint smile touched her lips. 'In a little while soon my husband come home,' she said quaintly. 'You wait – yes?'

'Yes, please.' The door opened wider and she stepped aside to let him enter the hall.

The computer-enhanced impression of the young woman who had claimed to be a spokesperson for Hizbollah was referred to the Identification Division of the FBI in Washington, DC, together with a brief description of her physical characteristics. The suspect was thought to be between five feet four and five feet six inches tall and to weigh approximately one hundred pounds. There had been a wide divergence of opinion as to her age amongst the witnesses questioned by the German police; the only thing they had agreed on was that she was over twenty-one but under thirty. Dean Rennert, head of the Identification Division, noted that at some time the suspect might have had her thyroid gland removed. If the scar was that obvious, he reckoned the operation must have been carried out in the last two or three years, which might or might not be helpful.

Although her country of origin was unknown, someone in Berlin had suggested the Middle East, which was all-embracing. Wherever the lady had originally come from, there were grounds for thinking she had spent a considerable number of years in America, possibly in Texas. The evidence for this was a tape recording of a conversation she had had with Police President Voigt, a copy of which had so far failed to arrive. Finally, she could speak both English and German fluently. It was presumed her first language was Arabic, or maybe Farsi.

In addition to combating organised crime, and Federal Law enforcement, the FBI was also responsible for National Security and Counter-Espionage. National Security entailed monitoring the activities of subversive organis-ations, neo-Fascist militias, extremist protest groups like Pro Life, who weren't above killing people, the Ku Klux Klan and far-out religious sects. The amount of infor-mation held by the Identification Division was awesome. As well as the vast library on convicted felons, the fingerprints of everybody who had served in the army, navy, air force, Marine Corps and Coastguard from World War Two onwards were on record. The number of people who had come to the notice of the FBI and found their way on to the data base as a result of their involvement with extremist groups was no less impressive.

Dean Rennert underlined the physical characteristics of the Jane Doe which he thought offered the most promising lines of enquiry. On a separate sheet of paper he wrote a brief memo. It read: 'Forget the crazies and religious nuts. Concentrate on left-wing activists and terrorist sympathisers but exclude fund-raisers for the IRA.' Then he sent for his senior computer analyst and told him to start trawling.

Roman Zborski was over six feet tall, thin as a rake and almost completely bald. His head resembled an upturned pudding basin with a two-inch fringe of wispy hair around the rim. In an effort to minimise his lack of hair, he had carefully trained long strands across the crown of his head. The smile which had been on his face when he let himself into the apartment faded when he saw Ashton waiting for him in the sitting room.

'No need to look so alarmed.' Ashton came forward to meet him, his right hand extended. 'Didn't your friend in the British Embassy tell you to expect a visitor from London?'

'Yes, but I did not think you would come here. It is very risky for me.' Zborski ignored Ashton's outstretched hand, walked past him and dumped his cheap-looking plastic briefcase in an armchair. 'If anyone saw you . . .'

'Nobody did.'

'We should have met on neutral ground. You had only to phone Maria and leave a message suggesting a time and place . . .'

'And you would have been there,' Ashton said, finishing the sentence for him.

'But of course.'

Like hell, Ashton thought. Ten to one, Maria would have hung up the moment she'd heard his English voice. And if by some remote chance she had talked to him and he had been able to make her understand, there was every likelihood that Zborski would have failed to show up at the designated RV. It was one thing to tell your case officer from the British Embassy that Pavel Trilisser was due in Warsaw on a certain date, quite another to disclose the Russian's detailed itinerary which would be known only to a few senior civil servants. It was the reason why Ashton had decided to corner Zborski when he was at home and feeling safe.

'What time does Trilisser arrive this evening?' he asked casually.

'You've missed him, his plane landed at 17.25 hours.'

'So who's he staying with – the Russian Ambassador?'

'Why are you interested in this man?'

'That's none of your business.'

'You are wrong, Mr Ashton, it is my business. I tell you nothing until I know.'

'What are you after? More money?'

'You think I do these things for dollars?' Zborski turned a bright shade of red and his voice rose in anger. 'I do these things for my country. Suppose you have been sent here to kill Pavel Trilisser? What good would that do Poland?'

'I promise you nobody is going to assassinate Pavel Trilisser. We don't go in for that kind of thing; the Foreign Office doesn't like it.'

'I am not happy, Mr Ashton. I need something more than your word. When you have the Russian bear for a neighbour you have to be very careful.'

For careful read wary. Zborski's father, Ladislaw, had learned that lesson the hard way. A reservist officer in the artillery, Ladislaw Zborski had been recalled to the active list when his anti-aircraft battery had been mobilised in August 1939. Assigned to the air defence of Warsaw, he had gone into hiding when the garrison had been forced to surrender on 27 September. The foundations of the Polish resistance movement had been laid the day Hitler had reviewed his victorious troops in the capital, and he had been amongst the first to join the *Armia Krajowa*, the Home Army. In 1939, the Polish Communist Party had refused to have anything to do with the organisation on the grounds that Stalin had signed a non-aggression pact with Nazi Germany.

The Communists had, of course, changed their tune when the Wehrmacht had invaded the Soviet Union. They had then demanded that the Home Army should attack the Germans at every opportunity regardless of the reprisals taken against the civilian population. It had not mattered to the Polish Communist Party that fifty Poles were executed for every German killed; their only concern had been to serve Moscow and assist the Red Army.

The discovery in 1943 that 4,500 officers taken prisoner by the Russians in 1939 had subsequently been murdered by the NKVD and buried in mass graves in the Katń Forest was something the Poles could not forget. Also buried deep in the national psyche was the memory of what had happened to units of the Home Army which had fought side by side with the advancing Russians. As soon as the Germans had been driven out of Lvov, the local Polish commander, his whole staff and several hundred rank and file had been shot by their so-called allies, while the survivors had been drafted into General Zygmunt's Polish Division which was loyal to Moscow. But the really poisoned chalice had been Stalin's cynical exploitation of the Warsaw Uprising. With the Russians virtually at the gates of the city, the Moscow-controlled radio at Lublin had urged the Polish Underground to attack the enemy. Thereafter, the Red Army had sat back for the next sixty-three days allowing the Wehrmacht a free hand to destroy the insurgents.

Born in 1949, Roman Zborski had spent nearly all his life under a Communist régime which had followed the Moscow line and denigrated the achievements of the Home Army. But the Poles had never seen themselves as a Russian satellite and Ladislaw had taught his son well. Although he had found it necessary to join the Communist Party in order to gain promotion to the higher ranks of the Civil Service, Zborski had remained a nationalist at heart and had always regarded Russia as a potential enemy. And Rowan Garfield had maintained this was the case when explaining to Ashton why the Pole was passing information to the SIS.

'I don't think you have been listening to me,' Zborski complained indignantly.

Ashton denied it but the Pole was right, he hadn't been paying full attention to him. He had been too preoccupied wondering just how much he could tell Zborski.

'We need Trilisser's help,' he said, coming to a decision.

'To do what?'

'To stop the Russian *Mafiozniki* from selling plutonium to terrorists.'

There was nothing in that statement which could be classified Top Secret, and declaring the task he had been given was not going to do lasting damage to the nation. The identity of the source might have rated the highest security grading at one time but after Gamal al Hassan had been murdered, the need for secrecy had died with him.

'Couldn't this be done through the usual diplomatic channels?'

'Pavel Trilisser and I enjoy a special relationship,' Ashton told him drily. 'We're like that,' he added and crossed fingers.

'Like my country and Russia.' Zborski shook his head. 'Why is it we are always underneath?'

'About Trilisser,' Ashton reminded him gently.

'He is staying with V. N. Ivanov, Minister Counsellor at the Russian Embassy. He has a large apartment at 52 Bory Promenada not far from the Warsaw Musical Society Building.'

'And the rest of his programme?'

'This evening he goes to the Opera House to see the ballet company perform *Swan Lake*. All tomorrow he will be at the Council of Ministers Building. Tomorrow night he will attend a farewell dinner in his honour at the Bristol Hotel. On Saturday morning he will fly back to Moscow.'

Ashton asked Zborski to repeat the itinerary so that he could commit it to memory, then quizzed him about the timetable.

'And how many are there in Trilisser's party?' he asked.

'Two. A junior official from their Ministry of Foreign Affairs and a secretary.'

'Well, now,' said Ashton, 'that wasn't such a terrible ordeal, was it?'

'That depends on what happens in the next thirty-six hours,' Zborski observed sourly.

The programme started running at 12.00 hours Eastern Standard Time and finished five hours later. The first cull, which was based on language qualifications and physical characteristics of the Jane Doe produced a list of twenty-six names. Of these, the vast majority had, at some time, worked for the government. Some had been employed by the Defense Department and had translated technical journals for Military Intelligence, others had worked as interpreters at the United Nations in New York while a few had been engaged by the State Department as tutors. All had come to the notice of the FBI because they'd had to be vetted before taking up their respective appointments. Not a single one of these had had the thyroid gland removed.

Regardless of their former security status, the twenty-six names were put through a second cull where the questions asked concerned ethnic origin, political activities and possible character defects of the subject. At the end of this programme, the original list was cut to just three names. In alphabetical order, they were:

Mary Jo Harnak, born San Antonio, Texas, on 25 November 1968. Caucasian (father German), blonde, blue eyes, height five feet six and one half inches. Weight 148 pounds. Subject educated UCLA, Arabic Studies. Anti-Semitic, fined 500 dollars by Sacramento District Court for malicious damage to Jewish property 17 May 1992. Last known address – 462 West Thirty-Fourth Street, Manhattan, New York, New York.

Louise Helen Kay, born Jefferson City, Missouri, 8 June 1960. Caucasian, brunette, brown eyes, height five feet four inches, weight 98 pounds approx. Bachelor of Arts Fulton University 1984, majored French, German. Politically active on campus – crypto-Communist, pro-Arab, fund raiser for Palestinian refugees, distributed literature supporting Popular Democratic Front for Liberation of Palestine. Wrote four abusive letters to President Reagan on subject of US subservience to demands of Israel. Embraced Muslim faith in 1989, changed name to Leila Khalif. Left US for Jordan 1990.

Thought to be still in Middle East. Mother deceased, father remarried, currently living Eureka Springs, Arkansas.

Noreen Tal, born Amman, Jordan, 26 February 1966. Dark hair, sallow complexion, brown eyes, height five feet five inches, weight 103 pounds. Trained as a nurse St Thomas's Hospital, London, England, 1985-1988. Married Karl Warlimont, German national, 19 July 1986 Paddington Registry Office. Separated twelve months later. Subject moved to New York September 1990, secured work permit, employed as staff nurse Roosevelt Hospital. Suspected of being implicated in bombing of World Trade Center. Detained Rikers Island, later released for lack of evidence and deported one week later. Present whereabouts unknown.

In forwarding the print-out to Dean Rennert, Head of the Identification Division, the senior analyst recommended that Mary Jo Harnak should be eliminated on the grounds that she did not match the physical characteristics of the suspect. Although Noreen Tal appeared to be the most likely candidate, he pointed out that she had disappeared without trace and questioned whether in view of this the Bureau should take any further action. There was, he thought, a case for a follow-up on Louise Helen Kay a.k.a. Leila Khalif. Photographs of all three women were attached to the print-out.

The Opera House or Grand Theatre was located in the Central District of Warsaw. Intended to be a showpiece replacement for the old opera house which had been totally destroyed in 1944, it occupied the whole of Teatrainy Square. Ashton thought the architect who had designed the building must have drawn some of his inspiration from the French Renaissance School epitomised by the Pantheon in Paris and mixed it with a large dollop of twentieth-century functionalism.

The ballet started at eight; Trilisser was due to arrive five minutes before the curtain went up. Although Ashton could have observed the Opera House from the monument to the martyrs of Warsaw across the square from the entrance, he wanted the Russian to see him. He had therefore positioned himself at the top of the steps, his back to one of the Doric columns where he was protected from the persistent drizzle. Nobody had bothered to put out the red carpet for the man from Moscow and the only police presence was a solitary prowl car away to Ashton's left at the corner of Senatorska Road.

The new free economy had not produced a great improvement in the lot of most people. Over half the audience were still poorly dressed by Western standards, but the nouveau riche were doing very well, thank you, the men in Armani suits, the women in little numbers by Calvin Klein and Yves St-Laurent and dripping with costume jewellery. Six years ago, the apparatchiks would have arrived in Ladas or chauffeur-driven Zils; today the emerging entrepreneurs and racketeers tended to own top-of-the-range BMWs, Mercedes, Volvos and Ferraris.

Trilisser and party arrived at 19.55 hours in a black Mercedes limo and were met at the foot of the steps by the front-of-house manager and two commissionaires carrying umbrellas. The junior official from the Ministry of Foreign Affairs wore an ill-fitting suit and appeared to be in his late twenties. The other member of his staff was an attractive dark-haired woman of roughly the same age who, even in high heels, only came up to Trilisser's shoulder.

As the party ascended the steps, Ashton stepped forward until he was almost within touching distance of the former KGB General. 'Remember me?' he said quietly in Russian.

Trilisser flinched as if someone had tried to slap his face and missed; then recovering his composure, he walked on into the theatre. As she neared the entrance, the woman looked back and glared at Ashton. He wondered what they would make of it when they returned from the ballet and found he had left his calling card at 52 Bory Promenada in their absence.

Chapter 16

It wasn't difficult to pick up a cab outside the Opera House or anywhere else in the town centre for that matter, but Bory Promenada was off the beaten track and Ashton thought it unlikely that any taxi driver would be cruising the area looking for a fare. The almighty greenback was, however, a very persuasive factor when you wished to retain the services of the cabby you already had. The Pole didn't know too much English and couldn't speak a word of German, but he could recognise Hamilton's portrait on a ten-dollar bill. Sign language also helped him to understand that the note was merely a down payment and that an extra twenty would be his if he waited for Ashton while he called on the Russian Minister Counsellor.

Number 52 Bory Promenada and the neighbouring apartment houses on either side were a little piece of Russia in the heart of Warsaw. Despite Hazelwood's absolute conviction that Trilisser wouldn't dare to raise so much as a finger against him in Poland, Ashton had an uncomfortable feeling that he was about to walk into the lion's den. From the outside, the building resembled the apartment house on Ujazdowskie where the Zborskis lived but, as he rapidly discovered, there were quite a few subtle differences.

The place was virtually a fortress. The first line of defence was a TV camera mounted above the lintel. The second and third lines didn't become apparent until he broke the invisible infra-red fence which automatically triggered two powerful security lights before he reached the entrance. The door was fitted with an electronic lock and looked solid enough to resist a 66mm anti-tank missile. The number of call buttons below the squawk box indicated there were only four apartments within. The names of the occupants were not listed. Faced with a multiple choice, Ashton pressed the top button and was answered by a harsh voice demanding to know what he wanted. Standing close to the microphone, he told the Russian he had an important message for Pavel Trilisser.

'Clear off, no one of that name lives here.'

'That's all you know,' Ashton told the voice. 'He's staying with V. N. Ivanov. Now let me in.'

'Who are you?'

'My name is Ashton, I'm a special envoy from London.'

'You should deliver your message to the Russian Embassy.'

'What I have to say can't wait until morning.' Ashton looked up at the TV camera above his head. None of the electronic defences was worth a damn unless somebody was monitoring them. It suddenly occurred to him that it didn't matter which button he'd pressed, he would still have ended up talking to a security guard. 'If Pavel Trilisser is not available, let me speak to Minister Counsellor V. N. Ivanov.'

'Impossible. You must go to the embassy.'

'OK. Fine. You've made the decision, but I wouldn't like to be in your shoes if the message doesn't get to Pavel Trilisser in time. Because, make no mistake, President Yeltsin is going to be very mad when he hears about it.'

Ashton turned away. There was no need to see Ivanov. The security guard would let Trilisser know that a Russian-speaking Englishman called Ashton had called at the apartment house claiming to have an urgent message for him. If Trilisser had been shaken by their encounter in Teatralny Square, the former KGB officer would be even more disquieted by the news that he'd been to 52 Bory Promenada. Ashton thought he'd done a pretty good job;

then, before he was halfway down the path, a security guard opened the door and called him back and suddenly the picture wasn't looking so rosy after all.

Ashton could have kicked himself for losing sight of the aim. Trilisser was the man he had to unsettle, not some damned security guard. He should have walked away when the man had told him to go to the embassy, but no, he'd had to go over the top and browbeat the Russian into submission. Now he would almost certainly be searched before he was allowed to see V. N. Ivanov and the bloody alarm and tear gas dispenser was in his raincoat pocket. No chance either of ditching it before he went into the apartment house. Although Ashton was now halfway to the sidewalk, the security lights were still on. He would have broken the infra-red fence several paces to his rear and the lights ought to have been extinguished automatically. That meant somebody had over-ridden the cut-out and put both lights on hold. In all probability, that meant he was up against at least two security guards.

Ashton turned about, unbuttoned his raincoat and holding it wide open, retraced his steps. He derived little satisfaction from observing that his deduction had been correct. There were, in truth, two security guards on duty.

'You want to search me?' he said truculently to the smaller of the two men. 'You'll find my passport in the breast pocket of my jacket.'

As the guard removed it, Ashton reached behind his back, tugged the left sleeve clear of the shoulder and shucked off the raincoat. Then he casually tossed the mac in the direction of the hall chair roughly six feet to his left. It could have gone horribly wrong had the CS gas dispenser made contact with the wooden frame or dropped out on to the floor. But he got it exactly right and the raincoat fell neatly across the seat.

He faced the security guard again, arms outstretched for a body search. The Russian returned his passport, tucking it into the breast pocket of his jacket, then quickly frisked him. It was tempting to ask if the precautionary measures meant they were expecting the odd discontented Chechen to visit them but their attitude suggested both men lacked a sense of humour and there was nothing to be gained by antagonising them.

'Do I get to see Counsellor Ivanov now?' Ashton enquired politely when the security guard had finished searching him.

Neither Russian condescended to answer; they had developed rudeness to a fine art. The taller man on the front desk picked up the internal phone, pressed one digit and then deliberately turned his back on him. He spoke in a low voice, the receiver close to his mouth so that Ashton shouldn't hear what he was saying.

V. N. Ivanov was marginally more polite when he appeared a few minutes later. Since the guards were not prepared to introduce them to each other, Ashton took it upon himself to do so and got a curt nod in return.

'A special envoy,' Ivanov repeated.

'That's right.'

'Presumably you are staying at the British Embassy?'

'No, and if you did telephone the Ambassador, he would deny all knowledge of me. Like I said, I am a special envoy.'

'So where are you staying in Warsaw?'

'The Forum,' Ashton told him unhesitatingly.

'And you have a message for Pavel Trilisser?'

'Yes. It concerns Gennadi Yasnev.'

'Who's he?'

'A former major in the GRU who can do him immense harm. Be sure to give Trilisser my name and tell him he can reach me at the Forum Hotel.'

'Why should he do that?'

'Because I imagine he would like to keep his job as Foreign Policy adviser to President Yeltsin.' Ashton picked up his raincoat. 'Please accept my apologies for disturbing you,' he said and let himself out of the apartment house. This time the security lights were extinguished before he reached the pavement.

The taxi driver was still waiting where Ashton had left

him. For that extra twenty dollars he would probably have stayed the night. Opening the nearside rear door, Ashton got into the cab, emotionally drained.

'Where you go now?' the cab driver asked him.

'The Central Station.'

'No understand.'

'The railway.' Ashton explained in basic English. 'Jerozolimskie Boulevard – near Palace of Culture and Science.'

The driver grunted, started the engine and made a three-point turn without either signalling his intention or bothering to check the road was clear in both directions. He headed west, shot across a main road and disappeared into a maze of narrow back streets which for the most part were poorly lit. Completely disorientated, Ashton asked him where they were.

'Mokotow District,' the driver told him. 'I know better place.'

'For what?'

'Nice girl – is that not why you go train station?'

'I want to make a telephone call.'

'You no want girl?'

'Not tonight.'

'OK.' The Pole shrugged his shoulders. 'You the boss.'

He made a right turn at the next intersection and headed north on a main thoroughfare. A few minutes later he pointed to a prominent building on their right just beyond a hospital and informed him it was the *Politechnike Warszawska*, the Technical University of Warsaw. 'Many students,' he added.

Presently, Ashton spotted a familiar-looking skyscraper up ahead, recognised it as the Lot Airlines building he'd seen on the way to the Marriott Hotel that morning and knew exactly where they were. On across Jerozolimskie Boulevard and into Warsaw Central Station, he then declined the driver's offer to wait for him, paid off the cab and walked into the terminus.

The clock in the main concourse was showing 21.18

hours; in London it was an hour earlier, in Washington, DC, it was ten minutes to four in the afternoon and British Airways Flight 217 had just landed. Deception time: 'Hi, Harriet, it's me, darling. Had a pretty good flight, just cleared Immigration and collected my luggage. How are you and Edward?' And in the background, clearly audible over the public address system, a Polish voice announcing the departure of the 21.50 to Grodzisk Mazowiecki. Terrific; you've already lied to Harriet and now you're lying again, and this time she will know it because despite a number of curious colloquial expressions on both sides of the pond, the English and the Americans do speak more or less the same language which was more than can be said for the train announcer.

Ashton veered away from the bank of pay phones with their PVC bubble hoods and ran straight into a hooker as he headed towards the exit. Blonde, pale, thin, knocking forty and listless; mutton got up as lamb in high heels, black leather micro mini, angora-wool red sweater and World War Two flying jacket. Mouth gashed in a smile that was as meaningless as the invitation she babbled to him in Polish.

'No, thanks,' he said and sidestepped past her.

A hand plucked at the sleeve of his raincoat and took a firm grip. 'Oh, you are American,' the woman said. 'I give you good time for forty dollars – Greek, French, any which way you like. OK?'

'Not tonight, not ever.' Ashton jerked his arm free and walked on.

'Faggot!' she screamed. 'Goddamn, lousy stinking faggot!'

The policeman standing twenty feet away looked through him, apparently not understanding a word she'd said. Ashton went on up the boulevard, turned left, and made his way back to the Forum Hotel on foot.

He would phone Harriet from the hotel room. What the hell did it matter if the charge did appear on the final bill? He was going to tell her the truth and try to explain why he had deceived her anyway, because if he didn't, it was bound to come out one day and how would she then ever learn to trust him again? But there would be no confession tonight, tempting as it was to get it off his chest. That would have to wait until they were face to face.

Dean Rennert had the greatest respect for his senior analyst and couldn't fault the way he had programmed the trawl. No area had been overlooked and he could follow the search pattern stage by stage. Rennert had no quarrel with the reason why Mary Jo Harnak had been eliminated from the list of three possible suspects. What he hadn't been able to accept was the implication that they should ignore Noreen Tal on the grounds that her present whereabouts were unknown and she would be difficult to trace. Consequently, he had deliberately arrived at the FBI Building on Pennsylvania Avenue half an hour before he was due to see Louis Freeh, the recently appointed Director, in order that he could spend the time in the Records Department studying Noreen Tal's file.

After reading the transcript of her interrogation by Federal Agents from the New York office, Rennert was satisfied that his initial reaction had been justified. In the time remaining to him, he wrote a brief memo commenting on the recommendations submitted by his subordinate and clipped it to the print-out. Then he signed a docket which allowed him to take the Noreen Tal file out of the records branch when he went to see the Director.

Louis Freeh had a quick and incisive brain. He could read a brief and assimilate all the salient facts in half the time it took the majority of men and women.

'Your analyst has done a good job, Dean,' he said. 'Please tell him so from me.'

'I will, Director.'

'As a matter of interest, whose idea was it to omit IRA sympathisers when programming the trawl?'

'Mine. And I stipulated fund raisers, not activists.' Rennert paused. While his father was of German descent, his maternal great-grandfather had been a company commander in the Tipperary Brigade of the IRA in 1920 and he felt compelled to set the record straight. 'It was a logical, not an emotional decision.'

'I'm sure it was, Dean.' Freeh compared the photograph of Louise Helen Kay, also known as Leila Khalif, and Noreen Tal with the computer enhanced likeness of the wanted terrorist. 'Who do you think most resembles the suspect?' he asked.

'Louise Kay, but for my money she's just an exhibitionist. What has Kay actually done apart from distributing subversive leaflets on the university campus, writing abusive letters to President Reagan and embracing the Muslim faith? Nothing. Tal is the one with the real track record. I know we had to let her go for lack of hard evidence but for a week or so she did live in the same rooming house as one of the perps charged with the car bombing of the World Trade Center. And she was in the vicinity of the building around the time we calculate the vehicle was left in the underground parking lot.'

'I'm not saying you're wrong, Dean, but I prefer to keep an open mind on this one. Let's fax the personal details and photographs of both women to Interpol Headquarters, St Cloud, for information to the Berlin *Kriminalpolizei*. We'll also let the CIA and Defence Intelligence Agency know the results of our trawl. OK?'

Rennert nodded. 'What should we do about the father of Louise Kay?' he asked.

'I think we should tell the field office in Little Rock to send one of their agents out to Eureka Springs to interview the man,' Freeh told him.

Ashton lay stretched out on the bed, legs crossed at the ankles, hands clasped together under his head. From time to time his stomach rumbled as if to remind him that, having declined the in-flight meal provided by Lot Airlines, he hadn't eaten anything all day apart from a slice of toast at breakfast. Yet he wasn't hungry; his appetite had, in fact, lost its edge after he had talked to Harriet. They hadn't quarrelled or even exchanged a cross word. On the contrary, she had been warm and outgoing, pleased to hear from him. Nor had there been any indication that she suspected he wasn't calling from Dulles International. He hadn't actually lied to Harriet, merely said it was the first opportunity he'd had to call her since his flight had arrived. He had also said he would try to call her again tomorrow around the same time but she wasn't to worry if she didn't hear from him because he would be home about lunchtime on Saturday no matter what. 'That's marvellous,' Harriet had said but she had also sounded a little puzzled as if unable to make out why he'd thought such a fulsome explanation was necessary.

The sudden jangle from the telephone made him flinch and he instinctively checked his wristwatch: 21.42 hours; the ballet still had eighteen minutes to run. Harriet? It couldn't be. How would she know where he was staying? Ashton swung his feet off the bed, sat up on the edge and slowly lifted the receiver. The English-speaking operator on the hotel switchboard checked his name, then announced she had a lady who wanted to speak to him. Before he could ask who was calling, she had put her through and he found himself conversing in Russian.

'I am Lisa Trilisserova.' The woman paused as if to give him time to draw the obvious conclusion, then said, 'I have been informed by V. N. Ivanov that you wish to see my father.'

'That's correct.'

'Very well, I will take you to him.'

'Hang on a minute—'

'I have a car waiting outside the hotel.'

'You're here now?'

'Yes, downstairs in the lobby.'

'How will I recognise you?' he asked, playing for time so that he could figure out what was going on.

'That won't be a problem for you, Mr Ashton. You saw me when we arrived at the Opera House this evening.'

219

'That brings me to my next point. How come we are talking to each other before the curtain has come down on *Swan Lake?*'

'My father does not like the ballet. He told the mayor he was feeling unwell and we left the theatre during the first interval.'

Ashton thought there could be an element of truth in her story. It was the sort of excuse Trilisser could well have made, but what had prompted it was another matter. Maybe Pavel Trilisser genuinely did hate the ballet and had left at the first opportunity. On the other hand, maybe V. N. Ivanov had contacted him at the Opera House during the first interval and he had decided that Ashton represented a threat he couldn't ignore.

'Are you still there, Mr Ashton?' Lisa Trilisserova asked in a sharp tone.

'Yes.'

'Well, are you coming with me or not?'

'I'd like to know where we are going first.'

'I've already told you, to meet my father.'

'Don't be obtuse. Are we talking about 52 Bory Promenada or some other place?'

'My father has no desire to be seen in your company. This meeting will take place on neutral ground in the open air.'

'So whereabouts is that?'

'You have five minutes to make up your mind,' she told him and put the phone down.

Ashton replaced the receiver, walked over to the window and drew the curtain back. Dark night, moon in the first quarter and not showing yet. Looked as if it were still drizzling. Did he go with Lisa to an unknown rendezvous or did he insist on meeting her father at a time and place of his own choosing? Suppose Trilisser would have none of it? What did he do then? Like the girl said, he had to make up his mind one way or the other. He turned away from the window, grabbed his raincoat from the wardrobe and checked to make sure the Close Quarter

Defence System was in the right-hand pocket before taking the lift down to the lobby.

Lisa Trilisserova was still in the blue chiffon number she had worn to the ballet but there was no commissionaire to hold an umbrella overhead this time and she had had to borrow a PVC mac from somebody who was much broader across the shoulders. She had also changed into a pair of low heels.

Pavel Trilisser was a tall, lean ascetic with startlingly blue eyes whereas Lisa's were brown. Furthermore, she in no way resembled the former KGB General, but if she wanted him to believe she was Pavel's daughter, Ashton was prepared to go along with the charade.

'Good evening, Lisa Trilisserova,' he said and dipped his head a fraction.

'Shall we go, Mr Ashton? I think we have kept my father waiting long enough.'

'I'm ready when you are.'

'Good. The car is parked in the side street.'

The black limo had been swapped for a smaller, beige-coloured Mercedes. However, the same burly chauffeur was behind the wheel.

'I want him out,' Ashton said curtly.

'What?'

'Tell him to get out of the car, give the keys to you and walk away. He isn't coming with us.'

For a moment he thought Lisa was going to object but then she apparently had second thoughts and bending at the waist, she tapped on the side window and spoke to the driver. There was a brief altercation in Russian, following which the chauffeur got out of the Mercedes, slammed the door and tossed the keys at Lisa before stomping off.

'There goes a happy man,' Ashton observed.

'He is very angry with you.'

'I'm going to lose a lot of sleep over that.' Ashton plucked the keys from her grasp. 'I'm driving,' he announced, 'but you get to ride up front where I can keep an eye on you.'

Ashton got in, waited for Lisa to join him, then started the engine and put the automatic gear shift into drive.

'Make a right turn on Jerozolimskie Boulevard,' Lisa told him sourly.

'OK.'

'And you're on the wrong side of the road.'

Ashton tripped the indicator and checked to make sure the road was traffic-free in both directions before he pulled away from the kerb and cut across the street. Filtering into the boulevard, they headed towards the Poniatowski Bridge only to make another right turn before they reached the Vistula. The avenue veered to the right and became much narrower beyond the Lot Air Tours building, then joined a dual carriageway where Ashton was told to make yet another right turn. A little farther on they turned left for a change into a potholed lane across open ground.

'Where are we?' he asked.

'Józef Pilsudski Park. There's a lake just ahead. When we reach it, make a U-turn and stop, then flash the main beams four times before switching off all the lights.'

Ashton followed her instructions without bothering to ask why the rigmarole was necessary. It was the sort of procedure which was second nature for a man like Trilisser who had spent most of his working life in the KGB's First Chief Directorate, the Foreign Intelligence Service. And in a curious way, Ashton felt reassured. The RV also looked right. Pavel didn't want to be seen in his company and on a filthy night like this they sure as hell had the park to themselves. There was nothing like a spot of rain to deter even the most hardy and passionate of lovers.

The lake was on his right at three o'clock; to the left at nine the orange glare from the streetlights in the distance silhouetted what appeared to be a stadium. Somewhere between nine and twelve o'clock he could hear a vehicle. No lights, the driver feeling his way in bottom gear and coming towards them. He could see it now, a small box masquerading as a car – a Lada. Well, you couldn't find anything more inconspicuous than that. Forty yards apart, the vehicle literally crawling along. Thirty yards apart, the driver coming to a halt and cutting the engine.

'My father,' Lisa Trilisserova said. 'We'll go and meet him.'

'No, you stay where you are,' Ashton told her and got out.

He walked forward and continued to do so even when Trilisser made no effort to leave his car and meet him halfway. One more precaution against anyone seeing them together? He heard Lisa get out of the Mercedes and scowled. Pavel's daughter was getting to be a real pain. The courtesy light came on in the Lada as Trilisser opened the door. Only it wasn't him; this man was too short and too well built. The junior official from the Foreign Ministry to his front and Lisa coming up fast behind him.

Ashton ducked and swivelled to his right. Something hard caught him a glancing blow behind the left ear before thumping into his shoulder. A sock filled with lead shot? No doubt the junior official from Moscow had one too. As Ashton swung round, Lisa stumbled past him and blundered into her accomplice. Two amateurs, he thought, but still dangerous. He pulled the gas dispenser and alarm system out of his raincoat pocket, aimed it in the direction of their faces and released a dense spray of CS.

There was no more effective nonlethal weapon at close quarters. The CS gas burned like hell, attacked the eyes, nose and mouth and made breathing difficult.

Lisa screamed, dropped the lead-filled cosh and rubbed her eyes. 'I can't see.' Her screams rose several decibels above the panic alarm. 'I'm going blind.'

Ashton grabbed hold of an arm and ran her to the lakeside. Behind him, the junior official was crawling around on hands and knees vomiting like a dog. He upended Lisa, pushed her face into the water, then yanked her upright.

'Face the wind,' he said curtly, 'keep your eyes open and don't rub them.'

'I can't breathe, I'm suffocating.'

'You can and you aren't.'

She choked on a glob of phlegm, spat it out and retched. When she was not vomiting mucus, Lisa mouthed a wide-ranging litany of swear words.

'Just shut up and listen.' Ashton shook her like a rag doll. 'I don't know if you are Pavel Trilisser's daughter and I don't care too much either way, but you tell him from me, if he tries to pull another stunt like this, he'll be moving out of the Kremlin to spend the rest of his life in the Lefortovo Prison. First thing Trilisser does tomorrow is telephone me because from here on I'm calling the shots.'

Ashton shoved her out of the way and walked back to the car. The junior official was still on hands and knees and in no state whatever to stop him driving off in the Mercedes.

Chapter 17

Ashton hadn't requested a wake-up call but he got one just the same at six o'clock sharp. Still half asleep, he reached out and lifted the receiver but instead of a cheerful voice bidding him good morning, the day began with a hint of malice. In a grating voice that set his teeth on edge, Trilisser asked him if he knew what the penalty was for grand auto theft in Poland.

'What are you talking about?'

'A beige-coloured Mercedes,' Trilisser said angrily.

'Would the licence number be 41856 dash 93?' Ashton asked him in a guileless tone. 'Because if it is, you owe me a vote of thanks.'

'I owe you what?'

'A little gratitude would not come amiss. Thanks to me, the police recovered your vehicle after it had been abandoned in Zurawia Road by a couple of joyriders'

'Liar.'

The police had also implied as much. Car thieves – yes, but joyriders were virtually unknown in Warsaw. Ashton, however, had had two things going for him: nobody had been around when he'd ditched the car in Zurawia Road, a side street one block from the Forum Hotel, and he couldn't speak a word of Polish, which had been a big handicap for the police. Every question they'd put to Ashton had had to be addressed through an interpreter. The consequent delay had given him plenty of time to come up with a foolproof answer; not that the police would have been able to shake his account had they spoken a common language. The best stories were always the simple ones and none could have been more straightforward than his. Last night, he had walked into the hotel, asked to see a receptionist who could speak either English or German and had told her that a few minutes ago, he had seen two young people running away from a car they had clearly just abandoned. He had wondered aloud how he should report the incident to the police and, surprise, surprise, the young woman had been eager to assist him.

'I doubt if the Mercedes belongs personally to you,' he said, interrupting Pavel Trilisser in the midst of a stream of invective, 'but the car's been vandalised. It looked to me as if they had used the key of their own old car to start the engine. Anyway the root was snapped off in the ignition, the courtesy light had been deliberately broken and one of the seats had been slashed with a knife.'

Ashton had inflicted the damage himself on the way back from Józef Pilsudski Park in order to support his story. It also accounted for the swelling behind his left ear.

'Incidentally, one of the joyriders tried to brain me with a cosh. A young woman, mid to late twenties, short dark hair, button nose. She came up behind me while I was grappling with the driver.' Ashton paused, then said, 'Recognise the description?'

'No, of course I don't,' Trilisser snarled.

'That's just as well then because I described her to the police.'

'I've had enough of this, I am going to hang up.'

'Yes, you do that and we'll talk again when you've cooled down – say eight o'clock.'

'Impossible, I have to attend a meeting.'

'Then make it seven thirty at the Bristol Hotel.'

'What is this?'

'I don't think we should discuss our private business over a party line,' Ashton said, and hung up before the Russian could come back at him.

In choosing to adopt a high-risk strategy, there was, he

calculated, a one-in-three chance that Trilisser would decide to sweat it out but when you were dealing with someone like the former KGB General, you needed to be dictatorial. And the Russian had already demonstrated that he could be manipulated; the fact that he had acted on the message Ashton had sent to him via Lisa was proof of that contention.

Ashton went into the bathroom, took a cold shower to freshen up, then shaved. Although the swelling behind his left ear was still there, it was now a good deal smaller than it had been last night. Returning to the bedroom, he laid out a complete change of clothing on the bed and dressed quickly. Breakfast consisted of an apple and banana from the fruit bowl that had been left in his room with the compliments of the management. While eating, he studied the Business and Tourist Map of Warsaw which he'd bought from the newsagent in the lobby. He then wrote a brief note on the hotel stationery and addressed the envelope to Pavel Trilisser, printing his name in both the English and Cyrillic alphabets. At ten minutes to seven, Ashton walked out of the hotel, flagged down a passing cab and, showing the map to the driver, indicated that he wanted to see the Tomb of the Unknown Soldier.

The monument was in Saski Gardens and lay within easy walking distance of the Opera House to the north and the Ministry of Culture and Arts, the Europa and Bristol Hotels to the east. The gardens were not yet a major tourist attraction, especially at a few minutes after seven o'clock on a not very promising morning. The sky was overcast and a force 3 to 4 north-east wind made the weather seem even chillier than it was. The taxi driver shook his head, bewildered that anyone, even a crazy tourist from England, should want to go sightseeing at such an early hour in the morning. Had he lingered in the neighbourhood after dropping Ashton off, he would have been even more convinced that his fare was touched with madness. As soon as the cab had disappeared into the distance, Ashton left the gardens and walked to the Bristol Hotel.

Like the mythical phoenix, the Bristol had arisen from the ashes of Warsaw, rebuilt stone upon stone to become an identical reproduction of the original. It was a throwback to a more gracious era between the wars when headwaiters in the Adlon chain wore tailcoats, boiled shirts and starched wing collars. But string quartets, marble floors and palm fronds in the lobby were *de trop* in the late twentieth century and whatever message the exterior appearance of the Bristol might have conveyed, it was essentially a modern hotel.

A cleaner was still hoovering the carpet when Ashton entered the lobby and went over to Reception. There were two front desk clerks on duty; approaching the nearest girl, he discovered her command of English was excellent.

'I want to leave this note for Mr Pavel Trilisser,' he said and produced the letter he'd written earlier.

'Is he staying here?' she asked, frowning.

'He will arrive very shortly.' Ashton smiled at her. 'I'd be grateful if you would give him the letter as soon as he does. Mr Trilisser is a representative of the Russian Government and the letter you are holding could affect the outcome of the talks he is having with your Council of Ministers this morning.'

'Are you from the British Embassy, Mr . . . ?'

'Ashton.' He took out his passport and waved it under her nose. 'I'm a special envoy from London,' he told her. 'Poland wishes to join the North Atlantic Treaty Organisation and Her Majesty's Government is determined that no undue pressure from Moscow should be exerted on Lech Walesa to withdraw the application.'

It was a long speech for Ashton and so full of blarney that it would have left an Irishman breathless, but it impressed the Polish girl no end and that had been the whole idea.

'How will I recognise him, Mr Ashton?'

'Mr Trilisser is taller than me, very slim and has the bluest, most unnatural eyes you've ever seen. He has also been told that an important document addressed personally to him is awaiting collection at the Bristol.'

'Then I will make sure he gets it,' the girl said.

Ashton thanked her, moved away from the counter and checked the number of one of the pay phones in the lobby on the way out. Yesterday evening while waiting for Trilisser at the Opera House, he had made a note of the nearest public callbox and knew there was one in Teatralny Square at the junction with Wierzbowe. He walked quickly towards it, conscious that he only had a few minutes in hand before the Russian was due to arrive at the Bristol.

At 07.28, he opened the door of the callbox, stepped inside and piled all the loose change he had on top of the coinbox. Was Pavel Trilisser going to be punctual or would he choose to be late? What would he, Ashton, do if he ran out of cash at a critical stage of their conversation? Ashton dismissed both questions from his mind, and looked at his wristwatch instead. On a more positive note, he assumed Trilisser would not be late for their appointment and allowed him a couple of minutes to read the note which erred on the generous side. As soon as the time was up, he lifted the receiver, fed the coinbox and rang the hotel. When the switchboard operator answered, he asked for Reception and was lucky enough to get the girl with whom he'd previously dealt.

'Remember me – Mr Ashton?' he asked.

'Yes, of course.'

'Is Mr Trilisser there?'

'No, he hasn't arrived yet.'

Ashton told her he would try again later and put the phone down. He rang a second time after waiting three minutes and drawing another blank, left the callbox and walked down the road to the Europa Hotel across the street from the Bristol. Unsuccessful once more at the third attempt, he then kept a discreet watch on the hotel, a vigil that was rewarded when Trilisser finally arrived some twenty-five minutes late in the same black limo he'd used yesterday evening. Ashton went back inside the

Europa, made a beeline for the one phone booth that was unoccupied and just managed to get there ahead of a French businessman who made his displeasure known with a few Gallic expletives. Ashton rang the Bristol for the fourth time, got through to Reception and eventually reached Trilisser.

'Turn about,' Ashton ordered him in a voice that brooked no argument. 'Directly across the lobby you'll see a number of pay phones. Take the one on the extreme left as you face it and wait for me to call. No questions, just do it.'

He hung up before the Russian could object and counted off forty seconds by which time he calculated even someone who could only get around with the aid of a zimmer frame should have crossed the lobby. He lifted the receiver again and ignoring the irate Frenchman who was tapping on the glass door like a demented woodpecker, dialled 26-66-97 only to hear the engaged tone.

The Frenchman started kicking the door which didn't improve Ashton's temper. He tried the number again and this time Pavel Trilisser picked up the phone.

'Let's keep this short,' Ashton told him. 'What message did Minister Counsellor V. N. Ivanov give you last night?'

'He said a man called Gennadi Yasnev could do me immense harm.'

'He will if you don't hand him over to us.'

'You're asking the impossible. The population of Russia is a hundred and fifty million–'

'This man is GRU,' Ashton said, talking him down. 'His picture appeared in *Izvestia* when he was awarded the Order of Aleksandr Nevesky for bravery against Afghan terrorists in 1983. In 1987 he was supposed to be a commercial attaché with the Soviet Embassy in Baghdad. He was recalled to Moscow in February 1990 allegedly on grounds of poor health. A routine X-ray is said to have revealed a shadow on the upper lobe of the left lung. Some Intelligence officers believe that was a cover story and that Yasnev was guilty of currency speculation. I don't subscribe to that view because you people would have had him shot had he been dealing in the money market . . .'

'This is all very interesting, Mr Ashton, but the GRU is an entirely independent Intelligence service . . .'

'Don't give me that crap; the KGB has always kept an eye on the Armed Forces. The Third Directorate was established for that very purpose. You even infiltrated your own people into Military Intelligence with the same kind of long-term commitment you showed in placing Colonel Rudolph Abel alias William Fisher in the States, and Konon Molody alias Gordon Lonsdale in England.'

There was a lot more he could have said but time was moving on and he wanted Trilisser to know what was expected of him before the irate Frenchman barged his way into the callbox.

'You are to pass everything you learn about Gennadi Yasnev to the British Embassy in Moscow as and when it reaches you. You are not to sit on any information.'

'You don't seriously expect me to walk into that bourgeois villa on Maurice Thorez Embankment, do you?'

'Of course not. You do what you're doing now; that way nobody gets to see you with our Head of Station.'

It was a tried and proven means of communication which Ashton had used himself the three previous occasions he had been in Moscow. In measured tones he told the Russian how he was to make the initial contact within twenty-four hours of his return to the capital. He also left Trilisser in no doubt that the SIS would pull out all the stops to destroy his credibility if he failed to comply.

'No arguments,' Ashton told him. 'You don't have any say in the matter, just get on and do it.'

He hung up and left the box. Determined to give Ashton a piece of his mind, the angry Frenchman followed him out into the street. He was still waving his arms and shouting when Ashton flagged down a cab and told the driver he wanted the Forum Hotel.

Breakfast didn't finish until 10.00 hours. It was, however, over for Ashton before he had time to order.

While he was consulting the menu, an embarrassed-looking receptionist approached his table and informed him that there was a small problem which she was sure he would be able to resolve.

The small problem came in the shape of two burly police officers who promptly arrested Ashton and informed him he was to be charged with rape.

The police barracks between Krochmaina and Grzybowska Streets didn't rate a mention in any of the official guidebooks Rowan Garfield had produced for Ashton's reading. Neither did the Pawiak Prison, though Ashton gathered he was likely to make its acquaintance before too long. The interrogating officer was a Major Janusz Karski who was sufficiently fluent in German to dispense with the services of an interpreter.

'I am a special envoy from London,' Ashton told him, 'and I insist you inform the British Embassy of my present whereabouts.'

'I understand you told the hotel staff you were a business-man. Are you now claiming diplomatic immunity?'

Ashton hesitated. The Foreign Office didn't know he was in Warsaw and his name had been removed from the Blue List when he'd resigned from the SIS in 1993, which meant that no one in the embassy would vouch for him. He thought of referring the police to Roman Zborski, then rejected the idea because it meant turning the spotlight on the Polish civil servant, and the one thing you never did was betray a source.

'Are you holding an identity parade?' he asked.

'No, it isn't necessary; the complainant has already picked you out.'

'When was that?'

'As soon as you entered the charge room; the complainant was watching the whole scene through a one-way mirror.'

'And what's the name of this invisible lady?'

'Larissa Grushkova.'

Yesterday evening she had called herself Lisa Trilisserova; this morning she'd had to use her real name because the police would have asked to see some means of identification.

'Has Miss Grushkova been examined by a police doctor, Major?'

'Yes.'

'Then he'd better do a DNA test on me.'

'That won't be necessary, Mr Ashton.'

'What are you talking about? The doctor will want to compare my semen with whatever traces were found in her vagina. There should also be seminal stains on her clothing and underwear . . .'

'Penetration did not occur,' Karski said flatly. 'There was no premature ejaculation either.'

'So what am I doing here?'

'You are to be charged with attempted rape, assaulting and occasioning actual bodily harm to her companion, Vasili Ivanovich Sokolov, stealing a Mercedes Benz 190 and deliberately vandalising said vehicle.'

Vasili Ivanovich Sokolov was undoubtedly the junior official from Moscow whom Ashton had last seen crawling around on hands and knees.

'Have either of those two made a statement yet?' he asked.

'They both have. Their evidence was recorded in Russian and Polish.'

'I'd like to see a copy of them, Major.'

'You may, once their affidavits have been translated into English.'

'There's no need for that, I'm fluent in Russian.'

'I can see you're a man of many parts, Mr Ashton.'

'And an important part of me is famished.'

'Why is that?'

'Because your officers dragged me off before I could order breakfast. Now I'd like something to eat and drink. I also want to see the British Consular Officer.'

'What's wrong with Her Majesty's Ambassador

Extraordinary and Plenipotentiary?' Karski asked sarcastically.

'That's a pretty good joke, Major, and I should treasure it if I were you because you are in very, very serious trouble. Matter of fact, I don't think you'll have anything to laugh about in the future if you don't get your act together and put a stop to all this nonsense.'

Ashton hoped he had struck exactly the right note. He had been cool, disdainful and intimidating without resorting to bluster. Unfortunately, Major Janusz Karski didn't appear to be the least bit impressed, possibly because he had heard it all before.

Dean Rennert was one of those early birds who made a point of being at his desk not a minute later than seven thirty. However, this morning there were others who had beaten him into the office, amongst them FBI Director Louis Freeh. Before Rennert had had time to open his combination safe, the phone had rung, summoning him to Pennsylvania Avenue.

'We have a problem with Louise Helen Kay,' Freeh said, getting straight to the heart of the matter without any preamble. 'The CIA claim she is one of theirs.'

'What?' Rennert was conscious that his voice sounded as if somebody had gotten a tight grip on his gullet and was trying to strangle him. He cleared his throat. 'That's crazy,' he protested, passing judgement before hearing all the facts.

'Nevertheless it's true,' Freeh said, unruffled. 'She is what's known as an agent in place.'

'Jeez-us.' Rennert exhaled slowly and closed his eyes. 'Don't those SOBs at Langley know what Louise Kay has been up to? For Chrissakes, she could be the bitch who walked into the *Schwarz und Weiss* on Berlin's Oranienstrasse, picked up a limey operative called Moresby and delivered him to his executioners. If I and the rest of the team are right, this is the sweet lady who revelled in the news that thirteen people had been reduced to offal by a bomb one of her so-called brothers planted in the English Bookshop. I mean, doesn't this mother-fugging Louise Helen Kay-cum-daughter-of-Islam Leila Khalif know which goddamn fugging side she's on?'

'That's a long speech for you, Dean.'

'I'm sorry, Director, I guess I got carried away.'

'It's understandable,' Freeh said reasonably. 'The feeling at Langley is that she didn't have much choice. Deputy Director Operations, Near East, thinks Louise Kay found herself in a position where she had to go along with it or risk exposure.'

'Thinks?' Rennert intoned with heavy irony. 'Does that mean he's just guessing, Director?'

'No, it's his informed opinion.'

'In that case, what do you want me to do about the information we've already passed to Interpol, copy to the Police President, Berlin? Do I come up with some cockamamie story about how our records were regrettably out of date and we've just learned that the lady died a couple of years back?'

'No, we leave things as they are, Dean. There's a risk involved in whatever we do but this way we actually improve her credibility with Hizbollah. If we shift into reverse, we could end up by putting her life in jeopardy. So we'll call on Mr Kay in Eureka Springs as planned and find out what he has to say concerning his daughter. I'm also arranging for our people in New York to check out Mary Jo Harnak at her last known address in Manhattan.'

Rennert began to wonder where all this was leading and in particular what, if anything, was required of this Identification Division. Director Louis Freeh did not keep him in suspense for long.

'Meantime, I'd like you to take another look at the trawl programme and see if we can't widen the scope a little. On reflection, it was a mistake to exclude the crazies and the religious nuts.'

'How about fund raisers for the IRA? Do we continue to leave them out of the reckoning?'

'Might as well throw them into the melting pot and see what rises to the surface. OK?'

Rennert nodded and had half turned away to leave when it suddenly occurred to him that a correction was needed to the data on Louise Helen Kay. 'We don't have a marker against her,' he explained. 'Nobody at Langley has ever indicated that she was one of theirs.'

'We'd better put that right, Dean.'

'So what colour code do we give her?'

'Grey,' Freeh told him, which said it all.

Chapter 18

The Third Secretary, Consular Affairs, was in his mid twenties, on his first overseas posting and decidedly earnest. He was also very friendly, which Ashton thought was a new departure for the Foreign and Commonwealth Office whose representatives in his experience tended to be aloof when dealing with Britons abroad. This was probably because most of the people who went to the embassy or the consulate had money problems of one kind or another and expected Her Majesty's diplomats to advance them whatever amount of cash they needed. In keeping with this apparently new approach, the Third Secretary had asked Ashton to please call him David when he'd introduced himself.

'Have the police charged you yet, Peter?' he asked after learning the reason why Ashton had been arrested.

'Not officially,' Ashton told him. 'They've taken my fingerprints and photographed me, head and shoulders first, then left and right profiles.'

'That's standard procedure; it doesn't necessarily mean you will be arraigned.'

'And if I'm not, what then? Do the police give us the photographs and the negatives?'

With his face already known in Moscow, Ashton had no desire to reach a wider audience. It could limit his employability and since he wanted to rejoin The Firm on a permanent basis, that was a handicap he could ill afford.

'Let's take one step at a time, shall we?' David smiled.

'First thing we need to do is examine the evidence and see what sort of case they've got.'

Ashton pushed the affidavits across the table. 'The top copy is in Russian, the one underneath is the Polish version.'

He wondered if he should offer to give the younger man a quick oral summary of the statements but ultimately rejected the idea. If David was fluent in Polish it was a good idea to let him read the evidence for himself. That way, Ashton figured, he would rapidly learn if there was a major difference between the two. In this instance, however, rapid proved to be the wrong choice of word. Watching the Third Secretary carefully reading each statement line by line, his lips moving slowly like a six-year-old grappling with a *First Reader*, Ashton came to the conclusion that 'eventually' might have been a more appropriate adverb.

'I see Larissa Grushkova and Vasili Ivanovich Sokolov both state that, having approached you to ask how they could find their way back to 52 Bory Promenada after getting themselves lost in the back streets of Warsaw, you volunteered to guide them but led them instead to Józef Pilsudski Park.'

'That's the weak part of their story. The fact is, Larissa Grushkova collected me from the Forum Hotel and when we arrived at the park, Sokolov was already there waiting for me.'

'I see.'

From his doubtful tone it was obvious to Ashton that he didn't. He wondered just what the consular affairs officer had been told before he had set off for the police barracks.

'What did Major Karski say to you when he rang the embassy?' Ashton asked.

'He didn't. I was told by an official at the Ministry of the Interior that a Mr Aspen was in police custody and was about to be charged with a number of serious offences.'

It was, Ashton thought, a typical cock-up. The official at the Ministry of the Interior had got his name wrong, which explained why Aspen hadn't rung any bells at the embassy. The quick solution was to disclose exactly who he was and what he was doing in Warsaw. But there was a major snag. The new Poland might have all the trappings of a democracy but Major Karski had started his career under a Communist régime and old habits died hard. Ashton was prepared to bet a month's pay that this interview room which had been set aside for them was wired for sound and every word of their conversation was being recorded. The tape would then be transcribed into Polish and analysed. In view of this, he wasn't prepared to say anything that wasn't strictly necessary.

'What about the rest of the evidence, Peter? Did you incapacitate Mr Sokolov before assaulting Miss Grushkova?'

'I didn't assault either party,' Ashton told him. 'I acted in self-defence and sprayed CS vapour in their faces.'

'Where did you get an aerosol can of Mace? You can be prosecuted in England for having it in your possession.'

'We're in Poland,' Ashton reminded him.

'Quite so. Miss Grushkova claims she managed to escape after hitting you about the head with her handbag.'

'Shades of Margaret Thatcher.'

'This is no joking matter, Mr Ashton.'

'Neither was the lead-filled cosh she used. She caught me behind the left ear with it.'

'Did you take their Mercedes Benz?'

Ashton sighed. 'You have to admire their audacity, David. They took certain undeniable facts and turned them around to fit their story. None of it would stand up in a court of law back home, even if the Director of Public Prosecutions were of a mind to proceed with the case. But as I pointed out just now, we are in Poland and obviously the police have a much freer hand over here.'

'And did you subsequently vandalise the interior of the Mercedes 190 after abandoning the car in Zurawia Road?'

'That's a matter of opinion.'

'Really? Well, in my opinion, Mr Ashton, the best thing I

can do is find you a good lawyer.'

'I wish to make a complaint,' Ashton told him.

'Indeed. What about? Police brutality?'

'Wrong. I've no complaints regarding Major Karski, he's looked after me rather well. The cuisine in this place may leave a lot to be desired but at least it's edible.' Ashton leaned forward, rested both elbows on the table. 'Have you got anything I can write on?' he asked in a low voice. 'A pocket diary, an old envelope, anything at all?'

David went through his pockets and brought out a slim appointments diary. He looked at it dolefully as though reluctant to despoil any of the blank memo pages at the back. Then a bright smile lit up his face. 'I know, why don't I summon a police officer and ask him to bring a few sheets of scrap paper?'

Ashton pinched his eyes between thumb and index finger. 'Yes, you do that,' he said wearily, 'and he'll bring a pad and stand behind me while I write a confidential note, and when I rip the top sheet off and give it to you, he will take the pad away and forensic will read the indentations on the second sheet under an ultraviolet light.'

'Couldn't you remove the top sheet and rest it on the table?'

'And if the police officer says, "Oh no you don't" – what then?'

'You don't think this is a little far-fetched?'

'This is a private message to my wife. I don't mind you and Mr Jarrard seeing it but I draw the line at anyone else.'

Ben Jarrard was the SIS Head of Station, Warsaw. The consular affairs officer blinked several times as if he had just been caught with a sucker punch to the jaw and was technically out on his feet. His mouth opened and for a moment Ashton thought he was about to say something which both of them would rapidly come to regret. But although this was only his first overseas posting and the Cold War had officially ended before he had joined the embassy, the young Third Secretary responded with all the aplomb of a seasoned warrior.

'Yes, of course you must send a message to your wife.' He gave Ashton the appointments diary and a Biro. 'It was very remiss of me not to have asked if there was anyone back home you wished to inform.'

On one of the blank pages at the back of the slimline diary, Ashton wrote a brief note to Ben Jarrard instructing him to contact Pavel Trilisser at either the Council of Ministers or at the residence of V. N. Ivanov at 52 Bory Promenada. The message he had for the former KGB General was simple and direct. Unless Larissa Grushkova and Vasili Ivanovich Sokolov retracted their statements by 19.00 hours, his continued detention by the police would be regarded as a hostile act and appropriate retaliatory action would be taken against him.

'This note will make sense to the recipient, will it, Mr Ashton?'

'Absolutely. We have a very special relationship.'

'And it will have the desired effect?'

'I think so.'

Ashton had based his strategy on the assumption that without consulting him, Trilisser's siblings had acted on their own initiative last night. When he had discovered just how much their misplaced endeavours had screwed things up, he had decided on remedial action. Ashton was sure Trilisser's aim had been to take him out of circulation until he was safely back in Moscow. If everything had gone according to plan, the police would have arrested him at the Forum Hotel before he departed for the Saski Gardens. But no plan was ever foolproof and the police had taken longer to react to the complaint than Trilisser had allowed for and, as a result, the Russian had been forced to keep his appointment at the Bristol.

Although his analysis of events was based on pure conjecture, it did explain why Mr Yeltsin's special adviser on foreign affairs had driven things right up to the last minute before putting in an appearance. And with a conference scheduled for eight o'clock, he had been unable to prevent the police investigating Larissa

Grushkova's phoney complaint. But at the end of the day, it was still only a theory and Ashton had never been inclined to put all his eggs in one basket.

'Mind you find me a good lawyer, David,' he smiled. 'Just to be on the safe side, you understand.'

Hazelwood sat at his desk in shirtsleeves, the made-to-measure jacket by Gieves and Hawkes draped across the back of his chair which he thought was better than hanging it from the old-fashioned umbrella and hatstand provided by the Property Services Agency. It was an exceptionally warm day for the end of September and the office was a suntrap. Air conditioning was a dirty word as far as the Treasury was concerned and they had statistics to prove that installing a Westinghouse model would be a waste of public money since long hot summers occurred only once every ten years. In a moment of inexplicable generosity, Roy Kelso had volunteered to provide a Venetian blind from the maintenance fund, an offer which the Administrative Assistant Director must have subsequently regretted because there was still no sign of the blind four months later.

Hot, sticky and unable to summon up enough enthusiasm to smoke one of his favourite Burma cheroots, Hazelwood was not in the best of moods. His temper was not improved when Garfield poked his head round the door to announce that his presence was urgently required by the DG. Muttering under his breath, he put on his jacket and left the office, locking the door behind him.

Stuart Dunglass looked grim, though it was hard to tell whether this was due to his ill health or whether something had happened that put the SIS in a bad light and therefore reflected adversely on his stewardship. Enlightenment followed soon after he had waved Hazelwood to a chair.

'Your protégé has been making waves again, Victor. This time he's got himself arrested for rape.'

'Actually, I think the charge is attempted rape,' Garfield

said, diffidently correcting the Director.

'Who's the alleged victim?' Hazelwood asked.

'A Russian woman called Larissa Grushkova.'

'Well, I take it no one here thinks there is any substance to the report?'

'With respect, Victor, that's not the point.'

Hazelwood began to wonder who was sitting in the chair – Dunglass or Garfield. 'You want to tell me what is, Rowan?' he rasped in a voice that grated like sandpaper on metal.

'He sent a memo to Ben Jarrard via the consular affairs officer instructing him to deliver an ultimatum to Pavel Trilisser.'

A Head of Station was only marginally outranked by an Assistant Director in charge of a department at Vauxhall Cross. In his heyday, Neil Franklin had enjoyed direct access to the DG, bypassing both his department head and the Deputy DG. Of course, that had been before Stuart Dunglass had been appointed to run The Firm, but there was no getting round the fact that Ashton had overstepped the mark.

'I don't think Peter meant to tread on Ben's toes,' he said, pouring oil on what he thought were troubled waters. 'I imagine he was trying to inject a sense of urgency.'

'Ben hasn't taken umbrage.'

'He hasn't?' Hazelwood frowned. 'Am I missing something?'

'The thing which both puzzled and alarmed Ben Jarrard was the fact that Ashton was able to tell him where he would find Pavel Trilisser. That's why he called me on the cipher-protected satellite link.'

Ashton knew the itinerary the Polish Government had arranged for Mr Yeltsin's special adviser on foreign affairs, which was more than HM Ambassador and the SIS Head of Station did.

'Peter must have got the programme from Roman Zborski,' Hazelwood said, voicing the only possible conclusion.

'And broke every rule in the book by doing so.' Dunglass took a sip from a glass of water. 'His first duty was to protect our Polish source and I'm afraid he's put Zborski at risk.'

'I don't believe Ashton had much choice, Stuart.'

Hazelwood didn't think it was necessary to remind both men that all they had been able to tell Ashton was the date' and time of Trilisser's arrival in Warsaw. They'd had no idea how long the former KGB General would be in Poland or where he would be staying. That had still been the case the morning of Ashton's departure when Garfield had seen him off from Heathrow. Ninety-nine times out of a hundred, there was no need to disclose the identity of the source but Ashton's mission had been the exception, the one case where the rules had to be waived. Everyone had mentally crossed their fingers, hoping Ashton wouldn't find it necessary to home in on Roman Zborski. Somewhat unrealistically they'd counted on Ashton dogging Trilisser from the moment his plane touched down, living in his shadow until an opportunity arose for him to make contact.

'Peter is a good agent,' Hazelwood said, striking a positive note. 'He will have checked to make sure nobody was following him before he contacted Roman Zborski. That's one thing we can be certain of.'

'Tradecraft is not the issue here,' Garfield said. 'I know Ashton's good. Unfortunately, due to circumstances beyond anyone's control, he was forced to adopt a high-risk strategy which has resulted in this bogus charge of rape. He may or may not have scared the pants off Pavel Trilisser but in Ben Jarrard's opinion, he's likely to have caused our Polish friend to have a heart attack.'

Head of Station, Warsaw was also convinced that whatever the outcome, the SIS had lost the services of their highly placed source for good. Even if his cover remained intact, Roman Zborski would never trust the British again and would take steps to distance himself from his case officer. Hazelwood had known Ben Jarrard ever since he had been a junior desk officer at Century House. Even in those far-off days he'd earned a reputation for being a pessimist, the sort of man who looked at a bottle of whisky that was half full and pronounced it half empty. Little, it seemed, had changed with the passage of time.

'Ben just hopes that we gain more than we stand to lose.'

'There won't be any doubt on that score if Trilisser delivers Gennadi Yasnev to us, Rowan.'

'I wonder.' Dunglass toyed with the glass of water, tapping a fingernail against the Waterford crystal to make it ring, then took another sip.

'Look at it this way,' Hazelwood said. 'With any luck he can lead us to The Czar. God knows Rowan's people on the Russian Desk have been working night and day to identify him but they are no closer now than when they started.'

'The Defence Intelligence Staff at the MoD haven't been able to assist us either,' Garfield added. 'Same goes for 22 SAS up at Hereford.'

'Well then, I suppose we'll have to await developments in Warsaw.' Dunglass consulted his wristwatch. 'Four thirty-five,' he announced in a weary-sounding voice. 'What time did you say Ben was hoping to catch Pavel Trilisser?'

'About now; Warsaw is an hour ahead of us.'

'Do you expect to hear from him again today?'

Garfield nodded. 'Ben will talk to me over the crypto-protected satellite channel if he has anything, Director.'

'Good. Please let me know what he has to say for himself.'

Both men waited expectantly until it finally dawned on them that Dunglass had nothing more to say. Hazelwood murmured something about clearing the in-tray and quietly left the office with Garfield hot on his heels.

'I don't get it, Victor,' he said once they were out of earshot. 'I mean, the DG specifically told me that he wanted to see you urgently and then he ends up saying nothing. He seems unable to concentrate on anything for

more than a few minutes. The grip's just not there.'
   'He's a sick man, Rowan.'
   'If you ask me, he shouldn't have come back.'
   'I think Stuart knows that,' Hazelwood told him.

They called Eureka Springs the Little Switzerland of America and with some justification in the opinion of Special Agent Leroy Manfull. Maybe the mountains weren't so high but you couldn't beat the scenery, which was a hell of a lot more varied than it was in the land of the cuckoo clock. It wasn't all fir trees out there; mountain ash, red oak, plane, maple – you name it, Eureka Springs, Arkansas, had it. And in the fall you never saw such a splash of colour, from the deepest of reds to pure gold. Born in Rosedal, Bolivar County, Tennessee, Leroy Manfull had never been out of the United States.

He was a heavy man, tipping the scales at 217 pounds. Since Manfull was also a couple of inches under six feet, most of his peers at the FBI field office in Little Rock would have said he was fat had they been asked to describe him. With his florid complexion, overhanging stomach and thick southern accent, which he liked to put on in the company of northerners, he was everybody's preconceived idea of a typical redneck. But nothing could have been farther from the truth. In 1965, at the age of seventeen and while still in High School, he had joined civil rights campaigners on their march from Selma to Montgomery, Alabama, under the leadership of Dr Martin Luther King. It was the memory of the brutal police methods employed by Governor George Wallace to disperse the marchers that had drawn him to the FBI after graduating in Law from the University of Tennessee. While there, Manfull had met his future wife, Sandra-Lee, a honey blonde from Pine Bluffs, Arkansas. Getting himself assigned to Little Rock four years after they had married was all he had ever aspired to.

Manfull turned off State Highway 62, drove through downtown Eureka Springs, past the red-brick Corner Store and on up the hill flanked by colour-washed, two-storey Victorian buildings. As the street got narrower and the turns tighter, he stole a quick glance at the town plan unfolded on the passenger seat.

The Kays lived on Osage Drive, which was not too far from the Inn of the Ozarks but a series of No Entries made it hard to find the quickest way there. He came round a tight bend and catching sight of a street sign, swung right beyond the Episcopalian church. To leave enough room for another vehicle to get past, he ran the '89 model Pontiac Bonnville up on to the grass verge on the left side of Osage Drive close to the hedge fronting the Kays' property, then crawled across the adjoining seat and got out.

The neighbouring property was some fifty or more feet away. Through the gap and on the forward slope of the opposing hill, he could see the upper half of a huge statue of Christ in solid white stone, arms outstretched, palms uppermost. Below the statue and out of sight in a re-entrant was a man-made amphitheatre where the great passion play was performed nightly. He walked through the gap in the hedge, rang the bell and was greeted at the door by a buxom redhead in her mid thirties.

'I'm Leroy Manfull,' he said and produced his shield. 'FBI, Little Rock. I guess you must be Mrs Kay?'

'Yeah, I'm Donna.'

'Your husband is expecting me, I called him early this morning.'

'Oh really?' Donna Kay frowned. 'He didn't mention it to me. You want to come in and wait for Jack?'

Manfull blinked. Kay hadn't said anything about not being in when he had phoned him. Little Rock to Eureka Springs was 182 miles; he hoped it wasn't going to be a wasted journey.

'When are you expecting him to return?' he asked.

'Any time now. Jack's down at the depot with a bunch of tourists. Soon as they're safely on board, he'll come home.' She stepped back a pace. 'So what do you want to do?'

247

'I'd like to wait for him.'

'Fine. The den's on the left. What can I get you – coffee, home-made lemonade, Seven-Up, root beer, or maybe something stronger?'

'A glass of lemonade would be great,' Manfull told her.

The den was a microcosm of the life and times, hobbies and interests of Jack Kay. Popular novels, biographies, several histories of the American Civil War 1861–1865, and a library of textbooks covering macro- and micro-economics crammed the bookshelves from floor to ceiling down the whole of one wall. The opposing wall was a picture gallery of photographs. An enlarged snapshot of Kay in uniform taken in London's Trafalgar Square towards the end of World War Two, sergeant's chevrons on his arms, air gunner's badge, 8th Air Force shoulder patches and looking no more than sixteen. Kay at university on the GI Bill in the immediate post-war years; on a hunting trip in the Rockies; on the landing dock with a marlin he'd caught off Monterey. On his installation as Dean of Phelps County Community College; with Donna on their wedding day and even more recently, in a loco engineer's uniform. There were, however, no photographs of his first wife and their daughter.

'Have you seen the one where Jack is shaking hands with President Eisenhower?' Donna asked.

Manfull turned about and accepted the glass of lemonade she was holding out to him. 'No, I was looking for a picture of Louise,' he said calmly.

'Is she in trouble again?'

'Have you heard from Louise recently?' he asked, ignoring her question.

Donna nodded. 'Ten weeks and one day ago. Thursday, 21 July. She always phones on the anniversary of her mother's death, loves to take it out on Jack and make his life hell.'

'Why?'

'Because in her warped little mind he killed her. Plain truth is Veronica killed herself.'

'She committed suicide?'

'You could say that. Veronica was a lush, drank all day and every day. Coming home from the country club that fateful afternoon, she wraps the family Chrysler around a tree and goes out through the windshield because naturally she had neglected to fasten her seat belt. Louise was sixteen at the time.'

'That's rough,' he said, but Donna appeared not to hear him.

'Sometimes I think Louise is out to kill Jack. He's got a bad heart and could have a fatal coronary at any time. Just talking about her gets him agitated. I'm telling you all this, Mr Manfull, because I don't want you upsetting him.'

Manfull recalled what he had said to Kay on the phone, recalled too how flat the man had sounded at the mention of his daughter. But more significantly, he hadn't said a damn thing to his wife before leaving the house.

'Where did you say Jack had gone?' he asked, interrupting her in the middle of a monologue on her husband's poor state of health.

'The depot, North Arkansas Railway; it's one of the tourist attractions.'

'Right.' Manfull swallowed the rest of the lemonade and returned the glass to Donna Kay. 'Thanks for the drink.'

'You're leaving?'

'Yes. There's no need for me to see your husband, you've answered all my questions.'

'I have?' she said doubtfully.

'As sure as I'm standing here.'

Manfull couldn't wait to get out of the house. Kay was trying to avoid him, could be he had driven off some place and wasn't planning to return until nightfall. He almost ran out into the narrow road, unlocked the Pontiac and opening the nearside door, scrambled across the passenger seat and got behind the wheel. Firing the engine, he shifted into drive and pulled across on to the right-hand side of the street. The temptation to floor the gas pedal was almost overwhelming, but this was touristville with narrow roads, bric-a-brac stores and pedestrians spilling over the sidewalks. He left the Pontiac in a parking lot near the bus station and followed the directional signs for the preservation railroad. The depot was a brick, late Victorian building with a raised bell tower above the ticket hall. The train on the nearest track comprised three day coaches in the predominately wine-coloured livery of the North Arkansas Railway hauled by a 4-6-2 steam loco.

The last passengers were boarding the end coach and Manfull had a clear view of a tall, thin, round-shouldered old man talking to the engineer in the cab. He didn't have to look twice to know who it was. Some instinct prompted Kay to look in his direction and although they had never met, the seventy-year-old suddenly turned away and broke into a shambling run.

Manfull called out his name and went after him. He saw Kay cross the track in front of the steam-driven loco and seconds later lost sight of him. He could hear the throb of a modern diesel shunting engine on a parallel track and above it a nerve-jangling scream. The sight which greeted him when he too crossed the inside track was easily the bloodiest and most unnerving he'd ever seen. What was left of Jack Kay was under the middle driving wheel of the 0-6-0 diesel.

Chapter 19

With a population numbering only nineteen hundred, a 911 call in Eureka Springs was answered by Carroll County PD. The community had its own volunteer fire department, funeral director and several doctors, one of whom had arrived on the scene minutes after receiving an urgent phone call from the train supervisor of the North Arkansas Railway. After pronouncing the victim dead, a formality required by the fire department before they could remove the body, he had then treated the engineer of the shunting loco for shock. A number of the people on the first coach who had witnessed the fatal accident had also looked pretty green around the gills when their tour guides had rounded their charges up and ushered them out of the depot.

Leroy Manfull had felt pretty queasy too at the time but he was over that now. The need to chainsmoke his way through a packet of Marlboro owed more to a guilty conscience than a vivid recollection of the mangled remains the firemen had removed from under the central driving wheel of the 0-6-0 diesel locomotive. Exactly why he should hold himself responsible for what had happened to Jack Kay was something he found hard to explain. Whatever the reason, Manfull was glad that he had been spared the task of breaking the news to Donna Kay. That lousy job had fallen to the doctor who'd pronounced her husband dead and who happened to be a close friend of the deceased.

Manfull had encountered a certain amount of hostility from the two police officers from Carroll County PD who'd answered the 911. The blond sergeant had gotten really uptight with him when he had refused to say what he was doing in Eureka Springs until he'd consulted his Bureau Chief in Little Rock. Unfortunately, the Bureau Chief had declined to give him the guidance he needed without first clearing the line they should take with Washington. By the time he'd called back, the number of law enforcement officers eager to question him now included a hard-nosed US marshal from Fayetteville some fifty-eight miles away.

'I hear what you're telling me,' the marshal said after Manfull had described what had happened. 'But what made Kay run?'

'Don't think I haven't asked myself the same question a hundred times and I still can't make it out. The guy hadn't done anything wrong so far as the Bureau is concerned, and he sounded perfectly normal when I spoke to him on the phone early this morning.'

'That's not what Mr Austin told us,' the blond sergeant from Carroll County PD said, chipping in with his ten cents worth.

'Who's he?' Manfull asked.

'The engineer Kay was talking to when you showed up. He said the old guy was definitely edgy.'

'His daughter is running around with a bunch of Arab terrorists. Right?'

'No, that's not strictly correct, Marshal. There's only a possibility that she is.'

'There's nothing like splitting hairs,' the sergeant said in an aside to his partner.

'The daughter is a real sweetheart,' Manfull said, ignoring the snide observation. 'According to the second Mrs Kay, she enjoyed making him miserable. Personally, I think there was more to it than that. I've a hunch she scared the hell out of him.'

'Enough to make him panic and run when he saw you?'

'That would be my interpretation, Marshal.'

'If you'd never met him before, how come he knew you were from the Bureau?'

'I can't answer that until I've questioned Donna Kay.'

And that wouldn't happen right away without incurring headlines like, 'FBI Intrudes upon Widow's Grief'. He could imagine how well that would go down with the Director.

'Remind me,' the marshal said. 'When did Jack Kay last hear from his daughter?'

'Ten weeks and one day ago.'

'Do you believe that?'

Manfull shook his head. 'No way.'

First thing he was going to do when he was back in Little Rock was to get the phone company to run a check on the Kay household. Louise Helen Kay a.k.a. Leila Khalif struck him as the kind of loving daughter who would place a collect call for the sheer hell of it. And if he was right about that it would show in the phone company records.

Little, ring, middle, index, thumb; Hazelwood drummed the fingers of his right hand on the desk as if performing a repetitive exercise on a piano. Six o'clock in London, seven in Warsaw and still no word of Ashton's release from Head of Station. Either Trilisser was cutting it damned fine or the Poles had prevented Ben Jarrard from delivering his ultimatum. There were a couple of other possibilities which Hazelwood instantly dismissed from his mind because they were equally negative. For someone who was used to making things happen, the realisation that he was unable to influence events was hard to accept. With nothing to do and time crawling past at a snail's pace, he was almost grateful when Jill Sheridan tapped on the door and asked if he could spare her a few minutes.

'With pleasure,' Hazelwood said, and meant it for once. 'What's the problem?'

'Remember the artist's impression of the woman who collected Moresby from that bar on Oranienstrasse?'

'I should do. Voigt sent copies to practically every agency under the sun. We got ours via Gerald Willmore and the Foreign Office.'

'One also reached the FBI and they came up with two possible names.' Jill Sheridan leaned forward and placed the thin beige-coloured folder she had been nursing on Hazelwood's desk. 'Louise Helen Kay and Noreen Tal; you'll find their personal details inside.'

Hazelwood opened the folder and spent less than a minute digesting the potted biographies of both women. 'How did we get hold of this data when it's not addressed to us?' he asked.

'Gerald Willmore told me the Kripo had sent copies of the artist's impression to Interpol Headquarters at St Cloud for worldwide distribution. I then rang the Interpol cell at Scotland Yard and asked to be kept informed of developments.'

She had also taken it upon herself to express an interest on behalf of MI5, the Security Service. Terrorists from the Middle East had been active on the streets of London from Gaddafi's hit teams in the early 1970s to the short-lived bombing campaign against Israeli business establishments in the early part of the current year. In those twenty plus years, the Security Service in conjunction with the Metropolitan Police Special Branch had compiled a vast data bank on Mid East nationals who had come to their notice for one reason or another.

'That was pretty smart of you,' Hazelwood told her.

'Really? I thought it was simply common sense. Anyway, we've nothing on Louise Kay or Noreen Tal and neither has MI5.'

'Why not? This Noreen Tal was suspected of being involved in the bombing of the World Trade Center. How did the FBI know she was in London from '85 to '88 training as a nurse at St Thomas's Hospital if they didn't ask the Met?'

'I can think of one possible explanation.'

'And another thing,' Hazelwood said before she could

say anything more, 'they also appear to know that she married a German called Karl Warlimont at Paddington Registry Office in July 1986. Don't tell me they plucked that information out of the air?'

'Tal was employed as a staff nurse by the Roosevelt Hospital on Tenth Avenue. The hospital administration would have wanted proof of her qualifications before they took the Jordanian girl on. My guess is the FBI got their information from the hospital authorities.'

Jill was right, he thought. There was something else he should have noticed: Noreen Tal had moved to New York in September 1990 and had been living there for over three and a half years when the World Trade Center had been bombed. The life she had led in London was history, so were the friends she had made. The FBI had been more interested in finding out what Noreen Tal had been up to during those forty-three months she had spent in New York prior to the bombing. And evidently they'd soon come to the conclusion that she had not been involved in the terrorist outrage.

'That's why the Bureau didn't approach MI5, Victor.'

'End of story then?' Hazelwood suggested.

'That rather depends on you.'

'Would you care to be a little more explicit?'

'I recommend someone with plenty of clout should ask MI5 to do some homework on Noreen Tal.'

'You've come to the wrong man,' Hazelwood told her. 'You should be talking to the Director General.'

'Stuart went home early this afternoon. I doubt very much we'll see him in the office again.'

Jill spoke with great authority, as if she were a cancer specialist giving a prognosis based on her expert knowledge. Her arrogance ruffled Hazelwood and it was on the tip of his tongue to ask how she could possibly know that. He bit it back because no one could match Jill's antenna; time and again she had been one step ahead of everybody else.

'What do you see MI5 doing?' he asked.

'Their first task would be to compile a nominal roll of everyone who had trained with Noreen Tal at St Thomas's from '85 to '88. The list should also include the teaching staff, State Registered and Enrolled staff nurses.'

'Why stop there?' Hazelwood enquired acidly. 'Why not include all the ancillary workers?'

'I don't want to sound snobbish,' Jill told him, completely unfazed by his sarcasm, 'but in my experience, like usually mix with like.'

Compiling the list was the easy part; once that had been accomplished, MI5 would have to trace and interview every name with a view to learning all there was to know about Noreen Tal. Specifically, they would be looking for anyone who might still be in touch with the Jordanian girl.

'Have you any idea of the number of man-hours this will take?' Hazelwood asked.

'Yes, it will run into thousands, but so what? Right now we have two women who appear to fit the bill; think what it will mean if we can eliminate Noreen Tal from our enquiries. We would then be able to concentrate all our energies on hounding Louise Helen Kay until her life becomes one long nightmare.'

'We?' Hazelwood repeated quizzically.

'Ourselves, the CIA, the Russian Intelligence Service, the *Bundesnachrichtendienst* and the Kripo in Berlin. I don't believe we have a cat in hell's chance of catching the people who tortured and killed Moresby and Gamal al Hassan but we can turn the spotlight on them and force the cell to disband. That would be a victory, wouldn't it?'

'Of a kind,' Hazelwood agreed.

'There's also her husband, Karl Warlimont. Let's not overlook him because even he might know of her present whereabouts.'

Listening to Jill Sheridan, Hazelwood had to admit that she had done her homework. To find Warlimont she had in mind a three-fold approach. This embraced the Registry Office in Paddington to ascertain where he had been living at the time of his marriage, the Immigration Service to see whether the German was still in the UK and finally the Office of Population Censuses and Surveys to cover the rest of the field.

'I admit the process will be time-consuming and the end result could be negligible.'

'That's why we're not going down that particular avenue,' Hazelwood informed her before she could make a case for doing so.

'What about my other suggestion?'

'I'll talk to my opposite number in Five.'

'Thank you, Victor.'

'He may turn me down,' Hazelwood warned.

'Perhaps you could sweeten the pill by offering to share the workload once they've produced the list of nurses and trainees?'

'I see. How many desk officers can you spare from your department?'

'Well, none, but wouldn't something like this be right up Peter Ashton's street?'

'I think they'll want a bigger contribution from us than just one man, good as Peter undoubtedly is.'

'Couldn't Roy Kelso let you have one of his vetters?'

'Like who, for instance?'

'Brian Thomas?'

Her suggestion came as no surprise to Hazelwood. Even as he asked the question, he had known she would nominate the ex-Detective Chief Superintendent who had made Henry Clayburn get all hot and bothered under the collar. There was, he thought, no one quite like Jill Sheridan for killing two or even three birds with one stone.

The detention cells at the police barracks were an improvement on Moscow's Lefortovo Prison but that wasn't saying a lot. Although the food was better in Warsaw, you were still looking at four blank walls, a bedboard on the floor and a shatterproof glass slit high up near the ceiling which allowed a glimmer of daylight into the room. However, compared with the treatment he had received at the hands of the Russian militiamen who'd arrested him, Ashton reckoned the Polish law enforcement officers had behaved like perfect gentlemen. In Moscow there had been no hope of an early release; in Warsaw he had every reason to believe that he wouldn't see Pawiak Prison from the inside. All the same, he was beginning to think he might have been a shade optimistic in his assessment when one of the uniformed officers unlocked the door and Major Karski walked into the cell.

'If you would like to come with me, Herr Ashton,' he said in German.

'Where are we going?'

'To collect your personal effects from the property room.'

'You mean I'm free to go?'

'We've no longer any reason to detain you. We have, of course, informed the consular affairs officer at the British Embassy of our decision.'

Ashton followed Major Karski out into the corridor and instinctively fell in step with him. 'What made you change your mind?' he asked.

'Larissa Grushkova has withdrawn her allegation. She now says you are not the man who attacked her last night. Her friend, Vasili Ivanovich Sokolov, admits to making a similar mistake.'

'I don't remember lining up on an identity parade.'

'We dispensed with that formality,' Karski said in a droll voice. 'They looked at you through a one-way mirror in the charge room. Saved a lot of time.'

'How long ago was this?'

'Approximately twenty minutes. I wanted them safely out of the way before you were released.'

'I wouldn't have made any trouble, Major.'

'Perhaps not, Herr Ashton, but I don't believe in leaving things to chance.'

Neither did the sergeant in charge of the property room. Through Karski, he insisted Ashton count the money in his wallet to make sure it was all there. Ashton was then required to sign a docket acknowledging the return of his passport, wristwatch, airline ticket and wallet containing 750 US dollars, 5280 zlotys, Gold Mastercard and a head and shoulders snapshot of Harriet.

The Omega was showing 18.25 hours, which was exactly thirty-five minutes inside the deadline he had set Trilisser. But since Karski admitted delaying his release in order to avoid a possible confrontation with Grushkova and Sokolov, it was evident the Russian had wasted no time in complying with the ultimatum Ben Jarrard had delivered.

'I'm sorry we had to arrest you, but we had no choice.'

'Don't worry about it, Major.' Ashton grinned. 'I'm not a man to harbour a grudge.'

'Please, I would personally like to drive you back to your hotel. Will you allow me to do that?'

'It would be my pleasure, Major,' Ashton told him.

You could tell the people who were on to a good thing in the new Poland by the top of the range BMWs, Mercedes, Volvos, Audis and Maseratis they rode around in. Like their uniformed colleagues, the criminal investigation officers had to make do with a Lada Riva, one of the many Fiat models of the early 1970s which had been built under licence throughout the old Eastern Bloc. Whether unmarked or not, the vehicle was a dead giveaway.

'Try shadowing a suspect in a car like this,' Karski said. 'Soon as he sees a Lada in the rear-view mirror, he knows who you are.'

Ashton got the impression that, in the opinion of most police officers, having to observe the new procedures for interviewing a suspect and the need to advise every wrongdoer of their rights were the main reasons for the increasing crime rate. Several complaints later they arrived at the Forum and parted company.

There was a note waiting for Ashton when he collected his room key from reception. Addressed to him in spidery handwriting, the enclosed invitation was the Russian equivalent of 'Mr Pavel Trilisser requests the pleasure of Mr Ashton's company at the Bristol Hotel on Friday, 30 September at 19.45 hours'. There was no RSVP or any indication of the sort of hospitality he could expect to receive, only a claim that the get-together would be to their mutual advantage.

For sheer effrontery, Ashton thought, the former KGB General was hard to beat. Trilisser's minions had tried to put him in hospital and when that plan had miscarried, Larissa Grushkova had alleged he'd tried to rape her. Now, despite everything that had happened, Trilisser calmly assumed he would agree to meet him.

Ashton took the lift up to his room on the eleventh floor. On the last sheet of hotel stationery in the folder on the writing desk, he wrote a brief letter to Ben Jarrard. It read: 'In case nobody at the Embassy speaks Russian, the enclosed is an invitation from Pavel Trilisser to meet him at the Bristol Hotel tonight. Since I don't believe the man is foolish enough to chance his arm a third time, I've decided to take him up on it.'

If London enquired after his whereabouts on Monday, Head of Station, Warsaw would know that he'd got it wrong. Ashton folded the note in two, slid it into an envelope with the invitation from Trilisser and addressed the letter to The Consular Affairs Officer, The British Embassy, Number 1 Aleja Róz, Warsaw. Then he rang the Lot Airlines desk at the airport and managed to get himself on Flight L0281 to Heathrow, departing at 07.55 hours. Before leaving the hotel, he checked the internal letter rate with the concierge, bought a stamp at the desk and mailed the letter.

Seven years ago, any communication addressed to the British Embassy would have been intercepted, opened and read by the Polish Security Force, the SB. Depending on its content, the letter would then either be conveniently lost in the post or sent on to the Embassy once a highly skilled technician had reinserted the correspondence with the aid of a thinner version of the metal key used to open a tin of sardines. But in this new enlightened era, Ashton had every confidence that the letter would be delivered untouched and unseen by the Secret Police.

The invitation from Trilisser had specified the Paderewski Suite named in honour of the Polish President and concert pianist of yesteryear who had been the principal shareholder of the old Bristol Hotel between the wars. The Russian was on his own – no junior official from the Ministry of Foreign Affairs, no Larissa Grushkova and more importantly, no muscle-bound bodyguards.

'I wondered if you would come,' Trilisser said and offered his hand in a perfunctory gesture of friendship.

Without thinking, Ashton automatically shook hands with him. 'I was curious to hear what you had to say.'

'It concerns a *Mafiozniki* they call The Czar. I wanted you to know that we are equally determined to discover his true identity and deal with him. The Police Chief of Moscow, Major General Gurov, has been ordered by me personally to give this task absolute priority.'

'Well, bully for you,' Ashton said caustically.

'However, I doubt if Major General Gurov will be successful.'

'You do surprise me.'

'I am by no means convinced that this so-called Czar is to be found in Moscow.'

'Oh yes? Suppose you tell me how you reached that conclusion?'

'My information on The Czar came from our resident in Berlin. Where did yours come from, Mr Ashton?'

'The CIA – also in Berlin.'

'You take my point then?'

Ashton nodded. There was only one conclusion to be drawn. Provided Trilisser's claim could be taken as gospel, then neither the CIA station in Berlin nor the equivalent cell of the Russian Intelligence Service would ever have heard of The Czar had he not been operating on their bit of real estate. It was of course a mighty big proviso. The decommissioning of the Soviet nuclear arsenal and the fear that some munitions might end up in the wrong hands was a constant nightmare. Should a number of sub kiloton artillery shells go astray, any request by President Yeltsin for a further two-hundred-billion-dollar loan to keep the Russian economy afloat was likely to be rejected out of hand. Given these circumstances, Trilisser had good reason to pretend that The Czar was out of Moscow's reach.

'It pains me to admit this, Mr Ashton, but the withdrawal of our armed forces from the former German Democratic Republic was not conducted with the efficiency one associated with the Red Army.'

'And not every last round was backloaded from the ammunition depots in the Eastern Zone?'

'There is that possibility,' Trilisser said, and began to steer him towards the door.

'Is there anything else you would like me to pass on to London?'

'I don't think so.'

'Enjoy your dinner then.'

'Well, I am the guest of honour.'

Ashton opened the door, then looked back. 'A word of advice,' he said. 'Stick to Gennadi Yasnev; he's real and we expect the RIS to find him.'

'If he exists, they'll get him.'

'Alive.'

'There's always that hope.'

Ashton left the Paderewski Suite, took a lift down to the lobby and walked out of the hotel. Trilisser had wanted to remind him of their last meeting and was counting on this fact to substantiate the suggestion he had tried to plant in his mind.

'Nice try,' Ashton said aloud, 'but it isn't going to work.'

The *Schwarz und Weiss* was always crowded on a Friday night. By the time Kommissar Eicke arrived at ten after eight, the place was heaving and the clientele were reduced to breathing by numbers. It therefore took him a few minutes to spot the transvestite who called himself Claudia. Usually she was to be found in one of the booths; this evening however Claudia was perched on one of the bar stools having an intimate conversation with an athletic-looking gay in skin-tight black leather jeans and a matching waistcoat. For reasons that had nothing to do with sartorial taste, this had deliberately been left unbuttoned for the purpose of displaying a large gold medallion and a hairless but well-muscled chest that glistened with oil. They were locked in a passionate embrace when Eicke tapped Claudia on the shoulder and spoiled things.

'This will only take a second,' he growled and thrust the facsimile the Kripo had received from the FBI under her nose. 'Just say which of these two women is the one you described to the police artist.'

'That one,' Claudia said unhesitatingly and pointed to Noreen Tal.

Eicke thanked her, went looking for the waiter who'd pressed one beer after another on Moresby and asked him the same question, only for the man to pick out Louise Helen Kay. The bartender who had also helped the Kripo to produce the likeness didn't think it was either woman.

Chapter 20

Until almost the last minute Ashton hadn't known whether or not Harriet would come with him. She had been very receptive when he'd told her they had been invited to spend Sunday afternoon on the river at Marlow and had only turned against the idea when he had mentioned that Hazelwood would be there. Suddenly there had been a hundred and one difficulties, all centred around four-month-old Edward, which made the whole thing impracticable.

Harriet had never liked Victor and believed the Deputy DG abused the loyalty shown him. Eight days ago Ashton had returned from Warsaw still nursing a swelling behind the left ear the size of a sparrow's egg and had confessed to deceiving her. 'No excuses,' Ashton had told her and had waited for the fireworks, but most of Harriet's anger had been directed at Victor Hazelwood on account of the letter from Roy Kelso which the postman had delivered that same morning. It had offered her the post of resident housekeeper on a retainer of £10,000 per annum, an opening which Victor had indicated might be hers when they had moved into 84 Rylett Close. The letter couldn't have arrived at a more inopportune moment; the timing had convinced Harriet that Victor had only made the offer in writing to keep her off his back.

'I don't care what you say, Peter,' she had told him fiercely, 'he talked you into going. And when that letter was posted, he'd already heard that you had been arrested.'

265

And there the matter was left until he was about to leave, when Harriet had appeared with Edward strapped into a baby seat and had blithely announced that they were joining him. In the two years Ashton had known Harriet, she had never ceased to surprise him. Grateful for her company, he did not ask what had prompted her to change her mind until they were a mile from Junction 4 on the M4 Motorway.

'I thought my presence might deter Victor.'

'From doing what?' he asked.

'Sending you to Outer Mongolia.'

Harriet was noted for her dry sense of humour and he wondered if what she had just said was one of her famous throwaway lines. It was difficult to tell because she was sitting with Edward in the back of the Vauxhall Cavalier and he couldn't see her face in the rear-view mirror.

'Who did you say was lending us this cabin cruiser?' she asked.

'Cyrus Verlander.' Ashton moved into the slow lane, then tripped the indicator to show he was leaving the motorway. 'But he isn't coming along. Our host this afternoon is Walter Maryck.'

'The name sounds familiar.'

'He's the CIA Chief in London. His wife's name is Debra and they have two children, a nine-year-old boy and a girl of eight.'

'And what does this Cyrus Verlander do for a living?'

'The man is a film producer, raises money all over the place.'

And did very well out of it too from what Hazelwood had told him. Verlander was the proud owner of The Oaks, a six-bedroom, twentieth-century, mock Tudor riverside house set in two acres of prime real estate a mile outside Marlow in the direction of Crookham. Within easy commuting distance of London, it would, Hazelwood reckoned, even in the recession-hit housing market, still fetch a cool one and a half million should Verlander ever consider selling it.

'Not much farther now,' Ashton said.

'Doesn't matter, Edward's fast asleep.'

Ashton dipped into the pocket of his plaid shirt, took out the sketchmap Hazelwood had photocopied for him and laid it on the adjoining seat. Following the directions, he drove through Marlow, crossed the suspension bridge over the Thames and turned left beyond the Compleat Angler. Five minutes later, he made another left turn into a narrow lane that led to The Oaks. A directional sign planted in the grass verge pointed the way to the boathouse and landing dock.

There were two cars parked on the grass to the right of the boathouse, Hazelwood's Rover 800 and a sleek, dark blue Mercedes that obviously belonged to the Marycks. The whole nuclear family was there, mother, father and two children, all of them casually dressed for a trip on the river but looking as if they'd stepped out of the centrefold of a glossy fashion magazine. Hazelwood was his usual dishevelled self and was minus Alice.

'Sensible woman,' Harriet murmured.

Edward started yelling the moment he was lifted out of the car and didn't stop until his mouth closed round the rubber teat of the bottle Harriet had thought to bring with her along with enough Pampers, cleansing lotion, cotton wool and baby foods to open a branch of Mothercare. The Maryck kids thought he was a pain and wrinkled their noses in disgust.

The cabin cruiser looked brand-new and was the last word in luxury. Judging by the boat shows he had seen on television, Ashton thought Cyrus Verlander couldn't have seen much change from £300,000. For that kind of money the movie producer had got himself a fifty-footer with a flying bridge, a well deck large enough to hold a small drinks party, a six-berth cabin, galley, diner, closet, shower, washbasin and a powerful twin six diesel. In what was obviously a well-rehearsed scenario, Debra Maryck suggested Harriet would feel a lot safer with her and the children in the well deck. Following another suggestion,

Ashton found himself casting off the mooring lines fore and aft before joining the other two men on the flying bridge.

Maryck started the engine, engaged drive and then headed upstream. 'Remember that tape you gave me?' he asked, looking at Hazelwood.

'Yes. Is that why the three of us are here on the river on a Sunday afternoon?'

'You could say that. Fact is, I sent the tape on to Langley for attention Deputy Director Operations, and he had the guys on the Near East Desk listen to it. And they made a positive ID. The spokeswoman is Louise Helen Kay.'

'Oh, shit,' Hazelwood said wearily. 'We've wasted God knows how many man hours on Noreen Tal.'

'That's a bit of an exaggeration, isn't it?' Ashton said quietly. 'I only got the list of names on Friday morning; all I've done is make a few phone calls.'

'I was referring to the Security Service; they put the list of nurses together.'

'The thing is, she's one of ours,' Maryck told them in a low voice.

Hazelwood blinked. 'Would you mind repeating that?'

'Louise Kay is an agent in place.'

'When did you learn this?'

'Last Tuesday.'

'So why did you withhold the information from us until now, Walter?'

'Because it was addressed to me personally. There was also a caveat which read "FOR US EYES ONLY".'

In ignoring that stricture, Ashton thought it likely that Maryck had committed an indictable offence under Federal Law. Faced with a long term of imprisonment if he was arraigned and convicted, Ashton reckoned it was no wonder that the American had gone to extreme lengths to set up a clandestine meeting with British Intelligence.

'Tell me something,' Hazelwood said. 'Did Louise Kay contact her case officer before the English Bookshop was bombed?'

'I don't know, Victor.'

'Well, has anyone heard from her since then?'

'If anyone has, Deputy Director Operations didn't see fit to inform me.'

Approaching a convex loop in the river, Maryck eased back on the throttle. By the second week in October, most pleasure craft would normally have disappeared from the water, having been laid up for the winter. But this Sunday afternoon happened to be warm and sunny and that general rule of thumb wasn't applicable.

'Maybe she never had an opportunity to make contact,' Maryck continued. 'Perhaps the other members of the cell were watching her too closely?'

Hazelwood looked sceptical and from his tone of voice Ashton was pretty sure the American didn't believe it either. If Maryck had come to the conclusion that Louise Kay had changed sides, it would explain what had motivated him to ignore the instructions he had received from Langley.

'I'll tell you one thing, Victor. That Police President in Berlin is one hell of a smart cookie. He not only sends everything he has on the mystery woman to Interpol St Cloud in the sure knowledge that one of the packs will go to the FBI, he also drops a bundle on Caspar Lemberg and your Consul General in Berlin.'

'I don't mean to sound rude,' Hazelwood said, 'but could you please get to the point, Walter?'

'The point is the FBI had already told Interpol that Louise Kay was a possible suspect before we informed the Bureau that she was one of ours. A number of our people at Langley wanted the FBI to cable Interpol retracting the information but were overruled by the Deputy Director Operations. He figured it would help to strengthen her cover if she remained on the wanted list.'

'But you think Louise Kay doesn't need to have her cover embellished because she's no longer on your team. Is that it?'

'You want to know what really bothers the hell out of

me, Victor? It's having one American and one British agent
in the same cell. What are the odds against a coincidence
like that?'

In Ashton's experience, there were never more than five
terrorists in any one cell. 'About a trillion to one,' he said,
quickly answering Maryck's question. 'I believe there was
more than one cell operating in Berlin. Furthermore, I
don't think either the SIS or the CIA had an agent in place.'

'Would you care to enlarge on that statement?'
Hazelwood said ominously.

'When did a terrorist cell need more than one PR representative?'

According to Willie Baumgart, the Kripo had received
two anonymous phone calls the day the bodies of Moresby
and Gamal al Hassan had been found in the builder's yard.
The man had called Gamal al Hassan a traitor and said he'd
been executed. The woman had made her entrance
approximately forty-eight hours later following the
destruction of the English Bookshop.

'There were two teams,' Ashton continued. 'One lot was
there to protect the money man while the second group
were the designated custodians of the atomic weapons.
Could be they were also tasked to carry out the nuclear
strikes.'

'Strikes?' Hazelwood queried.

'I doubt if these people went into the market place to
buy just one device.'

And if they were of a mind to acquire sub kiloton
munitions, the *Mafiozniki* would want to be sure of a
sizeable order before they were prepared to do business
with Hizbollah.

'Why don't you look into your crystal ball again and tell
us how many 130mm shells they're after?' Hazelwood said
acidly. 'Is the order in single figures or double?'

Ashton recognised the tactic and wasn't offended. This
was Hazelwood acting the part of the aggressive sceptic,
pushing him to justify his assumptions to see if he had
thought it through. 'Single, over two but under nine. Every

round above five increases the risk of interception while the munitions are in transit.'

'So money isn't a limiting factor?'

'Not if the Iranians or Colonel Gaddafi are bankrolling them.'

And they would need every penny they could get from their backers. Whatever the true cost of a 130mm nuclear warhead, the purchase price would be inflated several hundred per cent. There were palms to be greased: the officer commanding and senior staff of the ammunition depot, the 'mules' who would transport the nukes, the border guards, customs officers and any number of parasites with outstretched hands along the way. Could run to as much as four maybe five million. Dollars, of course – everybody wanted dollars. Anybody who had to carry that amount of cash around would need a body-guard, correction, several bodyguards.

'We sent Steven Quorn into Berlin with 250,000 dollars,' Hazelwood said reflectively. 'Gamal al Hassan claimed he had infiltrated Hizbollah and the money was the down payment for information he could supply.'

Ashton made no comment. Miles Dempsey, the former Head of Station, Kuwait had been less than impressed with Gamal al Hassan and his performance during the Gulf War. It was Jill Sheridan who'd created the myth that the Palestinian was a major asset and she had done so in the interests of furthering her career. And Jill had continued in the same vein when she was back in London, attributing to Gamal much of the high-grade material which passed across her desk. Ashton was not alone in thinking this; listening to his old guide and mentor, it was evident Hazelwood had reached the same conclusion. The joke was that Gamal had finally come good and in all probability no one had been more surprised than Jill.

'This blue chip of yours,' Maryck interjected, 'how was his libido?'

'I'm beginning to think his brain was located below the navel,' Hazelwood said, going over the top.

'A beautiful woman isn't necessarily a tigress in the sack.'

'Now there's a profound observation, Walter. May one ask what prompted it?'

'Louise Helen Kay will never make the cover of *Playboy* magazine but from what I hear, she's been putting it about ever since she reached puberty. I guess you could say it was Gamal's bad luck to make her acquaintance.' Maryck glanced over his shoulder, then spun the wheel and came about to head back to Marlow. The wash from the launch lapped the near bank and drew an angry shout from a lone fisherman. 'Of course, her case officer and the rest of the Near East Desk still think she's a jewel,' he continued in the same flat voice, 'but I don't buy it.'

'Somebody ought to tell Voigt not to waste time looking for Noreen Tal,' Hazelwood said.

'Like who?'

'Like you.'

Maryck emphatically told him to forget it. He was the only man who had been told that the voice on the tape belonged to the woman whose likeness had been circulated through Interpol. If Police President Voigt prevailed upon Bonn to ask the State Department for a recent passport photograph of Louise Kay, it wouldn't take the CIA's Deputy Director of Operations long to work out who had been responsible for pointing the police chief of Berlin in her direction.

'It would seem the job's yours, Peter.'

'Don't tell me,' Ashton said wearily, 'you'd like me to leave on Monday.'

'Well, there's no point letting the grass grow under your feet,' Hazelwood said, choosing what he deemed to be an apt maxim.

'I'll give you another adage – more haste, less speed. First thing we have to do is come up with a convincing line which will point Voigt towards Louise Kay without making things difficult for Mr Maryck here.'

'The name is Walter,' Maryck told him quietly.

Ashton nodded. 'Walter then.'

'Do you have one in mind?' Hazelwood asked. 'A line, I mean.'

'Suppose I tell him we have traced Noreen Tal and eliminated her from our inquiries?'

'It's risky. Voigt may have located her ex-husband and learned a great deal about the lady and her movements.'

'Look, if the worst comes to the worst, I'll tell Voigt the truth and make him understand why he can't attribute the information to Walter. OK?'

'It is by me,' Maryck said. 'The sooner everybody homes in on Louise Kay, the better. The way I see it, she's the only promising line of inquiry we've got. I am of course assuming that you guys are still waiting for Moscow to deliver Gennadi Yasnev?'

In diplomatic language, the American was suggesting that Pavel Trilisser was proving a big disappointment, and he was right. The former KGB General might have established contact with Head of Station, Moscow, using Larissa Grushkova as a go-between, but all he'd produced so far was a photocopy of Gennadi Yasnev's Record of Service in the GRU up to the date of his discharge on 3 December 1992. Perhaps it was still early days yet but Ashton had a feeling that the Russian was deliberately dragging his feet.

'Being something of an optimist,' Hazelwood said apropos of nothing in particular, 'I believe it's possible the on-going Kripo investigation has forced the Hizbollah cells to disperse.'

'Well, that's one way of looking at it,' Ashton said. 'However, being something of a realist, I think that if they have moved out of Berlin it's because they are about to take delivery of their nuclear toys some place else.'

The drop zone Gennadi Yasnev had chosen was approximately fifty miles north-east of Berlin and twelve miles due west of Greiffenberg in Pomerania. The countryside was flat, open and uninteresting, suitable for dairy farming and growing root crops but not much else. The six-acre field he'd rented from a greedy farmer was more than adequate for his needs. The equipment he was using had been stolen from the Russian Air Force and consisted of a small audio homing beacon and ten battery-powered recognition lights. The means of delivery was an Antonov An-26, codenamed Curl by NATO. A twin turboprop with a cruising speed of 273 miles an hour and a range of 1500 miles with maximum fuel/minimum payload, the aircraft was primarily intended for cargo carrying. It could however be easily adapted to meet a paratroop or paradrop role.

The plane had taken off from the Kutuzov military airfield north-west of Kaliningrad at 20.10 hours local time and keeping within Russian airspace the navigator had plotted a course which would take them out over the Baltic. Shortly after crossing the coast, they would descend to fifty feet to drop below the radar screen before making a ninety-degree change of course. To minimise the risk of detection, the pilot would maintain that altitude when he entered German airspace, only climbing to 600 feet as he approached the drop zone.

It was a hazardous flight by any standard and Yasnev didn't need this sallow-faced bitch who spoke English with a transatlantic accent to point out just how many things could go wrong. The pilot could misjudge his altitude and plough into the sea; they could wander off course and fail to pick up the signal from the homing beacon; they could hit a power line and crash.

'They're late,' the girl said in a low but fierce voice.

Yasnev glanced at the face of his luminous wristwatch. 'Less than four minutes,' he growled. 'That's nothing.'

'How do you know they haven't been intercepted and forced down?'

That was one possibility he could discount. Peace had broken out; nobody downed a plane for violating airspace these days. Besides, this was a Sunday night and the German Air Defence Command would be on minimum manning.

'This pilot of yours,' the girl continued, 'has he done a lot of low flying?'

'You can bet on it. He worked with the Spetsnaz in Afghanistan, carried out any number of low-level missions.'

'But not over the sea?' she persisted.

'You want to try flying up a valley to free-drop supplies with the mountains towering above you on either side. Wave top over the sea is nothing compared with that.'

'You'd better be right.'

'Hold it.' Yasnev waved a hand to silence her and crooked his head as if that would somehow improve his hearing. The whine of a turboprop aircraft in the distance, though faint, was nevertheless unmistakable. 'You can stop worrying,' he said, 'they're here.'

The Antonov An-26 came in at 600 feet and made just the one run over the DZ. The pallet weighed 415 pounds and floated to earth under four parachutes. Two would have been enough but Yasnev wasn't taking any chances.

'About time,' the woman said.

She had no idea what the mission had entailed, what skills had been demanded of the pilot and navigator. They had flown 418 miles at practically zero feet by dead reckoning and they'd hit the aiming point right on the nose. That had to be a near-incredible feat but Yasnev knew he would be wasting his breath if he tried to explain their achievement to her.

'Well, what are you waiting for?' he snapped. 'Go get it.'

The woman took a flashlight from the pocket of her anorak and flicked it on and off to summon the Transit van that had been parked in the far corner of the field some 400 yards away from the aiming point. In a curious way, this was the most dangerous time of all. The woman had two suitcases at her feet containing six and a half million dollars; out there on the DZ there were five steel containers lashed to a wooden pallet which might or might not contain an equal number of 130mm nuclear shells. To resolve a potentially explosive situation, the principals had agreed that each would have two bodyguards excluding the van driver and the gunman Yasnev had left at the farmhouse to watch the German family. Despite meticulous planning, it took them far longer to recover the load and clean up the DZ than had been allowed for. The overrun was entirely the fault of the Palestinians who insisted on making a detailed examination of each munition before they were prepared to hand over the money.

'Are you satisfied now?' Yasnev enquired angrily.

'I will be once the loose ends have been tidied up,' the woman told him.

Yasnev knew what she meant. Together they walked over to the farmhouse and went inside. The family were in the kitchen – mother, father, two sons in their early twenties and a pudding-faced daughter aged about sixteen. All five were watching a dubbed version of a Clint Eastwood Western on TV and were not aware that their guard was no longer alone until Yasnev tossed a small brown paper parcel on the kitchen table. The farmer lost interest in the movie and quickly unwrapped the package, expecting to find 10,000 Marks but discovering instead that only the top and bottom banknotes were real. The rest of the wad consisted of blank sheets of paper cut to the same size.

'Surprise, surprise,' the woman said, then produced a 5.45mm PSM self-loading pistol from the waistband of her jeans and coolly shot the old man through the right eye.

A split second later, Yasnev and the gunman who'd been watching over the family opened fire and went on shooting until the kitchen resembled a slaughterhouse.

He went under the name of Feliks. He was twenty-six years old and had short blond hair which had been clipped close to the skull so that what remained resembled a field of wheat stubble. Feliks had a round smiling face but his eyes told you he was a hard man and an untrustworthy one at that. He was a sergeant in Moscow's Anti Organised Crime

Division, which was a sick joke because he was on the payroll of the Babushkin gang, a Mafia family whose leader hailed from that particular district of the city.

The Scheherazade was part of a chain of restaurants, bars and casinos owned by the Babushkin *Mafiozniki*. More up-market than most casinos, it was located on Georgiijevski Street, a mere thirty metres from the Bolshoi in Theatre Square and close enough to the plush Metropole Hotel to draw Westerners who wanted to see what Moscow's night life had to offer without getting themselves mugged in the process. But in the main, it was the favourite haunt of the local nouveau riche, the commodity brokers, currency speculators, bankers and dubious entrepreneurs who would have been put up against a wall and shot in Brezhnev's era. Almost without exception, the clientele had already paid a handsome premium to the *Mafiozniki* for an all-risks policy to protect their businesses against fire and theft and insuring themselves against personal injury. In frequenting the Scheherazade, they were allowing the *Mafiozniki* to relieve them of a further slice of their disposable incomes.

Feliks assumed they regarded an evening's entertainment at the casino as money well spent, even though the roulette tables imported from Las Vegas had a double zero which practically guaranteed the house would always be the heaviest winner. The restaurant served good food, the barman could fix any cocktail you cared to name and the liquor hadn't come from a still in the forest. The croupiers looked glamorous in strapless, designer-label evening gowns and were available for other forms of entertainment after the casino closed in the early hours of the morning provided you could afford the asking price for their services.

Much as he would like to have a quickie with one of the girls or even a hand job in an alley, he would have a hard time finding the wherewithal for even a couple of champagne cocktails at the bar. Yet, for all that his purse was invariably thin, Feliks was no stranger to the casino. Familiar with the routine, he unbuttoned the hip-length leather jacket that was now showing obvious signs of wear and tear and allowed himself to be searched by one of the two strong-arm men on the door, both of whom he knew to be off-duty police officers. After being pronounced clean, he left the top coat with the hat-check girl in the vestibule and went inside.

There was not a space to be had at the roulette tables. Easing a path through the crowded room, Feliks made his way over to the bar and grabbed a vacant stool.

'I'm here to see Oleg,' he told the barman.

'You Feliks?'

'As ever.'

'Oleg isn't here yet.'

'That's OK, I'm early. Meantime, you can fix me a French 75 on the house.' He snapped his fingers and pointed to the array of bottles on the glass shelves behind the bar. 'And none of your domestic crap. The brandy has to be Remy Martin and I want it topped up with French champagne.'

'There's nothing like having expensive tastes when somebody else is picking up the tab,' the bartender said nastily. 'Let's see, snitches like you are allowed two freebies, right?'

Feliks told him to shut it and turned away to look at the couples on the minute dance floor. Dimmed lights, soft piped music and loads of sexy-looking talent; it was better than watching a porno movie the way some of the couples were wrapped around each other. He reached behind him, found his glass unerringly and raised it to his lips, his eyes never leaving the dark-haired girl in a red sheath. She was a little on the plump side but he liked his women to have some meat on them, and so apparently did the Westerner who was dancing with her. Except dancing wasn't in it; the lucky bastard had a tight grip on her arse and was as close to screwing her as a man could get without actually unzipping his pants.

'Enjoying the floor show?' Oleg asked, coming up behind him.

'I don't know a better way of killing time.'

'Well, now you don't have to, so let's hear what you've got for me.'

Feliks drained his glass, turned to face the bar and ordered another French 75. 'Does the name Gennadi Yasnev mean anything to you?' he asked.

'Never heard of him.'

'Ex-GRU, big-time *Mafiozniki*.'

'Who says?'

'Major General Gurov, Chief of Police – that's who.'

'He must have a fertile imagination,' Oleg said dismissively.

'Last Monday, he tells the Anti Organised Crime Division that Gennadi Yasnev is public enemy number one. Doesn't matter what else is on our desks, we're to drop everything and go after him.'

'Why do you insist on giving me all this shit when I've already said I've never heard of the guy?'

'This morning they put a price on his head and the General says the Kremlin will authorise payment in hard currency.'

'How much are they offering?'

'Ten thousand pounds, provided he's brought in alive. That's the equivalent of seventy million roubles, so you can bet every police officer in Moscow will be looking for him, especially as his photograph has been sent to every precinct house. I tell you, somebody in the Kremlin wants this guy real bad.'

There was a long silence, then Oleg pulled out a roll of US dollars. 'I think you've just earned yourself a nice fat bonus,' he said and gave him a measly twenty.

Chapter 21

The school bus left the major road and turned into a narrow, unmade-up lane that in places was barely wide enough for two vehicles to pass with any degree of comfort. Although the track ran arrow straight between the fields like an old Roman road, the driver changed down into third. A dynamic, ever-expanding economy and, with it, a better way of life had been virtually guaranteed following the reunification of East and West Germany, or so his friends and neighbours kept telling him. But as yet, nobody had got around to giving the lane an asphalt surface and five years after the Wall had come down, it was still a potholed cart track which threatened to shake the school bus to pieces. Not that he would shed too many tears over its demise; the damned thing was already overdue for the scrap heap, the spur tooth gearbox was shot and the clutch was on its last legs.

The driver eased his foot on the accelerator and, touching the brakes at the last moment, came to a gentle halt by the cart track that led to the Stroops' farmhouse a hundred metres back from the lane. Rain or shine, Karen Stroop would invariably be waiting for the school bus perched on top of the five-barred gate. If she was sick, one of her brothers or Frau Stroop herself would be there at the roadside with a note for her teacher but this morning, for the first time ever, no one was there to meet the bus.

The driver sounded the horn more in hope than expectation that the discordant blare would carry as far as the farmhouse. He was not a man to give up easily and he repeated the process several times before accepting defeat.

'All right,' he said loudly, 'who's going to call for Karen?'

The Stroops' daughter was not the most popular girl in the school. Karen was plump, had bad breath, often smelled as if she hadn't washed and was inclined to be spiteful. It was therefore hardly surprising that nobody would sit next to her if they could possibly avoid it. The bus driver also suspected that the chances of anyone volunteering to call on her were about zero and was proved right by the deafening silence which greeted his jocular invitation.

'Well, give me a name then,' he suggested.

'Wilhelm,' a girl at the back shouted and giggled. 'Irmgard,' another called out, then a boy asked what was wrong with Johan, and suddenly the whole bus was chanting, 'Gun-ther, Gun-ther, Gun-ther.'

'Seems you're elected, Gunther,' the bus driver announced cheerfully when he could finally make himself heard.

A tall, rangy adolescent who looked as if he was rapidly outgrowing his strength got to his feet and stormed off the bus, the mutinous expression on his face occasioned by the burst of applause and mocking cheers from his companions.

The driver cut the ignition and ignoring the No Smoking signs, lit a cigarette and leaned back to enjoy the first one of the day. He switched off, closed his ears to the rhubarb of noise, and didn't even react when a pheasant broke cover to amble across the lane practically under the front wheels of the bus. However, Gunther returned a lot sooner than he had expected. The fourteen-year-old youth had stalked off towards the farmhouse in high dudgeon; now here he was running back as if the devil himself were snapping at his heels.

'You look as if you've seen a ghost,' the driver observed jocularly. 'What happened, did Herr Stroop set his dogs on you?'

Gunther shook his head, then took a deep breath. 'They're dead,' he said in a rasping voice.

'What, all of them?'

'Yes. They've been shot.'

Gunther was renowned for his practical jokes but one look at his ashen face convinced the bus driver that this was not a hoax. He reached for the Cellnet phone on the dashboard, the one piece of up-to-date technology the local education authority had seen fit to provide since reunification, and alighted from the bus.

'Let's you and me take a look, Gunther.'

'Do I have to?'

'All I want you to do is show me how you got into the house.'

'Through the barn; there's a door near the back which opens into the kitchen.'

Gunther dropped farther and farther back until in the end he had to shout at the top of his voice to make himself heard. 'It wasn't locked,' he yelled.

The bus driver waved a hand above his head in acknowledgement and walked on. Herr Stroop had a couple of Dobermanns which he kept chained up during the day but allowed to roam free at night. There were a lot of foxes about and the dogs were there to make sure they didn't get at the chickens. But there was no sign of the Dobermanns in the yard this morning and he hoped they weren't about to spring on him when he walked into the house.

What he knew about farming, particularly dairy farming, could be written on the back of a postage stamp. However, it did seem to him that the cows were unusually restive and even though their udders didn't look as if they were bursting, he wondered when they had last been milked.

The kitchen door was wide open. Even though Gunther had prepared him for what lay inside, the carnage still shook him to the core. Herr Stroop was slumped over the kitchen table, his head over on to the right side of his face in a halo of blood and brain matter. A fistful of blank pieces of paper was still clutched in his left hand. Frau Stroop lay flat on her back on the floor, legs bent at the knee and supported by the upturned seat of the chair she had been sitting on. On the other side of the table, her two sons were sprawled on top of one another as if in a loving embrace.

Karen Stroop had tried to run away, or so it seemed to the bus driver. She had left the table but instead of making for the other door which opened into the hall, she had gone the wrong way towards the outside wall. It looked as though Karen had tried to find a refuge in the space between the long sideboard and the pedestal-mounted Grundig television. At any rate, she had been sitting on the floor in a puddle of urine when the killers had shot her. Again, he assumed the family had been gunned down by more than one intruder, a supposition based on the amount of damage that had been done to the furniture and the number of empty cartridge cases lying about.

Unnerved by what he had seen, the bus driver retreated to the barn, leaned over one of the stalls and vomited. When he finally stopped retching, he rinsed his mouth under a tap out in the yard, then recovered the Cellnet phone from where he had dropped it in his flight from the kitchen. His hands still trembling, he punched out 110 and told the operator he wanted to report a murder. 'Well, several murders,' he added, correcting himself in a voice that quavered.

Life, Ashton thought, was never dull when you worked for Victor Hazelwood. Sunday afternoon on the river, Monday morning in Berlin; no time to go to the bank, no time to do anything other than ring round the airlines and get himself on the earliest flight possible, using his Gold Mastercard. Roy Kelso had also had a busy Sunday evening, though this had only become apparent when Ashton had gone to the British Airways desk to collect his plane ticket and had found an officer from the Pay Section waiting for him with a bundle of American Express traveller's cheques and the equivalent of a hundred pounds in Deutschmarks. In addition, the senior pay clerk had produced a docket acknowledging receipt of both sums which Ashton had been required to sign before he would part with the money.

It had all been a little shambolic. Nobody had indicated how long he might be in Berlin so he had packed a bag and stopped off at the Zoo Station where he'd rented a locker before going on to the *Polizeipräsidium* on the Tempelhofer Damm. No one, of course, had thought to warn Heinrich Voigt that he was coming and his reception had been less than ecstatic. The duty officer had demanded to know why he wanted to see the Police President and Voigt's PA had tried to refer him to Eicke on the grounds that the Kommissar was in charge of the murder investigation. He had nothing against Eicke but there were things he was prepared to tell Voigt which he could not disclose to the Kripo Chief of the Central District. So he had sat it out in what had become a battle of wills until the PA had finally cracked and informed the Police Chief he had a visitor.

'Mr Ashton.' Voigt stood up as he entered the office and dipped his head before shaking hands with him. 'This is indeed a pleasure, I hadn't expected to see you again quite so soon.'

Given the Police President's aversion to the SIS, Ashton found it difficult to believe that Voigt was happy that he'd returned to Berlin. If the truth were known, the German had probably hoped he'd seen the last of him. Any lingering doubt that he could be mistaken was dispelled when Voigt asked him how long he was proposing to stay this time.

'I'm flexible,' Ashton told him. 'Could be a day, maybe a week, perhaps even longer. Depends on what comes out of the woodwork.'

'Quite so,' Voigt said and nodded sagely even though it was evident from his baffled expression that he hadn't understood the idiom. 'What is it you wish to tell me?'

'Among the woodlice is Gennadi Yasnev.'

'The man who told Ella Franklin his name was Georgi Mugrowski when he introduced himself after the funeral service? We know all about him, Mr Ashton. Ex-GRU, served in Afghanistan with Soviet Special Forces, was on the staff of the Soviet Embassy in Baghdad in 1987 masquerading as a commercial attaché. Now he's probably working for the *Mafiozniki*.'

'When did you learn all this?'

'Twelve days ago in a telex from Bonn. The photographs arrived later; I presume they were originally supplied by the CIA.'

'Have you had any luck with them?'

'Luck?' Voigt looked indignant. 'We don't rely on luck, Mr Ashton. Kommissar Eicke and his team of detectives have shown Yasnev's photograph to every innkeeper in the city and have found no trace of the man. He has disappeared, possibly to the Middle East with the other terrorists.'

'You know for a fact that they have left Germany?'

'No, but it's a reasonable supposition. The people who blew up the English Bookshop are not fools; most of them would have left Berlin before the bomber struck. For all we know, the woman who spoke to me could have been calling from Paris, Rome, Brussels or any other city.'

'They haven't given up,' Ashton said doggedly. 'They came here to buy themselves a nuclear capability and they won't go away empty-handed.'

Somehow he had to make Voigt see that, for Hizbollah, the destruction of the English Bookshop had simply been a means to an end and not the end itself. The immediate threat to the terrorist cell had been eliminated when they had cut Gamal's throat. They had then gone after the SIS Head of Station in Berlin because they had mistakenly assumed that Neil Franklin had been running the Palestinian and the *Mafiozniki* had made it clear they were unwilling to sell them any nuclear weapons until

Yasnev was satisfied the SIS no longer posed a threat. Unfortunately, there were no material facts to support his contention and that alone was enough to ensure he failed to persuade the German.

'You are wasting my time, Mr Ashton,' Voigt said impatiently. 'You told my secretary that you had certain information which was for my ears only.'

'That's right. It concerns the identity of the spokeswoman for Hizbollah.'

'You mean Noreen Tal?'

Ashton shook his head. 'No, we have eliminated that lady from our enquiries.'

'Then you have made an error.'

Of the two suspects identified by the FBI from their records, Voigt had always felt that the Jordanian girl was the one the Kripo should be looking for. She identified with the Palestinian cause more readily than Louise Kay ever could, even though the American woman had changed her name to Leila Khalif. Distributing leaflets on a university campus in support of the Popular Democratic Front and writing abusive letters to Ronald Reagan was a soft option compared with Noreen Tal's commitment. Voigt also had the greatest respect for the Federal Bureau of Investigation and reasoned they wouldn't have arrested her unless they had good cause for believing that she had been involved in the bombing of the World Trade Center. The fact that Claudia had identified Noreen Tal as the woman who had collected Moresby from the *Schwarz und Weiss* bar was not the only clincher.

'We traced her ex-husband, Karl Warlimont, to Aachen where he was interviewed by one of my officers. He told us some very interesting things about Noreen Tal. Her parents originally came from Umm el Fahm and were driven out of Palestine during the first Arab-Israeli war of '48.'

More fortunate than most refugees, they had brought out enough gold to establish themselves in Amman where Noreen Tal was born.

'She has two brothers older than herself, both of whom joined Fatah in their teens and are still active in the Palestine Liberation Organisation.' Voigt picked up a ruler from the desk and tapped it against the palm of his left hand to emphasise the point he wanted to make. 'Warlimont said she was almost psychotic in her hatred of Israel.'

'Did Warlimont hear the tape?' Ashton asked.

'Yes, and he was positive the spokeswoman was his ex-wife.'

'How can he be so sure? The marriage barely lasted twelve months.'

'They lived together for the better part of two years before they married.'

'And when were they divorced?'

'January 1988.' Voigt laid the ruler aside. 'Why do you ask?'

'Karl Warlimont seems to have it in for his ex-wife. I just wondered if she had taken him to the cleaners. There's nothing like a wacking great alimony to make a man go off at the deep end.'

'The deep end?' Voigt asked, frowning. 'What does that mean?'

'It's another way of saying he was very angry and upset.'

'It was an amicable divorce; there was no rancour over the division of property. Both parties considered the settlement a fair one.'

'If you say so.'

'I am merely repeating what Herr Warlimont told my officer.'

'Has he heard from his ex since the divorce?'

'No, and he has no desire to either. He is now happily married to a German woman and they have two children under four.'

And more than six years after they had split up, he was still harbouring a grudge against Noreen Tal and was only too eager to trash her. Warlimont had probably taken his cue from the attitude of the police officer who had interviewed him and had told him what he had wanted to hear. Ashton wondered what the Jordanian girl could have done to him to have incurred such lasting hatred. Whatever the cause, it was unlikely that Voigt could be persuaded that he was going after the wrong woman unless he was confronted with incontrovertible proof.

'The CIA claim that Louise Kay is one of theirs,' Ashton said. 'And it's her voice you've got on tape.'

'I don't understand. Why was she listed as a suspect by the FBI?'

'Because they were quick off the mark. By the time the CIA received the tape-recorded message from Hizbollah, the FBI had already acted on your request for information and had given the two names to Interpol. No remedial action was taken because the CIA felt Kay would be a lot safer if things were left as they were.'

'How do you know all this?' Voigt asked suspiciously.

'We made a copy of the tape you gave me and sent it on to Langley. They recognised the voice and told us who she was.'

'Well, no harm has been done. We're looking for Noreen Tal, not Louise Kay.' Voigt scowled. 'The Americans must be very proud of her – such dedication.'

'She's a phoney,' Ashton told him curtly. 'Her case officer may believe she is working for the Agency but he must be one of the few desk officers who does.'

'Would you care to name some of these dissenters?'

It was the last question Ashton was prepared to answer. Maryck had put his career, possibly his freedom on the line and there was no way Ashton was going to betray him. All he could do was invite the Police President to take his word for it and was just about to say so when the telephone rang. The ensuing conversation was brief, largely one-sided and therefore unintelligible. It did however get him off the hook.

'It would seem you are right,' Voigt said after he had put the phone down. 'The Hizbollah are back in town; they have left their calling card near the Victory Monument.'

'Is that where you are off to now?'
'Yes. I'm sure you will understand that this incident must take priority.'
'Can I cadge a lift?'
'To the Victory Monument?'
'Where else?' said Ashton.

The whole of Strasse des 17 Juni was blocked off from Ernst-Reuter-Platz to the Brandenburg Gate, a precautionary measure which had brought traffic in the Mitte and Tiergarten Districts to a virtual standstill. To get to the incident from the *Polizeipräsidium*, Voigt had his driver make a wide detour through the Schöneberg and Charlottenburg Districts but still hit trouble north of the Kurfürstendamm. From there on they would have made better time had they got out of the Mercedes and walked the rest of the way. Barely moving at a snail's pace, the driver had crossed Kantstrasse and headed north towards Ernst-Reuter-Platz. With vehicles double-banked, the only way forward had been to mount the kerb and drive on the sidewalk with the siren warbling.

The calling card had been left on the south side of the Strasse des 17 Juni in the narrow strip of saplings and secondary undergrowth between the road and the Bremer Weg footpath and cycle track inside the Tiergarten. It was also approximately four hundred yards west of the towering Siegessäule column which was crowned with the gilded bronze statue of Winged Victory. The traffic police were out in force and had placed sawhorses across the highway. Between the barriers closing off Ernst-Reuter-Platz and the Victory Monument on the circle of the Grosser Stern, there were two ambulances, four fire engines, a communications vehicle and a van belonging to the bomb squad. As a matter of diplomacy, Ashton stayed well back while Voigt consulted with the fire chief and the police officer in charge, then followed him into the wooded strip between the road and the footpath-cum-cycle track.

The calling card was a hinged, chocolate-coloured metal container approximately three and a half feet long by twelve inches wide and nine deep. The stencilled Cyrillic letters on the lid showed that it had been manufactured by the State Armament Factory, Bryansk, in August 1983. The lot and batch numbers indicated the particular production run of the 130mm shell. The yellow triangles incorporating a death's head denoted the type of munition; the Geiger counter belonging to the bomb disposal expert lent substance to Ashton's hunch that the symbols indicated a nuclear warhead.

'The container's empty, Herr Polizei Präsident,' the bomb disposal officer told Voigt. 'I think some practical joker must have put it here as a prank.'

Voigt nodded. 'Probably a student from one of the universities,' he said, looking hard at the police officer in charge. 'Better prepare a statement on those lines for the TV and press reporters. No point in alarming people unnecessarily.'

He also wanted photographs taken of the ammunition container in situ and the surrounding area before it was searched with a fine-tooth comb. Forensic were to dust the container for latent prints and endeavour to establish from the crushed bracken how long it had been lying there. The nearside lane was to remain closed during the search, but apart from this restriction, the traffic police had Voigt's permission to reopen the Strasse des 17 Juni.

'Hizbollah were determined to ensure we took them seriously this time,' Voigt said as he and Ashton walked back to the Mercedes. 'Their spokesman rang the police station on Invalidenstrasse north of the Tiergarten as well as the one on Keilbelstrasse to the south. He told the desk sergeant at each station precisely where to look for the nuclear ammunition box. The spokesman added that the Great Satan should take note of the destructive power which Hizbollah now possessed.'

'That's a pretty naked threat,' Ashton said. 'What's their price for keeping the peace?'

'He didn't say.'

'Maybe they aren't ready yet; that would make sense if they are going for more than one target.'

'No.' Voigt stopped by the car and motioned the driver to stay put. 'No, I'm prepared to accept they may have smuggled one round across the frontier but I don't believe our border guards are so lax that they could have brought in a whole arsenal.'

'I think you'll find the *Mafiozniki* delivered the munitions by air.'

'You mean they used a helicopter?'

'It's a question of range,' Ashton said. 'If he's to avoid detection, the pilot won't want to overfly Poland. So I figure he will stay within Russian airspace until he's over the Baltic, then he'll head inland across Usedom Island. At a guess, that would make the round trip close on six hundred nautical miles and even the Mi-26 Halo, which is the largest logistical support helicopter in service with the Russian Air Force, would need to be refuelled before setting off on the return leg.'

'You're very knowledgeable, Mr Ashton.'

'It was part of my job to know this kind of data when I was in the Ministry of Defence. Anyway, I reckon they would have used a fixed-wing aircraft, stayed down at tree-top level to make tracking difficult for the radar operators before climbing to six hundred feet as they approached the drop zone. They would then have kicked the pallet out and gone home adhering to the same flight pattern.'

'It's an interesting theory,' Voigt said, 'but I think hiring a military aircraft plus a very experienced aircrew is beyond the *Mafiozniki*.'

'I'm not so sure. Everything's up for grabs in St Petersburg and Moscow these days. I imagine the same applies elsewhere in Russia.'

'Perhaps.' Voigt frowned. 'I suppose it would do no harm to check with the air force,' he said thoughtfully.

'It's got to be worth a try.'

'Quite so. Can I give you a lift anywhere?'

'Well, that's very kind of you but I suspect I'm going in the opposite direction.'

'To the airfield?' Voigt asked hopefully.

'To Clayallee.' Ashton smiled. 'I want to have a word with the representatives of the Great Satan. But don't worry, I promise not to leave Berlin without saying goodbye.'

The expression on Voigt's face suggested he was willing to forgo that courtesy if it meant Ashton delaying his departure.

Chapter 22

As had happened on the previous occasion, the Marine Corps sentry outside the US Consulate directed Ashton to the enquiries desk inside the entrance where Sharon Pezzi was once again on duty.

'Hi,' Ashton said, 'remember me?'

'Sure I do.' Pezzi flashed him a grin. 'Never forget a face, just can't remember the name, that's my problem.'

'I won't hold it against you.'

'Thanks. So how can I help you?'

'I'd like to see Mr Caspar Lemberg.'

'Now I remember.' Pezzi snapped her fingers. 'You're Mr Ashman. Right?'

'Pretty close; it's Ashton.'

'Oh, sorry.'

'Don't be, I've been called worse.'

Ashton took out his passport and placed it on the desk. In return, Pezzi gave him a visitor's pro forma to complete. 'Is Mr Lemberg expecting you?' she asked.

'He doesn't even know I'm in Berlin but hopefully he will find time to see me.'

'I'm sure he will.'

Ashton completed the pro forma, then killed time looking at the pictures of the Berlin Airlift of '48 displayed in the hall while Pezzi checked to see if Caspar Lemberg were available.

'No problem,' she announced presently and quickly made out a visitor's pass.

In a rerun of the previous visit, the same Marine Corps sergeant escorted him up to the same interview room on the second floor. This time however he was not subjected to an electronic body search and Lemberg didn't keep him waiting.

'It's good to see you again,' he said. 'What brings you back to this neck of the woods?'

'A lowlife called Gennadi Yasnev.'

For a moment it looked as if Lemberg were going to pretend that he'd never heard of the Russian but in the end common sense prevailed. The man who had claimed to be Georgi Mugrowski had been identified by the CIA's Operations Directorate. When they'd authorised Walter Maryck to release the information to British Intelligence, the Agency would have automatically sent a copy of the signal to their Station Chief in Berlin.

'I guess you think Gennadi Yasnev is back in town,' Lemberg said slowly.

'Who can doubt it after what has happened this morning?'

Again there was a slight pause while the American considered what line he should take. 'Could be a hoax,' he said. 'I imagine it wouldn't be too difficult to lay hands on an old ammo box. All you've got to do is give it a lick of paint and slap on a few warning signs–'

'I've seen the container they left near the Victory Monument,' Ashton said, interrupting him. 'It's no fake; the lot and batch numbers look authentic and the symbol denoting a nuclear warhead is straight out of the *Manual of Staff Duties* which used to be issued to senior officers of the Red Army.'

'Yeah? Well, I kid you not, the Russians really caught the spirit of free enterprise. They were selling the shirts off their backs before they left Berlin. Even now, if you go down to the Unter den Linden at the Brandenburg Gate you can buy yourself a whole chestful of Soviet medals and one of those full dress peaked caps which look as if the hatters were blind drunk or stoned out of their minds when they made them.'

'Are you telling me these hawkers of memorabilia can produce an ammunition container to order?' Ashton gave the American time to respond and wasn't surprised when Lemberg didn't say anything. 'I doubt if you are going to tell me what Louise Kay said either.'

'Louise Kay?' Lemberg frowned as though he couldn't place the name. He even managed a puzzled inflection in his voice, but it was the sudden blink which let him down and told Ashton he was right on target.

The terrorists had phoned two police stations and the incident had been reported all the way up the chain of command until it had reached Voigt. At no stage had the Kripo alerted the American Consulate. When Ashton had left the scene of the incident, the press and TV reporters were still being held a long way back from the Victory Monument and weren't in a position to report what had happened. Had the police spokesman made a statement before he'd reached the Consulate, Lemberg would have explained how he'd heard about the incident. He'd also left himself wide open on another score.

'It's futile to pretend you've never heard of Louise Kay,' Ashton told him bluntly. 'Voigt faxed a request for information to Interpol and before the CIA got wind of what was happening the Bureau had named Louise Kay as a possible suspect. After consulting the Near East Division, the Deputy Director Operations decides it's safer to leave things as they are. By now, the voice tape has reached Langley and they know that Kay was in Berlin recently. So, if you'd never heard of the lady before, you certainly did after the Agency had listened to what she had said to Voigt. She was operational on your patch and there was no way they could leave you in ignorance. Right?'

Lemberg spread his hands as if he found the suggestion utterly preposterous. 'It's your scenario,' he said dismissively.

'You mean that isn't standard procedure with you guys?' Ashton said, deliberately setting out to needle him. 'What kind of Intelligence organisation do you belong to?'

'The biggest and the best,' Lemberg said heatedly.

'That's what I'd expect you to say, but I can tell you're unhappy.'

'I am?' Lemberg echoed mockingly.

'Louise Kay contacted you this morning and now you're asking yourself why she didn't touch base with you soon after the Hizbollah cell arrived in the city. You find it hard to accept that she didn't have an opportunity to do so before Moresby and Gamal al Hassan were murdered, before the English Bookshop was reduced to rubble.'

'That's some crystal ball you've got,' Lemberg said.

'It would be interesting to know when she was last in touch with her case officer,' Ashton continued relentlessly. 'But you know full well the Deputy Director Operations would have pushed her on to you a lot sooner had she warned the Near East Division that the cell was moving to Berlin.'

Even though Lemberg's office number wasn't in the public domain, getting through to him would not have been a problem for Louise Kay. He had been in post for over two years and that was certainly long enough for the Russian Intelligence Service to identify him as the new Chief of Station. That information would have been automatically passed to the GRU. If Gennadi Yasnev had been able effectively to destroy the British network in the city, there was every reason to suppose he was equally well informed about the names of every CIA officer in the capital.

'The phone number of the US Consulate is no secret,' Ashton said. 'It's listed in every guide book to Berlin, never mind the local directory. When the switchboard operator took her call, Louise Kay asked for you by name.'

'I won't deny it,' Lemberg said.

'So what message did she give you?'

Ashton waited. He could understand Lemberg's reluctance to confide in him. Despite the weight of circumstantial evidence against her, the American wanted to believe that Louise Kay was still controlled by the CIA.

It was almost an article of faith with him.

'Face it,' Ashton said bluntly, 'you lost her a long time ago. She went across in 1989 when she embraced the Muslim faith and changed her name to Leila Khalif.'

'Maybe.' Lemberg scowled. 'The hell with it, you're only saying what I'm thinking privately. Kay said that the cell she had infiltrated call themselves the Abu Nidal Group. And you were right about her claiming that this morning was the first opportunity she'd had to make contact. She said the others watched her all the time and that it was only now that she'd finally won their trust. Anyway, Kay wanted me to let the Agency know that the Group had just taken delivery of five sub kiloton nukes which means they now have a multi-strike capability – her words. That was the sum total of her knowledge. I asked where she was calling from and in a panicky voice she told me Daoud was coming and hung up.'

'Did you hear any background noise when she was on the phone?'

While some people tap their front teeth with a fingernail as an aid to concentrating their minds when asked to recall something and others distort their features or tug on an earlobe, Lemberg simply closed his eyes and pinched the bridge of his nose between thumb and index finger. 'I remember a faint humming noise in the distance and I think I heard a jet. Sounded like a military aircraft, but I could be wrong.'

'What time was this?' Ashton asked.

'Eight minutes past noon. I logged it when I took the call.' Lemberg snapped his fingers. 'Something else; the switchboard operator told me she thought Louise Kay was on a crossed line when she put her through, but I didn't hear any other voices.'

'A pay phone not too far from one of the autobahns?' Ashton said, thinking aloud. 'Could be she and this Daoud had stopped at a rest house. It's also possible there is a military airfield in the vicinity.'

'So where do we start looking?'

'Your guess is as good as mine,' Ashton told him. 'We might be able to narrow it down if we knew where and when the nukes were delivered. If you can bring yourself to do it, I think you should tell Voigt about the phone call from Louise Kay. You don't have to mention her by name.'

'You're damned right, I don't have to,' Lemberg said.

Manfull turned into Osage Drive and this time parked his '89 model Pontiac Bonnville on the grass verge bordering the right side of the road opposite the Kay property. He had waited a full ten days before returning to Eureka Springs. In that time, a coroner's inquest had been held and the body of Jack Kay laid to rest in Forest Lawn Cemetery. The fall had also arrived and the huge statue of Christ in white stone surrounded by evergreens and deciduous trees was now set against a backdrop of every hue of red and gold. Manfull locked the Pontiac, crossed the narrow road and walked through the gap in the hedge fronting the house. Donna Kay met him at the door before he could ring the bell.

'Morning, Mrs Kay,' he drawled. 'It's good of you to see me. Lots of folks in your position would have found some reason not to.'

'Yeah, well, I guess I'm different.'

Manfull could see for himself that she certainly was. Her eyelids weren't puffy and there were no dark shadows underneath; the grieving widow it seemed was through with crying. Donna Kay hadn't gone into mourning either; she was wearing a pair of figure-hugging slacks and a red silk blouse that matched her hair.

'I thought we'd use the sitting room, it's more comfortable than Jack's old den.'

'Whatever suits you, Mrs Kay.'

'Donna,' she said, flashing him a smile over her shoulder as they moved through the hall. The widow, it appeared, was ready to do a little flirting. She obviously wasn't averse to him admiring her butt the way she kept wiggling it. He wondered if she had indulged in the same sort of body language with other men when her husband had been alive.

'Coffee?' she asked. 'Home-made lemonade, Seven-Up?'

It was all there, neatly arranged on a tray which she had placed on the low round table in front of the settee. Determined to make him feel welcome, she had also provided a plate of cookies.

'A glass of home-made lemonade would be dandy,' Manfull told her.

The Bureau Chief in Little Rock had not been in favour of Manfull interviewing the widow. The Coroner's jury had returned a verdict of accidental death and in his opinion that was the end of the matter. The reason why the Bureau Chief had finally relented was the fact that he couldn't explain why the old man should have run away from one of his agents.

Manfull couldn't explain it either, except he just knew it had everything to do with Louise Kay. He had gotten the phone company to run a check on the household to see if she had placed a collect call at any time after Thursday, 21 July, when she had last spoken to her father, but had drawn a blank. Her mother, Veronica Kay, had been killed in a traffic accident on the same date in 1976 when Louise had been sixteen years old. Hoping to find something which might indicate why Kay was terrified of his daughter, Manfull had obtained the traffic accident report from the Cole County Police Department.

'I don't know how to put this,' he began.

'It's OK. Don't worry about me, I know you've got a job to do.'

Manfull drank some of the home-made lemonade, then said, 'Remember you telling me that Veronica was a lush and how she had wrapped the family Chrysler around a tree?'

'I'm not likely to forget,' Donna said.

'Did Jack ever talk about that fateful afternoon?'

'Not directly. He said Louise accused him of driving her mother to drink for a whole mess of reasons. None of them true, I might add.'

'Did Jack tell you that he was with Veronica at the Country Club that day?'

'No.' Donna stared at him, her mouth open. 'Who told you that?' she asked.

'It was in the accident report. Apparently, Jack met her for lunch and there was a big row; the maître d' thought he'd deliberately provoked a quarrel. The investigating officer went one better and wondered why Mr Kay had made no effort to stop his wife leaving the club when he knew she was way over the limit. He hinted that maybe Jack didn't care that there was an even chance she could have a fatal accident.'

'I don't believe it.'

Neither had the DA's office in Jefferson City when they saw the report, but it might explain why Louise had hated her father with such a deep and abiding intensity.

'I can't think what spooked Jack.' Manfull finished the rest of the lemonade and put the glass down on the tray. 'It couldn't have been me. We'd never met and he didn't sound worried when I phoned him before I left Little Rock. Someone else must have phoned Jack that day.'

Donna opened her mouth, then closed it hastily and in that instant Manfull knew she had telephoned Kay down at the depot of the North Arkansas Railway. She had told her husband what he was wearing and Kay would have known that he'd seen his photograph in the den. It was one of the missing pieces of the jigsaw but the picture was still a long way from being complete.

'Has anything unusual happened in the last ten days?' Manfull asked as tactfully as he could.

'I had a letter from one of the local realtors concerning the lease Jack had taken on an office on Main Street here in town.'

'When did he do this?'

'July 25 this year.'

Exactly four days after Louise Kay had telephoned her father; Manfull was convinced there was a connection. 'You didn't know anything about the office until the realtor wrote to you?' he said, backing a hunch.

'Damned right. Jack had paid three months' rent in advance and the realtor was anxious to know whether I wanted to continue with the arrangement.'

'Have you been down to the office?'

Donna shook her head. 'Not yet.'

'You got a key?'

'I found one in Jack's desk.'

'Well then, would you mind if I took a look at the place?'

'Sure, why not? I'll come with you.'

The office was above a beauty parlour and adjoined a toy bazaar. Access was via a wooden staircase on the right side of the building. The furniture consisted of a table, chair, filing cabinet and a telephone. Street maps of Chicago, Detroit, New York, Seattle, San Francisco, Los Angeles, San Diego, New Orleans, Austin, Boston and Memphis were in the top drawer of the filing cabinet, the other two drawers were empty. Pinned to the wall above the table was a cutting from an unknown newspaper which read: 'Vacation brochures wanted. Write Box 870, Postal Station A, Toronto.'

It didn't make a damned bit of sense to Manfull.

Every guide book to Berlin agreed that the California on the Kurfürstendamm was a moderately priced hotel which Ashton thought would please Kelso no end when he submitted a claim for expenses. It had been a big mistake to use the secure speech facility at the British Consulate to phone Hazelwood after he had seen Caspar Lemberg. Had he used a normal open line, Victor would have been compelled to be a lot more circumspect. Consequently, he could have pretended to have misunderstood him and caught the first available flight back to London. That would certainly have pleased Harriet who had done her best to take the news philosophically when he had told her that Victor wanted him to stay on in Berlin for the time being.

From the Consulate he'd gone to the Central Tourist Office on Martin-Luther-Strasse to find out what hotel accommodation was currently available in the city. The short answer was precious little. Every single room at the Bristol Hotel Kempinski, the Schweizerhof and Inter-Continental was taken. Hecker's, where he had stayed before, was booked solid, as were all the other hotels in the same category. After trying several other numbers, the tourist information officer was able to get him into the California. All he'd had to do then was collect his suitcase from the locker at the Zoo Station and settle in.

The California had survived the war intact and should have been a listed building, but it wasn't, and as a result the hotel now rubbed shoulders with a brand new McDonald's. Apart from comfortable-looking sofas which were scattered haphazardly about, the lobby also boasted a mini fountain and a chunk of the Berlin Wall. There was one other oddity: the lift only stopped between floors so that guests had to walk up a flight of twelve steps to reach their rooms.

Ashton finished unpacking, helped himself to a beer and a packet of salted peanuts from the mini bar and switched on the TV. He flicked through the channels from SFB to ARD before staying with an old black-and-white movie on RTL, the second station of the Public Service Network. He caught only the last five minutes of the dubbed version of *Great Expectations*, then almost before the credits had finished rolling, a newscast anchor man appeared on screen sharing the desk with a well-groomed blonde in her mid forties who read the headlines from the autocue. For once, the ethnic cleansing of Muslims by Serbs in Bosnia-Herzegovina was relegated into second place by the cold-blooded murder of an entire family of five at an isolated farmhouse near Greiffenberg. Near was an understatement; the sketch map which appeared briefly on the screen showed that the Stroops' farm was at least twelve miles from the small market town of Greiffenberg and approximately fifty miles north-east of

Berlin. The sketch map was replaced by an on-the-spot roving reporter standing in the middle of a field, the farmhouse some distance to his rear.

Ashton paid scant attention to what the reporter was saying; instead he took a long hard look at what he could see of the landscape. Flat, open, miles from anywhere, an ideal location for a DZ. He picked up the remote control and put the TV on standby, then lifted the telephone and rang Heinrich Voigt.

'I've just been looking at the early evening news,' he told Voigt when the PA patched him through to the Police President. 'I've a hunch that there is a connection between what happened to the Stroops and the incident this morning.'

'Where are you calling from?'

'My room at the Hotel California.'

'I think you had better come round here,' Voigt said.

'So do I.' Ashton cleared his throat, wondered how he could tactfully suggest that several heads were better than one and decided there was no way of doing it without sounding unctuous. 'It might be helpful if Caspar Lemberg sat in,' he said.

'That thought had also occurred to me,' Voigt told him and hung up.

Even on the Kurfürstendamm, getting hold of a taxi wasn't easy in the evening rush hour. Although Lemberg's house in the elegant residential district of Dahlem was farther away from the *Polizeipräsidium* than the California, he owned a Volkswagen Golf and knew all the short cuts that avoided the traffic. Consequently, he was already ensconced in Voigt's office by the time Ashton arrived.

'You missed your vocation as a clairvoyant,' the German told him. 'I took your advice and rang Air Defence Command. The radar station at Usedom which covers the approaches to the former city of Stettin picked up a low-flying intruder at 21.10 hours last night.'

The radar operator had lost track of the plane soon

afterwards but twenty-one minutes later it had reappeared on the screen, this time heading out over the Baltic. Complaints about a low-flying aircraft from a number of residents in Prenzla suggested the intruder had gone at least fifty miles inland before turning back.

'What about Herr Stroop and his family?' Ashton asked.

'Their bodies were found by the school bus driver at twenty minutes to eight this morning. In the opinion of the police doctor who made a preliminary examination on the spot, all five were dispatched upwards of an hour before midnight. The local Kripo could find no apparent motive for the multiple killing. Herr Stroop had been counting what he believed was a bundle of money when one of the executioners shot him through the right eye. There were a couple of one-hundred Deutschmark notes on the kitchen table and ninety-eight blank sheets cut to the exact same size. It therefore seems logical to suppose he'd expected to receive 10,000 Marks for services rendered–'

'Like allowing one of his fields to be used as a DZ,' Ashton said, cutting short an account which gave every indication of being a very long story if it was left to the Police President.

'Quite so,' Voigt said. 'The Kripo discovered a wooden pallet and four parachutes buried in a shallow ditch bordering one of the hedgerows. They didn't have to look very hard to find them.'

Ashton calculated that the plane would have been over the DZ at 21.30 hours and reckoned it would have taken the terrorists about forty minutes to collect the munitions and remove the homing beacon and navigational lights.

'The investigating officers also found a number of tyre tracks,' Voigt continued. 'These suggested that two, possibly three vehicles had been used to transport the munitions and personnel.'

Ashton listened to him with half an ear. The Kay woman had phoned Caspar Lemberg at 12.08, some fourteen hours after the Abu Nidal Group had cleaned up the drop zone and bugged out. Given that timescale, it was possible to clock up 800 miles on the autobahn, but of course that didn't allow for rest stops, refuelling or diversions.

'Something puzzling you?' Voigt asked.

'Only a time and space problem,' Ashton said and explained what he meant.

'It would have taken them at least an hour to reach the autobahn from Herr Stroop's farm,' Voigt told him.

'There's something else I think you should consider, Peter,' Lemberg said, chipping in. 'If I were Daoud, I would avoid travelling during the small hours of the morning. There would be a fair amount of traffic on the roads up to about 01.00 hours but after that it would thin out quite dramatically and the truckers would have the autobahns pretty much to themselves. The way I see it, anyone driving a car, a van or a pick-up is going to be a lot more conspicuous.'

'So when would you start rolling again?'

'Just after sunup, say 06.45 hours.'

Ashton went over his figures again. Reducing the time-scale to eight hours, he upped the number of miles they might reasonably expect to cover in one hour from fifty to sixty, then converted the total distance into metric for Voigt's benefit.

'I figure Daoud had clocked up 768 kilometres when Louise Kay rang the US Consulate.'

Voigt opened the bottom drawer of his desk and took out a small-scale road map covering the whole of Germany, Czechoslovakia, Austria and Switzerland. Then, using a ruler as a crude sort of compass, he described a semicircle on the map with a radius equating to 768 kilometres centred on Greiffenberg. Cities as far apart as Prague, Nuremberg, Frankfurt and Cologne lay within the circumference.

'Of course it's only a rough guess,' he said apologetically.

It was all of that, Ashton thought, but even so, it demonstrated the fallacy of his calculations. Without further and more definite information, they were simply groping in the dark.

'Those tyre tracks the Kripo found . . .'

'They are visiting all the neighbouring farms,' Voigt said, anticipating his question. 'If they find anyone who remembers seeing any strange vehicles on the Stroops' property, I'll be the first to hear.'

'Well, I guess that's it,' Lemberg said. 'I've nothing more to contribute.'

'Neither have I.' Ashton frowned. 'But I think we should stay in close touch, maybe set up something on the lines of an anti-terrorist Intelligence team?'

'That's a policy decision only Bonn can take,' Voigt said curtly.

'And Washington,' Lemberg added.

'I've no quarrel with that but somebody should start the ball rolling.'

There was a lengthy silence, then Caspar Lemberg told Ashton that it seemed he had been elected.

Office hours for the British Consulate were strictly nine to five and it had gone six o'clock when the meeting at the *Polizeipräsidium* had broken up. It was Gerald Willmore's bad luck that Ashton had been given his private telephone number. Not unnaturally, he had been reluctant to return to the Consulate on Uhlandstrasse simply to allow someone who wasn't even a member of the Diplomatic to use his crypto-protected telephone link. Ashton however was nothing if not forcefully persuasive.

With Berlin an hour ahead of London, Ashton saw no point in ringing Hazelwood at Vauxhall Cross. However, that wasn't a problem. A secure speech facility had been installed in Victor's house on Willow Walk the day he'd become the Deputy Director under Stuart Dunglass. Following a brief summary of his meeting with Voigt and Caspar Lemberg, Ashton told him what he had in mind.

'If we don't pool our information and work together, we're never going to catch these people. We need a co-ordinator and an expert on the various terrorist factions in the Mid East.'

'Where are you staying?' Hazelwood asked, interrupting him.

'The Hotel California, Room 314.' Ashton paused, then picked up on the point he had been trying to make before Victor had put him off his stride. 'I'd like to know why these people claim to be Hizbollah one moment and the Abu Nidal Group the next.'

'Fine. I'll send Jill.'

'Jill? You mean Jill Sheridan?' Ashton said in disbelief.

'Yes. Is that a problem with you?'

'No, but I think you may have one with Harriet when she gets to hear about it.'

'Ah,' Hazelwood said with feeling.

Ashton laughed. 'Cheer up, Victor,' he said, 'it may never happen. If Voigt has anything to do with it, Bonn will probably veto the whole idea.'

Chapter 23

Bonn didn't veto the idea. Whatever objections Voigt might have had, Chancellor Kohl was not about to reject an offer of assistance from the SIS when there were a bunch of lunatics running around his country with five nuclear shells. When there was a life-threatening situation in the offing, it was remarkable how swiftly politicians, civil servants and career diplomats could move. Ashton had had no idea what had been going on behind the scenes until Hazelwood rang the hotel at 07.00 to inform him in commercial language that The Firm was going to reinforce his sales team. He was also told that they would be on the Lufthansa flight arriving Berlin-Tegel at 12.45 hours and would he kindly meet them at the airport with a car.

Ashton looked up the car rental firms in the Yellow Pages of the telephone directory under *Autovermietung*, found that both Avis and Hertz had an agency on Budapesterstrasse, and hired a Volkswagen Passat from the latter because it happened to be the nearest. Cutting it a shade close, he arrived at Berlin-Tegel in time to see Jill Sheridan emerge from Customs and Immigration into the concourse looking elegant and businesslike in a well-cut trouser suit. The shoulder bag and executive briefcase Jill was carrying suggested she wasn't expecting to stay more than a few days in Berlin. Then Steven Quorn appeared in her wake loaded down with a large Vuitton suitcase in addition to his own bag and it was evident that she was prepared for every eventuality.

'Good of you to meet us, Peter,' she intoned without sincerity. 'I hope you've rented a car?'

'A Volkswagen Passat.'

'I would have preferred something larger, but never mind.' Jill divested herself of the shoulder bag and gave it to him. 'Where have you left the car?'

'On the cab rank,' Ashton told her curtly.

'You'd better lead the way then, this is my first trip to Berlin.'

Ashton walked towards the exit, pushed the swing door open, and without bothering to wait for Jill, went on down the circular staircase to the slip road. He unlocked the car, opened the boot and dumped the shoulder bag inside, then left it to Quorn to put the suitcases away and close the lid.

'It's central locking,' he told Jill in case she was waiting for him to open the door for her.

'Thank you for pointing that out,' she said icily and got into the passenger seat, leaving Quorn to get in the back.

'Where are you staying?' Ashton asked.

'Let's try the Schweizerhof.'

'All the single rooms have been taken.'

'Then I'll ask for a twin bed.'

'And Steven?'

'The same.'

If you were an up-and-coming Assistant Director it seemed Kelso would rubber-stamp your claim for expenses. The same criteria seemingly applied to the eager beaver whose principal job apparently was to carry her bags on and off the plane.

'This is an emergency,' Jill added.

'Well, I can see that would make a difference.' Ashton pulled away from the kerb and joined the stream of traffic heading for the town centre. 'There's been a new development since Victor rang this morning,' he continued. 'The Kripo have found a witness who was driving past the Stroop place on Sunday evening when three vehicles, which were coming towards him from the direction of Angermünde, turned off the road on to the track leading to the farmhouse.'

'When was this?' Jill asked.

'The witness wasn't too sure of the time but thought it must have been around 17.30 hours because the night was beginning to close in. It wasn't dark enough, however, for him to need his headlights.'

The leading vehicle had been a beige-coloured Mercedes; two grey Transit vans had followed it at a respectful distance. The witness had only been a matter of a few yards from the farm track when the driver of the second Transit van had cut across the road in front of his vehicle, forcing him to stamp on the brakes.

'The guy was so mad he stopped his car and got out. That's how he managed to get part of the registration number of the tail-end vehicle before it disappeared into the distance.'

'Part of the number?' Jill said with heavy emphasis.

'Two letters and two digits – M blank R 84 blank blank.'

'Pity he didn't take a closer look.'

'I imagine he thought about it,' Ashton said, 'then decided discretion was the better part of valour. I'd have done the same in his shoes.'

'I doubt it,' Jill said.

'You're wrong. There were three vehicles in convoy which meant the odds would have been at least three to one in the event of a rough house. In the circumstances, I would have looked the other way to avoid a confrontation. Anyway, it's irrelevant; the police have circulated descriptions of all three vehicles plus the partial registration number.'

'Do you know if they ran a computer check using the incomplete licence number and vehicle description?'

'I didn't ask them, Jill, and I recommend you don't either. I think we will get on with Voigt a whole lot better if we don't tell him how to do his job.'

'I wasn't planning to.'

'Good. How do you see the three of us operating?'

As he rapidly discovered, Jill had very definite ideas on the subject. Quorn would be the police liaison officer and would be based at the *Polizeipräsidium* while Jill worked from an office which the British Council had been requested to provide. As for Ashton, he was to stay in close touch with the CIA's Head of Station and pick up what scraps of information he could. However, for the present, his main job was to chauffeur Jill around.

Jill Sheridan was one of those people blessed with the happy knack of always falling on their feet. Ashton couldn't think of anyone else who had been promoted after requesting a home posting on the grounds of sexual prejudice by the indigenous population. She had also married a man whose business activities and unsavoury character traits would have cost any other woman her security clearance. And nobody who'd presented material gleaned from other agencies as if it had come from their own sources would have weathered the subsequent storm and come out of it with their reputation still intact.

It therefore came as no surprise to him when she had absolutely no difficulty in obtaining two twin bedrooms at the Schweizerhof. The fact that Voigt almost fell over himself in his eagerness to find a niche for Steven Quorn at the *Polizeipräsidium* did however leave Ashton a little breathless.

Although nominally independent, the British Council received grants from the Foreign and Commonwealth Office and a request from the purse holders in Whitehall carried more weight than the Ten Commandments. The room set aside for Jill Sheridan was only marginally smaller than that of Her Majesty's cultural representative in Berlin.

'Jill Sheridan walks on water,' Ashton observed after the Council officer had left them.

'Is that meant as a compliment?'

'No, it's a glimpse of the obvious. I think you can get away with anything, and you know it. Which is why you won't mind answering a question off the record.'

'Depends what it is, Peter.'

'Why did you phone Anthea Vise?'

'What makes you think I did?'

No prevaricating, no pretending that she'd never heard of Anthea Vise, just a sharp intake of breath before she challenged him to prove his contention.

'You weren't happy about Moresby,' Ashton told her. 'I imagine you saw the military documents of the four ex-servicemen the Armed Forces Desk had obtained from the Ministry of Defence and had had no objections when Moresby was provisionally selected. You weren't invited to sit in on the subsequent interview because Rowan Garfield's outfit was running the show in Berlin. But when you heard that Moresby had told the panel that he wasn't emotionally involved, you didn't believe him. So you did a little checking on your own account and rang the offices of Sentinel Alarms Limited in York.'

'I trust you don't think I got that from his Military Record of Service?'

'No way. Frank Warren's Security Vetting Section turned up that information. There had been no time for them to do more than update the security clearance Moresby had held when he was serving in the Military Police. Anyway, when Anthea Vise answered your call, you put on what she described as a lah-di-dah accent. I don't know what you said to her but the way she must have reacted told you Anthea Vise and Jack Moresby were partners in every sense of the word.'

'Is this still off the record, Peter?'

'Absolutely.'

'Then the answer's yes.' Jill smiled. 'Now you want to know why I didn't pull the plug on Moresby?'

'I already have a pretty shrewd idea.'

'Well, you don't need much grey matter to realise there was no time to find a suitable replacement.' Jill perched herself on the edge of the desk, legs crossed at the ankles. 'What was I supposed to do? Advise Rowan Garfield to call it off? Believe me, he wouldn't have needed much encouragement to cancel the operation. I couldn't allow that to happen, not when this particular group of terrorists were determined to acquire a nuclear capability. Besides, at the end of the day, what did I have against Moresby? The fact that he had lied about his sex life? It seemed a minor blemish to me at the time. It still does.'

Jill could have gone to Hazelwood and dumped the whole problem in his lap, but that wasn't her style. In her eyes, it would have been a sign of weakness, a failing which she believed her peer group would have seized upon and used against her. Ashton realised there had been another consideration. Jill was a very ambitious lady and meant to go all the way to the top. Gamal al Hassan had been her agent in place; if the operation had been successful, nearly all the credit would have gone to her, if it had been a disaster, Rowan Garfield would have carried the can because his department had been responsible for running the op. It was a classic example of heads I win, tails you lose.

'Why so silent, Peter?'

'I'm wondering why it took me so long to figure out that you were the lah-di-dah lady. Victor and I thought it was some woman Moresby had been seeing on the side. We were worried she would surface and sell her version of what had happened to her boyfriend to the highest bidder.'

'Well, it's all water under the bridge now. Personally speaking, I think looking back is a waste of time, especially when we've got more important things to do.'

'Like what?'

'I want to meet Helga von Schinkel. I know Voigt has spoken to her at length and so have you, but a woman may have more luck in jogging her memory.'

Ashton thought there was no harm in trying. It beat sitting around waiting for something to happen. 'Afternoon visiting hours are from two to four,' he told her. 'You've got roughly forty minutes to play with.'

'That will do me.' Jill straightened up. 'Better ring the *Polizeipräsidium* and let Steven know where we're going.'

It sounded like a verbal reminder to oneself. Ashton was therefore slow to grasp that Jill expected him to do it.

Gennadi Yasnev came home to Moscow the long way round. From the Stroop farm he and his three bodyguards had gone north towards the remote hamlet of Schwede and then slipped across the border into Poland, driving cross-country and without lights for six kilometres either side of the demarcation line. There had been no need to exercise anything like the same degree of caution when leaving Poland; all they'd had to do was grease a few palms and the road to Kaliningrad had been wide open. After making a detour to pay off the pilot, co-pilot, navigator, loadmaster and two air dispatchers, they had driven on into the city and had deposited the remaining five and a half million dollars with the Novgorod Merchant Bank, one of the many financial institutions controlled by the Babushkin *Mafiozniki*.

The bodyguards had been personally chosen by The Czar and had been given two quite separate tasks. Their first job was to make sure that no rival faction attempted to rob Gennadi Yasnev; they were also there to take whatever remedial action was necessary should he be tempted to make off with the money himself. Throughout the long journey to Kaliningrad, he had lived in fear, wondering if they would take it into their heads to kill him and disappear with the six million. Not surprisingly, he had been heartily relieved to see the back of them after the money had been left in the vaults of the Novgorod Bank.

Yasnev had spent Monday night at the best hotel in town and had sold the Mercedes to a kerbside street trader before catching an Aeroflot plane to St Petersburg. He'd had no business to do in the city and had gone there simply because he had been unable to get a seat on the one flight to Moscow. Yasnev had had no better luck in St Petersburg and had been forced to complete the rest of the journey by train. The apartment house on Moskovskaja Malaja near the permanent exhibition site devoted to the

Economic Achievements of the old USSR had never looked so welcoming. He trusted his mistress, Irena Mushkova, would be equally welcoming.

Yasnev paid off the unofficial taxi and walked briskly into the lobby. The six-storey apartment house had been completely gutted and refurbished in a joint venture with the Swedes. Not only did the lifts work a hundred per cent of the time but where Comrade Stalin's architects had made provision for twelve workers' flats on each floor, there were now only four luxury apartments. The tenants of yesteryear who had been privileged to live there had been evicted long ago.

Yasnev stopped by the bank of lifts, pressed the call button and found he was presented with a choice of three cars. He took the nearest and went up to the fifth floor, a lascivious smile on his face at the thought of the fun and games he was about to have with Irena. She was twenty-five years old, intelligent, well-educated and voluptuous. Irena had trained as a ballerina but had never made the grade with the Bolshoi. At twelve, she had been a slender waif; with the coming of puberty, she had shot up and put on weight. When Gennadi Yasnev had met her, Irena had been scratching a haphazard living as a part-time fashion model while running a ballet class for the children of Moscow's nouveau riche. Alighting from the lift, he turned right in the corridor, walked to the far end and let himself into the flat. Leaving his travelling bag in the hall, he went into the sitting room.

Irena Mushkova was curled up in one corner of the settee, her legs bent in a V, ankles tucked under her buttocks. She was holding the TV remote control loosely in her right hand and was watching a basketball match on Channel 1. Within reach on the low table by the armrest was a bottle of pepper vodka, tonic water and a glass with a slice of lemon floating on the dregs in the bottom. Irena gave every sign of having had too much to drink. She looked befuddled, had difficulty focusing her eyes and was unsteady on her feet when she stood up.

'What are you doing here?' she asked in a slurred voice.

Yasnev didn't reply. No explanation was necessary for what he intended to do to her. He reached out for Irena Mushkova and pulled her against him, then raised her dress and slip to waist level the better to cradle her buttocks in his hands. Irena kicked off her shoes and wrapped both arms around his neck to lift herself up until her toes were just brushing the floor as he waltzed her out of the room, across the hall and into the master bedroom. Setting Irena down, he gave her bottom a playful slap, then pushed her back on to the bed and unzipped his pants. As always, he made love like a rutting stag; as always, she responded with little cries of pleasure. That she faked it didn't bother him one iota. Finally spent, he rolled off Irena and lay on his back.

'I'm surprised you came to the apartment,' she said presently.

'Why shouldn't I? I bought the damned place; I also pay for the clothes on your back and the food in your belly.'

'The police are looking for you,' Irena told him with evident satisfaction.

'Rubbish. We practically own the entire force.'

'Nevertheless, it's true, Gennadi Yasnev. They are offering a reward in hard currency for information leading to your arrest. Ten thousand pounds, the policeman said.'

'What policeman?'

'The one from the Anti Organised Crime Division who was here yesterday morning.'

Yasnev felt his heart begin to race. How the hell did they know about the apartment house? Vera Kiselnikova, the harridan he had divorced three years ago; she knew the address of the apartment he'd bought for his fancy woman, as she called Irena. She had told the police where to find him.

'I telephoned you last night from Kaliningrad. Why didn't you warn me then?'

'Don't be angry with me,' Irena said in a brittle voice. 'I thought the police might be listening to us.'

They had tapped the phone. He had never known the police to be so efficient, but of course it wasn't every day that one of Moscow's finest could pick up a small fortune in hard currency for simply doing his job. He'd been lucky not to be arrested when he'd stepped off the train at the St Petersburg station. Ten thousand pounds; Yasnev shook his head, it was unheard of. Another even more alarming thought occurred to him. What would Arkadi Petrovich Zaytsev, The Czar of the Babushkin *Mafiozniki*, make of it? He was one of the very few men who could identify Arkadi. That being the case, Yasnev asked himself what conclusion he might draw if their positions were reversed and knew he wouldn't trust Arkadi to keep his mouth shut if he were arrested.

'The policeman who came here,' he said hoarsely, 'was he in uniform?'

'No, neither was his bodyguard.'

'Bodyguard?'

'A big man, very broad, very powerful. He was armed with an automatic rifle.'

'A Kalashnikov?'

'If that's what you call it.'

The bitch could smell the fear on him and revelled in it. He wanted to lash out, to beat her face into a bloody pulp, but satisfying though this would be, she would scream the place down while he was doing it. 'Stay here,' he rasped, 'and don't make a sound.'

Yasnev left the bedroom and walked into the sitting room which overlooked the street. He switched off the lights, went over to the settee and picking up the remote control, put the TV on standby. Once his eyes had become accustomed to the dark, he moved to the window and parted the curtains.

In what had become a distinctly up-market neighbourhood, on street parking had become the norm. But amongst the BMWs, Mercedes, Audis, Jaguars and Volvo estates, the Lada on the opposite side of the road stood out like a sore thumb even though the vehicle was in the dark shadows between two streetlights. As he watched, Yasnev saw the glow from a cigarette inside the car. The smoker would have a partner; two men could keep awake and stay alert better than one. Off duty police working for the *Mafiozniki* or officers of the Anti Organised Crime Division? No matter; they would kill him in the sure knowledge that it was safer to shoot first and ask later.

Yasnev went into the kitchen and checked the alleyway which separated the apartment house from the next one on the right. Although he couldn't see anyone, he sensed they were there watching the block of flats. The two men in the Lada must have seen him arrive and had summoned help. So why were they waiting if they had the place surrounded? The answer was obvious when you thought about it. The best time to take an armed man was in the small hours of the morning when he was at his lowest ebb. Only Yasnev wasn't armed. To avoid detection at the airport he had ditched his automatic before boarding the plane to St Petersburg, and the only self-loading pistol in the flat was a standard 9mm Makarov with just one clip of eight rounds. But even if he had a whole arsenal of weapons at his disposal, he would not survive a shoot-out with the police. All the same, he didn't like being naked; bending down, he opened the cupboard under the sink and retrieved the 9mm pistol he'd taped to the waste outlet. Then tucking the pistol into the waistband of his slacks, Yasnev returned to the sitting room and poured himself a large vodka.

There had to be a way out of this mess if only he could think straight. Arkadi Petrovich Zaytsev was arguably the biggest racketeer in town but nobody had put a price on his head in hard currency. And how had the police chief, Major General Gurov, managed to lay his hands on £10,000 when everybody knew his force was strapped for cash? And how was it his minions knew where Vera Kiselnikova was living? Then it suddenly dawned on him that they must have got her address from his army documents. The whole thing had to be political and that meant some bastard in the Kremlin was pulling the strings.

Yasnev got to his feet, moved the two armchairs up to the settee and emptied the rest of the vodka over the furniture plus another bottle which he found in the drinks cabinet. That done, he fetched Irena Mushkova from the bedroom and told her to pick up the phone.

'Dial 01, give your name and address and tell the operator the apartment building is on fire.'

'On fire?' she echoed.

'That's what I said.' Yasnev struck a match and ignited the pool of alcohol on the settee. 'Better get a move on otherwise you'll succumb to smoke inhalation.'

The flames rapidly took hold and the latex foam upholstery began to burn. Panic-stricken, Irena lifted the receiver and dialled the number of the fire service. As soon as she had finished the emergency call, Yasnev felled her with a savage downward chop across the neck. Moving swiftly, he closed the door to the sitting room behind him and left the flat. He hit the swing door next to the lifts on the run and went down the internal fire escape taking the concrete steps three at a time. When he reached the lobby, Yasnev waited by the side exit until he heard the wailing siren of the fire engine as it turned into Moskovskaja Malaja and finally stopped outside the apartment house. Then he stepped out into the alleyway and raced towards the street, making for the footpath on the other side of the road.

The fire on the fifth floor was a perfect diversion and nobody came after him. All he had to do now was stay alive until he could contact Major General Gurov in the morning.

Chapter 24

Yasnev stirred, gradually became aware that it was getting light and reluctantly opened his eyes. The whore he had picked up near the Minsk Hotel was lying flat on her back breathing through her open mouth and snoring loudly. She answered to the name of Natasha which he didn't believe for one moment was her real name; she was allegedly just thirty, also a pretty suspect claim if the lines on her face were anything to go by. She had hair the colour of straw but the roots were dark. Thinner than most Russian women of her age, Natasha had a pretty good figure except for her breasts which resembled a couple of withered pears.

He was expected to believe that Natasha was an intern at the Central Hospital in Gorki Street who had become a prostitute in her spare time simply in order to make ends meet. However, although she was better educated than the vast majority of hookers, Yasnev thought it more likely that she was a nurse. In her secondary occupation Natasha performed like a robot, but he did not feel cheated; he had not paid good money for the satisfaction she could give him in bed. All he had wanted from her was a roof over his head and somewhere to hide until morning, and this she had been able to provide.

The roof over his head was a small room in the loft above a disused stables that at one time in the long distant past had belonged to the local branch of the dairy workers' co-operative. Yasnev neither knew nor cared what had happened to the horses, the milk carts they'd pulled or the

323

delivery men themselves. They had probably all vanished from the streets of Moscow before the Great Patriotic War; at any rate, he could not remember seeing them at work and he was no youngster.

The stables were located in a courtyard off Bronaja Street. It was a part of Moscow the tourists never saw even though it was only a short walk from Gorki Street and the noise of the traffic on the inner ring motorway was clearly audible.

Yasnev reached under the grubby bolster for the 9mm Makarov and the billfold containing 380 US dollars which he had placed there for safekeeping. Taking care not to disturb Natasha, he folded the blankets and quilted eiderdown aside and got out of bed. His jacket was draped around a ladder-back chair, the slacks and shirt lay across the seat, the black shoes side by side underneath. He tucked the billfold into the breast pocket of the jacket and left the pistol on the chair, then padded over to the dormer window and looked out. It was a grey, depressing morning, the sky overcast, and there was a persistent drizzle that was likely to last all day and could turn to sleet if he was any judge of the weather.

Seven thirty-six; if you could believe what he'd told the press and TV reporters, Major General Gurov had already been at his desk for over half an hour. Faced with a crime rate that made Washington, DC, seem like a haven of peace in comparison, the Chief of Police had to give the impression that he was doing something about it. But too much was at stake for Yasnev to take anything on trust and he therefore decided to wait until 09.00 to make absolutely sure that Gurov was at his desk when he called.

Yasnev turned away from the window, retrieved his socks from under the bed and balancing on one leg at a time pulled them on, then reached for his slacks. The Makarov pistol landed on the floorboards with a loud clatter and woke Natasha.

'What was that?' she asked in a breathless voice that betrayed her alarm.

324

'Nothing, I dropped one of my shoes.'

'You're leaving?'

'Not just yet.'

'What time is it?'

Yasnev bent down, picked up the automatic and tucked it into the hip pocket of his slacks. 'A quarter to eight,' he told her.

'Holy Mother, I'm supposed to be on duty at eight.'

'You can afford to be late for once.'

'That's all you know.'

Yasnev pulled the billfold out of his jacket. 'Twenty dollars says I'm right.'

Natasha looked at the money he had dropped on to the bed. 'I guess it does,' she said and laughed throatily.

'I plan to stay another hour.'

'For twenty dollars you can spend the whole day here.'

'I'm going to use your bathroom. OK?'

'You know where it is.' She smiled. 'I like a man who keeps himself clean.'

The bathroom was in an alcove screened by a curtain and was in keeping with the hovel where Natasha entertained her men friends, as she coyly referred to the 'Johns' she picked up on the street. There was no bath, no shower and no proper washbasin, only a sink with a cold water tap. And the toilet was the Asian variety he'd become familiar with in Afghanistan, the bowl set in concrete at floor level with ridged footholds on either side and a cistern mounted on the wall. He rinsed his hands and face, found a square of cloth that served as a towel and dried himself off.

'How can you bear to live in a place like this?' he asked her from the bathroom. 'There's no kitchen, not even an electric ring . . .'

'I don't live here; this is where I do my entertaining. Unless a friend wants to stay the night with me, I go home at midnight. I live with my mother and daughter and we have a nice three-room flat in the Ramenki District near the University of Moscow.'

Yasnev brushed the curtain aside and walked through. 'You talk too much,' he told her.

'Oh.' Natasha kicked off the blankets and quilt. 'You want to do the other thing?'

She had gone to bed in her oyster-coloured slip and was still wearing it, only now it was screwed up sash-like around her waist. Her body looked stringy in daylight and he noticed her pubic hair was dark.

'You'll catch a cold like that,' he said.

'You don't want to make love?'

'No, I don't.'

Natasha pouted. 'You're a difficult man to please.'

'So I've been told.' Yasnev finished dressing, then sat down on the upright chair and lit a cigarette. 'Do you know where the nearest pay phones are?' he asked.

'There's a row of four near Puskinskaja Metro station. That is no distance from here.'

There would be a couple of militiamen on duty in the entrance hall of the Metro station; they constituted the visible evidence of Major General Gurov's highly publicised law and order campaign and were not specifically on the lookout for him. He had more to fear from the unknown foot soldiers of the Babushkin Mafia than the police. Yasnev dropped the cigarette on to the floor and crushed it under the heel of his shoe. It was still drizzling and he would look a little conspicuous in only a jacket. He went over to the hanging cupboard and looked inside.

'Who owns this?' he asked, holding up a cheap plastic mac which was about his size.

'A friend,' Natasha said. 'He forgot to take it with him when the vice squad raided the place and he had to leave in a hurry.'

Now she tells me, he thought. The damned stables was a knocking shop and he was lucky the police hadn't visited the place again last night. 'I'm borrowing it,' he said. 'Any objections?'

'You can keep it, for all I care.'

'Thanks. Maybe I'll see you again some night.'

Yasnev left the squalid room, ran down the wooden staircase, opened the Judas gate in the large stable door and stepped out into the courtyard.

The office assigned to Pavel Trilisser was on the top floor of the Council of Ministers Building. Located on the south-east side and almost under the great dome, he had an unrivalled view of the Kremlin Theatre and little else, other than a glimpse of the Saviour's Tower. Had he been given a room overlooking Red Square from the Arsenal Tower to St Basil's Cathedral, it would not have made a jot of difference to him. As the special adviser on Foreign Affairs to President Yeltsin, he was far too busy to spend time looking out of the window.

This morning was no exception. The Iranians wished to build a nuclear reactor for peaceful purposes and were willing to pay through the nose to acquire the fissionable material and the necessary technology. Moscow could supply them with everything they needed and could use their petrodollars. President Yeltsin was not averse to the deal but wished to know what sort of reaction he could expect from the West before making up his mind. The short answer was that the Americans wouldn't like it one bit and might well impose all kinds of economic sanctions. Worse still, it was likely they could persuade the British, French and German Governments to take similar action and then the fat would really be in the fire. That was the gist of the assessment Trilisser intended to put before the President for his consideration and was in the process of drafting the paper when the telephone rang. Annoyed at the interruption, he reached out, lifted the receiver and tartly asked who was calling.

'It's me, Gurov,' an equally terse voice informed him. 'Can we talk? It's important and confidential.'

'Then we'd better not converse in clear language.' Trilisser depressed the button on the cradle to activate the secure speech facility and waited. 'Now, what can I do for you?' he asked a few seconds later.

'I've just had a phone call from a man claiming to be Gennadi Yasnev. He rang my office direct, didn't come through the 02 switchboard operator.'

Trilisser couldn't understand why Gurov should be surprised that a member of the *Mafiozniki* knew his phone number when half his personal office staff were probably on the payroll of the Babushkin family. 'What did he have to say?'

'Yasnev wants to give himself up, but there are conditions. He will surrender only to me personally. He says he has seen me on television and knows the sound of my voice. He also thinks I can be trusted. That reward you told me to put on his head has really got him going. If you ask me, he is scared stiff his own people will put a bullet through him.'

'Never mind that,' Trilisser said impatiently. 'How do you propose to take him into custody?'

'Yasnev is going to ring again at three minutes after ten and give me a rendezvous. As soon as I know where he is, I'll have my officers pick him up.'

'No, I'm afraid that's not good enough, General. You are the only one he trusts so you have to be there.'

'I have better things to do with my time. You seem to forget I am the Chief of Police.'

'You will do as I tell you,' Trilisser informed him in a cold rage. 'Otherwise you will be lucky to find a job as a road sweeper. Choose three good officers to go with you, men you would trust with your life. When you have Yasnev, take him out to your house.'

'My house?' Gurov exclaimed as if unable to believe his ears.

'You are responsible for his wellbeing, General, and I can't think of a safer place. Do I make myself clear?'

'Perfectly.'

'Good. Call me as soon as you have Yasnev in your custody.'

Trilisser hung up, then buzzed Larissa Grushkova on the intercom and told her to come in.

'I have a job for you,' he announced when she entered his office. 'I want you to get in touch with your friend at the British Embassy and arrange to meet him this evening. You can imply that you have some vital information concerning the present whereabouts of Gennadi Yasnev, alias Georgi Mugrowski.'

Ashton was in the middle of breakfast when Quorn telephoned the hotel and informed him in the usual guarded language that there had been another fresh development and his presence was therefore required forthwith. Yesterday they had been busy, busy, busy, getting nowhere fast and Ashton had a feeling that today, Wednesday, 12 October, was going to be a repeat performance. The army had a saying for it – 'When in doubt, run about, scream and shout.' To give Jill Sheridan her due, she always knew what she was doing and never lost her head. She was, however, hyperactive, like a person with a thyroid problem, and rather than play a waiting game, would happily go down a blind alley as she had done with Helga von Schinkel yesterday afternoon.

Contrary to what Ashton had anticipated, Jill and Helga had got on like a house on fire. No two women could have been less alike but a stranger observing them in animated conversation would never have guessed it. Yet despite the rapport between them, Helga had been unable to recall anything she hadn't already told Heinrich Voigt.

Jill had drawn an equal blank with Caspar Lemberg, whom she had decided to call on when they left the St Francis Hospital on Budapesterstrasse. Although the CIA Station Chief had greatly admired her physical attractions, he hadn't been prepared to jeopardise his career on her behalf. The only information they had on Louise Helen Kay had been gleaned from the cable the FBI had sent to Interpol Headquarters, St Cloud. The full biography which almost certainly contained a great deal of material the Bureau was unaware of, was locked away in the vaults at Langley. But whatever doubts Caspar Lemberg might have about the trustworthiness of the woman who now called herself Leila Khalif, he had refused to ask the Deputy Director Operations for a print-out of her file. His attitude was understandable; Langley had told him all he needed to know and to ape Oliver Twist and ask for more would be asking for the same kind of trouble.

Ashton left the hotel and drove round to the Schweizerhof. Although Quorn hadn't said so, he assumed Jill would expect him to pick her up. Turning into Budapesterstrasse, he spotted her waiting on the pavement outside the hotel. He could have sworn she was tapping her foot and discovered he hadn't been mistaken when Jill got into the Volkswagen and informed him he was late.

'What do you mean, late? I only heard from Steven a few minutes ago.'

'Where were you then? He rang me at seven thirty.'

'Hey,' Ashton said. 'Why are we having this spat? It won't be the end of the world if we keep them waiting a few minutes.'

In the event, they were more than a few minutes late. The rush hour was in full spate, the *Polizeipräsidium* on the Tempelhofer Damm was a fair way across town and they seemed to hit a red at every set of traffic lights. They were met in the entrance hall by an agitated-looking Steven Quorn who whisked them up to the office of the Police President on the top floor where Caspar Lemberg was awaiting their arrival with some impatience. Voigt himself looked relaxed and unperturbed. In the short time they had been acquainted, Ashton couldn't recall when he had been quite so cheerful. The reason why Voigt was in such a good humour became clear when he announced that one of the grey Transit vans had been found near Münster.

'At a small town called Handorf off Route 51,' he added. 'The vehicle had been abandoned on the forecourt of a disused filling station on the outskirts. It was found at 21.09 hours last night by two patrolmen. The full number of the vehicle is M dash HB 9132.'

'Surely that can't be right?' Jill frowned and glanced at Ashton. 'I was given to understand that the delivery van seen at the Stroop farm was M blank R 84 blank blank.'

'Indeed, that was the incomplete number reported by the witness, Miss Sheridan.'

'Then how do you know this other vehicle was at the farm?'

Ashton closed his eyes. Jill should have allowed Voigt to tell her why in his own way instead of leaping in like a sniffer dog. Now, she was about to be cut down to size.

'The Ford Transit van was made in England,' Voigt said with evident relish. 'The number plate belongs to an Audi. Also the original colour of the van was dark blue. We know that because the driver backed into something and scraped the rear-wheel housing.'

'Looks as though the vehicle was stolen to order,' Ashton said.

'So it would seem.'

'Be interesting to know the name and address of the real owner.'

If one van had been stolen to order, so had the other, and by the same gang of car thieves. Both vehicles had been given a quick spray job, fitted with false UK plates and delivered to an address on the Continent within twenty-four hours of being lifted off the street. Either C1O, the stolen motor vehicle investigation branch of the Met or the Criminal Intelligence Unit would have a shrewd idea which crooked dealer had done the job. Find that man and lean on him hard enough and he might be persuaded to name the client or the client's agent on the Continent. But first it was necessary to start with the vehicle.

'The Driver and Vehicle Licensing Centre at Swansea would have the original owner on record,' Ashton continued, tactfully feeling his way. 'All they need are the chassis and engine numbers.'

'I'm assured the matter is in hand.' Voigt turned to Caspar Lemberg. 'You've heard nothing more from your source?'

'Not a word.'

'But now we have a better idea where she was calling from. Yes?'

'I heard a jet and the noise of traffic in the background. If there's an airfield near Handorf, I'd say we did. We'll have an even clearer notion when the second Transit van is found.'

'You believe they've dumped it somewhere?'

'Don't you?' Lemberg countered.

'Yes. I think the nuclear explosives have been transferred to another vehicle, perhaps more than one vehicle. It depends on how many targets they intend to hit.'

Voigt was also certain in his own mind that wherever the Hizbollah-cum-Abu Nidal terrorists were now, they were definitely off his patch and were unlikely to return. Berlin to Handorf was approximately 300 miles and that was a long way to drive merely to create a diversion.

'There are really no juicy targets in this city. With this nuclear capability they've got, threatening the seat of government would make a great deal more sense.'

'We're talking about Bonn?' Jill said.

'Or Paris, Miss Sheridan, or perhaps even London. In the circumstances, you may wish to reduce the size of your team in Berlin.'

Ashton thought he had a point even if it did sound like a none too subtle invitation to leave. To his surprise, Jill agreed with the Police President. However, she did want to leave Quorn in place for a couple of days or so just in case something did crop up. After Voigt had indicated such an arrangement was OK with him, it was handshakes all round and time to leave. Jill Sheridan planned to call on Gerald Willmore before flying to Bonn where she intended to give the SIS Head of Station a run-down on the Abu Nidal and Hizbollah terrorist organisations.

'And you?' she asked as they drove away from the *Polizeipräsidium*.

'I'm going home,' Ashton told her. 'This is strictly a

police job and there's nothing for me to do in Berlin.'

The scenery had become so familiar that Manfull didn't need to look at the Pontiac's odometer or catch a road sign to know how far he was from Eureka Springs. Sixty miles to go before another head-to-head encounter with Donna Kay, only this time he wouldn't be treating her like she was a fragile piece of china. The lady had not been entirely honest with him, a fact he should have recognised when he had first made her acquaintance and she had shown him into her husband's den. Amongst the popular novels, biographies, several histories of the American Civil War and textbooks covering micro- and macroeconomics which crammed the bookshelves from floor to ceiling down the whole of one wall, there had been a collection of leather-bound diaries. Kay had been a regular Samuel Pepys and hadn't missed a year from 1971 to 1993. The thing was, there had been no sign of the one he had been keeping for 1994 and Manfull found it hard to believe he'd broken what appeared to be the habit of a lifetime. A gut instinct told him that for some reason Donna had hidden the diary, maybe even destroyed it.

But the imminent confrontation with Donna Kay was not the only difference about this particular trip compared with the other two. This time around, Eureka Springs was merely the first stop on what could be a long and protracted journey. He had been entrusted to find out everything he could about Louise Helen Kay, going right back to her formative years in Jefferson City and Fulton. Normally, the investigation would have been conducted by the appropriate field office in Missouri but Director Louis Freeh had wanted him to do it which Manfull thought was very flattering, though his wife, Sandra-Lee, wasn't too thrilled with the news that he would be away from home for several days.

An essentially modest man, he couldn't really understand why Director Freeh should have such faith in him but the fact was the Bureau had sent him the unabridged photocopy of their file on the Kay woman which nobody outside Washington had ever seen before. Apparently, it was all down to the advert he'd found in Kay's office in downtown Eureka Springs. 'Vacation brochures wanted. Write Box 870, Postal Station A, Toronto.' The Royal Canadian Mounted Police had been asked to look into it; although they had been unable to identify which newspaper had run the advert, they had ascertained that the box number had been rented for six months with effect from Wednesday, 20 July, by a woman calling herself Noreen Tal.

Ashton turned into Rylett Close and parked the Vauxhall Cavalier in the nearest vacant space to number 84. It had been one of those journeys where anything which could go wrong had gone wrong, starting from the moment a myopic old gentleman had shunted into the Volkswagen at the last set of traffic lights before the rental agency on Budapesterstrasse. Had Ashton returned the car to Hertz at the airport, he wouldn't have been involved in a stupid traffic accident. But he hadn't wanted to leave Berlin without saying hello and goodbye to Willie Baumgart and he'd figured to kill two birds with one stone by ringing Blitz Taxis and asking Willie to drive him to the airport. What had seemed to be a good idea had failed to gell. Sorting out the traffic accident had taken for ever and when he had rung the taxi office in Theodor-Heutssplatz the girl in the dispatcher's office had told him that Willie was off sick.

That had only been the beginning of Ashton's troubles. It seemed a significant percentage of the indigenous population wanted to leave the city and he had had to settle for a flight that went via Düsseldorf. The plane had been ten minutes late taking off and had then been held in a stack over the Ruhr because of some problem with air-traffic control. As a result, he had missed his connecting flight and had spent an hour in the departure lounge waiting for the next one to London. The final straw had occurred at Heathrow when he'd collected the Vauxhall Cavalier from the long-stay car park and found the rear offside tyre was flat.

The world suddenly became a better place when he let himself into the house, announced that he was home and Harriet came running to throw her arms around him.

'That was some welcome,' he said when they finally disentangled.

'You wait until tonight,' Harriet told him.

'So why don't we go to bed now?' Ashton glanced at his wristwatch, and grinned. 'It's gone eight.'

'Dinner will be on the table in five minutes.'

'Well, we can't pass that up.'

'Not after all the trouble I've gone to keeping the food hot without it drying up.'

Ashton went upstairs for a quick wash and a peep at his sleeping son, then returned to go through the letters on the hall table. Besides bills from British Telecom and British Gas and a wad of unsolicited mail, there was an official-looking envelope. The letter inside was signed by Roy Kelso. In view of the content, Ashton thought that putting his signature to it must have really stuck in his craw.

'They've agreed to take me back,' he said jubilantly and walked into the kitchen to show the letter to Harriet. 'See for yourself.'

The offer was everything he could have hoped for. To be sure, there was a slight catch, but the loss of a year's seniority was something he could live with. The Treasury weren't insisting that the golden handshake he'd received on resigning from the SIS should be refunded at once; they were prepared to see the repayments spread over five years at a nominal rate of interest. That was the worst case; if Harriet's brother did go ahead and buy their house in Lincoln, they would be able to repay most of the debt in one go and they could then think about getting a mortgage on 84 Rylett Close.

'What exactly is a Desk Officer Grade One (O and GD)?' Harriet asked.

'I haven't the foggiest idea. I'll ask Victor when I phone him to accept the offer.'

Harriet supposed a minor celebration would be in order and suggested he nipped round to the supermarket which was still open and bought a bottle of champagne. When they finally got around to it, dinner was something of a burnt offering, but the Lanson Black Label went down very well and they were both on a high. The downer came with *The Nine O'Clock News* on BBC 1 and pictures of the aftermath of a car bombing on the Boulevard Périphérique near the Pont de Chatillon in Paris's 14th *Arrondissement*.

Chapter 25

Hazelwood sensed the air of expectancy as soon as he entered the conference room to hold the usual morning prayers. It was evident that neither of the two announcements he wished to make would come as a total surprise to the assembled company. That news of Ashton's reinstatement had become common knowledge was perhaps only to be expected. The initial application and subsequent correspondence with the Foreign Office and the Treasury had been processed through the Administrative Wing and while Roy Kelso wouldn't have said anything, it was possible the clerical staff would not have observed the same degree of confidentiality amongst themselves. How they had become aware of the other matter was beyond him, but clearly word must have got out since, against all the odds, Jill Sheridan had returned from Bonn in time to attend morning prayers.

'You got your skates on, Jill,' Hazelwood observed. 'We weren't expecting you back until much later this morning.'

'I finished earlier than expected and managed to catch the last flight from Düsseldorf yesterday.' She smiled fleetingly. 'Head of Station, Bonn was kind enough to provide me with transport to the airport.'

'Glad' rather than 'kind' would have been the more appropriate word, Hazelwood thought sourly, but then he had always found that a little of Jill Sheridan's company went a very long way.

'Two points,' he said briskly. 'First, I regret to inform you that the Director has tendered his resignation on grounds of ill health. I'm sure we are all going to miss Stuart.'

Everybody round the table nodded in unison. Going one better, Garfield cleared his throat and added, 'Hear, hear.'

'The question of who is to succeed him in the long term is currently under discussion.'

In breaking the news of Stuart's resignation last night, the Cabinet Secretary had informed Hazelwood that he was in the running for the appointment. He had also been advised not to read too much into it because there were two other very strong candidates for the post. No names had been mentioned and Hazelwood hadn't bothered to ask; the only man he had to beat was himself and he had no intention of losing that contest. His reputation for taking what others deemed were unacceptable risks counted against him. But the end results nearly always justified his actions, like the subsequent air drop of nuclear weapons at the Stroop farm had for the Berlin operation. Sure, he'd been lucky, but that was an essential element. All the brains in the world were of little account if you didn't have a lucky winning streak.

'The other piece of news is that Peter Ashton is rejoining us in the newly created appointment of Operations and General Duties.'

Under General Duties, Ashton would be responsible for the syllabuses of all courses held at Amberley Lodge, liaison with MI5, the Security Service, on matters of common interest, and the co-ordination of military assistance from the armed forces whenever applicable. He would also be responsible for technical services, which meant he would inherit Mr Terry Hicks, a sea change that had met with the whole-hearted approval of Roy Kelso who couldn't abide the electronics king at any price. So far as operations were concerned, Hazelwood was anxious to make it clear that this did not involve Intelligence gathering. Heads of Departments therefore had nothing to fear and would continue to exercise absolute control over their own fiefdoms.

Jill stopped making notes on her scratchpad and looked up. 'So who's he answerable to, Victor?' she asked slyly. 'The DG?'

'Yes.'

'I see. Does this mean that the Treasury is now prepared to restore some of the cuts in the establishment we've been forced to make?'

Hazelwood was ahead of her. What Jill really wanted to know was how he had managed to get financial approval for the post when every department had had its budget slashed to the bone. It was none of her business but nevertheless he felt constrained to explain how economies in other non operational areas had made it possible. Jill had lost a champion in Stuart Dunglass, she had made a bad marriage and there was a messy divorce in the offing which might damage her career. Her professional conduct while running the Intelligence setup in the United Arab Emirates had also been called into question and no one was more dangerous than Jill Sheridan when she had her back to the wall and was feeling vulnerable.

'The Treasury hasn't relaxed its grip on public expenditure,' Hazelwood began, then completely lost the thread of what he was about to say as he attempted to anticipate what Jill's next point would be. Help came from the most unexpected quarter.

'Perhaps I can explain how the post has been funded,' Kelso said, and immediately turned to Jill Sheridan. 'It's really very simple. In future, we shall be sharing the Training School at Amberley Lodge with the Security Service. This means that half the running costs will be borne by MI5.'

'Stuart would never have sanctioned that proposal; he wanted to retain Amberley Lodge for our sole use.'

'I'm afraid you are mistaken, Jill,' Kelso said acerbically. 'So far as that particular issue was concerned, Stuart had thrown in the towel over a month ago.'

'Thank you, Roy,' Hazelwood said with genuine feeling. He looked around the table; it was time to get things back on track and he could see from his animated expression that Garfield had some news to impart. 'Yes, Rowan? You have something to tell us?'

'We've got Gennadi Yasnev,' Garfield said triumphantly. 'He gave himself up to Major General Gurov.'

'When did this happen?'

'Late yesterday afternoon, though Head of Station, Moscow wasn't informed until 22.00 hours local time.'

Had he been wearing a hat, Hazelwood would have thrown it high into the air. It had been his idea to offer a reward of £10,000 for information leading to the arrest of Gennadi Yasnev. He had found the money out of the Director's contingency fund and in doing so had broken all the rules, but it had worked.

'Head of Station has a list of questions to put to Yasnev,' Garfield continued, 'but he may want something in return, like political asylum for instance.'

'I think that's a matter you and I should discuss later,' Hazelwood said judiciously. 'What about the bombing on the Boulevard Périphérique? Any word on that from Paris?'

'Nothing specific. It's probably down to the Algerian fundamentalists and is part of their campaign to punish the French for supporting the unelected military régime in their country.'

'I expect you're right.' Hazelwood pointed to the Assistant Director responsible for the Pacific Basin and Rest of the World Department. 'What have you got for us, Roger?' he asked.

The welcome Ashton had received when he'd walked into Vauxhall Cross had been akin to that afforded the prodigal son. Frank Warren, the head of the Security Vetting and Technical Services Division, had been waiting for him in the entrance hall with a temporary pass, but that had only been the beginning of the red carpet treatment. The office he had been allocated on the fourth floor was half as big again as the one he'd had in Benbow House and the riverside view was a thousand per cent more pleasing to the eye than the rooftops of Southwark.

'You're spoiling me rotten, Frank,' he said with a grin.

'Well, it's good to have you back.'

'I can tell you it feels good to be back.'

'Even if it means seeing more of Roy Kelso?'

'A small price to pay. How do you feel about losing Terry Hicks to me?'

'It's no skin off my nose, Peter.' Warren frowned. 'Does this mean you will be responsible for the spring cleaning programme?'

Spring cleaning was the in-house jargon for an electronic security check. In practice, this meant Hicks descended on a number of different embassies every year and swept the secure areas in each one to make sure none of the offices had been bugged.

'I haven't the foggiest idea,' Ashton told him. 'What's the present state of play?'

'The programme for 1995 is fixed.'

'Then let's wait and see what happens. OK?'

'Sure. You need a new ID card so I've told Hicks to have one of his photographers take your picture at 10.30 hours, if that's convenient.'

'No problem. Where do I meet him?'

'He has a studio of sorts in the basement.' Warren hesitated, shifted his weight from one foot to the other as if acutely embarrassed. 'We also need to update your vetting status. It's all very well for Victor to blithely announce that he has restored your security clearance but there's nothing about it on your file and a lot of water has flowed under the bridge in the last twelve months or so. I mean, so far as the paperwork is concerned, you are still a single man.'

'In other words, you want to arrange an in-depth interview.'

'Yes, I'm afraid it has to be done.'

'Fine. Who's going to grill me?'

'Well, Brian Thomas is available,' Warren said and did another soft-shoe shuffle.

Ex-Detective Chief Superintendent Brian Thomas had certainly lit a fire under Henry Clayburn with his searching questions.

'I know he can be very offensive,' Warren continued awkwardly, 'and he's duty bound to ask for a detailed account of your financial position, but–'

'It's OK, Frank,' Ashton said, interrupting him. 'I know what to expect and it doesn't bother me. Are you still using him as a sort of unofficial liaison officer with the Met?'

'Brian has his contacts at Scotland Yard.'

'Good. There's something he can do for me.' Ashton told him about the Ford Transit van which had been found on the forecourt of a disused filling station outside Handorf and something of its history. 'The local Kripo are supposed to have sent the engine and chassis numbers to Scotland Yard so that they can check the details with Swansea. I want to know what the Met has turned up, whether any other Ford Transit went missing within a fifty-mile radius of the stolen vehicle and the name of the most likely candidate for the job.'

'Anything else?'

'Yes, I'd like Brian to encourage the Met to piss on the thief until he gives us the name of the client who placed the order.'

'I'm not sure they will be willing to do that,' Warren said doubtfully. 'They could find themselves in hot water if the dealer's got a smart lawyer.'

'Then get me his name and address,' Ashton said, 'and I'll piss on him.'

Major General Gurov left the rococo-style building, which at one time had belonged to the All Russian Insurance Company, by the back door. Before he boarded the armour-plated Zil limousine which was parked in the alley between Police Headquarters and the Lubyanka Prison, two militiamen checked to make sure the passageway was clear. In the good old bad days, the entire Politburo and every top-ranking Soviet apparatchik had been driven everywhere in a bullet-proof car even though the odds against somebody attempting to assassinate them had been astronomical. Today the threat was very real, with newspapermen, judges and senior police officers the principal targets. Worse still, the *Mafiozniki* had demonstrated that an armour-plated limousine was no protection against a man armed with an RPG-16 rocket launcher which could inflict crippling damage on a T72 main battle tank.

Dzerzhinsky Square, as Gurov preferred to remember it, was no distance from the Kremlin, but in his hyper-anxious state, the journey seemed to take for ever. He did not begin to unwind until his driver swept through the gates of St Saviour's Tower and circled round the former Presidium of the Supreme Soviet to deliver him safely outside the Council of Ministers Building.

Gurov took the lift up to the top floor and sought out President Yeltsin's special adviser on Foreign Affairs. Although Larissa Grushkova must have consulted the great man when she had made the appointment on his behalf, there was nothing civil about the way Pavel Trilisser received him.

'You've got five minutes, General,' he said icily.

'This is important.'

'So is my time.'

Gurov struggled to contain his anger. 'This concerns Gennadi Yasnev and the list of questions you wanted my officers to ask him.'

'I told you to conduct the interrogation.'

'It doesn't matter what you said,' Gurov exploded. 'Yasnev refuses to open his mouth until he is guaranteed immunity from prosecution and political asylum in the West.'

'Tell him that isn't negotiable.'

'And then what?'

343

'You keep chipping away, he'll crack in the end.' Trilisser plucked a file from the in-tray and opened it at the page that had been flagged up for his attention. 'Now, if you've quite finished, I'd like to get on.'

Gurov remained seated. 'I want this piece of filth out of my house.'

'Impossible,' Trilisser said without looking up from the file.

'Every foot soldier in the Babushkin *Mafiozniki* is after his hide and he knows it.'

'All the more reason why he should stay with you. Your home is a fortress.'

'You call a few security lights, a couple of TV cameras and a mangy guard dog with an alcoholic handler a fortress?'

'And four dedicated police officers. Let's not forget them, General.'

'I haven't. I'm just wondering how long I can rely on them; it doesn't take an IQ of a genius to figure out that the *Mafiozniki* know where to find him by now. You said yourself that half of my officers were on the payroll of some mob.'

'But not, I hope, the men you picked to guard Gennadi Yasnev.'

'When are you going to leave this ivory tower and step out into the real world? My officers are not facing a bunch of thugs armed with Makarov pistols and Kalashnikov assault rifles. These people have access to weapons that will reduce my house to a pile of rubble before the switchboard operator on the 01 exchange can answer up. Of course, that's assuming some upright citizen bothers to call in and report what's happening.' Gurov leaned forward and pointed a stubby finger at Trilisser. 'I'm telling you that if this situation isn't resolved by this time tomorrow afternoon, I will transfer Yasnev to the Lubyanka and to hell with the consequences. Some warder will probably cut his throat or string him up for a consideration but it will be no more than the bastard deserves.'

'I'm beginning to think a tour of duty in Chechnya will do you the world of good,' Trilisser said, and stretched his mouth in a smile that had all the warmth of a Siberian winter. 'Chief of Police, Grozny; now there is an appointment going begging.'

'When can I leave?'

'Don't be stupid. Promise Yasnev whatever he wants but get him talking. You shouldn't find it too difficult; after all, he insisted on surrendering to you personally because he believed you could be trusted.'

'I was a face he had seen on TV, a voice he'd heard. That was the sole basis of his trust. It does not extend to disclosing information to me or any other Russian. Furthermore, Gennadi Yasnev would not believe any promise I made him.'

'He would believe it if you threatened to turn him loose on the streets of Moscow.'

Gurov shook his head. Pavel Trilisser was a highly intelligent man, brilliant even. He had received accelerated promotion to lieutenant general and at one time he had been the youngest Deputy Head of the KGB's First Chief Directorate. However, in this instance, he was not living up to his reputation and was being just plain stupid. Yasnev might have maintained a vow of silence like some damned monk but he had listened to all the questions and had realised he had been dealt an incredibly strong hand.

'You couldn't be more wrong,' Gurov told him and explained why he was convinced that Yasnev would call his bluff. 'He knows the Yankees and the English are behind this and calculates that we daren't offend Washington.'

'It occurs to me that we may have to arrange a face-to-face meeting with one of the diplomats from the British Embassy.'

'That's still no good. Yasnev will only talk to somebody he knows by sight.'

'Does he have anyone in mind?'

'Yes, the man he saw at the funeral in Berlin.' Gurov frowned. 'He thinks his name is Ashmore.'

'Ashton,' Trilisser said. 'He means Ashton.'

'So?'

'So I'll have to see what can be done.'

Dean Rennert was a perfectionist. Given a job to do, he demanded the same degree of commitment from the staff of the FBI's Identification Division. Consequently, the senior computer analyst and his team had almost lost count of the number of programmes they had been required to write since the initial trawl had thrown up the names of Mary Jo Harnak, Louise Helen Kay and Noreen Tal. Initially, they had been told to ignore the crazies and religious nuts and exclude fund raisers for the IRA; then, in a complete about face, Rennert had instructed them to include them. Nothing else had changed; they were still looking for a woman of the same age and same physical characteristics as before. The computer had spewed out literally hundreds of names, including one goofy lady from Phoenix, Arizona, who'd actually had her thyroid removed in 1992; she had subsequently been eliminated when, as a result of further enquiries, it was discovered that she was currently serving five to ten years for aggravated assault, having stabbed an old woman who had referred to her religious sect as a bunch of perverts.

The final programme Rennert had asked them to write had been the most baffling of all. They had pulled every known extremist, male and female, and then matched the resultant list of names against the profile of Louise Helen Kay to see if at any time one of them might have crossed her path. The computer analyst had no idea what the Bureau proposed to do with this information, he merely underlined a couple of possibilities and gave the print-out to Rennert. After studying the document for some fifteen minutes, the Head of the Identification Division walked it over to Director Freeh's office on Pennsylvania Avenue.

'We've come up with two names,' Rennert told him, 'but

I recommend we forget the woman. She might have been born in the same town but she moved away from Jefferson City when Louise Kay was four years old. That leaves us with the man.'

Rennert didn't need to elaborate; the whole known biography of the suspect was summarised in the print-out.

Nathan B. Ungley, born Kansas City, Kansas, 5 August 1952. Married: first Ruth Fischer, 4 July 1970, divorced 19 April 1973. Married: second Elvira Hess, 20 February 1975, divorced 24 September 1978. Served in Vietnam with 1207th Artillery Battalion from October 1971 to March 1972 when unit withdrawn from Theatre of Operations. Attended Fulton University 1982, dropped out same year. Current address – Cook Road, Elk Prairie, Missouri. Self-styled company commander Missouri Militiamen.

'What does the initial "B" stand for?' Freeh asked.

'I don't know, Director. I could check with the Pentagon?'

'It's not that important. I see Ungley would have been at Fulton when Louise Helen Kay was a second-year student,' he said, looking up from the print-out.

'Yeah, that's the only connection. There's no evidence to show they ever met, but she was politically active in 1982.'

'OK, we'll fax these details to Little Rock for immediate attention Agent Manfull. He can look into it, maybe find a link.'

'Right.'

'Do we happen to know the strength of this crackpot outfit Ungley commands?'

'Five, including himself, Director.'

Freeh moved the print-out to the pending tray. 'That's some army,' he said derisively.

Hazelwood thought there had been a subtle change in the attitude towards him by Heads of Departments. 'The King is dead, long live the King.' It was almost as if they knew he would be confirmed in the appointment even though the selection process hadn't yet started. Every Assistant Director had made a point of dropping by his office metaphorically to touch their forelocks. Even the Commandant of the Training School down at Petersfield had phoned him twice to discover what assistance he could expect to receive from Ashton, despite the fact that this had been clearly spelled out in the establishment proposal. Nobody had called on him more often than Rowan Garfield, but there was a lot going on in his area and Hazelwood wasn't surprised when he appeared yet again. A not unreasonable hope that there had been further developments in Moscow evaporated in less than a minute.

'I'm afraid this is about the incident on the Boulevard Périphérique.' Garfield closed the door behind him, then pulled up a chair and sat down. 'It's more serious than we thought. The explosion was the result of a traffic accident caused by a Renault truck. Apparently the vehicle in front of it was overloaded and shed several crates of bottled beer which shattered on impact. A couple of tyres on the Renault were ripped to shreds by the broken glass and the driver lost control. He hit the crash barrier at one hell of a lick and the truck flipped over at least twice before coming to rest upside down. The vehicle burst into flames almost immediately and the fire was so intense and engulfed the Renault so rapidly that nobody could approach it. Unfortunately, the truck then blew up, killing several people who'd tried to rescue the driver. This was shortly before the fire brigade arrived on the scene. It seems the Renault was carrying a load of oxygen cylinders and at first it was thought a number of these had exploded.'

'But now we know this wasn't the case?' Hazelwood suggested.

Garfield nodded. 'From fragments recovered at the scene, it appears the vehicle was carrying at least one nuclear sub kiloton artillery shell. Thank God the munition hadn't been armed and only the conventional detonating charge which sets off the chain reaction went up.'

'That was fortunate,' Hazelwood said and was conscious of sounding trite.

'Yes, wasn't it? Question is, where do we go from here, Victor?'

'That's easy,' Hazelwood told him. 'I want you to phone the Paris Station and instruct them to get hold of every picture of the incident they can and send the lot over by special courier tonight. As soon as we have the photographs, one of your officers is to deliver them to the Atomic Weapons Research Establishment, Aldermaston, with a request that they estimate how many shells it had taken to cause such widespread destruction.'

Chapter 26

Ashton gazed at the triangular desk calendar which showed January to June on one face and July to December on the reverse. Made of thin cardboard and published by Her Majesty's Stationery Office, it was issued to all government offices. It had absolutely no artistic merit but there was nothing else to look at apart from the river, and that meant turning his back on Brian Thomas. To make matters worse, he had nothing to occupy him; the In, Pending and Out trays were empty and likely to remain so until Heads of Departments decided to send him the odd file for information. He had already set the combination on the office safe and now, ten minutes into Friday morning, he was reduced to twiddling his thumbs while ex-Detective Chief Superintendent Thomas perused the financial statement which he and Harriet had prepared yesterday evening.

'Have you got a prospective buyer for the house in Lincoln?' Thomas asked, looking up from the statement.

'Yes, Harriet's brother wants it; he's leaving the RAF and plans to settle in that part of the world.'

'Let's hope he doesn't change his mind then.'

There was no need for Thomas to elaborate. If for any reason brother-in-law did back out, the Ashtons could find themselves strapped for cash. Mortgage interest and the endowment policy on the property were gobbling up £800 a month between them and while the Treasury had agreed he could repay the golden handshake over three years at a minimal rate of interest, it would still amount to another £1,400. Tax, national insurance contributions and the premium on a Personal Equity Plan made a big hole in what was left of his salary after these deductions. Most of the basic housekeeping already came out of Harriet's money and were it not for the fact that they were living rent-free at 84 Rylett Close, they really would be up against it.

'If you do have to find another buyer, will the house fetch the asking price?'

'I think so, but who can tell?' Ashton shrugged. 'The bottom's dropped out of the housing market, but we'll survive whatever happens.'

'I'm sure you will.' Thomas slipped the financial statement into the folder he was nursing on his lap. 'Is there anything else you want to tell me in strict confidence?'

It was the stock question every vetting officer asked at the end of an in-depth subject interview. They had discussed his attitude towards drugs, sex and alcohol abuse yesterday afternoon and he had told Thomas that he had never experimented with uppers, downers, angel dust or any other mind-blowing drug. He had also informed the ex-Detective Chief Superintendent that he was a normal heterosexual, was not having an extra-marital affair and was not addicted to alcohol. Trite as the concluding question might sound, Ashton knew from his days as Head of the Security Vetting and Technical Services Division that it often elicited a startling disclosure. He recalled one candidate who'd confessed to being a transvestite who liked to be spanked by other men.

'You've heard the whole of my life history, Brian.' Ashton smiled. 'Now, is there anything you'd like to tell me?'

Thomas closed the file and put it into his briefcase. 'I thought you were never going to ask,' he said. 'Your friend, Heinrich Voigt, wasn't misinformed; the local Kripo did send the engine and chassis numbers to Scotland Yard. According to Swansea, the registered owner of the Ford

Transit is Woodnut and Son, Florists, of Somerset Road, New Barnet. The vehicle was reported missing on Monday, 5 September.'

Four days before Gamal al Hassan had contacted Head of Station, Cairo to report that he was on the way to Berlin, and exactly one week before Quorn and Moresby had flown into the city with a cool 250,000 US dollars in cash. Right from the beginning Ashton had thought Hizbollah had two cells operating on the Continent: an assault team of natural-born killers and a logistic support group. The date order of the incidents suggested he was right.

'Was another Transit van stolen around the same time?' Ashton asked.

'There most certainly was. The cheeky bastards lifted a BT van out of a secure compound at Neasden. It was a real pro job. They cut a hole in the steel mesh fence, put the guard dog to sleep with a tranquillising dart, hogtied its handler and drove out through the main gate.'

'And the date?'

'Sunday, 4 September. The scumbag in the frame for both jobs is a Mr Ronnie Aylesford.'

'Where does he hang out?'

'Raynes Park, south of the river. Describes himself as a Used Car Dealer, trades as R.A. Motors Limited. Part of his business is legit; he's registered for VAT, gets the returns in on time and employs a very sharp accountant to keep the Inland Revenue off his back. Above all, he never fouls his own doorstep; that's why these two vans were taken from locations in North London.'

Every police officer in V District knew that Aylesford was making a fortune out of insurance write-offs, that registration documents of vehicles damaged beyond economic repair in traffic accidents were being transferred to cars that had been stolen off the street. Proving it was another matter.

'They've never been able to catch him at it. Aylesford uses subcontractors to do the business; he tells them the make and year and they go out and steal it to order. The vehicle is then driven to some lock-up in London where it's given a paint spray to conform with the description of the insurance write-off and is fitted with the requisite plates.'

'What's V District doing about this latest caper?'

'They've already done it,' Thomas said. 'They took him in for questioning and rattled his cage but he laughed in their faces. He's got a solicitor who's just as smart as his accountant and he walked out of the New Malden nick within two hours of being arrested.'

'And that's it?'

'They'll keep an eye on him as they've been doing all along.'

'Well, let's attack the bastard from another angle. Suppose you get me the name and address of his smart-arsed accountant?'

'What exactly do you have in mind, Mr Ashton?'

'I'm going to make that accountant piss in his pants.'

Ashton intended to put the man under surveillance even if it meant going outside The Firm to hire private detectives from a reputable agency. He would have the little creep followed everywhere, night and day, and at some stage would make sure that Aylesford's financial wizard was aware of it. He also had the services of Terry Hicks on call and if necessary was prepared to bug a whole directory of telephone numbers.

'And then what?' Thomas demanded.

'I'll put the VAT and Inland Revenue inspectors on to him until he gets the message and tells us what he knows about Aylesford.'

'You haven't got a prayer.'

'You're forgetting something,' Ashton told him curtly. 'Until a year ago, Harriet was a middle-ranking desk officer in MI5. She's got a list of contacts as long as your arm who'd still be only too happy to do her a favour.'

'What you're proposing to do could take for ever and I understood time was something we didn't have.'

'You're right, we don't.' Ashton narrowed his eyes without being conscious of it. 'But I'm a vengeful man;

Aylesford is sitting on information and I mean to set his balls on fire.'

Hazelwood had always maintained that the newly constituted European Department was too large and too diverse to be managed by one man. Although Garfield was never going to admit it, there was more on his plate than he could handle. The purple smudges under his eyes indicated what it was costing him to stay on top of the job. It was partly of his own making. What had happened to Moresby and Neil Franklin had shaken him to the core and for the past month he had got into the habit of staying late and coming in early. For him, morning prayers was now on a par with Prime Minister's Question Time in Parliament and he was determined to anticipate every question and have all the necessary facts at his fingertips.

This morning, Hazelwood had deliberately stolen his thunder by suggesting Garfield brief him about events in Paris and Moscow after the others had departed. He had done so because Rowan had brought enough notes with him to keep morning prayers going for at least an hour longer than usual and he considered the other Assistant Directors had better things to do with their time. Hazelwood also preferred to adjourn to his office where smoking was permitted.

'The floor is yours, Rowan,' he said after telling his PA he was not to be disturbed.

'Larissa Grushkova has been in touch again.'

'When was this?'

'Last night at approximately 21.50 hours Moscow time. They spent over an hour riding the Metro, then Head of Station had to debrief the go-between, after which he drafted what amounted to a verbatim account of their conversation . . .'

Hazelwood wished he hadn't asked. Garfield wanted him to know that the delay in passing on the information could not be blamed on him.

'The draft was then pre-recorded and transmitted in one

quick burst over the crypto-protected link,' Garfield continued relentlessly. 'It was received by my duty officer at 22.19 hours Greenwich Mean Time and I saw the text about thirty-five minutes later. There wasn't much traffic about at that time of night so I was able to make good time into the office. Unfortunately, part of the text was corrupted and we had to ask for the gobbledegook to be verified. It took–'

'Never mind all that,' Hazelwood said impatiently. 'Just give me the meat.'

Garfield turned a delicate shade of pink. 'Yasnev has refused to answer any of our questions, says he doesn't trust Gurov or any Russian official. He wants immunity from prosecution and political asylum. I don't know whether you can stomach the latter demand considering he probably participated in the massacre of the Stroop family.'

'I think I'm best placed to make any moral judgement, Rowan.'

'Yes, indeed.' Garfield cleared his throat, one of his involuntary mannerisms. 'Yasnev is not prepared to talk to our people in Moscow either,' he continued. 'They are complete strangers as far as he's concerned and could be impostors.'

'Impostors?'

'English-speaking Russian Intelligence Officers.'

'So who is Yasnev willing to confide in?'

Garfield sighed deeply. 'Ashton,' he said. 'He was quite specific it had to be Ashton. Apparently he is only willing to deal with people he knows by sight and he saw our Peter at Neil Franklin's funeral.'

'What's your opinion of Trilisser? Is he trying to pull a fast one?'

'I'm convinced he isn't, so is Head of Station, Moscow.'

'Well, I'm not going to send Ashton into Moscow; his face is too well known there and I don't trust Trilisser or the people around him. In Warsaw, Vasili Ivanovich Sokolov and Larissa Grushkova did their best to put Ashton in hospital and when that failed she alleged he'd tried to rape her.'

'I doubt if the Russians will allow Yasnev to leave the country before they've got what they want from him. However, they might agree to him meeting Ashton in one of the Baltic States – Estonia, Latvia or Lithuania. Do you think Peter would go along with that?'

Hazelwood didn't know. Ashton had once told him that he would never again set foot in a country which had once been subservient to Moscow but he'd broken that vow when he'd flown to Warsaw. And maybe he could be persuaded to make one more trip.

'Any word from Aldermaston yet?' Hazelwood asked to give himself a breathing space while he gave it some thought.

Garfield shook his head. 'I'm hoping to hear something later today.' He leaned forward and placed a flat manila envelope on the desk. 'These are some duplicate photographs we received from Paris. I thought you might want to see them.'

'Thank you, Rowan. Is there anything else we need to discuss?'

'Moresby's father is still making waves. Although the national press hasn't taken up his cause so far, I have a nasty feeling some newspaper will eventually pick it up. I'm wondering if someone could have a word with Moresby, tell him his son died a hero and explain why we can't acknowledge it publicly. I'm sure he would accept it if we gave him a sanitised version of the truth.'

'I'll think about it.' Privately, Hazelwood believed it was better to leave well alone; take Moresby into their confidence and there was no telling how he would react. 'I'd like to have you draft a signal to Head of Station, Moscow for my approval, suggesting Ashton and Yasnev should meet in Riga this coming Monday. I want to get Ashton in and out on the same day if that's possible. Should this be impractical, he can stay overnight in Helsinki on the way back.'

'Right.' Garfield stood up, replaced the chair and moved towards the door.

'And let me know the minute you hear from Aldermaston,' Hazelwood added.

'I certainly will, Victor. I'd like to pull Quorn out of Berlin, if that's all right with you?'

'Give it another twenty-four hours.'

'Whatever you say,' Garfield said, and closed the door quietly behind him.

Hazelwood opened the carved box that enjoyed pride of place on his desk and took out a Burma cheroot. All he had to do now was come up with a powerful argument which would convince Ashton it was his duty to go in harm's way.

Lemberg knew who was calling before he even lifted the phone. Extrasensory perception had nothing to do with it; the Paris office had chattered to Bonn on the teleprinter and the report of the incident on the Boulevard Périphérique had been immediately repeated to Berlin.

'You're late,' he snarled, barely giving Louise Kay time to identify herself. 'What's the excuse this time?'

'Who the hell do you think you're talking to, asshole?'

'The kind of undercover agent who tells you something that's already happened. You'd have earned yourself a medal if we'd had prior warning of the para drop at the Stroops' farm but no, we only hear about the five sub kiloton nukes after they have been delivered. Now I'm going to be told that one of the nukes was destroyed when that truck blew up on the Boulevard Périphérique.'

'There were two nukes on the vehicle,' Kay yelled in a voice that conveyed her anger.

'Yeah? What happened to the other three, or is that an unfair question?' Lemberg held the phone away from his ear anticipating another blast but this time she didn't rise to the bait. The silence extended until Lemberg felt he had to break it. 'Are you still there?' he asked.

'Yes. I thought I saw Wadia looking for me.'

'Oh yeah? What happened to Daoud?'

'He was driving the truck which blew up.'

'Let's try another question,' Lemberg said acidly. 'Where are you calling from?'

'Bad Cannstatt.'

'Where the hell is that?'

'It's a suburb of Stuttgart and I'm calling from a payphone outside a goddamned *Konditorei*. What are you trying to do? Get me killed? How long do you think I can stay here talking to you without being missed?'

'Take it easy.'

'I'm trying to, goddamn it. I can do without all these interruptions. Just hear me out. OK?'

'I'm listening,' Lemberg assured her.

'Fine. For your information, two of those nukes you want to know about are on the way to Marseille. They are planning to ship them over to Alexandria on some rustbucket of a freighter. There's talk of one of the shells being used to atomise President Hosni Mubarak of Egypt, American lackey and friend of the Jews. Their words, not mine.'

'Right.'

'I don't know what they plan to do with the remaining shell. I'm getting out as soon as I learn where they're taking it. I'm living on a knife-edge here.'

'I've got the message.'

'Just don't give me any hassle next time I call. OK?'

Louise Kay hung up on him before he could answer. Lemberg replaced the receiver and waited expectantly. If Voigt had been dumbfounded when he had requested a phone tap on his Bundespost number, he could imagine how the Deputy Director Operations at Langley would react should he ever hear about it. But the end result would justify his decision. By provoking her, he had made Louise Kay finally give him something which could be verified.

When the phone rang again, he almost knocked it off the desk in his eagerness to answer it. Then the German Post Office engineer told him that the incoming call had been made from Bad Cannstatt and his stomach began to churn. His bowels went into free fall when he learned the Post Office had traced it to a payphone outside Bergdorf's *Konditorei* in the Hauptstrasse.

Mouth dry as dust, Lemberg telephoned Voigt and pleaded with him not to act on the information he had received as a result of the phone tap.

'I'm beginning to think she must be on our side after all,' he said weakly.

Manfull left the motel, outside Fulton, drove north to the interchange with US Highway 40 and then made for St Louis, which he was sure would prove to be one more fruitless journey. He'd gotten very little from Donna Kay other than an admission that, contrary to what she'd told him the first time they'd met, her husband had in fact become a mite agitated after learning that the FBI wanted to interview him. Not, she had hastened to add, that she'd been aware it was the FBI who'd called him. She remembered seeing the diary in his hand when he'd left the house but couldn't think what he had done with it after that, and had then wondered if it was still in the Buick. With her permission, he had searched the car but of course there had been no sign of the diary.

Manfull had left Eureka Springs certain in his own mind of two things. If the one for 1994 had been anything like the preceding journals he'd seen, it would have told him what worries and fears Kay had had before his death. And he wouldn't have somehow disposed of the diary unless some of the entries could have been pretty incriminating.

He had gone on to Jefferson City in Missouri to spend the rest of Wednesday retracing the route Veronica Kay had taken from the Country Club to her family home on Bel Air Drive. He had also tried to find somebody who'd known the family, but the fatal accident had occurred back in 1976, and eighteen years after the event the neighbours on either side had moved away. And those directly across the street had only set up house a bare five weeks before

Veronica Kay had been killed and had been on no more than nodding terms with the family.

All day yesterday he had spent at Fulton, making the rounds in the hope of meeting somebody who remembered Louise Kay and had finally run down the den mother of her sorority. There had been some talk of the class of '84 holding a reunion in June but that had apparently fallen through. The den mother had however been able to put him on to the woman who had mooted the idea and who happened to be living in St Louis. Manfull didn't expect to get much joy from her but at least he would be killing two birds with one stone. Yesterday evening he had telephoned the Bureau Chief in Little Rock and had been told to pick up a fax on a guy called Nathan B. Ungley from the Federal Building on Market Street.

The files were beginning to pass across Ashton's desk, background stuff Department Heads thought he should read to acquire the broad picture. The dossiers Jill Sheridan had sent him were the bulkiest of all and filled both the In and Pending trays to a respectable height. 'A brief history of the Arab world,' the Chief Archivist of the Middle East Department had told him with a grin, 'and very good for the soul it is too.'

To ensure he assimilated the essential facts, Jill had attached a brief covering the fundamental split in Islam between Shia, the minority sect who preferred the heredity principle of leadership devolving through Ali, husband of the daughter and sole heir of the Prophet, and the Sunni, who had chosen to elect one of Muhammad's companions as their leader.

The question of which authority was legitimate had split Islam and had led to an irreconcilable quarrel which had persisted down the ages between Sunni and Shia. 'A bit like Catholic and Protestant,' Jill had written in brackets, 'only different because the sects claimed a greater obligation from a Sunni or Shia than the country in which the individual had been born.'

But this was only the broad division. Throughout the centuries, Muslims had fragmented in further offshoots, each legitimised in its own opinion by other lines of descent from the Prophet. Divided on religious grounds, blood feuds between the various factions extended to the organisations dedicated to the liberation of Palestine. Abu Nidal had enrolled in the Palestine Liberation Organisation only to break with Yasser Arafat in 1972. Between 1977 and 1984 he and his followers had murdered hundreds of Palestinians at the behest of Libya or Syria or Iraq, who at varying times did not wish to see a political arrangement with Israel.

From what Ashton could make out from the brief, Hizbollah were pro-Iranian and waged war against Israel and America as much for Tehran's sake as they did on behalf of the Palestinian cause. On the other hand, the Abu Nidal group wanted to take over the PLO in order to continue the armed struggle against Israel. Alliances were made and broken with head-spinning regularity. Consequently, Jill believed there were two possible reasons why the terrorists who had killed Neil Franklin and twelve innocent Germans had claimed to be Hizbollah one moment and Abu Nidal the next. Either the on-going operation was a joint venture or else the outrage had been committed by a third party who had called themselves Hizbollah and Abu Nidal to confuse the various Intelligences ranged against them.

'Getting yourself educated?'

Ashton looked up from the brief and then got to his feet. 'Confused would be more accurate, Victor.'

'Then you won't mind breaking off for a few minutes.'

'It'll be a pleasure.'

'Gennadi Yasnev is being a nuisance.' Hazelwood pulled up a chair and sat down. 'He insists he will only talk to you.'

'Tell him to get stuffed.'

'Trilisser already has. So has Major General Gurov and he won't budge.'

'I'm not going to Moscow, Victor.'

'Of course you're not.'

'Well then, I'd say you've got a problem because I doubt if Trilisser will allow him to come here.'

'On the other hand, he might agree to a meeting on semi-neutral territory – Latvia, for example.'

'Oh no. I told you over a year ago that I was never going behind what used to be known as the Iron Curtain again.'

'You've just been to Warsaw,' Hazelwood reminded him in a mild voice.

'And look what happened.'

'Misplaced enthusiasm on the part of Larissa Grushkova and Vasili Ivanovich Sokolov. No serious harm was intended.'

'Well, that's certainly a load off my mind,' Ashton said acidly. 'I thought it was kind of personal at the time.'

Hazelwood opened the manila envelope he was clutching and laid a small gallery of photographs on the desk, twisting them around so that Ashton could see them properly. 'Stills from Paris,' he said, 'and a pretty sobering picture they make too.'

It was a typical Hazelwood understatement. The Pont de Chatillon in the 14th *Arrondissement* was not an area Ashton was familiar with, but local knowledge wasn't necessary to appreciate the extent of the damage. Although most of the blast had travelled upwards, there was still an enormous hole in the anticlockwise lanes of the Boulevard Périphérique and a mountain of rubble had fallen on to the road below. Windows had been shattered and slates swept from the roofs of buildings up to half a mile away in either direction.

'The experts at Aldermaston are convinced the damage was caused by the initiating charge of a single 130mm nuclear shell.' Hazelwood paused before delivering the punch line. 'That means there are four other shells unaccounted for. Just think of the damage they could do if they were armed for a nuclear explosion before detonation.'

There were a number of ways in which Hazelwood could have twisted his arm. Victor could have said that he owed him, that he couldn't pick and choose what assignments he was given, but that wasn't his style. Hazelwood was too Machiavellian for that; he knew how to make a man feel craven.

'All right, Victor,' Ashton said wearily, 'you win. When do I leave?'

'As soon as we hear from Moscow.'

'Everybody wants Yasnev – us, the Russians, but most of all the *Mafiozniki*.'

'I know. It could be a volatile cocktail, but don't worry, we'll take good care of you.'

Ashton couldn't help thinking that he had heard that one before.

Chapter 27

His name was Crawford; he was thirty-two years old and came from Malton in North Yorkshire. He had enlisted in the Household Cavalry at the age of seventeen and had received accelerated promotion to Corporal of Horse before transferring to 22 Special Air Service Regiment. For the past two years he had been seconded to the SIS in the rank of warrant officer class two. In looking for somebody to watch his back, Ashton knew Victor could not have picked a better man for the job.

This was not the first time they had been paired off. A year ago, the SAS warrant officer had accompanied him to Estonia on what should have been a quick in-and-out job had everything gone according to plan. It hadn't, which shouldn't have been altogether surprising since even with the most meticulous planning, it was impossible to anticipate every hiccup. Crawford had saved his bacon on that occasion thanks to a .357 Ruger Speed Six revolver they'd smuggled into Estonia, courtesy of airport security, Heathrow.

Unfortunately, this time around they were going in naked. It was impossible to fly to Riga and back in a day from London and they'd had to spend Sunday night in Helsinki. This meant the Finns would not accept the Heathrow security tags because they had broken their journey and their baggage would therefore be X-rayed again before it was loaded on to the plane. Ashton just hoped the *Mafiozniki* hadn't learned of their meeting with Gennadi Yasnev because they would have no trouble driving into Latvia with a whole arsenal of weapons.

Finnair Flight AY 30 had departed at 09.25 hours and was due to touch down in Riga fifty-five minutes later. Ashton looked out of the window hoping to catch a glimpse of the city, but there was an impenetrable overcast. The No Smoking/Fasten Seat Belt sign came on with a warning ping loud enough to rouse Crawford from a light slumber.

'You ever been to this place before?' he asked, instantly wide awake.

'No, on my limited income, Riga has never featured on our list of cities we'd like to visit.'

'Well, at least you're getting to see it for free,' Crawford told him. 'I guess that's one advantage of working for the government.'

The plane descended through the murky overcast and suddenly Ashton could see the Gulf of Riga, grey, inhospitable and so polluted to a depth of ten metres that bathing was prohibited. The mouth of the Daugava River, which divided the city, came in sight briefly, then the plane rapidly lost height and the panoramic view disappeared and it started to rain. Welcome to Riga, Ashton thought sourly.

The Immigration officer in the arrival hall didn't appear to know what he was looking for and stamped their passports on the first pristine page he came to. Once clear, they ignored the directional signs for the baggage claim area and walked on through Customs. To have lugged a couple of overnight bags around with them when they would only be in the city a few hours would have been plain silly. They had therefore left them with Her Britannic Majesty's representatives in Helsinki, much to the annoyance of the Head of Chancery who didn't see why the SIS should use the embassy as a glorified left-luggage office.

The airport was on the south-western outskirts of the city, roughly eight miles from the Hotel Latvia on Elizabetes Street where Gennadi Yasnev and his police escort would meet them. The cab driver mistook them both for Russians and was pretty offensive until Ashton put him straight, which turned out to be something of a mistake because thereafter he didn't stop talking. Mercifully, he chose the quickest route through the old town, crossed the October Bridge and went on up Liberation Avenue past the war memorial, finally turning left into Elizabetes Street beyond the park.

The Latvia was a typical In Tourist hotel. Ashton had seen its like in Warsaw, Tallin and Moscow, a square tower twenty-something storeys high serviced by two slow-moving lifts. The consular affairs officer was waiting for them in the lobby, seated at a small round table near the reception counter to the right of the entrance, exactly where Garfield had said he would be. To be used as a pseudo-Intelligence officer was not the reason why he had joined the Diplomatic. He was there purely to hand over the keys to the conference facility on the mezzanine floor and he was keen to discharge that responsibility as quickly as possible. Ashton asked if he'd noticed anything unusual while he had been waiting and he assured him the Russian delegation had not yet arrived, which was not quite the same thing.

'I guess we'd better take a look,' Crawford said after the consular affairs officer had departed.

Two flights of wooden steps led to the mezzanine floor where there was also a restaurant, beauty parlour and a business office which provided a secretarial service. The conference centre was next door to the business office and consisted of a large hall and half a dozen committee rooms arranged in line down the right-hand side of the auditorium. Eight rows of tubular steel chairs with plastic seats and backrests faced a raised podium between the emergency exits at the far end of the hall. The embassy had hired the entire centre for one day; where the meeting was actually held was up to them.

'Let's start with the committee rooms,' Ashton said and entered the first one on the right.

All six were identical, oblong boxes ten feet by eight

with large picture windows which extended from above the radiators to a foot below the ceiling. They were situated on the east side of the hotel and looked out across a grassed area to a row of apartment buildings.

'I don't like any of them,' Crawford announced after the briefest of inspections. 'A sniper on the third floor of any of those tenements across the street can look down into all six committee rooms. OK, his view of those on either extremity would be restricted to a very oblique angle but a good shot with a scope could hit the target.'

'We could lower the venetian blind,' Ashton said, 'then he wouldn't be able to see anything.'

'We're talking *Mafiozniki*; from what I hear, they wouldn't hesitate to rip the whole room apart with a rocket launcher. I know that sounds pretty extreme but can you afford to rule out the possibility?'

'No. We'll use the hall and arrange a few chairs in a circle in the middle of the room.'

Crawford looked around him with a professional eye. 'Do we know when the embassy hired this place?' he asked.

'Saturday.'

'And when would the Russians have known we were proposing to hold the meeting at this hotel?'

'The same day,' Ashton told him. 'We had to get their agreement.'

'So in the worst case the *Mafiozniki* might have had over thirty hours in which to jack up an unpleasant surprise for us?' He smiled. 'I know that's also a very large assumption . . .'

'You check the hall, I'll do the committee rooms,' Ashton said, wanting to get on with it.

He had set himself the easier task because this happened to be an area where Crawford had more practical experience of what was involved than he did, and there were a considerable number of nooks and crannies in the hall where a bomb could be hidden. The committee rooms were stark and functional, each one furnished with only a table and a few chairs. There were no cupboards and the radiators were not boxed in. Given enough time with undisturbed and unlimited access, a bomb could have been placed under the floor or between the rafters and reinforced steel joists, but thirty hours was insufficient.

A command-detonated bomb was not the only threat they had to consider. Fire regulations stipulated that there should be at least one emergency exit. The ones at the back of the hall opened into a passageway which extended from the restaurant to the internal staircase on the east side of the hotel and led to a cafeteria.

'This hotel is wide open,' Crawford said grimly. 'A gunman can enter the cafeteria from the street, walk on through and come up the back stairs.'

'It's too late now to change the RV,' Ashton told him. 'We shall just have to put someone on the passageway as well as the front landing above the lobby.'

The Russian delegation arrived fifteen minutes late at 11.37 hours. In briefing Ashton, Rowan Garfield had said that Yasnev would be accompanied by two police officers and a senior lawyer from the State Prosecutor's office. He had either forgotten to mention it or else he hadn't known that Larissa Grushkova would also be in attendance. Ashton assumed she was representing Pavel Trilisser, only to discover that she was effectively in charge of the delegation. The fact that he and Crawford had already searched the whole place counted for nothing and a further hour and a quarter was lost while the Russians went over the same ground again. There was another dispute over the number of sentries they needed. In the end, Ashton accepted that Grushkova would never trust the SAS warrant officer and agreed that her people should guard the passageway and front landing.

'Now can we begin?' he asked.

'Provided we converse in Russian.'

'That's OK by me.' Ashton turned to face Gennadi Yasnev. 'Suppose you tell me when and how these Arab terrorists first approached you?'

369

'Let us first discuss the question of asylum.'

'Fine. Have you been granted immunity from prosecution?'

'He has,' Larissa Grushkova said, answering for him.

'Well then, I'm authorised to say that we are prepared to accept you.'

'When?' Yasnev demanded.

'I'm on the Latvian Airlines flight to Helsinki which departs at 16.00 hours. There's a seat on it for you.'

'How do I know you aren't lying?'

Ashton took out a plane ticket and gave it to the Russian. 'Have a look at the voucher inside, it's got your name on it.'

'I'd like to ring the airline and have it verified.'

'We haven't got all night,' Ashton growled. 'There are some things you have to take on trust.'

'Quite so,' Gennadi Yasnev said, 'but this plane ticket doesn't happen to be one of them.'

Manfull unbuttoned the single-breasted jacket and sucked in his stomach, hoping this would disguise the spare tyre around his waist and make him look slimmer. He felt uncomfortable in more ways than one. The suit no longer fitted him; the jacket was tight across the shoulders and pulled under the arms. Also the zipper on his pants refused to stay up and kept inching down in what was a losing battle of the bulge. But what made him feel really ill at ease was the prospect that before too long the ash-blonde, well-groomed PA facing him behind her desk in the outer office was going to announce that Director Freeh was ready to see him and would he please go right in. The thought made his hands sweat and he instinctively rubbed both palms on his thighs to dry them before realising what this would do to his pants.

'Aw shit,' Manfull said in a voice louder than he'd intended.

The ash-blonde stopped hitting the keyboard of her word processor and looked up with a perplexed frown. 'Pardon me,' she said. 'Did you say something?'

'It wasn't important,' he mumbled and despite all his apprehensions was relieved when the green light above the communicating door suddenly illuminated. 'I think the Director's free now,' he said.

'So he is.' The PA stood up and smoothed down her immaculate skirt, then walked round the desk, opened the door and said, 'Mr Leroy Manfull, Director.'

Manfull started towards the communicating door, remembered his briefcase and turned back to collect it. His face burning with embarrassment, he finally made it into the office. He had never met the Director or his predecessor. In fact, Clarence Kelly, the former Chief of Kansas City Police, was the only Director he'd been introduced to and that had been after Kelly had addressed the FBI Academy. He wished somebody had told him precisely why he had been summoned to Washington. Instead, Manfull found himself answering questions about his wife and family, how long he had been with the Arkansas Bureau and where he had stayed Sunday night in Washington. Then suddenly their conversation turned on Nancy de Jeanney, who had tried to organise a sorority reunion.

'Tell me about her,' Freeh said.

Manfull cleared his throat. 'She's thirty-four, same age as Louise Kay, is married to a dentist and has three boys aged seven, five and three.'

'A very organised lady?' Freeh suggested with a smile.

'She is,' Manfull agreed. 'Spills over into her social life, except for the reunion, but that was down to a lack of support for the idea.'

'And she knew Louise Kay at Fulton?'

'Yes, sir. Once she started reminiscing it was surprising how much Mrs de Jeanney had to say about her.' Manfull picked up his briefcase which he'd placed beside his chair. 'I've got a tape recording of our conversation if you'd like to hear it.'

'I'd sooner hear it from you,' Freeh said.

'Oh, right.' Manfull put the briefcase down. 'The first thing you have to keep in mind, Director, is that she really disliked Louise Kay. Nancy de Jeanney admitted to me that if they hadn't lived in the same fraternity house, she would never have had anything to do with her. They'd practically nothing in common; Louise Kay was hypercritical of our foreign policy, embraced every left-wing cause, was sexually active, and was always bad-mouthing her father. It seems she claimed her mother had become a lush because of his sexual proclivities, the things he expected her to do in bed.'

'You believe that?'

'I never met Kay, Director, so I don't feel qualified to make a judgement. However, I do believe Kay was unfaithful to his first wife.'

Before being appointed Dean of Phelps County Community College, Kay had been a lecturer at Lincoln University in Jefferson City. Amongst other vindictive accusations, Louise Kay had alleged that her father had had an amorous relationship with one of his students while her mother was still alive.

'Mrs de Jeanney could only recall that her first name was Donna.'

'Who eventually became the second Mrs Kay?'

'I haven't had a chance to check it out yet, but I'd bet my shirt on it.'

In malicious hands, the illicit relationship could be used against Kay to show that he had had a motive for killing his first wife. Manfull also believed this was the hold Louise had had on her father.

'The way I figure it, she was always threatening to denounce him and Kay was sufficiently intimidated to do whatever she asked of him. I don't know what passed through his mind when I made arrangements to see him about his daughter but he surely lost his head. I guess the thought of meeting me really spooked him.'

Manfull hoped the Director would tell him why the Bureau was so interested in learning all they could about Louise Kay, but his question went unanswered. Instead, the Director wanted to know what he'd learned about the friends she had made while at Fulton.

'She was doing a number with a physicist called Abbas Din,' Manfull told him. 'His parents had originally come from the Lebanon but he had been born in this country. A dishy-looking guy according to Nancy de Jeanney – very popular too – people who moved in his circle called him Abe.'

'What about Nathan Ungley? Did Louise ever meet him?'

'The picture which came through on the fax was pretty blurred but Mrs de Jeanney was adamant she recognised Ungley even though she couldn't put a name to him. I was convinced because she told me he was a Vietnam vet and was therefore older than the other college students. She had no time for the guy, said he was always griping about something and was lucky to get a place at Fulton studying Political Science because he wasn't up to it intellectually and she wasn't surprised when he dropped out after the first year. One of the last things he did at Fulton was to hand out leaflets accusing the Israelis of behaving like Nazis towards the Palestinians. He didn't empathise with the Arabs, he did it for Louise.'

'Have you met Ungley?'

'I didn't know I was supposed to,' Manfull said.

'Don't worry about it, we've got a phone tap on his place and our people in Missouri have been keeping a discreet eye on him ever since he got involved with the Militia.'

'That's good to hear, I thought I'd fouled up.'

'How about Abbas Din, was he active on behalf of the Palestinians?'

'Not according to Mrs de Jeanney.'

The Director was firing questions at him with machine-gun speed which were so wide-ranging that it was difficult to see the connection, let alone what lay behind them.

'You've done a great job,' Freeh told him. 'Now I want you to concentrate on finding out what Kay was actually doing in that office he'd rented. I want to know precisely what sort of brochures he was collecting for his daughter.'

'His daughter?' Manfull frowned. 'I don't get it, I thought

the box number had been rented by Noreen Tal.'

'We sent the Canadians two photographs and asked they show them to the Post Office clerk who'd dealt with the lady. He picked out Louise Kay, which means she had used Tal's name as cover. There's no evidence to show that she ever met the Jordanian girl but Tal was believed to have been involved in the bombing of the World Trade Center in New York and her name was splashed in all the newspapers at the time.'

'So this Louise Kay is definitely a terrorist?'

'We thought so, the CIA never did. They've always maintained she is one of theirs and there has been one major development in the last seventy-two hours which could well support their claim.'

'Do we know how they came to recruit Louise Kay, sir?'

'No. And they're not likely to tell us either.' Freeh paused, then said, 'You can put that down to Nixon and Herbert Hoover.'

In 1970, on the order of President Nixon, a committee composed of all the Heads of the various Intelligence agencies was set up to consider how to counteract the wave of civil disorders which were then sweeping the United States. Breaking into and entering certain premises with a view to establishing covert electronic surveillance had been one of the recommendations accepted by the President. Hoover had refused to have anything to do with it and had stopped all liaison with every agency whose representatives had attended the committee meetings, which had included the CIA.

'People in Washington have long memories,' Freeh said cryptically. 'The CIA has not forgotten, nor have they entirely forgiven the Bureau.'

In the light of what had happened so far, Manfull couldn't help wondering what might be the cost of this long-standing estrangement twenty-four years later.

The French authorities were nothing if not thorough. Although the CIA had immediately alerted their counterparts, the *Service de Documentation Extérieur et de Contre-Espionage*, the moment they'd learned that two nuclear shells were to be shipped out to Egypt through Marseille, the fact remained that their information was dated. When the agent in place had contacted the CIA's Chief of Station in Berlin, more than five days had elapsed since the terrorists had taken delivery of the nuclear weapons.

In view of the incident which had occurred on the Boulevard Périphérique on Wednesday evening some forty-eight hours before the CIA had heard from their source, the Foreign and Counterespionage Service were of the opinion that the consignment had probably reached Marseille around the same time. To be absolutely sure, they began looking at all the shipping movements that had taken place from Tuesday, 11 October.

There were an impressive number of sailings every day from Marseille – ro-ro ferries to Corsica, container ships to North Africa, the Levant and the Black Sea ports, tankers to collect crude from Libya and freighters delivering to and picking up cargo from every port in the Med. All sailings from Marseille were prohibited and ships in port were ordered to discharge their cargoes on to the dockside. The names and destinations of all vessels which had left Marseille from Tuesday, 11 October, were ascertained from the various shipping lines and the ports of call warned accordingly. Every crate and container on the docksides and in the sheds awaiting shipment was then opened and checked, a Herculean task which involved hundreds of customs officials, dock labourers, stevedores, police officers and bomb disposal experts. Shortly after midday, a crate of machine tools destined for Alexandria on the 10,000 ton freighter *Isle de Porquerolles* was opened and found to contain two 130mm nuclear artillery shells packed between four lathes.

Ashton looked at the notes he'd made and reflected on how long it had taken to get so few hard facts out of

Gennadi Yasnev. The Russian was a born salesman, the slippery kind who could make a big production out of very little. He had also proved adept at evading difficult questions and would digress whenever Ashton had pressed him for an answer. 'How much will your government pay me when I am in England?' was a question Yasnev had put to him time and again when he needed a breathing space to assess which way the interrogation was likely to go. In every case it had taken Ashton a good ten minutes to get Yasnev back on track.

So much of what Yasnev had told him would be difficult if not impossible to verify from another source. He had given a very full account of how he'd come to meet representatives of Hizbollah during his travels in the Mid East earlier on in the year but that was ancient history and not immediately relevant.

In those areas where it mattered, he had been negative. Asked if he had ever met a terrorist called Daoud, Yasnev had replied he'd never heard of him. He had also denied all knowledge of Wadia, the other name Louise Kay had dropped when she'd contacted Caspar Lemberg. Pertaining to what had happened to the Stroops, he had been far away when they had been massacred. And naturally he'd had nothing to do with the bombing of the English Bookshop on Budapesterstrasse and was in fact astounded to learn it was run by the SIS. Yasnev was a consummate liar and difficult to shake.

He had admitted to knowing Leila Khalif and to show willing had described two of the terrorists who had been present at the DZ, one of whom Leila had consulted before the ammunition containers were loaded into the Transit vans. Ashton thought it was worth trying to mine a further nugget from that particular seam.

'This man whom Leila consulted,' he said, 'why did she do that?'

'She wanted to make sure we were selling her the real stuff,' Yasnev laughed. 'That bitch wouldn't trust her own mother.'

'This man was some kind of expert?'

'A nuclear physicist no less. At least, that's what she said he was.'

'Describe him.'

'I already have.'

'Humour me,' Ashton told him, 'do it again.'

'A tall guy, about your height only thinner and much better looking, pale olive skin, dark hair flecked with grey, spoke English with a Yankee accent. She seemed to like him a lot but I judged she was the sort of woman who'd have the hots for any stallion in the field.'

'Did she ever address him by name?'

'Yeah, she called him Al. No, I'm a liar, it was Abe.'

'Make up your mind,' Ashton said.

'I have, it's Abe.' Yasnev glanced at his wristwatch. 'It's gone three o'clock,' he said. 'We ought to be making tracks for the airport if you're serious about catching that flight to Helsinki.'

'Of course I'm serious.' Ashton caught Larissa Grushkova's eye. 'If that's OK with you?'

'What's it got to do with her?' Yasnev demanded.

'She's got a plane to catch too.'

It would be the same one Yasnev would find himself on and it wouldn't be going to Helsinki.

'I think we should leave by the emergency exit,' Larissa Grushkova said.

'After you then,' Ashton told her and waved a hand towards the exit.

Larissa Grushkova walked out into the rear passageway and was followed by one of the police officers. The shooting started as soon as Gennadi Yasnev left the hall. There was no reverberating crash of gunfire, just a series of hollow coughs, the hallmark of a semi-automatic fitted with a noise suppressor. The only one of the triumvirate to make it back to the hall was Larissa Grushkova and she was bleeding profusely from the mouth. She pointed an accusing finger at Ashton as though he was responsible for what had happened, then both legs buckled under her and she went down, eyes glazed and sightless.

'Let's get the hell out of here,' Crawford snapped. 'There's nothing anybody can do for her now.'

'Too right,' Ashton said and made for the emergency exit.

'For Christ's sake, where do you think you're going?'

'The back way down. The killers will be long gone by now; they've got what they came for and won't bother with us.'

Ashton walked out into the passageway, stepped carefully over Yasnev and the dead police officer and headed towards the staircase. There was no sign of the officer who had been detailed to stand guard in the corridor, which could only mean that either his body had been squirrelled away or else he had been party to the assassination. With Crawford close behind, Ashton went on down the staircase and calmly walked through the cafeteria to reach the street. Then he stepped out into the rain and flagged a cab from the rank.

The eight-mile drive to the airport seemed more like eighty. He kept wondering how long it would be before a member of the hotel staff discovered the carnage on the mezzanine floor and raised the alarm. Ashton asked himself what sort of time-lag there might be before the police thought to alert the airport security staff, and then decided it was pointless to speculate. Outwardly he looked calm and collected but his mouth was as dry as dust and his heart was pounding like a runaway train.

He did not begin to unwind until Latvia Airlines Flight PV 753 to Helsinki lifted off nine minutes late at 16.09 hours.

The Boeing 707 which had touched down at Toronto at 16.30 hours local time belonged to Airspeed Cargo Services operating out of Frankfurt. Amongst the freight it had delivered was a container of office equipment destined for a nonexistent firm of office suppliers in Niagara.

Chapter 28

Nathan B. Ungley prowled through the woods, the perfect hunting animal, silent, alert, equipped mentally, physically and materially to deal with any situation. He wore rubber-soled jump boots, a disruptive-pattern combat jacket and pants and a camouflage baseball cap. On the web belt around his waist there were two ammunition pouches for spare magazines, a water bottle, and a pistol holster containing a .45 M1911A1 Colt automatic, the most beautiful-looking handgun in the whole world in his opinion. Two fragmentation grenades and an AN/PRC-68 (X) Transmitter/Receiver were clipped to the D-rings on the harness which supported the web belt and prevented it from slipping down over the hips. The volume on the PRC walkie-talkie had been turned down to eliminate the background mush and he held the AR 15 Armalite rifle at the high port across his chest, left hand gripping the stock, right hand folded around the pistol grip, trigger finger outside the guard.

Stealth was essential because there were six Feebies in the clearing up ahead and they hadn't assembled there for a cook-out. Goddamned federal agents wouldn't allow a man no peace, always poking their noses into other people's business. Ungley moved forward, one step at a time, lifting each foot high to avoid brushing the undergrowth and putting it down gently where there was no danger of stepping on a twig. It took him fifteen minutes to cover twenty-five yards, but time was not a factor in his reckoning. The clearing was now just a few yards farther on and he listened intently to catch the sound of voices, but the Feebies were equally silent. Killers in waiting, he told himself, and boy, weren't they in for a big surprise.

Ungley inched forward, kneeled down on one knee and methodically searched the clearing, noting the exact position of each target. Holding the assault rifle with his left hand, he carefully unbuttoned the flap on the pistol holster, then moved the selector switch on the rifle to automatic. One, two, three, go, he mouthed the words to himself, got to his feet and charged into the clearing.

Some guys he knew would have gone in screaming and yelling, supposedly to put the fear of God into the enemy, whereas in reality they were scared shitless and needed to psych themselves up. Well, he didn't need any of that crap, he was a pro, ice cold and ruthless. Ungley took out the nearest agent on his right with a short burst, then went for the look-out in the tree before doing a forward somersault to take himself out of the line of fire. He came up into the crouch to present the smallest target to the Feds and engaged the trio who were spread in an arc. Longer bursts this time, traversing left to right and back again. No return fire, just bits and pieces flying off the targets as the 5.56mm rounds ripped them apart.

The sixth and last man was lying on his left hip, trying to hide in the long grass. Ungley couldn't see him but knew where he was; popping up like a jack-in-the-box, he rapped out a burst. The Armalite chattered a couple of times, then stopped on an empty magazine. He held on to the rifle with his left hand, snatched the Colt from the holster, thumbed the hammer back and walked forward shooting at the prone figure.

'Got you that time, cocksucker,' he yelled. 'Didn't figure I had one in the breech, didya?'

Bam, bam, two more for good luck, the .45 semi-auto kicking in his hand, the empty cases flying out of the ejection slot.

Ungley stopped firing, cleared each weapon in turn, then collected in the wooden figure targets and examined his marksmanship. Hot damn, that was some shooting, chest and head wounds in every target. Couldn't wait to do it for real. But right now, he needed to pick up all the empty shells, couldn't leave them lying around where the Feebies would find them. The cawing of the birds died away to nothing, and in the ensuing silence he could hear a familiar voice whispering on the radio. Ungley turned up the volume and extended the aerial.

'Where the hell are you, Nathan?' Chrissy asked in her earthy nineteen-year-old voice. 'Have you suddenly gone deaf or something? Don't you know I've been calling you for the past half-hour?'

Ungley hit the transmit button when she paused for breath. 'This is India One,' he grated. 'Use correct voice procedure, India Two. Over.'

'Aw shit, India One, you know who this is, but what the hell, you want me to play soldiers, I'll play soldiers. I'm India Two, Dog Crap wants to talk to you, says he'll call back on the other means in ten, so get the lead out of your ass and fly back to me. India Two, over and out.'

'India One. Now you listen to me,' he roared and knew he was wasting his breath.

Ungley forgot about the targets and the empty cases and set off back to the house, running like a man half his age. How many guys of forty-two had a body without an ounce of spare flesh on it and were able to run a mile in full battle order in four minutes twenty like he could? Legs pumping, he emerged from the woods and raced across the open ground towards the shack where Chrissy kept house for him and looked after the cow, the hogs and chickens when he had other more important things to do. Course, she needed a firm hand now and then, otherwise she got uppity, like she had done this morning, bad-mouthing him on the radio and not using correct procedure like she'd been taught.

Ungley came to a halt outside the front porch and

commenced running on the spot, part of the punishing régime he observed to keep in trim, ready for the big day. The exercise completed to his satisfaction, he went into the house and yelled for Chrissy.

She was a tall, slender girl, waif-like in appearance, and wore her blonde hair in a pony tail. She had been his common-law wife since the age of fourteen and without in any way being cowed or intimidated by him had learned to know her place.

'What's the first thing I told you about a field radio?' Ungley demanded as he removed the web equipment and stripped off his combat jacket.

'It ain't like a telephone,' she told him, arms folded across her chest.

'So why'd you forget that elementary lesson just now?'

Chrissy shrugged. 'I guess I forgot.'

'You forgot.' Ungley repeated heavily. 'Well, I guess I'm gonna have to teach you a lesson that you won't forget in a hurry. So you go stand in a corner of the living room and face the wall with your hands on top of your head until I'm ready to deal with you.'

Ungley walked into the kitchen, took a carton of milk out of the fridge and started to gulp it down. The phone rang before he finished it. His subsequent conversation with the caller was brief and entirely one-sided. Moments after hanging up, he lifted the receiver again and dialled 616-4404.

'Hi, Beau,' he said, 'this is Nathan. I just had a call from our friend Abe to say the stuff we ordered has arrived. You want to get your truck out and go collect it?'

Beau said he would do that small thing and put the phone down. Ungley followed suit and then walked into the living room. Chrissy was facing the wall like he'd told her to, back ramrod straight, hands clasped together on top of her head.

'OK, soldier,' he said in a low dispassionate voice, 'you know what's coming to you.'

'Are you going to wop me, Nathan?'

'Like I never did before,' Ungley said and unbuckled the leather belt around his waist.

The eavesdroppers were based in Elk Prairie, two miles down the road from Ungley's place on Cook Road. The electronic surveillance was into the fourth day and had at last come to life after seventy-two hours of total silence. The Special Agent in charge of the covert operation wished it had been possible to back up the phone tap with a micro transmitter inside the house but there were insuperable problems about effecting an entry. The house was never left unoccupied, Ungley discouraged callers, and there were a couple of pit bull terriers roaming the yard who looked as if they were longing to bite a chunk out of any intruder.

He had thought about aiming a probe at the shack; the latest gizmo could pick up anything that was said inside the house from a thousand yards away. There was, however, a proviso: you needed a clear line of sight, and that was the problem because there wasn't a scrap of cover that close in. And, just to make life even more difficult, Ungley patrolled the boundary of his property armed with a shotgun shortly after dawn and again before dusk.

But now at last they had something they could get their teeth into. Two incoming calls, both from the same man, and one outgoing one which they had traced to the Silver Dollar Motel outside Buffalo, New York. Thanks to ITT, they now knew the incoming calls had been made from separate payphones in Niagara. The Special Agent in charge had never heard of Abe or Beau but their voices had been captured on tape and it was just possible somebody might recognise one of them.

The Silver Dollar Motel looked the most promising line of enquiry. Whoever managed the place had to know Beau pretty well to allow him to use the motel like an office to run his business.

It had been raining when Ashton left Riga, it had rained all the time he and Crawford were in Helsinki and now it looked as if the heavens were about to open over London, which in a sense they already had.

'You're not the flavour of the month with the Foreign Office,' Hazelwood observed.

Ashton could understand that. He and Crawford had been forced to do a quick bunk and there had been no time to warn the embassy. Consequently, the Ambassador had only learned about the massacre when the Latvian Minister of External Affairs had demanded an explanation, which meant Her Majesty's representatives in Riga had had to eat humble pie, something they were not accustomed to doing.

'Matter of fact, you're not too popular in Moscow either.'

Ashton found that even less surprising, principally because Pavel Trilisser had never regarded him with anything other than the utmost hostility. The way Yeltsin's adviser saw it, Moscow had paid a heavy price for co-operating with the SIS. They had lost Larissa Grushkova, Gennadi Yasnev and two honest police officers, including the one who'd stood guard on the landing outside the conference hall. According to what the embassy staff had been told, he had been bundled into the adjoining business centre where the two Latvian secretaries on duty had been compelled to tie him up before they themselves were similarly dealt with. As soon as all three were incapable of offering any resistance, the gunman had calmly kneeled down and shot the police officer in the head.

But it was probably the loss of Gennadi Yasnev that had really angered Moscow's Chief of Police. Without him, Major General Gurov had no case against The Czar or the senior ordnance officer who'd thrown his depot open and invited the *Mafiozniki* to help themselves to a few nuclear artillery shells. Ashton made the assumption that Yasnev had been persuaded to name the chief of the Babushkin family and the senior army officer before Gurov's men had taken him to Riga, but that was by no means certain.

'Any word on the third police officer, the one who was supposed to be guarding the passageway?'

'He appears to have vanished,' Hazelwood said.

'I'm not surprised. I figured he must have told the *Mafiozniki* where they were taking Gennadi Yasnev; now it seems likely he took part in the hit itself.'

'I don't think we need bother our heads about him,' Hazelwood said impatiently. 'We don't know his name, and even if we did, he's outside our jurisdiction. He's Gurov's problem now.'

'I only mentioned it in case you wanted to rebut Trilisser's accusations.'

'Pavel is just going through the motions for the record. He knows who blew the whistle on the operation and if it comes to a bout of in-fighting, he's worried in case his enemies try to lay it on Larissa Grushkova.' Hazelwood gazed at the ornate wooden box on his desk with apparent longing but refrained from opening it. 'I'm trying to cut down on the number of cheroots I smoke in a day,' he said.

'Sounds like a good idea.'

'So Alice keeps telling me. Let's talk about the late and unlamented Gennadi Yasnev, he's much more interesting. If he were such a consummate liar, how are we to believe any of the information he gave you?'

'I think we have to look at each disclosure and ask ourselves if it can be verified by another source.'

'You want to give me an example?'

'Yes. First of all, I do believe there is a nuclear physicist called Abe because Louise Kay would need somebody like him.'

Ashton knew what he was saying was at odds with the revised perception of the American woman. Louise Kay was now the heroic agent in place whose bravery had been instrumental in recovering two of the five sub kiloton nukes. But it was not how Ashton saw her.

'I'm no expert, Victor, but as I understand it, the 130mm nuclear shell can be set for either a high, low or ground burst as well as varying yields up to the equivalent of 500 tons of high explosive. Maybe doing that is not beyond your average terrorist but he would have to know how to kick-start the necessary chain reaction. It's a sight more complicated than lighting the blue touch paper and retiring to a safe distance.'

'And it would be Abe's job to solve the problem of how to create the super critical mass?'

'Well, either he does it,' said Ashton, 'or else they've got to lay their hands on a 130mm cannon.'

'All right. For the sake of argument, let's say you're correct. What do we know about this physicist?'

'Not a lot. Judging from Yasnev's description, it's likely his ethnic origins are rooted in the Middle East but I've a hunch he was born in the United States. In fact, I wouldn't mind betting this man and Louise Kay go back quite a long way.'

'You're denigrating the heroine of the hour again,' Hazelwood told him. 'And it won't stick unless you can explain why she told Caspar Lemberg about the shipment of nuclear weapons from Marseille.'

'Insurance,' Ashton said cryptically.

'What?'

'In case she was ever arrested. Maybe she saw one of the Wanted posters the Kripo distributed and felt the likeness was too close for comfort.' Ashton suddenly snapped his fingers. 'No, wait a minute, there's a deeper purpose. Louise Kay is going home and not for the reason she told Caspar Lemberg. And she won't be arriving empty-handed either.'

Unable to resist the temptation any longer, Hazelwood helped himself to a Burma cheroot and lit it. 'I presume she has sent her luggage on in advance?' he said between puffs.

'I would in her shoes,' Ashton said. 'The big problem facing Louise Kay is the fact that every law enforcement agency in Europe is looking for her, and maybe the FBI is equally concerned to run the lady to ground. That's why she needs the CIA to say, "Hey guys, let her go, she's one of ours. Think of the thousands of lives she has saved." '

'Abe the bomb maker,' Hazelwood mused. 'Doesn't say much for his skills if he made up the one which demolished the English Bookshop and killed the handler.'

'You still think the bomb exploded prematurely?'

'It's something to bear in mind.'

To what purpose? Ashton wondered. It wouldn't help them locate the other two nukes, but it was a comforting way of minimising the danger if you were so inclined.

'You'd better go home and pack a bag,' Hazelwood suddenly announced.

'I've only just got back from Latvia,' Ashton reminded him. 'In case you've forgotten, I stayed overnight in Helsinki on the way out and again on the way back.'

'This isn't a nine-to-five job, Peter. If Harriet doesn't like the unsocial hours, you can always look for alternative employment elsewhere.'

'That's uncalled for, Victor,' Ashton said angrily.

'You're right, it is, and I apologise.'

'So where are you planning to send me this time?'

'Washington, DC,' Hazelwood said with obvious relief. 'There is a plane departing at 16.00.'

'You mean I'm not *persona non grata* over there?'

'Put it this way,' Hazelwood said, 'I doubt you would be welcomed with open arms at Langley, but I think the FBI will be interested to hear what you have to say.'

Sunshine Vacations was the only travel agent in Eureka Springs and whatever brochures Kay might have collected for his daughter, he hadn't obtained any from that company. If he had sent away for them, Kay hadn't rented a box number and the postmaster couldn't recall delivering anything of that nature to his home address. However, the manageress of the beauty parlour had told Manfull that she remembered Kay arriving at his office on at least two occasions carrying a large cardboard box. She knew for sure that one of the packages had come through the US Mail because she had seen it on his work table when she took him up a cup of coffee.

It occurred to Manfull that he was placing too literal an interpretation on the advert for brochures. There was a bookseller and a stationer in town, both of which carried a limited stock of maps. As a result of talking to the respective proprietors, Manfull figured Donna Kay had some explaining to do. The lady was not best pleased to see him when he came knocking on her door.

'Oh, it's you again,' Donna said irritably. 'When are you going to stop pestering me?'

'When you stop lying to me,' Manfull told her.

'I've had enough of this, I'm going to call my lawyer.'

'Yeah, you do that,' Manfull snapped, 'because you're going to need him. I don't know what exactly is going on down here but it is certainly life-threatening, and you are involved right up to your pretty little neck. Believe me, if it comes out that lives were lost because you'd withheld vital information, I will make it my business to ensure you die in prison.' Manfull stepped across the threshhold. 'Now why don't you invite me inside for a pitcher of your famous home-made lemonade and let's see if we can't sort out this problem we have?'

Donna retreated before him in a state of shock, eyes almost bulging out of their sockets, her mouth wide open and emitting a harsh rasping sound as if she was asthmatic and was finding it difficult to breathe. 'In here,' she gasped and opened the door to the den.

'Thanks. Hopefully this won't take long.'

'It hadn't better,' Donna told him with a brief show of defiance.

'All I want from you is a couple of straight answers, beginning with the out-of-town accommodation address your husband was using.'

'I don't know what you're talking about.'

Manfull sighed. 'I'm talking about the office your husband rented four days after his daughter phoned him and those street plans we found in the top drawer of the filing cabinet.'

Manfull told her what he had learned from the bookseller and the stationer and how Kay had asked them where they obtained their Rand McNally city maps. He spoke of the friendship which had existed between her husband and the manageress of the beauty parlour, of the cups of coffee she would bring him, and how she remembered seeing a large package that had come through the US Mail.

'It had "Printed Matter – Books" stamped in red on the outside.'

'This is news to me,' Donna said in a hoarse voice.

'The hell it is. Your late husband may not have heard of a dead drop and a cut out was probably a foreign language to him, but he knew enough not to foul his own doorstep. He didn't want a load of maps delivered to the house or the downtown office, so he went out and rented an accommodation address some place far away from Eureka Springs. Now, save yourself a load of grief and tell me where.'

'Fayetteville.' There was no hesitation, no lip-chewing, no sign of anguish that he could see. 'Fayetteville,' Donna repeated, 'box number 311.'

'And he ordered street maps from who?'

'Rand McNally, North America Maps, Rohnert Park, California, Mitock Publishing Incorporated.'

'Anything else?'

'Yes. Louise wanted guide books on Chicago, New York, Philadelphia, Boston, St Louis and Washington, DC. She put them in order of priority; St Louis was near the top of the list, immediately below Chicago. We thought about going there.'

'Chicago?'

'No, St Louis. It was my suggestion. I thought that if we looked around the city, we might get some idea what Louise was planning.'

Buffalo, New York, to a lock-up on Tweedsmuir Street in Niagara on the Lake and back again with a load of office equipment supposedly in need of repair. A round trip of 120 miles; no problem going into Canada, none coming out; US Customs checked the paperwork, superficially examined one crate and waved him on. How easy could it get? The man called Beau switched on the radio and searched the waveband until he found a station dedicated to country and western.

The mobile rang just as he was about to light a cigarette. Steering the pick-up with one hand, he reached for the phone and answered it. The woman at the Silver Dollar Motel told him she didn't want no trouble.

'Who does?' he said.

'A couple of not so friendly acquaintances been here looking for you,' she told him. 'Best you go some place else.'

'I intend to,' Beau said and switched off. Like St Louis, he said to himself.

Chapter 29

The immaculate ash-blonde PA made Ashton feel scruffy and dishevelled. Truth be known, he probably looked as if he had slept in his clothes, which wasn't too wide of the mark. All the Business Class seats on the British Airways flight to Washington had already been taken when Kelso had made the booking, and although on stand-by for upgrading, there had been no last-minute cancellation. You were just a little pushed for elbow room in the Economy Class and the jacket which he'd carefully folded and stowed in the overhead bin had ended up under a video camera, with predictable results.

He also felt rough; 20.00 hours in Washington was Wednesday one a.m. in London and the stubble on his face had all the texture of sandpaper. A quick wash and brush-up would have done wonders for him but the timing of the appointment Hazelwood had arranged meant that he'd had to go straight from Dulles International to the FBI Building on Pennsylvania Avenue. Although the building was still ablaze with lights when he arrived, all the offices, except those on the top floor, were deserted. The PA was evidently used to putting in a long day at the office, but there were limits, and before he had time to do more than set down his bag, she had ushered him in to the Director.

'Mr Ashton.' Freeh walked round his desk to shake hands with him. 'It's a pleasure to meet you. Please take a seat and tell me all about yourself.'

Ashton couldn't remember being asked for a verbal

curriculum vitae before and kept it short, mainly because he didn't like talking about himself. He also couldn't see how it would help to know what he had done in the Falklands campaign and on the streets of Belfast with the army's Special Patrol Unit before joining the SIS.

'You've got an interesting record,' Freeh said when he'd finished. 'Now tell me what you've got against Louise Kay?'

It was the last question Ashton had anticipated. Hazelwood had sent him to Washington to see if the FBI had anything on a nuclear physicist born in the United States whose parents had emigrated from the Middle East. Rightly or wrongly they'd assumed the Bureau shared their perception of Louise Kay. He found it hard to believe that they would have done a complete about-face and could only surmise that he was being subjected to some kind of litmus test.

'One fact alone is enough to condemn her,' Ashton said bluntly. 'When Louise Kay contacted our courier in Berlin, she knew damned well that she was leading him to his death. I've heard people say she had no choice, but that's a load of crap. All the witnesses interviewed by the Kripo are positive she arrived alone. Nobody was watching her every move as the CIA were led to believe. She could have warned Moresby he was in danger, told him to make a break for it when they walked out of the bar. A couple of sentences, that's all it would have taken.'

'You're right,' Freeh told him, 'and for the record, we can't swallow the CIA's version of her conduct either. We are dealing with a young unstable woman who has got her hands on a nuclear weapon and believes extreme violence is the solution to every political issue. All she lacks is the technical know-how to cause an atomic explosion and from what I hear it's likely you can identify the man who can supply it.'

Ashton thought the Director was putting it a bit strong. All he had got from Gennadi Yasnev was a reasonably detailed description of the suspect, the rest was supposition. The accent alone was not sufficient to justify the assumption that the man was born in America. What they had to go on seemed even slimmer by the time he finished telling Freeh about the man known to his friends as Abe.

'Abe,' Freeh repeated in a neutral voice which made it impossible to second-guess what he was thinking.

'I also have the names of a number of physicists in both Iraq and Iran who are believed to be engaged in a nuclear weapons research programme.'

The list had been produced by Jill Sheridan's department at Hazelwood's behest. Ashton suspected Victor had felt the SIS had precious little to offer and had wanted to inflate what they did have.

'We thought there was a chance one of the names on the list might strike a chord with your National Security Agency, maybe the State Department or the Defence Intelligence–'

'I think we will stick with Abe,' Freeh said, bringing him up short.

'You will?' Ashton said, then asked why.

'Because Louise Kay had an intimate relationship with a physicist called Abbas Din when she was a student at Fulton. His friends called him Abe.' Freeh smiled. 'That's not the sort of coincidence we can ignore.'

'He's known to the Bureau then?'

'Not well enough, but we intend to put that right. Where are you staying in Washington, Mr Ashton?'

'I've a reservation at Loews L'Enfant Plaza.

'Good. I don't know when your people are expecting you to return, but if it's possible I'd like you to compare notes with Special Agent Leroy Manfull.'

Ashton said he was sure London would be happy for him to do that and they parted company. Less than twenty minutes after leaving the FBI Building, he climbed into bed and went out like a light.

The woman who owned the Silver Dollar Motel was a raunchy forty-three-year-old divorcée who invited even the most casual of acquaintances to call her Damaris. She had extended this privilege to the two Special Agents who'd followed up the trace while making it plain she had no time for the FBI. In her opinion, which she hadn't hesitated to express, the Federal authorities were a bunch of Nazis and the Bureau was their Gestapo, so were the State Troopers and the Buffalo Police Department.

Damaris had admitted to the Special Agents that a trucker called Beau had stayed at her motel. She had also maintained that he'd given the phone number of the Silver Dollar to his boss without her permission and had been real annoyed when she'd learned he was expecting a phone call. Truth was, she couldn't tell them too much about Beau even though he'd stayed at her motel a few times when he'd been passing through Buffalo. Beau was short for Beauregard; that she did know, and he was from Missouri, but he'd never talked about his folks. Sport was all he was interested in, didn't have much conversation outside of baseball, football and boxing.

The Special Agents had thanked her and departed, leaving Damaris with the distinct impression that they were satisfied with her account, which had been her first big mistake. Her second was phoning Beau because the Special Agents had obtained the necessary court order from a right-thinking judge and the phone tap on the Silver Dollar had been in place before they'd called on her.

The Special Agents had returned an hour later all smiles because they had this interesting little tape they'd like to play to her. And Damaris had heard herself say, 'I don't want no trouble, Beau. A couple of not-so-friendly acquaintances have been here looking for you. Best you go some place else.' 'And what's your reaction to that?' they'd asked, and she had told them it was a goddamned invasion of privacy and a denial of her civil rights.

The two Special Agents had immediately arrested Damaris and had taken her in for questioning, hands manacled behind her back, hoping she would feel intimidated. They had told her she was entitled to be

legally represented but she had waived that right which
had suited them fine. They had questioned her right
through the night and had found her a tough lady to crack.
Yeah, she had called Beau, but so what? They hadn't told
her why they wanted to see him and he was a friend and
you didn't betray a friend. And they knew what she
thought of the Feebies. Right?

Besides, Beau was a patriot; he believed it was the
sacred duty of every American to bear arms in the defence
of their country. Maybe he was in the militia but when had
the goddamned Federal government made that illegal?
Where was Beau going? Damned if she knew; it weren't
none of her business anyway. Didn't know where he had
been either and didn't care.

They had asked her to describe Beau and she had told
them he was an Elvis Presley lookalike. Asked if there was
anything else, Damaris had told them he had the biggest
pecker you ever saw and had almost choked with laughter.

They had known all along that they would eventually
release her but she had gone away thinking she had worn
them down. And that was her third big mistake because
she had told the Special Agents a lot more about
Beauregard than she realised.

Nathan Ungley slipped out of bed, pulled on a pair of jeans
and a roll neck sweater, then sat down and shoved his bare
feet into the rubber-soled jump boots. It was his proud
boast that he could be dressed and ready to move sixty
seconds after opening his eyes. He reached under the
pillow for the Colt .45 automatic and tucked it into the
waistband of his jeans, then bending down, he retrieved
the 12-gauge Ithaca shotgun which he'd left on the floor
where, if need be, he could grab hold of it without getting
out of bed.

Ordinarily, the handgun under the pillow would have
been sufficient, but after the phone call from Beau late
yesterday afternoon, he'd figured a little extra insurance
would not come amiss. They had done the wrong number

routine, Beau supposedly calling Winston's Garage to report he'd run off the highway and wrapped his pick-up around a tree after a tyre blow-out, then apologising when told he must have hit the wrong digit somewhere. The key word was blow-out; it told Ungley their security had been breached and he should therefore watch his back. The waif-like Chrissy was still lying on her stomach, head over to one side and breathing heavily through her open mouth when he left the bedroom.

The sun was just peeping above the horizon, lighting up a threatening sky when Ungley walked out into the yard. Whistling the dogs to heel, he set off to patrol the bounds of his property. If the Feebies were watching the house, he wanted them to see he was still observing the same old routine. He moved unhurriedly, like a man with nothing to do and all day to do it in.

Back at the house again, he made two mugs of instant coffee, took them into the bedroom and woke Chrissy.

'Have you got your wits about you, girl?' he asked when she was sitting up in bed, nursing the mug with both hands.

'Haven't I always?'

'Prove it. Tell me what you're going to do this morning.'

Chrissy sighed. 'Not again. I lost count of the number of times we went over this last night.'

Ungley grinned. 'You angling for another wopping?' he asked her quietly.

'OK. We'll do it once more. Right after breakfast I drive into Rolla and leave the Ford Mustang outside the supermarket while I rent a car from Hertz, paying the deposit and collision damage waiver in cash. I then park the rental near the Mustang and transfer the bag containing your city clothes. After that, I buy a week's supply of groceries from the supermarket before getting my hair done. Eventually, you will pitch up at the salon where I'll give you the keys to the rental before driving back here. OK?'

'Something else.'

'Oh yeah. I should keep my eyes open and check to

make sure I'm not being followed.'

'And drive carefully,' Ungley reminded her. 'Rolla is where India Troop of the State Highway Patrol is based.'

'OK, OK,' Chrissy said impatiently. 'You want to tell me how you will leave the house without being seen?'

'Well, I'm not planning to sneak out of here like some criminal. I'll walk out of the door in full battle order – combat suit, AK 15, Colt .45, two fragmentation grenades, water bottle, pouches for spare magazines and the walkie-talkie radio. I'll also be carrying a number of figure targets and the Feebies will think I'm off playing soldiers again. But under the combat suit I'll be wearing these jeans and roll-neck sweater. Soon as I'm deep into the woods, I'll strip off, hide the weapons and clothing and start walking.'

'Where are you going, Nathan?'

'To Rolla,' he said, deliberately misinterpreting her question. 'I'll make it in less than two hours, it's only eight miles from here.'

'No. I meant after you leave Rolla.'

'That's a military secret,' Ungley informed her. 'First rule of security – what you don't know, you can't tell.'

Ashton surfaced, opened one eye and stared at the dust motes swirling in the shaft of sunlight which entered the room through a chink in the curtains. Where the hell was he? Riga? Couldn't be; he'd been into Latvia and out again on the same day. Helsinki then? No, he had stayed there Monday night. It sure as hell wasn't London because he was in a king-size bed without Harriet, and Edward would have been bawling his head off by now demanding the first feed of the day. So what day was it and who the hell had set the alarm for this ungodly hour? Slowly it dawned on his befuddled brain that the shrill noise was coming from the telephone and, lifting the receiver, he brought it into bed with him and croaked into the mouthpiece. A cool feminine voice enquired if that was Mr Ashton?

'I'm almost sure it is,' he said.

'Sorry to disturb you,' the PA said brightly. 'I have Mr Freeh on the line for you.'

Suddenly wide awake, Ashton kicked off the bedclothes and planted both feet on the soft pile carpet. 'Good morning, sir,' he said.

'You're sounding very chipper,' Freeh told him. 'I thought you might be suffering from jet lag.'

'Doesn't affect me at all,' he lied. 'I'm used to travelling.'

'Good. How soon can you leave for Washington National?'

'Ten, maybe fifteen minutes.'

'Fine. I'll arrange to have you picked up from the hotel. There's a TWA flight to St Louis departing at 09.18 hours; your driver will have the plane ticket.'

'Right.'

'Agent Manfull is already in St Louis and will meet you off the plane. OK?'

'Yes, sir. One thing, how will I recognise him?'

Ashton closed his eyes. Jesus, that was a dumb question. He knew exactly what the Director was going to say before he told him Manfull would be holding up a piece of cardboard with his name printed on it in block capitals several inches high.

Beau stifled a yawn, pushed the dashboard lighter into the socket, then shook a cigarette loose from the packet of Marlboro on the seat beside him and stuck it between his lips. Buffalo; Cleveland; Columbus; Ohio; and Indianapolis were behind him now and the odometer was showing 503 miles which meant he had just 231 to go, say another four hours twenty-five minutes' steady driving. The lighter popped out of the socket and he pressed the glowing ring against the cigarette, then drew the smoke down into his lungs and slowly exhaled, the better to savour the aroma. So OK, maybe the Big C would do for him in the end, but an awful lot of nonsmokers were going to die prematurely before this day was over.

Nothing was going to stop them. Although there had

been one bad moment when Damaris had told him the Feebies were looking for him, he had quickly realised they would soon run into a brick wall, even if they did manage to turn up his full name and social security number. The colour of the pick-up he was driving used to be white; now it was dark blue and had different plates, something which wasn't recorded on any goddamned data base. There was no trail of credit card payments which the Bureau could follow either. He had paid cash for everything: gas, food and the motel on Route 44 where he had stayed last night.

Foresight and meticulous planning, that was the key. He hadn't greatly cared for Abe, and he most certainly hadn't liked the way the man had talked down to him, repeating everything twice as if he was some ignorant hillbilly who couldn't read nor write, but you had to hand it to the Arab, he'd thought of everything. Moving the nuke from Germany to Toronto and then on to the lock-up he'd rented in Niagara on the Lake had taken a lot of organising. A million things could have gone wrong along the way, but nothing had. The proof was there in the back of his pick-up hidden under a load of office equipment.

One hour and eighteen minutes after lifting off from Washington National, Ashton walked into the Arrivals Hall at Lambert St Louis International Airport and made his way towards the large man waiting by the exit who was holding a placard aloft with his name printed on it. Leroy Manfull was wearing a sports jacket with a broad check, which he had wisely left unbuttoned, and a pair of tan-coloured slacks. Ashton reckoned the American was about an inch shorter than himself and weighed something in excess of 200 pounds. He had a florid complexion, receding light brown hair and an overhanging stomach. But, as Ashton rapidly discovered when he introduced himself, the American had a friendly disposition and a warm smile to go with it.

'My car's out front,' he said, 'on the taxi rank. Cab

drivers don't like it but this little old shield of mine makes a powerful argument.'

'I could use something like that in London,' Ashton told him.

'That's my car over there,' Manfull said, pointing to a white four-door, 'that '89 model Pontiac Bonnville. It's beginning to show its age, especially after the pounding I've been giving it these last few weeks, but it's very comfortable and has never let me down.' Removing the overnight bag from Ashton's grasp, he tossed it on to the back seat, told him cheerfully to climb aboard, then walked round the vehicle and got in behind the wheel. 'You're going to tell me all about Abbas Din. Right?'

'Not all that much to tell, I'm afraid,' Ashton said and repeated everything he had learned from Gennadi Yasnev. It sounded embarrassingly little.

'You think he's got the know-how to detonate a nuke?'

'Oh yes, Louise Kay would never have accepted him if he wasn't competent in that area.'

'Yeah, I guess Louise ought to know, she's certainly been acquainted with him long enough. They were at Fulton together. So was a jerk-off called Nathan B. Ungley.'

'Who's he?'

'A militiaman. You heard of them?'

'Vaguely.'

'They're a ragtag and bobtail army, ready to defend America against people like me. We've got guys on the radio and TV advising people to blow the head off any Federal Agent who knocks on their door.'

'I can't believe Kay stayed in touch with these people all this time. I've seen the print-out you sent Interpol and she graduated in 1984. Furthermore, the lady is supposed to have been in the Middle East since 1990.'

Manfull opened the glove compartment, took out a fax and gave it to him. 'Read this,' he said, 'and you'll see how she did it.'

There was nothing to show from which organisation the Bureau had obtained their information. There was no originator's reference and the text had been carefully laundered to erase any reference to the identity of the subject as well as the case officer who had initially recruited the agent back in 1983. But anybody familiar with the background had little difficulty in recognising the source.

After leaving Fulton, Louise Kay had taken a postgraduate course at Chicago University where she had regularly submitted reports on fellow students and members of the Faculty deemed to hold radical views. In 1988, thanks to her case officer who'd pulled a few strings, she had become an aid worker employed by the United Nations in the Middle East. From 1990 on through to the beginning of 1994, she had returned to America at six-monthly intervals using a different passport supplied by the CIA on each occasion. Given that amount of licence and freedom of movement, Ashton could understand how she had managed to keep tabs on Ungley and those like him. Those members of the Palestine Liberation Organisation whom she had betrayed had in all probability been on the hit list of the rival faction she was secretly working for.

'Any idea why the CIA has suddenly released this information?' he asked.

'I guess you can't have caught any of the news bulletins this morning,' Manfull said. 'One of the newspapers in Paris has reported that the explosion on the Boulevard Périphérique was caused by a nuclear shell. I suppose you couldn't hope to keep a story like that under wraps for ever. Anyway, it surely encouraged the folks at Langley to take a cold hard look at their agent in place and suddenly they didn't like what they saw.'

'You mind if I ask what you're doing in St Louis?'

'It looks as though Louise Kay has been collecting information on a number of potential targets. St Louis is one, the others are Chicago, New York, Philadelphia, Boston and Washington.'

All six were considered to be equally at risk and the various police departments and law enforcement agencies had been alerted. A car bomb was good for attacking a single designated target; a 500-ton device which created a radiation hazard was an area weapon and there was little point in trying to protect individual buildings.

'We figure these terrorists will plant the bomb in the downtown area where it will do the maximum amount of damage,' Manfull continued.

And kill the most people, Ashton thought. Inflict enough fatal casualties and eventually the electorate would begin to question why their government was prepared to sacrifice the lives of its citizens in order to support Israel. That was the philosophy of the Islamic fundamentalists, according to Jill Sheridan.

'What you will see here and in the other target cities is a greater police presence in the centre. More prowl cars cruising the area but not so obtrusively that people begin to wonder what the hell is going on.'

'There'll be a radiation hazard extending some five to ten miles from ground zero.' Ashton cleared his throat. 'I guess they will want to be clear of the potential contamination area before they send a command signal to detonate the bomb?' he suggested.

'Yeah, we've thought of that,' Manfull told him. 'The airport is already covered and we'll be putting checkpoints on all the highways. These will be outside the city limits to make sure nobody can bypass them by using a combination of side roads. It's going to be chaotic, so we can't go to high alert state until we've reason to believe St Louis is the target. Right now, it's just a suspicion. What we need is a break, something to indicate at least one of the suspects may be in town.'

Manfull continued on Interstate 70 as far as the Fourth Street exit in Downtown St Louis, then made a right into Market Street.

The break came in a phone call from Elk Prairie shortly after they arrived at the Federal Building. Ungley had walked into the woods adjoining his property armed to the teeth half an hour after his common-law wife had driven off in their elderly Ford Mustang. After Ungley had been gone for more than two hours, the agent assigned to close surveillance had searched the woods and found his webbing equipment, assault rifle, .45 handgun, walkie-talkie and combat uniform hidden in the undergrowth along with two fragmentation grenades. From subsequent enquiries in Rolla, the Special Agents had learned that Chrissy Ungley had rented a '94 model Ford Taurus, licence number MO 51 8732 from Hertz.

'Where's Rolla?' Ashton asked.

'A hundred and eight miles from here,' Manfull told him. 'Probably means the bastard is already in town.'

The most prominent landmark in St Louis was the massive Gateway Arch, a brilliant feat of engineering on the banks of the Mississippi which soared to a height of 630 feet above the city. The entrance hall inside the arch boasted a museum, gift shops, a cafeteria, a double tramway to the summit and a small movie theatre showing the stage-by-stage construction of the project. There was no better place to kill time without appearing to do so, which was another reason why Louise Kay had chosen it as a rendezvous.

From Frankfurt she had travelled to St Louis via London, Detroit and Chicago, using American Express traveller's cheques supplied by the Arabian Bank of the Middle East in Damascus. Abbas Din had accompanied her as far as London where he had then flown on to Toronto to move the consignment of office supplies to the lock-up he'd rented in Niagara on the Lake. Although she had no reason to suppose that anything had gone wrong, it was still a relief to see him stride into the hall and make his way towards the bench seat outside the museum. Smiling, she went to meet Abbas and kissed him on both cheeks.

'How did it go?' she asked softly.

'Smooth as silk,' he assured her and patted the bulge in his jacket pocket. 'Just had a bleep on the mobile. You know what that means?'

Louise nodded. Beau had signalled to say he was approaching the Poplar Street bridge across the Mississippi.

'Something's bugging you,' Din observed. 'What's happened?'

'Nothing.'

'Come on, I know you.'

'Well, OK, maybe it's my imagination but on the way from the rooming house where I spent the night, there seemed to be an awful lot of police cars cruising the downtown area.'

'I hadn't noticed any unusual activity on the way in from the airport.'

'Well, like I said, it's probably my imagination.'

Abbas took hold of Louise by the arm and steered her towards the exit. 'It won't take me any time at all to arm the surprise package,' he said quietly.

'I know.'

'Then let's go find a cab and get the show on the road.'

Ungley was parked on level four of the multi-storey to the north of the baseball stadium located in the area enclosed by Walnut, Spruce, Broadway and Seventh Streets. It had taken him one hour forty to walk into Rolla, collect the keys to the Ford Taurus from Chrissy in the hairdressing salon and be on his way. Forty miles down the road, he had pulled into a Caltex filling station and had changed into his city clothes in the men's room.

He had been told not to bring any firearms with him but that was the kind of stupid order no good soldier could be expected to obey. He had therefore slipped a couple of revolvers into the bag containing his city clothes; a .38 Smith and Wesson for Beau and a Ruger Speed Six for himself, a handgun that had been specifically designed for clandestine operations.

From his vantage point he saw the dark blue pick-up turn into the multi-storey. Moving back in rear of the Ford Taurus, he waited for it to appear on the fourth level. When it did, Ungley signalled Beau to join him as soon as he'd found a parking space for the vehicle. Any minute now he expected Louise Kay and the Arab to arrive at the stadium in a cab and then the combat team would be complete.

Another piece of the jigsaw had fallen into place. The Special Agents from Buffalo who had questioned Damaris had asked the FBI's Identification Division in Washington if anything was known about a man whose first, possibly last, name was Beau or Beauregard, was aged twenty-five to thirty, came from Missouri and could be connected with the militiamen. From this scanty information, the Identification Division had been able to match the suspect, and fax his likeness to St Louis with the additional information that he had one conviction for burglary when aged sixteen and had been a member of the same gun club as Ungley in Rolla. This had given the St Louis PD, FBI Special Agents and officers drawn from the State Highway Patrol in Jefferson City three faces to look out for. The worrying thing was that the Ford Taurus had apparently disappeared.

Ashton couldn't think what he was doing in St Louis; he had nothing more to offer and was just a spectator taking up valuable space in the Federal Building. The hunt was being directed by the Chief of Police, there were two SWAT teams ready at a moment's notice to move, a communications network linking City Hall, Police Headquarters and the FBI office in the Federal Building. There were also a couple of mystery men from Special Forces lurking in the background who would have the unenviable task of disarming the nuclear device, and a whole bevy of psychologists all set to evaluate Louise Kay and suggest what she might do next. Logic told Ashton his presence was unnecessary, that the best thing he could do was get out of everybody's hair and go on home. His gut told him that some people might think he was concerned to save his own skin, and that was a very compelling reason for staying put.

Manfull was equally at a loose end. Outside of the CIA, he was the undisputed authority on Louise Kay; it was the only reason why he was in St Louis.

'I don't know how much longer I can sit here twiddling my thumbs,' he said. 'I need to get out and about, maybe look for this damn Ford they're turning into a bomb.'

'I don't believe that's why Ungley rented it. You told me Beauregard was invited to get his truck out and go collect the stuff they'd ordered. Right?'

'Yeah, that was the message he got from Ungley.'

'Then the nuclear shell has to be on his vehicle; all they've got to do is arm it. They need the Ford Taurus to get out of St Louis once the nuclear device has been positioned. Wherever that Ford is now, the truck is with it. They've all got to be together – Ungley, Beauregard, Louise Kay, Abbas Din. Some place where they're not likely to be seen – an abandoned warehouse, an underground car park . . .'

Without saying a word, Manfull left him, walked across the room and spoke to the Bureau Chief. Feeling at a loose end, Ashton went over to the window and looked out. There wasn't a cloud in the sky; on such a fine sunny day, it was difficult to believe that four crazies were about to embark on an orgy of death and destruction.

'They've already figured that one,' Manfull said, coming up behind him. 'The police have started checking out the parking lots and multi-storeys.'

Ashton nodded, felt about six inches high; of course they had thought of that possibility and acted on it.

'What's that building over there?' he asked to cover his embarrassment.

'It's the Old Union Station,' Manfull told him. 'In the age of the train, it was the gateway to the West and South-West.'

'So what's it used for now?'

'It's been refurbished and is now the Hyatt Regency Hotel, St Louis. The tracks down below have been converted into a shopping mall.' Manfull froze. 'Jesus H. Christ,' he said in a low voice, 'that's where they are going to plant the bomb.'

He yelled the same message to the Bureau Chief, then took off with Ashton hard on his heels. Ignoring the elevators, Manfull went on down the stairs, showing remarkable agility for a man who was overweight and looked out of condition. He hit the street and turned left and started running, holding the small radio in his left hand to his ear while somehow managing to extend the retractable aerial.

'They're on the move,' he gasped as Ashton drew level with him. 'A prowl car observed the Ford Taurus and a blue pick-up leaving the multi-storey near the stadium.'

'I don't hear any sirens,' Ashton said.

'Orders,' Manfull panted, 'unmarked car – silent tracking – follow and report.'

Five blocks and a slight uphill gradient all the way, dodging pedestrians on the sidewalk, his chest heaving, a stitch lancing into his side. If it was agony for him, Ashton wondered what it must be like for Manfull. The American stopped running the moment he reached Union Station. Still clutching the radio in his left hand, he nursed both rib cages with an arm while he fought to catch his breath.

'I guess we beat them to it,' he said.

Ashton looked up and down the street. There was no sign of either vehicle, which struck him as ominous. 'I think we should take a look round the corner,' he said and started running again.

He didn't know if Louise Kay was the kind of murderous fanatic who wouldn't hesitate to press the button and vaporise herself into the bargain, but there was no point in leaving it to chance. He sure as hell didn't like to think what the consequences would be if the police car which had been tracking them had hit a red light at the wrong moment.

Ashton turned the corner into a side street and suddenly there they were coming towards him, a red Ford Taurus licence number MO 51 8732 followed by a blue pick-up.

Both vehicles stopped just short of a service road which led to the shopping mall and two men baled out of the van. The bomb had been armed and they were about to make a run for it; there could be no other logical explanation.

'Shoot,' Ashton yelled to Manfull. 'Shoot the fucking driver of the car.'

Manfull dropped the radio, snatched a snub-nose .38 Smith and Wesson from his hip holster, then stepped off the sidewalk into the road and holding the revolver in a double-handed grip, aimed it at Ungley. 'Freeze,' he shouted and immediately opened fire without waiting to see if the militiaman was going to obey his command.

The windshield exploded like a bomb and he saw Ungley tumble out of the offside door. It was also evident that the bastard hadn't been hit and was holding a gun. Manfull had never shot to kill before, but he did so now, blowing Ungley's head apart with a double tap.

Ashton saw Abbas Din looking at something he was holding in his right hand and concluded it was a remote control initiator, then went at him like a bullet. They were just twenty yards apart and he hit him with the force of a piledriver, digging his right shoulder into the stomach. It was the kind of flying rugby tackle an England player would have been proud of and it lifted Abbas Din clear off his feet and dumped him flat on his back, cracking his skull on the sidewalk as if it were an eggshell. It didn't do Ashton an awful lot of good either; the whole world seemed to be revolving and he was sure he was hallucinating because he could hear the wail of sirens and there was such a cacophony of gunfire he was sure war had been declared. When his head cleared and he got to his feet, it was evident there had been a battle, if not a small-scale war.

'All four are dead,' Manfull told him. 'It's over.'

The Bureau Chief in St Louis told him the same thing, so did Louis Freeh when he arrived back in Washington on Thursday morning. Ashton wanted to believe them but a nagging doubt remained.

Leaving the FBI Building, Ashton made his way over to

the British Embassy on Massachusetts Avenue where, as a matter of courtesy, he touched his forelock to the SIS Head of Station before calling Hazelwood on the crypto-protected satellite link. In London it was almost half-past two in the afternoon and, judging by the mellow tone of his voice, he got the impression that Victor had enjoyed a very good celebratory lunch at the Atheneum.

'You've heard the news then?' Ashton said.

'Ages ago. Just about every Intelligence agency on your side of the Pond has been in touch.' Hazelwood paused, then said, 'You did us a power of good and, believe me, we're all very grateful, especially Jill Sheridan.'

'How's that?'

'You did a lot to restore her reputation.'

It was, Ashton thought, a crazy world when fiction could suddenly become fact. To further her career, Jill had purloined a low-grade source and presented him as a gilt-edged asset, attributing to Gamal al Hassan information that had been gleaned from other agencies. It was one of life's great ironies that the Palestinian had finally come good. Of course Gamal's information had not been a hundred per cent accurate but there was no denying he had at least pointed the SIS in the right direction. If the air drop, which Yasnev had organised, had gone some way to vindicating Jill's apparent blind faith in her source, events in St Louis had certainly removed the last vestige of doubt.

'Do I take it that Jill is back in favour?' he asked.

'Let's say she has acquired a number of fans at the highest level in the Foreign Office.'

Jill was off the hook. Her current security clearance would not be reviewed, which meant she wouldn't have to face ex-Detective Chief Superintendent Thomas and answer a lot of potentially embarrassing questions about her sex life with Henry Clayburn

'So where do we go from here, Victor?'

'I want you to come on home,' Hazelwood told him. 'You've done a great job and we can all sleep a little bit easier in our beds.'

'The *Mafiozniki* sent Louise Kay and her friends five 130mm nuclear shells.'

'Quite so,' Hazelwood agreed, 'and they have all been accounted for. Two blew up in Paris, two were recovered in Marseille and you helped to neutralise the fifth in St Louis.'

'Just a minute. Aldermaston said the damage to the Boulevard Périphérique had been caused by one shell only.'

'They've changed their minds, Peter.'

'Yeah? Suppose what happened in Missouri was merely a warning shot. Suppose the Atomic Weapons Research Establishment was right the first time around. Suppose there is still another nuke out there. What will you do then, Victor?'

'Pray,' said Hazelwood, and hung up on him.

Last activity date: 10-26-02
Total checkout: 19
Date: 4-22-03